A House Afire

Emma Kinna

PublishAmerica
Baltimore

First printing

Hardcover 978-1-4489-5828-3
Softcover 978-1-4489-9087-0
PUBLISHED BY PUBLISHAMERICA, LLLP
www.publishamerica.com
Baltimore

Printed in the United States of America

Prologue

The Party.

Jeremy Heron was my good friend Janelle's boyfriend. I would like to state the fact that he'd never said a kind word to me in my life. He always whispered nasty things to his friends when I walked by them in the hallway at school. He'd openly called me all kinds of names when I turned around and looked at him.

So what was I supposed to do? I wasn't a big strong person physically, I couldn't intimidate him. I'd been brought up to be kind to each and every person I met. It was discouraging. What had I done to him?

And it wasn't as if I could burn him, breathe out flames during class.

But the party was different. It was just kids in the backyard, in the pool, in the house. Janelle's older sister was the "adult" present. I wouldn't have gone, shouldn't have gone, but Janelle had told me she was going to have a fire, and she was the only friend I had.

I was alone at the party, mostly. I hung out with Cassie and Janelle until Jeremy and Trevor showed up. Then Janelle put on music and she and Jeremy started dancing, along with Cassie, Trevor and everyone else at the party.

Jeremy stopped after a few songs. "Hey Phyllis," he said. I saw him glance at Trevor, like *hey, check this out.* "Hey Phyllis, you wanna dance?"

"Nope, I'm good."

"C'mon Phyllis, you're the only one who's not dancing. Don't you want to dance with me?"

"Well, when you put it that way, no," I said.

"Hey," Janelle had said to Jeremy, "you're here to dance with me."

"Yeah, but Phyllis is *all alone*," Jeremy told her.

"Let's go in the pool!" Cassie had shouted. Everyone had cheered at that, and we headed out. A couple of the girls and I played catch with a beach ball in the deep end, while everyone else played Marco Polo in the shallow end. Janelle's sister brought out pizzas and soda, along with generic party snacks—chips, cookies, a punch bowl, and everything went quite well compared to my usual social experiences.

Until they built the fire.

We all sat around it, in the backyard. A bunch of kids went back in the pool and some others went inside to dance. That left me and a few others by the fire.

"Look at all the colors," said one of the girls sitting across from me. Her glance flickered to something behind me. I ignored it, stupidly.

"Yeah," I said, "I love fire."

And right after the words left my mouth, my head was doused in cold, red liquid. No, not blood.

Jeremy and Trevor had dumped the punch bowl over my head.

Everyone burst out laughing. Okay, so there were only five people who saw, but that didn't make it any less humiliating.

I ran and jumped into the pool with my clothes on. I didn't care, it was just a T-shirt and shorts.

Janelle came out of the house as I came out of the pool.

"Phyllis, you're all wet!"

"Yeah, don't worry, I'm just gonna go sit by the fire and dry off."

"Okay."

I went and sat by the fire. I was alone. There were a couple of guys kicking a ball around and two girls in the pool, but otherwise, everyone had gone back inside.

After a while I saw Jeremy come out. I looked at him, then at the fire, and, very quickly, I inhaled the fire. The whole thing, leaving behind just the pile of wood. The heat felt good in my lungs.

I stood up. Jeremy was flirting with the girls in the pool. They got out and left him to cover it.

"Janelle sent you out to cover the pool?" I asked.

He ignored me.

Now, that was just rude.

"Hey Germs, look out."

I don't know if he looked at me then or not, but either way, I blew the fire I'd inhaled at him with all the heat, smoke, and force I could. It must've looked like an explosion.

He screamed, flying backward to the other side of the pool. I breathed it back in.

I heard one of the guys on the other side of the yard say, "What the hell?"

But I didn't care. I walked around the pool, down to Jeremy.

"Are you listening now, Jeremy?" I said angrily. "I want you to leave me the fuck alone. Forever. Because I don't think you deserve to *live*."

He looked at me. I loved the look on his face. I had never scared anyone before. I hoped he was in shock. Sadly I had somehow managed not to burn him.

"Do you understand?"

He nodded, got up and walked away. Quickly.

After that I'd called my Aunts to take me home.

What Happened to Me.

The last time I saw my parents, I was five. I don't remember much about them, except for that my mother always seemed very tall, and they were both loud. They argued a lot.

My mother and father were scientists. Brilliant, but much too daring.

They thought they had invented an injection, a vaccine, that would fire-proof people. I remember they had a lot of mice, and once I dreamed that I was in my bed and the room was full of mice. I have a bad feeling that that might be an actual memory. My parents must have burnt up a lot of mice testing their shot. But eventually it worked.

My mad-scientist parents were not exactly accepted by society in the first place, so they didn't go around asking people if they could test their invention by lighting someone on fire. They couldn't find a human test subject.

So, they used me.

I don't think I'll ever forgive them, as confident as they were, for what they did. I'm not sure how they accomplished it, I'm going by fragments of memory and what my Aunts have told me.

They tied me to a chair, left the house. Then they set the house on fire.

I escaped with some scrapes and a broken arm from falling debris, but no burns. I don't remember the fire. It took the house and everything in it, except for the chair and me. People said it was a miracle. My parents said it was a success.

My parents are now in a mental institution.

I live with my Aunts, Chastity and Kippie Sorin. I also live with the ability to breathe fire.

The Sorins.

My family has always been unusual. My grandparents were Theodore and Leona Sorin. In the 20th century on the income of a nurse and an engineer, they raised their children in an electricity and running-water devoid old house. They said they didn't need material things in life; they donated most of it to their church and kept the rest in a bank account. (Once I was informed of this, I realized where my mother must have inherited her craziness from.) Their youngest, Patty Sorin, left vowing to never live such a primitive life again. She became a scientist and married my father, William Caramie. Their oldest child, Philip, ran off at 18 and was never heard from again. Born ten months apart, Chastity and Kippie were always close, the middle children. They were also the only ones sent to public school (Philip was home-schooled and developed "anger problems"; Patty was sent to private school). Chasey spent all of her time doing volunteer work at hospitals and for her church, and kept to herself at school. She was quickly shunned for being *too* good. Kippie was more than outgoing, the family rebel, and soon dubbed a slut. After being treated horribly for their differences, Kippie and Chasey found sanctuary with a group of people who were also treated badly for various "odd" qualities of their own, though they were truly all good people. Chasey and Kippie made a decision. They were going to spend their lives helping "different" people.

Which really just meant everybody.

They both made sacrifices, but they say it was all worth it. However, they wouldn't have been able to do this if their parents had not been killed, ironically, in a car accident.

Being the sole heiresses of the fortune saved by the under-lived Theodore and Leona (Philip was gone, my mother had been cut off long before making me a fire-breather), they live in a large house just outside the city, on the way to the countryside. They house several people and four cats. Makes life interesting.

The Renters.

I was shipped off to live with the Aunts as soon as possible, and I've been told the whole fire-breathing thing didn't really kick in until then. My first full, vivid memories don't come before I was seven or eight.

My mother hadn't been close to any of her family, though the Aunts say they tried to be close to her. They say they fought for me. And they won.

Living just far enough from the city to be considered part of the smallest school district, I went to a tiny little elementary-middle school, and had a tiny little group of friends.

But that doesn't mean my life has ever been boring. The Aunts have made a home, for many years, with many people. Most of them come and go, but there are some who have always stayed with us:

Quincy Herman Smith- a very nice, very stylish gay man, who loves Madonna and Pierce Brosnan. His dark hair and skin are radiant and his appearance is always professional. His best friends, Abe and Butch, visit the house so often that they're almost permanent residents as well.

Bill Charles- he's extraordinarily...uh...eccentric. He spends most of his time watching movies and then taking on the personalities of characters. He's known the Aunts since childhood. He's permitted to live with us as long as he doesn't cause any major disturbances. All in all, he's a good friend to have.

Anna Xesly—that's pronounced "SAY-lee." Anna is half French, half African-American. She travels around, touring and doing other things I'm not quite sure of. She has the longest hair as well as the longest fingernails I've ever seen. She stays in our house when she's off or needs to practice. She's an opera singer, but she also does kung-fu and collects boyfriends.

And then there's me, Phyllis. A quiet, emotional, intellectual, fire-breathing, music-loving young girl. Not completely normal, but hey, these days who is?

The cats—

Johnny, named for Johnny Depp. I got him out of the pound when I was twelve. He's quite friendly and loves a sun-soaked spot to sleep in.

Enrique The Spaniard, who belongs to Quincy. He considers himself King. He acts royal, but is obviously in love with Wonder Woman, our only female feline. He's also a sucker for laps.

Wonder Woman, named by Bill. She's the first to eat, go out, or sleep on the cats' couch, which is in the sitting room (not to be confused with the living room) in the back of the house next to the kitchen.

Xerxes, named after an emperor by the Aunts. He was the first cat I ever met, and he's the oldest. He spends most of his time sleeping in secluded places. We can go for weeks without seeing him, but as long as his food disappears and we find his hair and such, we know he's okay.

There have been others, people and cats alike. Some have stayed for years, some for minutes. But these are the ones that have always called our house home, and probably always will.

Part One

In the Car.

"Aerials, in the sky, when you lose small mind you free your life," I sang softly along with System of A Down. Long car rides are not to be tolerated without music.

I was sitting next to Sid in his car. It was almost 11 pm on one of the last days of August. My face was dotted with blurred stage make-up; I'd just been in my high school's summer musical, "Fiddler On the Roof." Because there weren't as many seniors and juniors participating (I suppose they had better things to do), I'd been lucky and gotten a part as one of the daughters in the play's main family. My Aunts, Bill, and Quincy had also attended the performance—it was the second and last—but Sid had offered to stay and wait for me to change and bid my farewells to everyone in the cast. I'd been in a couple of musicals before this one, and it was always sad when they were all over. But a ride home with Sid brightened my day anytime.

"I feel ancient," Sid told me. "I remember listening to Charlie Parker."

"You still do."

"Yeah, you're right." He paused. "You were great."

I shrugged. "Thanks."

"Really Philly. You didn't do one thing wrong. It's damn hard not to screw up in front of a crowd."

I smiled. "Thank you Sid." I leaned back against my seat, shielding my face as I yawned. "Did *you* ever mess up?"

"Me, mess up?" He half-smiled. "Yeah. But I still loved doing it."

"Messing up?"

"Prosecuting. Nothin' like putting a guilty man in jail." He said it as easily as I would say, "Nothin' like an ice cream sundae. Especially at midnight."

"You don't seem as...lawful now," I told him.

"It's nice not to have to worry about perfection anymore. When I was a lawyer someone might see me at a bar and turn it into 'Dominick Siddons is An Alcoholic'," he told me.

"You didn't go to bars a lot then, I gather."

"You bet I did. After I retired."

"But you're *not* an alcoholic.."

"No, just a drinker." Sid looked over at me slyly. "Would you still be in love with me if I were an alcoholic?"

Mr. Siddons.

Dominick "Sid" Siddons had obviously come to the Sorin house before. And I had been there. Because the day he showed up, he knew us all right away.

I was fourteen, sitting at the kitchen table with Aunt Kippie. I was writing an essay for school, I think, and complaining, which is one of the things I do best.

Suddenly the door opened, and in stepped the best-looking man I would ever see. He was tall, with very dark brown hair and eyes. His eyebrows were dark and defined, expressive in a subtle way. His eyes gleamed with a sureness of his surroundings. But they were also powerful, intimidating eyes. His nose was long, his lips were perfect, my brain stopped working...

"Kippie!" He greeted my Aunt.

Aunt Kippie froze. "Sid!" Then, faster than a speeding bullet, she was hugging him. "Where have you been all this time?"

"Everywhere," he said. He smoothed her hair, which was thick and lively, though dark grey was beginning to take over her curly brown locks. Her skin was pale, unlike mine and Aunt Chasey's. "You haven't changed a bit!"

"Yeah, right," she said skeptically with a shake of her head. "Look at you. As young as when I first met you..."

Then Sid looked at me and our eyes locked. I'd already been staring at him, of course, but now that he was staring back, I felt violated.

"Oh my God...Phyllis." He continued to look into my eyes. "Jesus, I remember when you were five or six...you must be what, fifteen?"

"Fourteen," I told him automatically.

"Wow." He sized me up, then looked to Aunt Kippie. "She got some of your looks, Kippie."

"Pish tosh, Phyllis is beautiful."

"Exactly." He gave her a smile, then looked back at me. "I remember when you set the couch on fire." He grinned. "Scared Anna out of her mind. And then you just...inhaled it back in. Can you still do that?"

I'd met him before? Oh no! What if we were related? Or he was gay, like Quincy?

"Show him Phyllis. Don't you remember Sid?" Aunt Kippie asked me.

I shook my head, still staring. I was young, I couldn't help it.

Kippie winked at Sid. "Wait until I tell Chasey you're back. Let me go find her."

Sid saluted with two fingers as she left.

He sat across from me at the table. He reached into his pocket. He had a lighter. I loved lighters! He opened it up and held the flame a few inches from my mouth.

"Go ahead, Philly."

With a sense of déja vu that I just couldn't figure out, I inhaled the flame.

He grinned. "C'mon."

I blew out flames that flickered a moment in the air, then disappeared.

"Jesus." He looked at me again, amused. "Do you remember me now?"

I remembered the lighter trick, the sound of his laughter, Anna's screaming..

"A little," I said. "Your name is Sid?"

"Dominick Siddons. But, do I look like a Dominick?"

No, he didn't. I smiled a little.

"Are Quincy and Bill still here?"

"Yes. Are you...a friend of Quincy's?"

Sid laughed. "I'm not gay, if that's what you mean. But I've been friends with your Aunts for a long time."

I figured they must have baby-sat him, or something. He looked mid-twenties. But then I remembered how Aunt Kippie had looked at him. No baby-sitter should ever look at a kid that way.

"I used to live here...I started dating Anna...do you still know Anna?"

Ah, he was one of the beautiful Anna Sexy Xesly's many beaus. I supposed I'd hear the story soon. "Yes. She's on tour right now, though. She's playing Carlotta in 'The Phantom of The Opera'."

"Hoo boy." He put a hand to his forehead.

"Meowrrr."

We both looked down to see my kitten, Johnny. He rubbed against Sid's leg. Can't say I wouldn't have done the same thing had I been a cat.

"Another cat. Do you guys still have Enrique? Quincy got him right before I left."

Enrique the Spaniard, Quincy's pride and joy. How he got his name remains a mystery. "Yes we do."

"Good. In Quincy's room?" He picked Johnny up. I was liking Sid more and more.

"Most likely."

He set the cat on the table. "Who's this?"

"That's Johnny."

"Is he Quincy's too?"

"Nope, Johnny's mine." I loved saying that.

Sid looked up, right at me again. "Johnny Depp, right?"

I felt my cheeks turning red, but I laughed a little and nodded. "Right."

His smile grew wider. "So have you—" He was cut off by my Aunts, Bill Charles, and Quincy, who all rushed into the kitchen.

"Oh Dominick! You're back!" Aunt Chasey gushed.

"Sid Siddons! Good to see you're in good health," said Bill, shaking Sid's hand. He'd been watching a lot of BBC lately and had taken up a British accent.

"Sid baby! Gimme' a kiss!" Quincy grabbed Sid and hugged him, kissing him quickly on each cheek.

"Hey Quincy, I'm not French. How are ya?"

Quincy smiled. "Oh, you know me." He put his hands on his hips. "And *I* know *you*! Why is it that *you* get to stay young-looking all these years? This is *not* fair. Would you just bite me please?"

"Hey," Sid said softly, gesturing to me so subtly I almost missed it.

"Oh Phyllis!" Quincy said excitedly. "Don't you remember Sid?"

"Well, I—" I started.

"Oh Dominick that's right! You were here for about a year after Phyllis came." Aunt Chasey looked at me affectionately. "Such a beautiful girl."

I wasn't really. I had plain black hair, tan skin, and a pimple couple on my forehead that was ready to reproduce.

"Oh yeah, Phyllis is the *best*! I'm going to find her the perfect man," Quincy said. He turned back to Sid. "Speaking of which, have you found anyone since Anna?"

Sid nodded. "A few. But my relationships don't last very long."

Quincy said to me in a mock whisper, "Sid can't commit."

Sid looked downward and offered a stifled chuckle.

Quincy put a hand on his shoulder. "I'm sorry."

"Don't be. What about you Quince? Still single?"

"Not for long. But if you want me to be, I can arrange that." Quincy blew him a kiss. I giggled a bit.

Quincy looked at his watch. "Oh shit, I'm late for work!" Quincy bid us good bye, and rushed out to the store where he worked. It was an expensive clothing shop in the city that sold designer brands. Quincy lived well, especially since he didn't have to pay a lot of taxes.

Aunt Chasey sighed. "I wish he wouldn't use such language in my presence."

"Oh Chasey, Quincy's such a nice boy. He's just had a rough time, like the rest of us," said Aunt Kippie.

My Aunts are a bit weird themselves.

"Yes well, Dominick is a nice boy too. I do hope you're going to stay with us again." Aunt Chasey looked brightly up at Sid.

"That's why I showed up," Sid told her. "In a year or so, I want to move back here. I just need to clear things with you two."

"Oh Siddie dear," said Aunt Kippie, "you know you're always welcome." She looked to me. "I'm sure Phyllis doesn't mind, do you?"

"I won't be offended if you say yes," Sid put in.

"Of course I don't mind," I blurted out.

"Thanks girls. Do you mind if I stay here tonight? It was a damned long drive this morning."

"Yes that's fine," Aunt Kippie nodded, "I do believe we have several extra rooms."

So I ate dinner with the Aunts, Bill and Sid. I tried not to look at Sid, because whenever I did, I started staring. I zoned out while looking at a candle instead, figuring that would seem normal.

My Aunts took in a lot of people, but not with as grand a reception as they had Sid. Was he simply a friend? No, none of my Aunts' friends were simple. They all had...defining qualities. So what was Sid's, besides the fact that he was as tall, dark and handsome as a chocolate-chip cremewich (one of Quincy's favorite sayings)? There had been a couple of remarks about how young he looked...Quincy had said "bite me" but that was sort of a Quincy thing...Sid had started to ask me something..I'd have to ask him about that. So let's see..he looked young for his age? But how old could he be? Forty at most, and I only say that because I thought Johnny Depp was in his late twenties when he was in his early forties. Maybe Sid was a cosmetic surgery addict? Could that even happen to a man?

I studied Sid. Nothing about that face looked fake, not even his expressions.

No matter. I'd just ask Aunt Kippie.

Did I mention I'm kind of nosy?

Aunt Kippie was much more daring than Aunt Chasey. She'd had wings tattooed on her back in her younger days. She's mellowed with age, but she is known to have a few drinks at big parties and such. And by a few, I don't mean a *few*, if you know what I'm saying.

Neither of my Aunts had children, but I had the feeling that Aunt Kippie had come pretty close. She'd been married and divorced before I was ever around. Aunt Chasey had warned me that it was a very sensitive subject, so I hadn't ever said anything about it. I was sure, though, that if it ever came up, Aunt Kippie would be fine. Kippie could talk about anything, even if it hurt. (I myself hadn't inherited that trait.)

Oh no! What if it'd been Sid?

I laughed at myself, and the voice inside my head, which intervenes periodically in my life, said, That's impossible. And why are you so interested anyway? He's at least ten years older than you.

Looking back on that particular thought now, I laugh hysterically. Not quite.

* * *

Sid left early the next morning. It was very quick.

"Bye Kippie." He hugged her.

"Good bye Sid. When will you be back?"

"I'll write to you, I promise," he said.

"You'd better," she warned.

"That's right," said Chasey. "And remember, you can drop by anytime." She hugged him too.

"Have a good trip old boy, have a good trip." Bill shook Sid's hand again. "Quincy'll have my head when he finds I didn't wake him." Quincy had stayed out late that night and was still asleep.

Sid smiled a little. He looked down at me.

"Bye Philly. It was great to see you again."

I smiled back, tiredly. As soon as he left, I was going back to bed. "I wish I remembered more," I told him regretfully.

He waved a careless hand. "You were only five. It might come back to you." He hugged me. And then he kissed me on the cheek. "Don't burn the house down."

"Bye," we all said. Well, mine was sort of like, "B..." I was in shock.

He drove away in his black car.

The Cinemas.

Later that Saturday, I was, again, sitting with Aunt Kippie. Aunt Chasey had gone to the grocery store.

"So how do we know Sid?" I asked her.

Her eyes looked past me dreamily. "He's been a friend of ours for quite some time."

I raised an eyebrow. "He didn't look that old to me."

Kippie gave me a dangerous look.

I held up my hands in defense. "I didn't mean that offensively! You're not *old*...he's just really young."

"Well I suppose we've been friends with his family for a while."

"Why?"

"Why not?" Kippie's favorite comeback.

I wasn't sure how to put the question. "In what way is his family weird" would sound a bit harsh.

"Well...why was he living here?"

Kippie sighed. "The poor man has lived a hard life. All of his kin are dead now. The last time he was here, Chasey, Anna, and I were the only people he had. He loved it when you came along. Always wanted children."

"Why didn't he and Anna get married and have some then?" I asked.

"Oh, you know Anna. She's a free spirit, and so is Sid. They...it just wouldn't have worked out."

"Is that why he left?"

"I suppose that could have been part of it. And he wanted to travel, though where he went I've no idea. He hardly ever wrote to us."

"How long was he around for after I showed up?"

"A year, give or take. I know he was here for your sixth birthday..." She looked at me in a sad sort of way. "You really don't remember him, at all?"

"I can remember his voice...I think I remember Anna yelling at him. I definitely remember his lighter."

Kippie half-smiled. "You should. He used it an awful lot with you. Sweetheart, Sid's the one who helped you control your fire. He taught you in the backyard with the lighter. He was always the one in the line of fire, as he put it. He wanted to be sure you'd be okay before he left."

"Wow." I wracked my brain. "Does he have a job?"

"Doesn't need one. He's filthy rich. Last I knew though, he was a...he wanted to be a lawyer."

"A lawyer?"

"A prosecutor."

"Wow," I said again. We had something in common; I watched "Law and Order" with Bill all the time. "You think he would've been good?"

"The best."

"How did he teach me to control it?"

Kippie shrugged. "That remains a mystery, my dear."

Bill entered the kitchen just then. "Phyllis, I would be honored if you would accompany me to the cinemas."

"I would be honored to accompany you, William," I told him. "Do you mind, Aunt Kippie?"

Kippie shook her head. "Just be back before dinner, and all will be well."

To Bill's delight, our house was within walking distance of a small theatre, and I would often go there with him. Once in a while we went to the enormous one in the city, but it was a long drive.

Bill was crazy, no mistaking it, but he was still fully aware of what was going on. He'd held up a few jobs, quit a few jobs, but never had been fired. And he had an extremely fascinating perspective when it came to everything. I decided to ask him about Sid.

"How are you this fine day, Phyllis?" he asked me.

"I'm delightful, Bill. Yourself?"

"Jolly good, jolly good."

"Bill did you know Sid well?"

"Sid Siddons? Why yes! He was my friend when I was a young lad! Known the chap for most of my adult life."

"How old is he?"

Bill was thoughtful. "Well Phyllis..I couldn't say! My recollection isn't what it once was, I fear. But I do remember serving with him in the war."

"The war?" Okay then. Like I said, Bill was crazy, no mistake.

Bill nodded. "Nasty Americans, always starting wars where they aren't wanted."

Are wars ever wanted? I thought. "Oh," I replied.

"I can't imagine life without Britain. Simply lovely."

"Those devilish Americans," I agreed.

Bill chuckled. "Oh, but Phyllis, don't you recall? You *are* an American!"

Quincy.

Quincy had three very close friends; Abe, Butch, and Maria. Abe and Butch were gay, Maria, straight. Abe was a very well-dressed man, who loved purple. He had shoulder-length white-blonde hair, and a face like an Abercrombie model, according to Quincy and Maria. Quincy had had a short relationship with Abe years ago, which led to their friendship. Butch had been friends with Quincy since before my time. He wore a lot of denim and had a buzz cut. At least, when he was Butch. Sometimes, he was Beatrix. I'd actually seen him in drag once...he'd have been very convincing if it hadn't been for his muscly arms. Maria Vetello was a successful business woman. The story of Maria and Quincy's meeting somehow centered around the fact that they both spoke Spanish. She often accompanied Quincy and the guys on shopping trips or out to dinner. Occasionally, they all came over for dinner at our house. Aunt Chasey loved this, because she loved to cook. And she was the best cook/chef/baker there was. She could make anything. This was good, because my Aunt Kippie couldn't do a thing in the kitchen, and neither could I. Chasey and Quincy did all the cooking.

Quincy was a dark-haired man of medium height, and very well-groomed. When Anna was around, she spent a lot of her time with him. The two talked, shopped, and criticized men together. Anna was queenly, while Quincy was, well, flamboyant. Anna wore lots of black, and had red nails practically filed to points. If she wanted you to do something, she could simply poke you until you did it. She had long thick black hair that was always brushed, and a slight accent.

And she had dated Sid, among others. Since Anna wasn't around, I decided that Quincy would be the best person to ask about Sid.

So, after school during the week after I'd met Sid, I found Quincy sitting on the couch in the living room watching "Heartbreakers" with Bill. I guessed that Quincy had picked the movie.

I sat next to him.

"Hey Phyllis! How was school?"

"Eh." I detested school. I had hardly any social life because the few friends I had were all slowly drifting away.

"Sounds like some fun. You want to go shopping?"

I shook my head. "I'm too tired. But thank you."

"Anytime."

"I feel so bad." That would hook him.

"Why?" He looked at me.

"I hardly remembered Sid."

"I don't see how you could forget him," Quincy admitted.

"Exactly," I agreed.

"But you have a right to, I think, since most of those mem'ries are blocked out."

"Mmm."

Quincy grinned. "But wasn't he the hottest thing you've ever seen?"

I giggled. "Anna was lucky he was straight."

"Oh you know it baby!"

"So what happened between them?"

Quincy sighed. "They really did love each other at first. They fought a lot, but they'd always kiss and make up. Then they stopped making up and just kept right on fighting. Sid's the only man I've seen who could handle Anna, in that respect."

"Yelling?"

"Yeah. He's sort of a dominant kinda' man, and Anna's a dominant kinda' girl, so it was challenge for both of them right off. They clashed like red and orange."

"Did they break up before me?"

Quincy shook his head. "During. He stayed a few months after it happened though, for you. He was crazy for you, hon." Quincy grinned. "He *loved* that you could breathe fire."

"He must've been...18 or so!"

"Sid's older than he looks."

Crap. "Oh. Well how old *is* he?"

The question seemed to catch Quincy off guard. "He's..gotta be..thirty?"

"Oh." I was fourteen, so...16 years?

No! I thought.

After that conversation, I tried my best to forget Sid. It wasn't too hard; he didn't come back for a year.

Sarah Lagano.

My first day of eighth grade was hell on earth.

I'd never been a social butterfly, possibly because I was older than the other kids. I'd missed most of my first year of kindergarten because of what my parents had done, and so I'd restarted it at six and finished at seven. Through winter to the end of eighth grade I was fifteen, seeming far older than I should have been.

I walked to school with Janelle Warner, who at the time was the closest thing I had to a best friend. Janelle and I had lost touch, though, ever since she'd started changing boyfriends once a week, and hanging out with a rather unpleasant group of people including Jeremy Heron.

"I hope we have the same classes," she was saying.

"Yeah," I agreed. I just wanted to skip the whole year. I'd been going to the same school for eight years now. I'd been ready to burn it down for five.

"So how are the Aunts?"

"They're the same as always."

"Well, that's good, right? Oh look, there's Cassie! C'mon!" Janelle paraded ahead of me.

"Gah," I muttered in frustration.

Hardly anyone spoke to me that day, and there were more handouts and homework than my ancient backpack could handle.

I walked home alone, and when I got there, I tossed my full bag onto the couch and headed into the sewing room where the piano was. I practiced mindlessly, trying to forget the cold environment that I didn't want to discuss with anyone.

Two weeks later I was working on a project, an essay I'll wager, on the computer in the sewing room, when there was a knock on the front door. I sat Indian-style in my chair with Johnny on my lap, and I couldn't get up without disturbing him.

Luckily, Aunt Kippie was in the living room. I heard her open the door.

"Hello, can I help you?"

"Yes. You have rooms?"

"Yes we do! Please come in." The door closed. "Phyllis, won't you come out a moment?"

"Sorry Johnny," I murmured. I picked him up off my lap and put him on my shoulder, and went into the living room.

I must've looked horrid. My math teacher was an evil woman who didn't teach, but only handed out homework. I had asked everyone in the house for math help, even Bill. Surprisingly, he knew it quite well, but Quincy was even better. The point is, I'd been up doing math homework and then some the last few nights, and looked like a raccoon.

"Hi," I greeted the girl who stood at the door.

"Hey."

I blinked, and got a good look at her.

Her hair was pulled back and blonde, unnaturally so, because black roots peeked out from under it. Her eyes were covered by cat's eye lenses. A green bandana stuck out of one of the side-pockets on her leg. Part of a green tattoo peered out at the collar of her jacket; another part at her left wrist. Her face wasn't made up except for bright red lipstick, but she held her chin up proudly. And later, I noticed that she had a long, deep scar under and behind one ear, as if it had almost been cut off. Like Van Gogh.

This was my first glimpse of Sarah Lagano.

"My name is Kippie Sorin. I own the house with my sister Chasey, and Phyllis, my niece."

"I'm Sarah Lagano. I'm 21 and I'm just gonna stay until my boyfriend comes up from California."

"You're from California?"

Sarah shook her head. "NYC."

"How nice. Let me get my sister and we can work out the details." Aunt Kippie went into the kitchen.

"Is..is that a dragon?" I asked.

Sarah lowered her eyebrows. "Huh?"

"Your tattoo."

"Oh." She smiled. "Yeah. Don't ever get one, they never go away."

"You can't get it removed?"

"Shit no, it practically covers all of me. I got it years ago, piece by piece." She shook her head. "I was in a gang."

"Really?" I asked stupidly.

"Yeah." She reached into her pocket and pulled out a green pocket knife. "We were knife fighters."

"Just don't pull a knife on anyone *here*."

"Oh no, I'm completely done with all that. Me n' my boyfriend, we're starting a new life together."

I nodded. Aunt Kippie and Aunt Chasey emerged from the kitchen.

"Hello there," said Aunt Chasey.

"Hey, I'm Sarah Lagano," Sarah introduced herself.

"How nice to know you. May I ask you a few questions please?"

"Of course."

The three of them sat at the small card table in the living room. I sat on the couch with Johnny and watched.

"How old are you?"

"21."

"Are you employed?"

Sarah shook her head. "No, not yet, but I have money until I get a job."

"All right. Where did you live previously?"

"California."

"And what brings you here?"

"I'm waiting for my boyfriend. He's going to come up in a few months and then we're moving to the city."

"In the case that you smoke or use any kind of illegal drugs,well, I strongly advise you against it. Either way, they are forbidden in the house." Aunt Chasey nodded to me. "Our Phyllis, she has a breathing problem." Heh.

Sarah nodded. "Of course."

"Do you drink?" I'd never tried alcohol. I was a little wary of what it would do to my internal workings. Plus I had no idea how my internal workings worked.

"Yes."

"Do you have any food allergies? You'll be eating with us if you don't buy your own food."

"None. That'd be great."

Aunt Chasey smiled. "Good." She pulled out a piece of paper. "And would you please sign this? It simply requests that you do nothing that could damage the house."

"Of course," Sarah said again. She signed.

Aunt Chasey took the paper and looked to Aunt Kippie. "Is that all of it Kippie?"

Aunt Kippie looked at Sarah. "Are you prejudiced in any way? Mainly, towards gays, African-Americans, the mentally ill, and older women?" She smiled.

Sarah smiled back. "Not at all."

"Do you like cats?"

"Love them."

"We have four. And just so you know, everyone in the house will hunt you down in the case that you hurt one of them." Kippie was completely serious.

"Oh, I could *never* hurt an animal."

"Good. Your room will be in Section Two of the upstairs and you'll be sharing the floor and its bathroom with two men. Bill is mentally ill, but completely able and harmless. Quincy is gay. Both are easy to get along with...as long as you are."

"Don't worry, I am."

Aunt Chasey stood. "We'll show you the laundry facilities."

The upstairs of the house was divided into two sections; in the first section, there were five bedrooms, including mine and the Aunts'. We shared a bathroom that connected Aunt Kippie's room and mine. Other renters in that section used a separate bathroom at the end of the hall, across from the fifth room. The first section was connected to the second section by a door at the end of the hall diagonally across from the bathroom and the fifth bedroom door. In Section Two, there were also several bedrooms, and now, three of them would be slept in. Anna's room, when she was here, was in the basement along with a TV room and the laundry room. There was an attic bedroom too, but no one had used it since Aunt Kippie'd been married. There were some extra rooms on the first floor too that we used for storage and such.

The Aunts pointed out to Sarah the back stairway which led directly to Section Two from the kitchen, then took her into the basement. I remained on the couch with Johnny.

* * *

Three days later, I hadn't seen Sarah since. I was sitting at the card table, telling Bill about my English teacher who nagged worse than my Aunts ever had, when Sarah entered. Her hair was bright red and she wore a mini-skirt.

"Hey...Phyllis."

"Hi Sarah."

"I'm gonna go mail some stuff...I might meet some friends..."

Bill was wearing a cape and a mask, because, in honor of Anna, we'd bought "The Phantom of the Opera," and, of course, he was now the Phantom himself. "There is no need to explain yourself. Go, go and leave us!" he exclaimed.

Sarah, unfazed by Bill, said, "Okay," and left.

Quincy rushed out of the kitchen. "Sarah!" he screeched.

But Sarah was gone.

"God DAMN IT!" Quincy kicked the couch.

"Hey hey hey watch it!" I cried. Aunt Chasey adored the couch, and abhorred profanity.

"She was playing this loud satanic shit last night! I did not sleep. At all." Quincy shook his head.

"Ah, the music of the night," said Bill dreamily.

"No man, I'm serious. That was some disturbing stuff."

"Satanic?" I questioned.

"Yeah. That...*stuff* was right out of 'Rosemary's Baby'. Only heavy metal."

I raised an eyebrow. I kind of liked "Rosemary's Baby," it was a good movie, but... "Whoa."

Quincy pointed to the door. "She is *not* pulling that again," he promised. He stormed into the kitchen.

I looked at Bill. "Oh boy," I sighed.

"Perhaps it is *she* who is the toad," Bill was muttering.

In the weeks that followed, it was made clear that Sarah was *not* trying to make a better life for herself. While the music apparently stopped, she was less than civil to Quincy (according to Quincy), and she left the bathroom a total mess. Which Quincy found unacceptable.

So, one day in late October, the guys came over to get revenge.

Sarah had gone "out" again, which meant she was either finding people to bring home (or go home with), drinking herself into oblivion, or performing some kind of mortal sin. My Aunts had tried to talk to her a couple of times, but Sarah always said she had "things" to do.

I stood behind Butch, Abe, and Quincy as they went through Sarah's room. I'm ashamed to say I helped them. The Aunts had stashed a set of keys to all of the rooms in my room. I wasn't supposed to actually *use* them, it was only there in case the other two sets got lost. But sometimes, drastic measures had to be taken.

"What is the point?" Abe muttered.

"What the hell is this?" Butch pulled out a hot pink and neon green lace dress.

"Hideous," Quincy replied. "Whoa." He pulled out a string of clothing, presumably an under garment. "Ouch!"

"It probably feels different when you're a woman," Butch suggested.

Quincy looked at me. "Does *this* look comfortable to *you*?"

I shook my head. "Nope."

Abe was looking under the bed.

"Hey. A photo album!" He pulled out a leather book.

"No shit?" Quincy kneeled down.

Abe opened it. "Oh my God." He slammed it shut and shoved it back under the bed.

"Do I wanna know?" Quincy questioned.

"Not at all," Abe told him. "Man, this is disturbing."

"Hey, it's Xerxes." Butch picked an angry Xerxes up out of the closet.

"Butch, man, let the poor bastard sleep," said Abe.

"Here Phyllis." Butch handed the cat over the bed to me. I put him on Bill's bed, in the other room. Afraid that she had locked him in the closet, I looked for signs of harm or starvation. There were none. He'd just been sleeping.

"Sorry Zerks," I apologized, giving him a kiss. I went back to Sarah's room.

"Uh oh," Quincy said, opening another drawer. He pulled out a bag. In it were substances I only recognized because I'd seen "Fear and Loathing in Las Vegas."

"She hit the jackpot," Abe said. "Let's get out the bongs."

"Shut up Abe," Butch said. He took the bag from Quincy. "Damn, this is the real thing. We gotta tell the Aunts."

"They're not *your* Aunts, man."

"Shut up Abe."

"You!"

"You!"

"You!"

"Guys! We can't tell the Aunts!" Quincy snapped.

In unison, we all said, "Why?"

"Because they'll question Sarah and she'll know we were going through her room."

"Crap," Abe muttered.

"So what do we do?" I wanted to know.

Quincy thought a moment. Then he snapped his fingers.

"I got it!" He pointed to me. "We'll burn 'em!"

"What?" I said, startled.

"In the backyard. We'll have a bonfire!"

"Now if burning drugs isn't just, I don't know what is," said Abe.

"I'm up for it, as long as nothing explodes," said Butch.

"Phyllis wouldn't let that happen." Quincy gave me a look.

I rolled my eyes and sighed. "Fine."

So, that afternoon, I set fire to all of Sarah's drugs. However, we watched the fire from the front porch because Butch said that if we got too close, the fumes would get us high. Abe did look a little dazed afterwards.

Sarah never said a word about her missing drugs, and Quincy continued to dislike her.

Fifteen in Blue.

Sid returned on my fifteenth birthday, the end of November and the middle of my eighth grade year. Being that Thanksgiving had just passed, I was up in my room listening to ancient (or timeless, however you want look at it) Christmas CDs.

"Doesn't it feel like Christmas? Doesn't it feel like Christmas? Doesn't it feel like Christmas? Yes, it feels like Christmas," I sang along with my old Destiny's Child holiday CD. Piled next to it were some Billboard Christmas CDs, Mariah Carey's Christmas CD, Jewel's, and and other assorted Christmas CDs and mixes. I believe in music to get you into the spirit. I picked up a nervous-looking Johnny and danced around the room with him in my arms. Suddenly I heard a noise. I turned down the music. It had come from under my bed.

I looked at Johnny, who probably thought I was insane. "What is it Johnny?"

Enrique the Spaniard and Wonder Woman scurried out from under my bed.

"Ah!" I gasped. "Get of here! You scared me to death you damn cats!" I chased them out of the room. I looked at Johnny again. "Sorry sweetheart, I didn't mean to swear." Yes, at fifteen, I swore because it was forbidden. And had conversations with cats.

Then I heard a car door shut.

"Quincy must've come back," I told Johnny. I went to Aunt Chasey's room, where there was a better view of the front of the house and the end of the driveway.

Ohhhh boy, said the voice exasperatedly inside my head.

Oh boy! I retorted enthusiastically.

There was Sid, going into the house.

I didn't rush. I checked myself out in the mirror and walked down the stairs, just in time to hear cries of, "Sid!" "Sid, you're back!" "We've missed you!" "How nice that you've come!" from the Aunts.

"Hi Kippie, hi Chase," was pretty much all he could say as they smothered him in hugs.

"Who's *this*?" Abe had been sitting on the couch. He was sizing Sid up intently.

I inferred that Quincy had met Abe after Sid left. I told Johnny this telepathically.

Johnny jumped out of my arms and headed for the kitchen. Food over Phyllis, I suppose.

"Hi Sid," I greeted him from across the room.

"Hey Philly." Sid pointed to me. "Happy birthday."

"Thanks!"

"Abe, this is Dominick Siddons, better known as Sid," Kippie introduced.

"Good to know you, Sid," Abe said, flirting. "My name is Abe, I'm Quincy's *best* friend."

"Really? Nice to meet you. Where's Quince?"

"He went out to run some errands," said Aunt Chasey. He was buying me a "surprise" ice cream cake.

"I see." Sid held up a bag. "I don't know if you'll like these, Philly, but I thought of you when I saw them." He handed me two wrapped objects.

"Thank you Sid." I looked to the Aunts. "I'm opening these."

"Fine, fine, it's your birthday," Aunt Chasey said.

The first present was a candle. It was made of black and red wax entwined beautifully. It came in a small black holder.

"I love it," I murmured.

"Light it," said Sid and Abe in unison.

I grinned and blew a flame onto the candle.

"Wow," said Aunt Kippie. "That's gorgeous." She took it and placed it on a table.

The other gift was a poster.

"Johnny Depp! Thank you!"

Sid smiled. "I remembered the cat."

I smiled back.

"How nice of you Sid!" exclaimed Aunt Chasey. "But you must have felt awfully strange purchasing it."

Sid chuckled. "It's all right. I don't make a very convincing gay man."

Abe sighed. "You're straight. Of course."

Suddenly the front door opened and in staggered Sarah. She looked at us all and blinked her eyes. Her hair was green and black, her face was worn and tired.

"H-hi," she said. She stared blankly at Sid.

"Sid, this is Sarah," Aunt Chasey informed him.

"I'm Sid," said Sid.

"Hi. Um..I'm just gonna go to my room for a little whi..a little while."

"It's Phyllis's birthday," Abe told her.

"Oh really? Happy birthday Phyllis. Trust me, it just gets worse." Sarah wandered to the back staircase and went upstairs.

"Intriguing woman," Abe said sarcastically.

"She came to us a month or so ago," Aunt Chasey told Sid. "I do wish I could help her."

"She's beyond all help, I'm afraid,"Aunt Kippie remarked sadly.

"Why's that?" asked Sid.

"The poor girl's on drugs, she's sleeping around, she's drinking. She doesn't want to be helped."

"She was in a gang," I added. "She told me she's a knife fighter."

"Her rent's always on time though," said Aunt Chasey, adding a happier note.

Sid half-smiled and it was glorious. "Where's she from?"

"California," said Aunt Chasey.

"New York," said Aunt Kippie.

"Hoo boy," said Abe. "And you're sure she hasn't stolen anything yet?"

"Abraham!" Aunt Chasey scolded.

"I'm just saying." Abe looked out the window. "Where the hell is Quincy? Can't he find a damned ice cream cake?"

"Abraham!"

Abe flinched. "Sorry Phyllis."

"Don't worry Abe, I already knew."

"No use keeping secrets from this one," Abe told the Aunts, gesturing to me with his thumb.

"Oh, by the way. I need to discuss my options with you two," said Sid.

"Options?" asked Aunt Chasey.

"For...every month."

"Well, if you can remember how much the rent was before, I'm sure that'll be fine," she assured him.

Aunt Kippie gave her a look.

An understanding expression came across Aunt Chasey's face. "Oh, yes, let's go into the kitchen and discuss that." She looked to Abe and I. "Why don't you two stay in here and wait for Quincy to get back with that cake?" She smiled, and the three of them went into the kitchen.

"That was odd," I told Abe.

Abe nodded. "Are you sure you want that poster of Johnny Depp?"

The basement door opened, and out stepped Bill.

"Hi-ya Phyllis! Abe." He sat next to me on the couch, and swung an arm around my shoulder. In a second, I could tell he'd been watching a Jack Nicholson movie, or at least a Christian Slater one.

"How's the birthday girl?" he asked me.

"I'm all right Bill...how 'bout you?"

"Lookin' forward to some cake. Where the hell's Quincy?"

"That's what we wanna know!" Abe said, annoyed.

"If he doesn't get here soon, things are going to get pretty ugly." Bill cracked his knuckles. "Yep, I might need to get out the old axe."

If Bill could've been slightly saner about who he really was, he could've been an actor. He didn't often change his appearance unless it was a very small change like a hat or something...but somehow he always made it perfectly clear who he was. Aunt Kippie had described Bill's condition (although she was no psychiatrist) as a "way to escape the real world and his true self." Whoever that was. I would never know.

Let's move on to another, better-looking subject — Sid. It had looked to me as though he and the Aunts were all keeping some big secret. No matter, I decided. The Aunts told me everything, what I wanted to know and what I didn't want to know. They'd tell me after he left, if not while he was here.

The door opened.

"Surprise! Quincy is *home*!" yelled Quincy, carrying the cakebox. Butch was behind him.

Abe got up. "Thank God. Holy crap Butch! Your eyebrows are blue."

"No shit, sherlock."

"Shut up, you guys! Kippie and Chasey hate cussing. You know that!" exclaimed Quincy.

"Sorry," they both said.

"But why are his eyebrows blue?!" demanded Abe.

Butch beamed. "I had myself a creative awakening."

Quincy shook his head. "Some people paint. Butchie dyes his eyebrows."

Abe raised a normally colored eyebrow and stared at Butch for a second. Then he shrugged. "If you like it, then I like it."

"I *love* it!" Butch looked at me. "What about you, Phyllis?"

"Oh Butch, you know I've been saying all along that you should dye those things blue." I did my best Quincy voice.

Butch and Abe laughed. Quincy smirked. "Very funny Phyllis."

"So does Sid know Butch?" I asked.

"Butch is my man! Of course he knows Sid. Why?"

"He's here," said Abe. "Why did you not tell me about this man? He's HOT."

"Sadly, he's also straight," Quincy sighed.

"He could be converted," Abe insisted.

"Hey, if I can't convert him then *nobody* can," Butch let them know.

"He used to date Anna," said Quincy.

"Sergeant Anna? The opera singer?" Abe winced.

"Dat be the one mon."

"Never mind."

"Hence the 'used to.' They couldn't handle each other."

"Ahem. Nice eyebrows Butch." Sid emerged from the kitchen.

"Homigod, Sid Siddons!" Butch rushed up and hugged Sid, who looked a bit disturbed, then relaxed. "You're back! I can't believe it!"

"Yeah, I'll be moving back in in a little while. I'm glad to see you're still pals with Quince. How long have you had those eyebrows?"

"Since yesterday, actually."

"You should do your eyebrows blue, Sid," I told him.

He bounced his eyebrows at me. "You think so?"

My mind almost totally wiped out. "No," I murmured, shaking my head.

"Hot pink might look nice," Bill spoke up. "Now let's open up that cake!"

On the Porch.

They sang the birthday song, and I blue—I mean blew—out the candles. Then we ate. Afterwards, the guys went down in the basement with Bill to watch movies and drink beer.

I went out on the screened-in back porch with my new candle, as well as a drawing pad and a new art set my Aunts had given me. The other gifts were clothes, jewelry, shoes, CDs, assorted sheet music and songbooks, and some candy cigarettes.

I liked to draw, but I loved music more. Aside from the "real" piano, I had a keyboard in my room, which I had saved up for myself at twelve. I'd taken dance lessons for three years, piano lessons for seven, and though I'd stopped taking lessons I still played on my own. I'd forgotten most of what I'd learned in dance.

I tried to draw Sid. It didn't work out well. I turned the page and tried again.

"Hey Philly." He came out and sat across from me.

I quickly flipped the page. "Hey Sid."

"Did you have a lucrative birthday?"

"Definitely. I'm glad you came." I paused. "How did you remember?"

"I probably wouldn't have, to tell you the truth, if I hadn't been writing to your Aunts."

"Oh." I smiled. "I love the presents you got me."

"Good." Sid slightly raised an eyebrow. "Why didn't Anna show up?"

"She's still on tour. We went to see her during the summer. She always comes back though."

"Ah."

"So you and Anna met through my Aunts?"

Sid nodded. "Pretty much."

There was a pause.

"What grade are you in, Philly?"

"Eighth."

"That means I'll be moving in here in the middle of your freshman year."

"If all goes well for me," I muttered. School was hard for me because my Aunts held up the idea that I was a genius like my mother and if I dropped below an "honors" grade on anything, I was in big trouble.

He looked me in the eye. "It will." It was almost a threat.

"Why aren't you moving in sooner?" I wanted to know.

"I traveled a little, then I went back to the old house my family left me. I've been staying there, I still need to make some arrangements for leaving it."

"Why *are* you moving in?" I blushed a bit. "Not that I mind you moving in, but..."

"You have every right to question someone you're gonna live with, Philly." Sid smiled slightly, and shrugged. "It gets lonely up there. But it's mainly because this place is close to the city."

"Oh." Why in God's name wouldn't a man like Sid have a girlfriend?

Sid rested his chin on an upright fist. "Are you happy?"

"Huh?"

"Being able to breathe fire. Blessing or curse?"

"Blessing." I breathed out some flames to emphasize it.

Sid grinned. "Do you show it off to all your friends?"

I laughed a bit. "No, I don't have the kind of friends you can share this type of thing with."

Yeah, those kinds of friends have to *exist*, said the voice.

"Can't keep a secret, or they'd get weirded out?"

"Both."

"That's a shame. You'd probably have all the guys after you if they knew you could breathe fire."

I smirked.

He smiled. "Can you do any tricks?"

Tricks? Hmm.. "Yeah, actually. I mean, I guess so. I kind of just learned to do this." I puckered my lips and, making sure I wasn't facing the wind, blew out smoke rings. They were small at first, and then they grew like ripples and disappeared.

"Whoa. That's sexy," he told me, impressed.

"Thanks." I didn't know what else to say, but the word sounded good coming out of his mouth.

"So why aren't your friends here?"

"I just...once I got to middle school, a lot of my friends changed. We still talk but I just don't like them as much. But, you know, it's a pretty small school."

"True. Once you're at the high school, you have most of the city to pick from."

"Did you go to school here?"

He almost laughed but didn't. "Nope." He didn't elaborate.

"Oh." I paused. "Do you know which room you're moving into?"

"I'm not sure which section of the upstairs. Would it be a violation of your privacy if I took the one at the end of the hall? You had the room next to it the last time I lived here."

"No, not at all." The room diagonally across from mine, at the end of the hall, was the biggest bedroom. It also had a skylight. Besides that there was only a small window, so it was usually pretty dark.

"Really?"

"Really."

Sid grinned. "Thanks Philly."

"My pleasure," I said.

"Did you draw anything?" he asked, glancing at the paper in my lap.

I shook my head. "Not yet."

"What can you draw?"

"People. Trees. Cats. Uh, mostly people, though, I guess since I see them most. But no one in particular."

"Fire?"

"Yeah, I draw fire, but it usually just looks like a bunch of wavy orange things."

"Draw a person."

"Why?"

"I want to see how good you are."

I chuckled. "What do you consider good?"

"I draw people too. I'll compare you to me."

Sid didn't seem like the drawing type. I was surprised.

"Yeah, I know," Sid agreed, reading my mind. "You pick up a lot of things when you've been alive as long as I have."

I raised an eyebrow. "And how long is that?"

Sid almost looked as if he had to think about it for a few seconds. "30 years."

"When's your birthday?" I inquired.

"Draw me a picture first."

"Oh, sorry." I began to draw.

Maybe poor Sid doesn't want to tell you his birthday, chided the voice.

He already knows mine, I mumbled. What's it matter?

Grow up, the voice retorted.

Grow up?! What's that supposed to mean? I demanded.

The mental confrontation would have gone on longer; however, Sid interrupted it by speaking. "How long have you been drawing?"

"Since..since before the fire. My Aunts told me that."

"Really?"

"Mm-hmm."

"But you don't remember that?"

"No, not at all."

"Would I be prying if I asked you what your first memory is?"

"You can ask me anything," I didn't mean to say.

"I'll remember that." He grinned. "What is it?"

I leaned back and rested my pencil, thinking hard.

My first memory...

"Well, there is a dream I have sometimes..I'm lying in my bed..it's a different bed and a different room than what I have now, but in the dream, it's completely normal."

"Great thing about dreams," Sid remarked.

"Yeah. And I sit up in my bed, and look down, and there are little white mice crawling all over the floor. My Aunts told me my parents experimented mainly on mice, so I do wonder if that actually happened." I paused. He said nothing, so I went on. "But I guess my first *real* memory is..." I stopped again, confirming the memory in my mind. "Aunt Kippie and Aunt Chasey reading to me. I think I remember bits and pieces of my sixth birthday, but not enough to totally remember your face."

Sid smiled. "Well, I looked the same."

Wonder Woman hopped up the porch steps and came in through one of our cat doors. She walked over to me and I let her rub against my fingers.

"Who's this one?" Sid wanted to know.

"Wonder Woman."

"Bill named her?"

"He did."

"He was always into superheroes."

"Yeah, I like them too."

"Do you draw them?"

I shook my head. "I can't draw *specific* people." I looked back down at the person, the girl I had drawn. I handed the drawing to Sid.

"She looks a little like you," he said. He was studying my face.

I didn't think I was that much to look at. My skin had gotten better; it was naturally tan thanks to a little Native American blood. I looked more like Aunt Chasey in that respect, being darker. My eyes went back and forth from being green to being yellowish brownish. My figure was hourglass but my waist wasn't exactly small.

I looked back at him. "You have good eyes. They're very dark. Sometimes I'm not sure if they're brown or black."

"Brown," he said. "Were you trying to draw yourself?"

"Not really." I crinkled my lips. "I think she looks prettier than I do." That was meant to insult my appearance, not compliment my drawing. Plus I wanted to see what Sid would say.

"Nope."

I glanced at him.

"It's not a bad drawing," he said, "you just look good."

I smiled. I wished I could tell him how good *he* looked. "I don't know, but thanks."

"I don't say things that aren't true, Philly." He paused. "Well, not when I can help it."

Quincy entered then.

"Sid! Phyllis!" He sat in the middle between Sid and me. "Did you have a good birthday?" he asked me.

"Lovely," I replied. "What'd you come out here for?" I tried to sound curious rather than angry because he'd spoiled my moment with Sid.

Quincy leaned over, his cheek almost touching mine, and squinting, pointed at Sid. "That man, right there. I figured I'd try proposing one more time before I lost hope."

"Very funny Quince. What's up?" Sid asked.

Quincy got down on his knees. "Sid Siddons, will you marry me?"

Sid threw up his hands in a helpless gesture. "Where's the ring?"

"The ring! Aw shit," said Quincy, standing up and running a hand through his thick black hair. "Abe is quite taken with you, Mr. Man."

"Where'd he come from?"

"I dated him for like a week. We decided to be friends." Quincy shook his head. "Now he and Butch are in love, but neither one'll admit it. What're you gonna do?" He gave Sid a look. "It's almost as frustrating as you and Anna were."

Sid held up a hand. "Stop it Quince. Worst relationship of my life."

Quincy's eyebrows shot up. "Your *whole life?!*"

Sid considered. "Well...maybe there was *one* who was worse."

"I should think so!"

"What happened to Anna? I mean, *with* Anna?" I asked.

"Nothing Philly, it was just a mistake on my part."

Quincy raised an eyebrow at Sid. "Have you had anybody since then?"

"Yeah."

"I mean a serious relationship, Sid."

"No."

"You gotta open up your heart, Sid. You'll never find your girl until you *look* for her."

Sid looked at me.

"Dr. Quincy," I told him.

"Phyllis is single if you wanna make your move." Quincy winked at me.

Sid bounced his eyebrows. "Maybe I will."

I just smiled. Out of the corner of my eye, I saw movement and looked through the glass door to into the house. Aunt Kippie was looking at Quincy and pointing to Sid.

"Oh, Sid, what I came to say was, the Aunts need a word," Quincy said.

Sid stood. "Great." He went inside.

Quincy remained.

"Thanks for the shoes," I regarded him.

"Anytime hon."

"So what's the deal with Sid?" I asked.

"He's movin' in next December, I think."

"Yeah, but what's all the hush-hush stuff?" I persisted.

"Oh, they're probably tellin' him not to start trouble if Anna comes back."

I was alarmed. "Why would he do that?"

Quincy shrugged. "Sid's got some wolf to him, I guess you'd say."

I laughed a bit. "Wolf?"

"Yep." He looked at me. "*You* seem to like Sid, like Sid just fine."

My face didn't turn red, which was surprising because it only did that at all the wrong moments.

"He's cool," I said. Needless to say, that was an understatement.

Summer Again, Seven Months Later.

Sid left that night, hugging me good-bye this time, and I went on with my eighth grade year. It was terrible and I'd rather not recall it, so I'm skipping in my story to the summer after, when I'd passed everything and there were no more worries until September.

It was that summer that Quincy met Damien, and it was that summer that Bill started working again. And it was that summer I met Taylor.

I was in the living room, happily contemplating my freedom—it was too good to be true, compared to the hell I'd just been through—when the doorbell rang.

Sid? was my first thought. I'd started picturing scenarios in which Sid would move in early. Sometimes he'd ask me to marry him, sometimes he'd turn out to be a secret agent and had to take me away...

I got up and opened it. There were Abe and Butch.

"Hey Sparky!"

"Heat-miser!"

I stepped aside to let them in. "Hi Butch, hi Abe."

"Where's Quincy?" Abe wanted to know.

"Upstairs," I told them.

"I'm in the kitchen!" came Quincy's voice from the kitchen.

I looked to Abe. "He's definitely upstairs."

Quincy came out and waved his new scarf around. It was pink and white and red and orange, and he'd gotten it at the store where he worked. Apparently, it was part of a "hot" new designer line they were launching, called "Crimson."

"Oh Quincy you are kidding! You're not promoting that 'Crimson' crap, are you?" Butch said, raising his eyebrows, which were, sad to say, no longer blue, but very nicely shaped.

"Damn right I am! You should too! Crimson's gonna be the next Versace, the next Prada, Dior, Guess," Quincy went on naming clothing stores, designers, and brands for about ten minutes or so.

Abe raised a hand. "We get it, oh Quincy, Fashion Guru."

"In fact," said Quincy, pointing to Butch. He clapped his hands. "I have it, I've got it! Do your eyebrows *crimson*!"

Aunt Kippie stuck her head out of the sewing room. "Quincy, are you all going or what?"

Quincy held out a hand in a stop gesture, like a traffic cop. "Say no more. Boys, let's go." And they did.

Aunt Kippie looked at me. "I love 'em to death, but they make so much noise!"

I laughed a bit. "Maybe Quincy'll get rich."

Kippie rolled her eyes and leaned back into the sewing room.

The phone rang just then.

"Phyllis, could you be a dear and get that?"

I stood. "Sure." I got up and walked over to the phone.

Sarah, I should mention, had left, but her stuff was still in her room and my Aunts found her rent on the table every week. We hadn't actually seen her since Easter. Anna was still gone as well, and the Aunts were a bit worried because she hadn't written since May. Sid had given us no word since his last visit. And I hadn't done anything with Janelle or anyone else since Janelle's end-of-school party. That had not gone well, what with my little problem with Jeremy and all.

The point is, out of everyone who could've called, it was Janelle.

"Phyllis?"

"Hi Janelle."

"Hi! What's up?"

"Nothing, you?"

"Oh same, Jeremy's gone, Cassie's gone. All alone."

Good, said the voice.

"Oh," I said.

"Are you going anywhere this summer?"

"No. I'm taking an art class though," I told her, because I was.

"You still draw good?"

Draw *well,* corrected the voice.

Shut up, I told it.

"Okay, I guess."

There was silence.

"Phyllis...can I talk to you about the party?"

"What about it?"

"Phyllis, you put out my bonfire!"

"I did not put out your bonfire!"

"All the guys swore they didn't touch it."

"So?"

"So, you were alone with it, for like a second, and when we came back it was out."

"Maybe you set it the wrong way. What's it matter?"

I had made a mistake. "Why does the fire matter?" I demanded.

"What happened with you and Jeremy? The guys said something happened and Jeremy refused to talk about it."

"He dumped the punch bowl over my head."

Janelle sighed. "Why didn't you tell me?"

"Wouldn't have made me any drier."

"Tuh. What'd you say after he did it?"

"You know me, Jan. I just walked away. I'm not good at dealing with that crap."

"Oh c'mon Phyllis. You know Jeremy's just kidding around. He thinks you're sweet. He likes all of my friends." She was an idiot.

"Oh. Hey Jan, I have to go."

"All right. Wait! Do you want to hang out tomorrow?"

"Sure, come on over. I'll see you tomorrow."

"See you."

"Bye." I hung up, shaking my head. Janelle wasn't my friend, and I wasn't hers. That was over, and we both knew it. Yet we were still pretending.

I called to Aunt Kippie. "I'm going for a walk."

"Be back by dinner!"

"Okay." I left. I walked down the street, around the corner, past Janelle's neighborhood at the edge of our district, and into the next district.

I needed new friends. I couldn't go to high school still being the class freak, a position I didn't even know how I'd acquired.

I shook my head. Was it my "family"? Did people know about them and think I was automatically weird? Maybe it was because I'd gone out with Trevor's friend Toby Rutledge for two weeks and then broken up with him? But, two weeks, did that really count? Toby had been nice to me *until* we dated; I decided not to count it, but that didn't mean he hadn't.

I sighed.

I neared the next corner, where I planned to cross the little bridge up ahead, then turn and swing around the block and head home. Or maybe I'd jump off the bridge.

It can't be more than eleven feet from the water below, said the voice.

Exactly, I said. I'm not brave enough to kill, and that includes myself.

Since when does it take bravery to kill? the voice wanted to know.

"Whatever you want to call it," I muttered to myself.

Suddenly I heard a dog barking. I looked down to see a girl and a dog standing at the edge of the river, by the bridge. The girl had short, blondish red hair that was sort of spikey, but not in a gelled way. It was more like she'd just woken up, but it worked. Her eyes were bright as she looked up at me and smiled.

"Shut up Dig," she told the dog. "Hi," she said to me.

"Hi," I said, walking down. I see a dog, I have to pet it.

"Sorry he barked at you."

"S'okay. Can I pet him?" The dog was a fluffy brown loud one who came up to my waist when standing on all fours.

"Sure," she said.

I pet the dog. "He's cute. What's his name?"

"Digger. He's actually not mine, he's my cousin's." She rolled her eyes and gave a little smile. "But they pay me to walk him."

"He's sweet," I said, rubbing Digger's ears.

"Yeah, he loves everyone who pets him."

I looked at the water. "Does he swim?" I'd never had a dog, and honestly didn't plan on it. But that doesn't mean I don't love the creatures as much as cats.

She nodded. "Yup. I'm waiting for him to jump in." She held up a leash. "That's why he's not on this." She smiled again. "I'm Taylor."

"I'm Phyllis."

"Do you live near here?"

"Yeah, just a few blocks away, down a street some...almost in the country, but not." I was ever so articulate.

"That's cool. I live up there." She pointed up the street.

"So you live right on the edge of the city?"

Taylor nodded. "I can see the tops of some of the buildings from my bedroom window. Have you always lived here?"

"Yep." Except for those first five years I don't remember.

"I wonder why I never knew you."

"Do you go to school in the city?"

"Yeah."

"That's why."

"Oh. What grade are you in?"

"Going into ninth."

"Me too." She nodded again.

"So you'll be at the high school next year, right?"

"Yeah, I'll probably see you there."

"Yeah. It's pretty big isn't it?"

"Oh yeah. I heard the freshman class is like 1000 alone."

"Whoa. There's like 20 per class at my school."

Taylor raised her eyebrows. "How do you stand it?"

I chuckled. "I don't. I didn't."

Water splashed us as Digger jumped into the river.

"Ah!" we both cried.

Taylor laughed. "Digger!"

"How old is he?"

"Four, I believe."

"That's cool." I grinned. "I just have a bunch of cats at my house."

"I *love* cats!" Taylor said excitedly.

Later we'd joke that that's what got her to invite me to walk with her the next Wednesday.

* * *

I walked into the house just as Aunt Kippie was calling Bill from the basement to have dinner.

"Oh Phyllis, how was your walk?"

"It was good. I met a girl, with a dog. She's in my grade."

"How nice! Come in and tell us about it."

"Tell us about what?" inquired Aunt Chasey as Aunt Kippie and I went into the kitchen.

"Phyllis met another girl on her walk," Aunt Kippie told her, sitting down. Bill came in and sat.

"What's for dinner?" He had a southern hint to his voice, and his eyes had a squinty expression, but I couldn't place it to a movie character.

"Who might you be?" I asked him.

"I'm Budd." He picked up a fork.

"Kill Bill Vol. 2?" I asked softly, and Aunt Kippie nodded. "Spaghetti, Budd," I told him.

"What was her name?"

I looked to Aunt Chasey. "Who?"

"The girl," she said, putting some spaghetti on my plate.

"Taylor Venchak."

Aunt Kippie looked up quickly from the cheese she was sprinkling. "Ven*chak*?"

I nodded. "Venn-chack," I pronounced.

"Oh my."

"What is it?"

Aunt Kippie looked to Aunt Chasey. "Isn't that the family who lost the little boy about two years ago?"

Aunt Chasey nodded. "The very same. David Venchak. He wasn't over 8."

My eyes grew wide. "What?"

"It must have been her little brother or cousin. There was a little boy who died in a car accident. Apparently the whole thing happened in the blink of an eye. No one saw it coming."

"Oh my God," I said. "Do you think they were really related?"

Aunt Kippie nodded. "Chasey went to the funeral, didn't you Chasey?"

"Yes, but I didn't see any of his siblings there." Aunt Chasey shook her head. "Probably stayed home, the poor girl." She looked at me. "But don't bring it up with Taylor. Just, as always," she reminded, "be as kind as you can be."

"These are damn good meatballs, Chasey," Bill/Budd told her.

"Thank you Budd."

Taylor.

Taylor invited me to her house after our next walk.

"Wow," I said as we neared her house. It wasn't large, but it had a little pond in the front and a gold knocker on the door.

"Go in, Dig," she said, opening the front door. Digger rushed in.

"Hello Digger," said a tall woman standing inside. She patted his head. "Did you miss me?"

"Hi Aunt Linda," Taylor greeted her.

"How was Digger?"

"Good, as always," Taylor told her. She gestured to me. "This is my friend Phyllis."

The woman held out her hand. "Hello Phyllis, I'm so glad to meet you! I'm Taylor's Aunt Linda."

"Hi," I said. "It's nice to meet you too."

"Call me Linda." Linda took the leash from Taylor. "Well, Digger and I have to get going. See you Taylor. Bye Phyllis. Have fun girls!" She walked out the door and Taylor closed it after her.

"Bye Aunt Linda," Taylor called as she shut it. She smiled. "Aunt Linda's very friendly."

I nodded. "Gotta love your Aunts. I live with mine."

"Really?" Taylor was thoughtful. "Wait, your last name is Sorin?"

I nodded again, waiting for her to recognize it. Somehow, everyone knew my Aunts.

Taylor pointed at me. "Kippie and Chastity Sorin?"

"Yup."

"My parents know them."

I rolled my eyes a bit. "Doesn't everybody."

Taylor smiled again. "They were very kind to us after my brother died."

I didn't know what to say.

"He was eight. I was twelve." She sighed. "It was the worst thing...the most horrible thing that could have ever happened."

"I...I can't even try to imagine what you felt, or what you still feel," I said carefully.

"Do you have any siblings?"

"Not in the sense of a blood brother or sister."

We went into her living room.

"I'll give you a tour in a minute, if you want."

"Sure. You have a very pretty house."

"Thanks. My dad redid a lot of it." She looked at me. "So...do your parents live with you too?"

I shook my head. I hadn't had to answer that question in a long, long time.

No, said the voice. They came to take them away, ha ha, to the funny farm, where life is beautiful all the time.

I closed my eyes. It's pretty sad when the voice in your head has to remind you your parents were insane.

I sighed. "I...I don't really know where they live. They...were unfit to take care of me." Understated that one. "I haven't seen them since I was five."

Taylor's eyes were wide. "Wow. I'm sorry."

I waved her apology away. "Don't be, it was for the best. I have a family, just not the conventional kind. You can come over sometime if you want, but you might find it...odd."

"Odd's good. I've hardly been anyplace out of the ordinary, let alone this town, since Davy died. After the first year, my parents decided to start going on vacations and stuff again." She shrugged. "I've been sort of a recluse. You're the first friend I've had over here in a while."

"Well, you can meet a lot of weird people at my house." I grinned.

"Really?"

I nodded. "Do you want to come over for dinner tomorrow?"

"That'd be great!" Taylor smiled. "Do you want to see the house now?"

Taylor took me all around the house, which, for a small house, had a lot of rooms, and I was glad. It was what I was used to. We ended up in her room.

She sat on her bed. "You can check out my stuff, if you want."

I looked around. One entire wall, of Taylor's room, was a bookshelf.

"Wow, have you read all of these?" I asked her, turning.

She nodded. "Yeah, I'm a bookworm. But I mean, they're good books, not a lot of educational crap." She grinned. I laughed. "There's some DVDs and CDs there too," she told me. "I love music."

"Me too," I told her, scanning the shelves. There were a lot of horror novels (she had all of the Hannibal Lecter books and the movies were next to them), some general teen novels, biographies of authors, actresses, actors. She had some classics too, Hemingway, Dickens and Twain. Poems by Robert Frost. A shelf for Stephen King and Anne Rice, and some Christopher Pike. Lots of sci-fi.

"You like Stephen King?" I asked.

She shrugged. "He's Stephen King. You can't *not* read him when you're as into books as I am." She grinned again. "But the best ones, my favorite ones are on the bottom shelf."

I kneeled down. The second-to-last shelf was all CDs. Upon looking at the bottom shelf, I saw the spines of a great many DC Comic Books.

Graphic novels, said the voice.

Yeah whatever, I replied.

"That's awesome," I told her.

"Thanks," she replied. "Batman's the love of my life."

I pulled out one that had a bunch of different heroes on the cover.

"Who are all of these?" I asked. "I know Batman, Wonder Woman, Superman, obviously...that's the Flash, and that's...Green Lantern?"

"I love Green Lantern too."

"I don't know much about him. But who's the green guy? And the rest of them?" Apparently I didn't know as much about superheroes as I thought I did.

"That's Martian Manhunter." She went on to point out Plastic Man, Hawkgirl, Hawkman, Green Arrow, Black Canary...

"Eesh," I said.

"Yeah. I've been obsessed with DC my whole life. Davy was too. They inspired me to want to be a prosecutor."

"A prosecutor?" Like Sid!

Taylor nodded. "Oh yeah."

"I know a guy who used to be a prosecutor. Or, at least, he wanted to be. Maybe he is."

Taylor laughed. "Who is it?"

"This guy...he's 30, so he can't be retired." I paused. "My Aunts rent out rooms. He's moving in next year." And he's quite lovely.

"That's cool."

Taylor didn't have a ton of CDs, maybe 50. And that's not a lot, not when I had at least 100, and that was back when I was fifteen. Most of hers were rock, old and new, and Billy Joel.

"I love Billy Joel," I told her. It wasn't easy to say that in front of someone my age anymore, but I loved anyone who played the piano. "I've always wanted to learn to play his stuff."

"You play the piano?" Taylor looked up at me, clearly intrigued.

I nodded. "Since I was six."

"That's *so awesome.*" She half-smiled. "I've played guitar for like a month, and the viola since third grade. I kind of play drums too, but I haven't learned formally. Just from my older sister."

I smiled. "We should start a band."

"Oh, totally."

Damien, Donuts, and Dinner.

Taylor did come over the next evening, but her mother brought her this time. My Aunts invited her to stay as well, and were, very politely, refused.

"We're having something Italian," I told Taylor.

Taylor was looking around. "Wow," she said. "Your house is huge!"

"Has to be. Just brace yourself for people," I told her. "Quincy is a man who lives here. He's gay, and he'll probably bring his friends for dinner—" I stopped. "You don't have a problem with gays, do you?"

Taylor shook her head rapidly. "Not at all. I think I could actually use some gay influence. I mean, look at my clothes!"

I laughed. "They're fine," I reassured her, gesturing to the couch and sitting down. "So there's them, and of course, my Aunts. There's a girl who uses one of the rooms upstairs, but we haven't seen her in months. Anna Xesly lives in the basement, but she's not here right now."

"Where is she?"

I explained about Anna's being an opera singer on tour.

"That's really neat," Taylor said.

"It's cool that you think so. A lot of people just hate opera."

"Yeah, but the Phantom of the Opera isn't your generic opera."

I nodded. "True."

"So who else lives here?"

I grinned. "Well, there's this girl upstairs, named Phyllis, but she hasn't come out in years."

Taylor smirked.

"There is one more person. Bill Charles. He's mentally ill."

"Oh no. Is it serious?"

"It...it's an interesting condition. He—"

As if on cue, Bill came down the stairs.

"Hallo Phyllis!" he greeted me. "Phyllis's lovely friend," he greeted Taylor.

"Captain Sparrow, you took my movie!" I accused, hoping Taylor would sort of catch on and not be too freaked.

"Borrowed it love, borrowed it," he corrected me.

I looked to Taylor.

"He's British?" Taylor inquired.

I shook my head and spoke swiftly and quietly. "The Captain here watches movies and then...starts...that is he...takes on the personality of a character from the movie. He just watched 'Pirates of the Caribbean'."

Taylor was, once again, intrigued. "So am I supposed to call you 'Captain'?"

"If you please," Bill said. He studied Taylor. "And who might you be, young miss?"

"The name's Taylor."

"Well Taylor, it's a pleasure." Bill took her hand and kissed it. Then he released it and looked at me. "Wonderful news Phyllis, wonderful news!"

"What is it Captain?"

"I've begun work again." He paused. "At the donut shop."

"You've got the accent down perfectly," said an awed Taylor.

"What accent, sweetums?"

Just then the front door opened. "Helloo-oooo?" Quincy entered with a couple of bags with the word "CRIMSON" printed on the side. "Hey Phyllis," he said. "I got you some presents for the new school year!"

"Thanks Quincy, you didn't have to."

"Yeah well," said Butch, who was entering, "he saw flames and for some reason he just thought of you," with a grin. Then he saw Taylor. "But uh, I don't know why though," he added quickly.

Abe came in behind him. "It's good to be back."

"I don't suppose you have anything for me in that bag, do you Quincy?" Captain Jack inquired.

Quincy pulled out a red-and-white-striped shirt. "Thought this would work for you."

Bill took it. "Thank you Quincy!" He began to pull a wad of cash from his pocket.

"I can't take that from you Jack," Quincy told him, recognizing who Bill was.

Jack shrugged. "If you say so." He put the money back in his pocket.

Quincy looked at us. "Is this the famed Taylor who is joining us for dinner?"

"Why yes. In the flesh," Taylor said, shaking Quincy's hand.

"I'm Quincy Herman Smith."

"And don't you forget it!" Butch said, imitating Quincy's manner of speech.

"Shut your mouth, Butch," Quincy ordered. He gestured to Butch and Abe. "This is Butch. That's Abe. It's okay if you get them mixed up."

Abe whacked him. Quincy laughed.

"Hello," Taylor greeted them. "It's nice to meet you all."

"You too," said Butch.

"We'll meet again, I'm sure," said Abe. "Once you come into this house, you're family for life."

"Yeah, it's like once you go black, you can't go back. Even though this family's mainly of European descent," Quincy told her.

"Do you all want to come into the kitchen?"Aunt Kippie asked, standing in the kitchen doorway.

"Wait-wait-wait-wait! I have to show Phyllis and Taylor the clothes I bought!" Quincy insisted.

Aunt Kippie shook her head. "After dinner, Quincy."

Even for Quincy, there were no arguments with Kippie or Chasey.

"What's for dinner, Kippie?" Abe wanted to know.

"Yes, do tell," said Captain Jack.

Kippie sighed. "Chasey made ravioli and lasagna." She smiled wearily at Taylor. "If you get to know our family, you'll find out that Chasey was the one who was made for the kitchen."

"Kippie can't cook," Quincy whispered.

"Oh you hush!" Aunt Kippie whacked him as he walked by.

We went into the kitchen.

"I love my ravioli," said Quincy, scooping up some onto his plate.

"Yeah, and now we know what else you love," teased Butch.

"The hell's that supposed to mean?" Quincy wanted to know.

"Quincy." Aunt Chasey gave him a look.

"Sorry."

"Yes, do elaborate for us Butch," said Bill, taking some lasagna.

"Quincy met a guy today," said Abe.

"*Damien*," said Butch, making fluttering motions with his fingers.

"Wasn't that the name of the evil kid in 'Omen'?" Taylor inquired.

"Oh honey, Damien's anything but evil," Quincy let her know.

"Who's Damien, Quincy?" Kippie asked him.

"*Damien* is one of our regular costumers," Quincy informed her.

"He's very..." Butch began.

"Bright-colored?" Abe offered. "Clean? Prissy?"

"Y'all are just jealous," Quincy told them. "At least Damien doesn't dye his eyebrows and dress in denim suits!" He glanced at Abe. "*Or* leave his hair ungroomed."

Abe leaned back and folded his arms.

Butch raised an eyebrow. "And what is wrong with any of *that,* may I ask?"

"At least *I* don't shut myself in my room with 'Ray of Light' on full stereo whenever I get depressed!" Abe cried.

"You got somethin' against Madonna?!" Quincy stood.

"Boys," Aunt Chasey protested.

"You got somethin' against denim?" Butch stood and put his hands on his hips.

"GENTLEMEN!" Bill/Captain Jack slammed his hand down on the table. "*I* would like to eat my dinner! And preferably, have a nice drink after it. In peace! If you want to fight, it's fine with me. But not while I'm trying to eat! Now, I suggest you all stop acting like BILL'S RATS...and eat this *lovely* meal which has been so kindly prepared for us."

It was all I could to keep from clapping for Bill's performance, which had been complete with wobbling, hesitations, and hand-gestures. But, similar as he sounded, I still preferred Johnny Depp.

The guys sat down.

"Thank you Jack," said Aunt Chasey. She looked sternly at Quincy. "Now I think it would be quite appropriate and do you three some good to apologize to one another. I don't know what your separate feelings are about Damien, but Abe, Butch...I'm sure Quincy wants your approval."

"Psh," said Quincy.

"I approve," said Abe. "I just meant that Butch and I, personally, thought he was a bit too girly."

Kippie burst out laughing.

"Just don't insult my Madonna again," Quincy warned. He looked to Taylor. "Do *you* like Madonna?"

Taylor nodded. "I can play 'Like A Virgin' on the viola."

"Truly?"

"Nope. But I *can* play the beginning chords of 'Ray of Light' on the guitar."

"Sweet!" said Butch.

"That's the coolest," said Quincy. "That's my *favorite* song." He snapped his fingers. "We have an old acoustic guitar! You should play for us."

"Quincy," I whined.

"Sure," Taylor said. She looked at Bill. "But after dinner."

Captain Jack raised his glass to her. "At the opportune moment."

* * *

After dinner, Taylor and I went upstairs.

"That's a *long* hallway," said Taylor.

I nodded, and pointed directly in front of us, explaining where all the rooms were and to whom they belonged.

"What's the door at the other end of the hall for?"

"That goes to the other section of the upstairs where Quincy and Bill's rooms are."

"That's so cool."

"And Sarah's room," I added. "But she's never here."

"That's weird. What happened to her?"

I opened my bedroom door, and shrugged. "She's probably been murdered and someone doesn't want us to know. Sarah wasn't exactly your model citizen. But she was kind of cool," I admitted. Except for the drugs, and the satanic music, and the whole gang thing...

"Think she'll ever come back?" asked Taylor, stepping in after me. "Nice keyboard!" she exclaimed.

"Thanks. Bought it myself."

She looked at me. "Ouch."

"Yeah. I'm broke. I'm always broke."

"Me too. Well, not really." She grinned. "I clean my house for money. So what can you play?"

"I have Vanessa Carlton, Alicia Keys, Fiona Apple, and some classical stuff from my lessons. But I like to play other stuff too. I want to get Billy Joel and that kind of thing. And I want to learn rock songs too."

Taylor nodded. "I have a book of classic rock songs if you want to check it out."

"That'd be awesome."

Taylor admired my poster of Johnny Depp. "Where'd you find this?"

"Sid gave it to me. He's the guy who might be a prosecutor. He's moving in this year."

"Oh yeah, I remember you mentioning him. Are you close?"

"Sort of. We'll *be* close though, no doubt."

She grinned. "I liked Quincy and Bill. Where's Quincy from?"

"He's Puerto Rican or Cuban...maybe a little bit African..I don't know, he's from an island somewhere," I told her cluelessly. Quincy's face was brown, like it had been carved out of some beautiful wood. He spoke Spanish, but he never spoke about his upbringing and could have learned it in school or something. One thing was for sure, he had great skin. "Daily exfoliation is very important," he always told me.

She laughed. "Everyone here is so much fun."

"Yep. I live with a mentally ill man who works in a donut shop."

"He doesn't seem ill. Just a bit...I don't know."

"Crazy." I chuckled. "No no, Bill knows what's going on...he just thinks he's anyone but himself."

"Wish I could do that," Taylor said.

"I know what you mean."

Sarah Returns.

Over that summer, Taylor and I grew closer. We went to the beach, we went to the mall, we went for walks, we had sleepovers...by the end of August, it felt as if we'd known each other for years. But I never told her I could breathe fire.

One rainy day, I called to invite her over, but she was school shopping. I sat on the couch with Aunt Chasey.

"No Taylor today?" she inquired.

I shook my head. "Nope."

"Dominick called."

I looked up right away. "Sid?"

She nodded. "He's moving in in January."

"What day?"

"In the middle, if I remember correctly. The fourteenth or fifteenth, perhaps." She smiled. "It'll be so nice having him here. And Anna wrote. She said she'd be back next April, the middle of the month."

"Next April?!"

"Yes."

"Why?"

"She didn't tell me, and I didn't feel it was that important. Probably the tour."

"Oh."

"I just hope she'll get along with Sid. The fights they used to have!"

"What about?"

"Everything! Sid, being a lawyer, was always very vocal. And Anna is naturally...what did Quincy call her?"

"Controversy in motion."

Aunt Chasey laughed. "Oh yes. They had some interesting discussions, but after a while it was just too much for the both of them." She put a hand on my arm. "But did Quincy tell you anything new about Damien?"

I shook my head. "Just that everyone's going out tonight."

Aunt Chasey sighed. "That's what Kippie told me. We're both so eager to meet him."

"Yeah—" I began.

But I was suddenly interrupted as the front door opened.

It was a short-haired, pale girl in a trench coat. She had changed a lot, but it was most definitely Sarah.

"Hi there Phyllis, Chasey."

"Sarah! How nice to see you!" Aunt Chasey greeted her.

"Hi Sarah," I said.

"I was wondering if you could possibly rent a room out to a friend of mine."

"Well I'll have to meet your friend. Are *you* planning to stay with us, Sarah?"

"Yes. I've just been...just been figuring shit out, you know?"

Chasey flinched at the word *shit.* "I hope you're doing better."

"I am, I am. So you say you have to meet him? My friend?"

"Yes, I most certainly do."

"Okay. I'll bring him by tonight. Would that be all right? 6?"

"Of course. I just need to ask him the procedural questions and such, you understand."

"Oh yeah, definitely. Thank you Chasey."

"You're welcome."

"I'll be back at six," Sarah called, walking out the door.

"That was odd," I said as the door closed.

"Who was that?" Aunt Kippie emerged from the sewing room.

"Sarah. She said she wanted to bring a friend over who wanted a room."

Aunt Kippie looked to the heavens. "Lord save us."

"Amen," Aunt Chasey agreed.

* * *

At precisely six o'clock that evening, I was playing the piano when the door opened again.

Upon my entrance into the living room, I saw Sarah holding hands with a tall, curly-haired guy. He had a pierced eyebrow and a Scarface tattoo on his arm.

"Hey Phyllis. This is Ben Andrews."

"Hey," Ben nodded to me.

"Hi," I returned the nod.

Aunt Chasey, Aunt Kippie, and Bill came out of the kitchen. Bill had watched "Casablanca" with Taylor and me a week or so before, because it was Taylor's favorite movie. Now he was Claude Rains, or Lieutenant Renault, and lately was acting more British than ever.

"Hello," my Aunts each said.

"Hi," said Ben. "I'm Ben Andrews."

"And you'd like a room here?"

"Only temporarily, a month or so."

"Please sit," Aunt Chasey motioned to the card table.

I went upstairs and lay on my bed. There were bags of new supplies sitting idly on the floor of my room. Binders, paper, pencils, notebooks, erasers, all kinds of school stuff.

I yearned to set it all on fire.

First Day of School Eve.

I was extremely nervous the Tuesday before school began. Freshman year. What if some evil seniors grabbed me and threw me in a trashcan or something?

Highly unlikely, given that you'd probably end up burning them, said the voice.

True, I admitted.

Quincy knocked on my door. I knew it was Quincy because he was the only one who knocked to the rhythm of "Flashdance...What A Feeling."

"Come in."

Quincy, and I quote, had not been a "happy camper" since Sarah's return. He swore he could hear the two (Ben and Sarah) performing obscene actions in the middle of the night. He insisted that Ben had threatened him in the living room one night after he'd come home stoned. (Ben had been stoned. Quincy had just been up late.) He wanted them out, but he had no proof to take to the Aunts.

So, he and the guys had been leaving tape recorders all around the house, which did no good for my nerves, and was the reason I was in my room with my school supplies.

"I have it Phyllis, I have it!" He held up a tape recorder.

"What do you have?"

"*Evidence*, Phyllis!" He closed the door behind him and waved the tape recorder around. "Listen, my child, and you shall hear." He pressed PLAY. There were lipsmacking sounds.

"Quincy—"

"I *didn't* record them screwing, just wait. I love the T-shirt, by the way." I was wearing a Crimson T-shirt, one of the shirts he'd bought me. It was a red shirt that said "CRIMSON" in a darker shade of red on the front. Taylor had looked at it and said, "Well *duh*." The best of the gifts I had received from Quincy were the red pair of sunglasses and the black shirt with red flames on the sleeves, forming the word "Crimson" on the back.

Ahem, said the voice. Pay attention!

"That guy's getting on my nerves," Ben was saying.

"Who, Bill?"

"Who's Bill?"

I reached out to pause the tape. "Where did you put this one?"

"I shoved it between her bed and the wall. Don't worry missy, I didn't steal your keys. But listen to this, dammit!" He pressed play, and Sarah's voice returned.

"The one who thinks he's British?"

"No, the fag."

"Quincy."

"Yeah, he's a fuckin' tight ass. We should jump him."

"That'd be fun. Think we'd get away with it?"

"Yeah, if we did it right. Just don't do anything a dragon would do."

"Ben that's over. I'm just selling the shit, not using it. For anything."

Quincy stopped it. "That's fucking proof enough for me."

I could feel heat rising in my lungs. "What did she mean?"

"The Dragons. I talked to Butch and he said they were a gang famous for killin' their victims through forced overdose."

"And knife-fighting?"

"She probably said that to sound cool, Phyllis."

"How does Butch know this?"

"Phyllis, Butch is a transvestite."

"So?"

"They got connections."

I ran a hand through my hair. "When did you tape this?"

"Sunday. Couldn't get it outa their room til yesterday."

I got up and hugged Quincy. "We'll get them out, I promise. Or else I'll fry 'em."

We went downstairs. Quincy played the tape for Kippie. Aunt Chasey was with her church group. I'd been confirmed at 14, and after that Aunt Chasey had said it was up to me to go or not. Before that she'd made sure I got a full religious education, done all the more quickly because of her expertise and participation in the religion. But, that's another story.

"Oh my," Aunt Kippie said. She looked to Quincy. "Are they here?"

"I'm not sure," said Quincy.

Aunt Kippie went to the back stairway. "Sarah? Ben?" she yelled. Aunt Kippie's yell could wake the dead.

"Yes?" came Sarah's voice.

"Could I please have a word with the two of you?"

"Yes." Minutes later, the two came down.

"What is it Kippie?"

"Sarah, I'm afraid there's an emergency. I have to ask you and Ben to leave."

"Leave?"

Aunt Kippie nodded. "I'm terribly sorry, but I can only give you until Thursday to have everything out."

"Thursday? What is this bullshit?" Ben demanded.

"Calm down please. There's nothing I can do, and for that I apologize, but we must have both of you out and your rooms empty by Thursday."

"This is fucked up."

"You just lost yourself a day, Mr. Andrews. If you're not out by tomorrow, I'm calling the police. If you need money for a hotel, I'm happy to aid you."

Ben shook his head. "You bitch."

"Hey!" I sputtered.

"What the hell is your problem?" Quincy cried. "The woman is *sorry!* There is *nothing* she can do."

"No, no." Ben reached into his pocket and pulled out a knife.

Reacting instantly, I blew fire at him.

"Ah!" Sarah cried.

"What the fuck!" Ben shook his arms. His jacket had caught fire.

I quickly inhaled it back in.

Ben looked at me, wide-eyed, clutching one arm.

I looked back. "If you get out in one hour, we won't call anyone. And I won't hurt you."

"Won't *hurt me*?"

His knife had fallen to the floor and he glanced at it. I blew at it and it went to the other side of the kitchen. I looked him in the eye.

"I'll light your godforsaken hair on fire first. "You like *dragons*?"

Ben knew I knew. He coughed and looked at Sarah.

"Let's go Ben," she said.

It only took them fifteen minutes to pack.

When Aunt Chasey returned, she could tell Kippie was rattled.

"Are you all right, Kippie?" she asked, putting her hat in the closet.

"Ben and Sarah are gone. Phyllis almost set Ben on fire," Kippie murmured.

"What?!"

We told Aunt Chasey what happened.

When we'd finished, Aunt Kippie stood. "I'm going to bed early. I'll wake you in the morning, all right Phyllis?" She went upstairs.

"Do you realize they could tell someone?" I cried.

"They couldn't find anyone who'd believe it," Quincy said.

"What if they come back?" I wanted to know.

Quincy pointed to me. "They won't."

"But they don't *know* how much we know about the drugs," I protested. "They could..."

"Phyllis. What are they going to do?"

I sighed. "I don't know."

Aunt Chasey put a hand on my shoulder. "Phyllis, I'm proud of you. You protected Kippie and Quincy. Now go to bed, and think about school."

"Maybe we should call someone or something," I suggested.

Quincy put a hand on my shoulder. "Who're we gonna call Phyllis? Don't worry about it." He chuckled. "Fuhgedda' bowdit."

I nodded tiredly. "All right."

"Go get ready for tomorrow," insisted Aunt Chasey.

So, I went upstairs, completely freaked out. I needed to vent, and I needed to vent to Taylor.

Which led to a bigger problem: I hadn't told Taylor about the whole fire-breathing thing.

Just a minor detail, said the voice.

How could I tell her? "Hey Taylor, watch this!"?

I brushed my teeth and washed my face and decided to tell Taylor what really happened to my parents the next time she came over. I couldn't talk to my Aunts about breathing fire. Taylor would be interested; the Aunts would just try to be understanding and not actually understand it. Maybe when Sid moved in I could talk to him about it.

Day One.

The next day, I was awakened...interrupted would be a better word...from a surprisingly peaceful sleep. I hadn't had any first-day nightmares, and even when Aunt Kippie opened my bedroom door, I was calm.

Then I remembered.

"Guhhhhrrr...." I groaned, rolling away from Kippie.

"Phyllis, it's time to get up," she said, trying to break it to me gently.

"I know."

"Chasey made brownies."

"No she didn't."

"Yes dear, she did."

"I'll be down in a minute."

The bus picked me up at a corner near the house. The ride was so long that I fell fast asleep. Luckily, or unluckily, I was awakened (interrupted) again by the jerk of the bus as it stopped in front of the high school.

I followed everyone else from the bus into the school. It wasn't as big as it seemed, really, but since it was a school, I knew it'd be a terrible place.

I found Taylor at the main stairway. We had ten minutes to get ready for homeroom, and five minutes between each class.

"Where's your locker?" I asked her.

"Down the hall from yours, I think." Taylor had seen my locker at our orientation, but she'd gotten the wrong one and hadn't had it fixed until that morning.

"What classes do we have together?" Our schedules had been sent in the mail. We compared them.

"Global. Math. Swimming. Lunch," Taylor said.

"Wow."

"Somehow I find it hard to believe we're in advanced math," Taylor remarked.

"Like I have a choice with the Aunts breathing down my neck. Any lower would be a threat to my life."

Taylor grinned. "I must be in it because I don't have a life." She snapped her fingers. "That can be our mission this year. Lives."

I laughed. "Good to have." I paused. "Taylor...can you come over this weekend?"

"Sure. Will there be food involved?"

"Of course. I have to tell you something, though."

"What is it?"

"A long story."

* * *

The day went by decently, and there wasn't much homework. Probably a bad sign.

First period I had biology. The teacher was a man named Mr. Busch, and like most science teachers, he seemed a bit odd. He let us know that he didn't "take attitude," and if we "gave attitude" he'd "give us directions to the office."

While calling the roll, he mentioned that his wife's name was Phyllis. I just gave one of those agreeable laughs and said, "Really?"

"Yes," he said. "Don't think it'll get you extra points though. If anything, it might bring you down. I'm kidding, I'm kidding."

My next class was French. I was seated next to a girl named Key.

"Hey," she said.

"Hey," I said.

We didn't talk much after that, but when she started drawing in her workbook after the teacher told us not to, I knew we'd get along.

Math looked okay, but it never was. Luckily, I was seated behind Max Spalding, the smartest kid in the city. He'd gone to my school, but he'd won national science fairs and gone to national spelling bees, and somehow, everyone knew who he was. We were almost friends.

"Hey Max," I greeted him.

"Hey Phyllis. How was your summer?"

"Way too short. You?"

"It sucked. I took this summer chemistry course, and I swear that all we did was review the periodic table. I mean, who doesn't have that memorized?"

"Shut up, Max," said some kid.

"No," said Max, simply.

Periodic table...oh yeah, I thought. All I remembered was that H was hydrogen, O was oxygen, and together they made water. I think.

English was a better subject for me, but I wasn't sure about the teacher. He was a very happy man who reminded me of Dan Aykroyd. His name was Mr. Hamil.

"This year you'll be reading Homer, Shakespeare, Twain, Dickens, Hemingway, and, if we have time, Steinbeck."

"Who're they?" someone said.

"What are you doing in honors English?" he demanded.

He asked us who had read "The Grapes of Wrath."

Max raised his hand. I'm sure Taylor would have too.

"Oh my God! Tom Sawyer?"

Two guys I didn't know (and Max) raised their hands.

"Oh you poor deprived children! Lucky for you, we'll be reading both of those this year."

There was a simultaneous groan from the class.

"I think we should read 'The Sisterhood of the Traveling Pants'!" said a girl sitting behind me.

"You'll be doing individual reports every two months, don't worry," Mr. Hamil reassured her.

My global teacher was even worse.

Her name was Mrs. Highman, which I heard several people giggling about as I entered the room.

At first, she seemed like a nice lady. She handed out a questionnaire, saying she wanted to know all of her students.

But then, one of the boys got up to throw something away.

"WHAT ARE YOU DOING?!" she screeched. "You're not allowed out of your seat without PERMISSION! Next time you get a DETENTION!"

"Sorry," said the startled boy, going back to his seat.

"I'd better pass out the rules," she decided.

What she passed out was not a list of rules; they were a way of life we had to follow. Taylor and I exchanged looks.

A girl raised her hand. "May I please get a tissue?"

"You don't have to ASK for a TISSUE! Just GET UP and GET IT!"

The guy next to me mouthed, "Oooookayyyy."

Taylor and I met in the hall after class, before swimming.

"I don't even know where the pool is," I confessed.

"I do," she replied.

Swimming was easy; we wouldn't actually be swimming for two weeks, so for now they were giving out surveys from one of the hospitals.

"Doesn't seem so bad," Taylor said.

"I'm not crazy about swimming right before lunch," I told her.

"I don't see why we have to take swimming anyway. I avoided it until this year because I don't want to take it my senior year," said a girl with long shimmery hair. She looked different to me, somehow, than everyone else there. I mean, she was still human. But there was something else. I wondered why I hadn't noticed her before.

"They require the whole year, don't they?" Taylor made sure.

The girl nodded. "I say that if you want to learn to swim, you sign up."

"I'm just taking it now and getting it over with," said Taylor.

"I'm taking it every year," I told her. I'd never liked gym. It was hard to keep my "breathing problem" hidden when I ran for long periods of time. With swimming, well, there was water, the sworn enemy of fire, and nothing to worry about.

"What grade are you guys in?" asked the girl.

"Ninth," we said hesitantly, in unison.

"I'm a junior. You should sit with us at lunch."

Taylor and I looked at each other, shrugging.

"Okay."

"I'm Marylin, but I prefer Mary."

I nodded to her. "I'm Phyllis."

"I'm Taylor." Gee, I wonder which one of us said that?

Between swim class and lunch, we found out several things from Mary, Key (who turned out to be friends with her), and the other people sitting at their table. Mrs. Highman was the spawn of the devil, according to one girl. Mary disagreed; she said Mrs. Highman was the devil's mother, and they were close.

"She used to teach English," said Mary. "She'll take big points off for spelling."

"What about Mr. Hamil?" I asked.

"He's gay," said Mary's friend Helen.

"He is definitely not gay," said Mary. "Unless you mean happy."

After lunch I had art class. The teacher just passed out blank sheets of paper, told us to draw something that was part of who we were, and then sat at her desk with a magazine and two Milky Way bars.

"What the hell am I supposed to draw?" said one guy.

"Draw a basketball," a girl suggested.

"I hate basketball."

"Well then draw something you like!" She looked at me. "Honestly."

"Well I like girls but they sure ain't a part of me."

She rolled her eyes.

"What are you drawing?" he asked her.

"I'm drawing a lacrosse stick."

"Lacrosse is stupid," said the guy.

"No, you are," she told him. She looked at me. "What are you drawing?"

"A face," I told her. "It's a part of me."

She laughed slightly.

"Maybe I'll draw an ice cream cone," the guy mused. "I like ice cream cones."

The girl rolled her eyes again. "I'm Delia," she told me.

"I'm Phyllis," I told them.

"I'm Zorro!" said the guy.

"His name is John."

"Hi Zorro," I said to him.

"Thank you," he replied, glaring at Delia.

"You're such an idiot, John," she snapped.

"My name is Zorro!"

They argued about it for the rest of the period.

The day ended with a study hall, which worked out quite well.

I got home around three o'clock, tossed my backpack onto the couch, and didn't have to talk about my day until I was interrogated at dinner time.

"How was school?" everyone said.

"See any hotties?" asked Quincy.

"Not really," I told him, "but it'll definitely be better than last year. I mean...I guess it couldn't exactly be worse, but..."

"There were no cute guys?"

I shook my head. I had high standards. And I'd had Sid on the brain since I'd met him.

Quincy waved my remark away. "You're just waiting for Sid to come back."

"Quincy!" Aunt Chasey scolded.

"What happened to Damien?" I wanted to know.

Quincy smiled. "He's still around."

"I know *I'm* waiting for Sid to get here," said Aunt Kippie. "I don't know why it's taking him so long."

"That's a big house he lives in," Aunt Chasey reminded her. "He's probably finding someone to watch it, cleaning it out, deciding what to bring here."

"Is he going to work here?" I asked.

"Well he's only coming because—" Aunt Chasey stopped. She paused. "Maybe he will. It must be dull for him to not work."

"How'd he get rich?" I asked.

"Parents," said Aunt Kippie.

"Why is he coming?" I looked to Aunt Chasey.

"He's a fugitive in hiding," said Quincy.

"Change of scenery, I suppose," said Aunt Chasey.

"No better place for that than here," Bill remarked. He was still Captain Renault, and, tiring of it, we'd all been showing him different movies trying to get him to change.

Quincy looked at me. "Hey Phyllis, why don't you show Captain Renault our local theatre?"

"I do love a good performance," Bill admitted.

"All right then," I told him. "Off to the cinemas."

Telling Taylor.

The trip to the cinemas hadn't worked, but, knowing that Bill liked superhero-type movies, Abe had brought over his copy of X-Men. Quincy and I both agreed that while it was a good change, Bill just couldn't pull off Wolverine's look. I told this to Taylor when she came over that Saturday.

"He looks good enough," she said. "Has he ever been Batman?"

I shook my head. "We'd probably have to buy him the batsuit."

She was thoughtful. "I'm gonna get you the movie and see what happens."

I shrugged. You couldn't dissuade Taylor.

We went into my room.

"So are we going to hire someone to whack Mrs. Highman?" she asked.

I nodded. "That's what I needed to tell you."

Taylor laughed. "I'll get my Mafia pals to do it." She paused. "So what *did* you need to tell me?"

I considered chickening out and saying, "That was it," but I didn't. I had to think to myself, This is Taylor. She's the best friend I'll ever have.

"Tay...if I had a secret, you'd keep it, right?"

She nodded.

"No matter what it was?"

"Unless you killed someone. But then, it'd depend on who it was." She grinned, then became serious. "Don't worry, I've had to keep a lot of secrets."

"Like what?"

"Can't tell you."

"Good enough." I took a breath. "I want to tell you what really happened...what happened with my parents and why I'm here."

She sat back, attentive. "I'm listening."

So I told her. I told her my parents had been scientists. I told her about the injection, the mice. Her eyes grew wide when I told her about the fire.

"How did you...they put the whole house up?"

"Burned to the ground."

She raised an eyebrow. "You were tied to a chair?"

"Yes."

"How did you get out?"

"I don't remember."

"So you're a miracle child."

I nodded. I hesitated. Then I said, "I wasn't burned at all Taylor. The vaccine worked."

"What? You're fireproof?"

I nodded. "Yeah."

"You made this up."

"No."

"Don't mess around with me Phyllis, okay? I've been through a lot."

"I'm not! Here...watch." I blew out flames.

Taylor moved off the bed. "Whoa! Oh my God!" She looked up at me from the floor.

I did it again. Her eyes were wide. I blew some smoke rings.

"How..." She gasped. "You have superpowers!"

I laughed. "No, I can just breathe fire."

"How does that make you...un-burnable?"

"I can breathe it in, too." I demonstrated for her.

"Do it again!" she ordered. I did.

"Oh my God. Oh my God."

"Taylor.." I got down on the floor next to her. She moved away a little. I grinned. "Scared?"

"A bit shocked is all."

"Taylor..you have to promise me. Promise me you won't tell anyone. Anyone. Not one single person."

"I won't. No one. But..what's it like? Do your Aunts know?"

"I don't know, it just sort of comes naturally...I don't remember ever being normal. Yeah, my Aunts and Quincy and Bill all know. So does Anna, so does Sid. So I figured I'd tell you."

"That is so cool. You don't know what happened to the stuff they made, do you?"

"It was destroyed."

"How?"

"My Aunts got it...after my parents were put in a mental hospital."

"Have you ever gone to see them...to show them?"

"Never. Well...I think we visited them once, when I was little. But that was like, right after the Aunts adopted me."

"Wow. Oh wow. Why'd they destroy it?"

"They don't believe it was meant to be released. If it fell into the wrong hands..."

"Comic book apocalypse," said Taylor. "Don't you think someone will figure it out eventually?"

"Not while I'm alive."

"That'll be interesting," Taylor mused.

"Indeed," I agreed.

"You must have been hard to raise. A fire-breathing six-year-old. How'd they do it?"

"Remember Sid?"

Taylor nodded. "The prosecutor who's moving in."

"Yeah. He lived with us, years ago...I hardly remember. But apparently.. Somehow, he got me to control it. I don't know how..my memory has a lot of things blocked out."

"Have you asked him?"

"I plan to. Definitely."

November.

My birthday came more quickly than usual that year, and, unlike the last year, I had a party with my friends.

Mary, Taylor, Key, and I went to the movies in the city, then we went shopping. We'd all become close in the last few months.

Afterward, Taylor and I went back to my house. Mary had a car and drove herself and Key home. Key was in tenth grade, but had known Mary for several years.

Taylor and I got a ride from the Aunts, of course.

"Soon I'll be able to drive," I said.

"I hope you don't think I'm buying you a car," said Aunt Kippie.

When we got into the house, the guys and Maria were already there. We opened presents and ate cake, and afterward Taylor and I decided to watch her birthday present to me: the 1989 Batman movie.

Bill entered, late from work. "Forgive me, forgive me," he said. "I'm sorry Phyllis, I didn't mean to be late." Bill had watched the movie "K-PAX" that morning, a movie in which Kevin Spacey plays a man who claims to be an alien, but we never really find out exactly if he is or not. Bill had gone to work as Spacey's character, Prot (and he was very specific; it was pronounced with a long o), who was from the planet K-PAX. Because Prot was sensitive to Earth's light, he always wore sunglasses. It helped to tell when Bill was and wasn't that particular character.

"That's okay Prot," I told him. He handed me an envelope. It was a card with money and a coupon from his donut shop inside.

Best gift so far, the voice remarked.

"Thank you Prot," I said, giving him a hug.

"You're very welcome, I thought you might like them."

"I do. Would you like to watch 'Batman' with us?"

He nodded. "Your entertainment here on Earth is much more interesting than that of K-PAX." Prot often compared life on Earth to his home planet's.

However, when the movie was over, he was from Gotham City.

Taylor yawned. "I'm...surprised he didn't decide to be the Joker."

"Yeah. Want to go upstairs?" I asked.

"Sure, I'm a bit tired."

"Go ahead, just let me grab something," I told her.

"All right." Taylor quickly went upstairs.

I took the envelope and followed.

In my room, after we'd changed, I opened it. I pulled out a card, and a piece of paper.

I took the paper and looked at it. It was a drawing, a sketch of me.

"Whoa," said Taylor, kneeling next to me. "That's good."

I pointed to Sid's signature at the bottom of the page. "This, Taylor, is the guy I'm gonna marry."

"I thought he was old."

I waved the comment away. "Age doesn't matter." Taylor couldn't say anything; Batman had been created before her parents were born. I paused. "He never did tell me when his birthday was. But, when you see him, you'll want to marry him too."

Taylor grinned. "So he drew that? He must be in love with you, too."

"That'd be nice," I sighed. I picked up the card.

On the front, there was a little cartoon. It showed a dragon sitting happily in front of a birthday cake, then blowing out the candles and accidentally setting the cake on fire. Inside it read in print, "Hope all goes well on your birthday."

I smiled, then read what Sid had written.

Happy Birthday Philly. Sorry I can't be there.
I thought you'd like the picture. I drew it after your last birthday.
See you in January. Keep blowing smoke rings.
- Sid

Taylor read the card. "Sounds like a good guy. Sounds like you have a chance with him too."

I laughed.

She stretched out on her stomach on my bed. "So how many boyfriends have you had?"

I snorted. "None. Just this one kid in the eighth grade for like a week. I don't count it. At all. What about you?"

Taylor shook her head. "No...I didn't talk to anyone much for a while after Davy..." She smiled nostalgically. "There was this one guy..Tony..who I really liked for a while, but the school year was almost over when I finally talked to him."

"Have you seen him at all this year?"

Taylor shook her head.

"What'd he look like?"

"Tall, blonde. Kind of skinny, but not bony. I don't like huge guys anyway. I figured he'd even out perfectly once he stopped growing."

"You like blondes?"

She nodded. "He was a golden-haired angel-face boy. I like those."

I giggled. "What about Bruce Wayne?"

She shrugged. "Yeah, he works too."

* * *

Taylor didn't find her "golden-haired angel-face boy" right away, but she did find Hawk. Yeah, his name was Hawk. He was in her homeroom and rode her bus, and later we discovered he had our lunch period.

I met him in December, a few days before the beginning of Christmas vacation.

Mary and I were sitting at the lunch table with Helen, Key, and Key's boyfriend, Dan.

"Hey Hawk," Mary said.

I looked up to see a brown-haired, muscular guy walking with Taylor. His T-shirt read LED ZEPPELIN, which meant one of two things—he wanted to be cool or he actually was.

"Hawk, this is Phyllis," Taylor said as they sat down.

"Hey Phyllis."

I nodded to him. "Nice to meet you. Like the shirt." I wanted to be cool.

"Yeah, they're one of my favorites," said Hawk.

"So tell us Hawk," said the ever-cool, ever-outgoing Key, "how did you acquire the name Hawk?"

Hawk shrugged. "Hippie parents."

I knew Taylor had been attracted to it because it reminded her of Hawkgirl and Hawkman, of DC Comics. I also knew that they had kissed shortly after he'd asked her out, which made me slightly jealous. I reminded myself that I had chosen not to kiss Toby in eighth grade, and that soon I'd be sharing a house with a man a bizillion times hotter than Hawk.

Hawk wasn't bad looking though; his hair was wavy, his eyes were green. He looked strong, like he'd be able to lift Taylor out of any trouble she got into. He wasn't much taller than she was, though. Taylor was about 5'6. I was 5'4. And Key towered above us at 5'8.

"Nice," I said.

Hawk looked at me. "Taylor says you know a guy who thinks he's Batman."

I nodded. "And many other people."

"Guess I'll have to watch out," he said, looking at Taylor.

And then it started.

Taylor and Hawk made out everywhere; in school, in the halls, at lunch, hello, good-bye, one more kiss. I called her house once and could hear him kissing her as we spoke. Not a long conversation.

Quincy and I were sitting in the living room during this phone call. I had told him *weeks* ago about the making out. I handed him the phone for a few seconds.

"See?" I mouthed, taking it back.

He nodded, lowering and narrowing his eyebrows.

I told Taylor I had to go, and hung up.

"That's *obscene*." Quincy was disgusted. "She's better than that."

"I know. And I never see her. Not even when she's sitting right across from me because her *face* is being sucked off!"

Aunt Chasey entered. "Whose face is being sucked off?" she demanded, horrified.

"Someone Phyllis knows, Chase," said Quincy.

"Oh. Well I just wanted to say that dinner is in five minutes. Chicken and mushrooms in white wine sauce," she announced, then went back into the kitchen.

"Mmmm." Quincy loved chicken, and anything involving wine.

I pulled my knees up and rested my chin on them.

"I miss her Quincy. I don't know what to do."

"Well you know *my* approach, honey," said Quincy. "I say tell her what you're feeling. I understand this is her first big relationship, but that's just rude!"

I sighed. I wanted the problem to work itself out. I didn't want to tell Taylor her kissing Hawk was gross. Couldn't someone else?

Nope, said the voice.

And for once, it was right.

I called her the next day, Saturday.

"Hey Taylor, what are you doing today?"

"I'm going to the movies with Hawk. I miss you though. Want to meet us?"

Eww. "No, thanks, I'm good. But um...Taylor?"

"Yeah?"

"Can I be blunt? Like, really blunt?"

"Uh oh. No, be sugarcoated." She laughed. "No no, do your worst."

"You've been making out with Hawk...to an obscene amount," I blurted.

Taylor burst into laughter. Then she stopped.

"Really?"

"Yes."

"What do you mean?"

"I mean, you're always with him. Kissing him!"

Taylor sighed, and was silent for a moment.

Finally she said, "I'm sorry Phyllis, I won't do it anymore."

"Really? Just like that? You don't hate me?"

"No! No, no, no! I just..Hawk never wants to do anything but make out. I liked it at first, but now it's just..."

Gross? the voice offered. I said nothing.

"I don't know Phyllis. I guess I'd better talk to him. I'm sorry."

"Me too."

"Why?"

"For saying that."

"Hey, honesty's the best policy, right? Nothing is of more value than a friend who tells the truth. It's hardly ever heard, you know." I knew she'd be all right, she was quoting Billy Joel.

I laughed. "All right, well I'll leave you to it. Give Hawk my best."

"Ha. I'm sure I will."

"Bye Taylor."

"Bye Phyllis."

I hung up.

That went better than expected, I thought.

That Monday I went to math review during lunch (I'd gotten an eighty-seven on a test and my worried Aunts insisted I make sure I was clear on everything). I didn't get much of a chance to talk to Taylor until the next day, the Tuesday before Christmas vacation began.

She came to me that morning. I was extremely tired because Aunt Kippie had made me go over my math with her ("You're so good at this, Phyllis, you just need to pay more attention!"), but I could tell something was wrong with Taylor.

"Tay?" Taylor looked worse than I did.

"I broke up with him, Phyllis."

"What?!"

"Hawk. I talked to him about the kissing thing on Saturday. And he said he'd tone it down, and he did. And then yesterday after school, I found him kissing Tiffany Mcbriston."

"Oh my God. You want me to fry him for you?"

Tears and laughter gushed simultaneously from Taylor.

"Sure, sure go ahead," she cried.

I hugged her to me. "Don't worry Taylor, you'll find someone else. I'm not going to say someone better, because that's obvious."

Taylor nodded, leaning away slowly. "Just give me some time."

"Whatever you need, Tay. I'm here."

She grinned sadly. "Thanks Phyllis."

It was all I could do not to burn out Hawk's eyes from his head.

Guys are just trouble, said the voice.

I sighed. Like I knew.

We spent the weeks before Christmas finding ways to torment Hawk and his new girlfriend. Key was the most daring of our group of friends and generally she was the one to think of ideas. We wanted to do something exciting that would result in Hawk getting covered in chocolate sauce or having to jump in the pool naked. But usually we just ended up doing something lame, like replacing his 2% with skim. Our pranks weren't very funny, but at least Hawk always ended up confused as hell. We stopped when Christmas was just around the corner, realizing that we'd better spend some time getting gifts.

Most of the people in my house were surprisingly easy. I got Quincy a gold earring, Bill a cape (I knew he'd use it for something). My Aunts were generally happy with practical things; Kippie liked knitting needles or thread, Chasey liked interesting cooking ingredients.

A few days before Christmas Taylor and I were making paper chains for our respective Christmas trees when Aunt Chasey walked in.

"Oh girls," she said pleasantly. "I wonder if I might recruit you?"

Taylor and I looked at each other. "Recruit us for what?"

"Caroling. My church group and I are going out on Christmas Eve and it would just be lovely if you two would join us."

I looked at Taylor. "What do you think?"

Taylor shrugged. "Hey, you're the one who can sing."

Just then, Quincy came in the front door. "I'm hoo-oome," he sang. "I got all your presents and now I gotta go wrap 'em."

I looked at Chasey. "We'll go if Quincy goes?"

Quincy raised an eyebrow. "Hmm?"

So, on Christmas Eve, Quincy, Taylor, the guys and I all followed behind Chasey's church group as we wandered around a local development for the elderly singing carols.

"I did *not* expect so much snow," said Butch.

"Don't tell me you wore sandals?" Abe demanded.

"I'm not *crazy*. Look, I wore socks under them."

Taylor caught a snowflake on her tongue. "I bet we could use all this snow for a prank."

"That doesn't sound like holiday-spirit-talk," said Butch.

"Prank? Who ya prankin'?" Quincy asked, turning.

"Ex-boyfriend," said Taylor.

"I know this is old hat, but I would go with tying his shoelaces together," said Butch. "I never get tired of that."

Abe rolled his eyes. "You think they should get him to trip on a banana peel too Butch?"

"Maybe we could *take* his shoelaces," Taylor mused.

"Oh, you know what's a classic?" Quincy said. "Replacing his shampoo with honey."

"Or ketchup!" said Abe.

"Aw, that's nasty," said Quincy.

"He *does* shower after gym..." said Taylor.

"All right everyone," called Aunt Chasey as we stopped in front of another house. "Oh Come All Ye Faithful."

"I think I forgot the words to this one," said Abe.

"Hey guys," Quincy said. "Guess who has a date for New Years?!"

"Ohmigod!" gushed Butch.

"*Finally.*" said Abe.

Aunt Chasey cleared her throat and I handed Abe my songbook. Carols were my specialty.

"Thanks Phyllis!" he whispered.

"Merry Christmas."

Once Again.

Christmas break went by more quickly than anyone would have liked and soon it was back to school.

Two Fridays after New Year's, I rode the bus home like any other day. I was a bit peppier than usual; Taylor and I had stolen an unopened bottle of Gatorade from Hawk when he wasn't looking. Not an enormous accomplishment, but it was worth it just to hear him ask Tiffany, "Where the hell's my Gatorade?"

Taylor was completely over Hawk now; she just was embarrassed that they'd ever gone out, made out. I assured her it was all right; at least no one had dumped a big bowl of punch over her head. Taylor loved that story, especially the ending.

I got off the bus, and noticed a black Honda in our snow-covered driveway.

I went into the house.

Sid was coming down the stairs as I came in.

"Sid!" I said, too excited for my own good.

"I'm all moved in," he said, smiling as the Aunts entered.

"Sid, I know you're a grown man, but are you sure you don't want to wear a sweater? It *is* January," Aunt Chasey told him. Sid was wearing a black T-shirt and jeans. Oh, those arms...

"I'll put something on if I go outside Chase, don't worry."

Aunt Chasey saw me. "Phyllis! How nice that you're home."

"Yes," said Aunt Kippie, pulling her coat off a hook by the door. She patted Sid's arm. "Glad you're settled." She kissed me on the cheek. "I'm going to the hospital now." She looked to Chasey. "Sorry I won't be here for dinner."

"Don't worry about it dear." She turned to me. "How was math?"

I sighed. "Fine."

"Any problems today?"

I shook my head. "Nope, it was good. Taylor stole Hawk's Gatorade."

Kippie chuckled. "Sweet revenge."

"Thou shall not steal," warned Aunt Chasey.

Aunt Kippie rolled her eyes. "Oh c'mon Chasey." She hugged and kissed me good-bye, then left.

"Hawk?" Sid raised an eyebrow. "Taylor? I take it you're having a good year."

"Tuh. I wouldn't exactly call it *good*, but..." I put my backpack by the piano in the sewing room.

Sid nodded. "Trouble in math?"

I shook my head. "Nothing serious, just...the Aunts, you know?" I grinned at Aunt Chasey.

Chasey sighed. "Just make sure your homework gets done. I have to clean." She went back into the kitchen.

Sid sat in the recliner, which would come to be known as Sid's Chair. I sat on the couch.

"So did you find any friends you could tell? About breathing fire?"

I nodded. "Yeah, actually I did. Her name's Taylor. Hawk was her boyfriend."

"Wish my name was Hawk." Sid grinned.

"You don't look like a Hawk."

He leaned forward in the chair. "What *do* I look like?"

My breath caught.

Pretty damn good.

"A Sid," I said articulately.

He smiled. "Is that good?"

"Definitely."

"Thanks." He leaned back again. "How's Quincy? I haven't seen him at all today."

"He's good. He's probably with Damien."

"Damien?"

"Boyfriend. Asked him out on New Year's Eve, I think. I've hardly seen Quincy since."

"Wow. He still lives here though?"

"Of course." Bien sûr. Crap, I had French homework.

"What about Anna?"

"April, I think." I blinked. "I mean, she's coming back in April."

"Did she still have the nails when you last saw her?" Sid made a claw in emphasis.

I nodded, surprised. "Yes. But, it's been almost 2 years now, so I guess she could've changed." Yeah, right.

"How long have you known Anna?"

"Ten years, I think." Only the part of my life I remember.

Sid shook his head. "She doesn't change." He laughed slightly. "But everything else does."

"She's a constant variable."

"She's definitely constant."

"You don't seem to have changed. I mean, not that I'd really know. But you look the same."

Sid nodded. "I've looked like this for a while." He grinned. "You changed though, a lot in one year."

"Really?"

"Yeah." The phone rang as he said it.

"Hold on," I told Sid. I got up and answered it.

"Hello?"

"Hey," said Taylor's voice. "Key just called and wants to know if we can go to the movies."

"Well.." I glanced at Sid. "I don't think I could get a ride."

"You can go via Taylor."

"What time?"

"Seven." Maybe she could meet Sid.

"You want to come over earlier? I mean, I guess you probably can't if your mom's driving, but—"

"I'll just walk over, and Mom can pick us up at 6:30."

"We're going to the big theatre?"

"Everything's big with Key."

"So you'll come over?"

"Sure. It might be a little while though."

"That's fine."

"I'll just show up."

"Go ahead."

Taylor giggled. "Bye Phyllis."

"Do you still have the Gatorade?"

"I drank it." Taylor's laughter was crazed.

I grinned. "I'll see you."

"Bye!" Still laughing, Taylor hung up.

I did too.

"I take it that was Taylor?" said Sid.

"Yes."

"She lives nearby?"

"Kind of. Just a few blocks, but it's a different school district, so we didn't meet until this summer."

"And she knows about it?"

"The fire thing? Yeah." I pursed my lips. "I should be more careful, though."

"You haven't told a lot of people, have you?"

"No." I thought of the party that summer. I changed the subject. "I loved the card you sent, Sid."

Sid held up his hands in a helpless gesture. "You were the first thing I thought of when I saw it."

Aunt Chasey stuck her head out of the kitchen. "Who called, Phyllis?"

"Taylor. She's coming over and we're going to the movies at 6:30." I held up a stopping hand before she could say anything. "But don't worry; Mrs. Venchak is driving us."

Aunt Chasey smiled. "Oh good. Please let her know I'm grateful. You'll be eating dinner, won't you?"

"Yup."

"And you, Sid?"

Sid stood. "No thanks Chase, I've gotta go."

She nodded and went back to the kitchen.

I raised an eyebrow. "Go? But you just moved in."

"I have to get some stuff in the city." Sid went over to the coat rack by the door and grabbed his leather jacket.

I went over to him. "How long'll that take?"

"Hour, two hours. Depends on how long it takes to find them."

"Well what're you looking for?"

Sid smiled down at me, close now. "Don't worry Philly," he said. "I live here now. We'll have time to talk. And," he said, turning to leave, "meet Taylor."

I sighed as he left.

At least he's interested in meeting Taylor, I thought.

He didn't answer the question, said the voice, pissed off.

"Oh well," I muttered.

I practiced "Piano Man" until Taylor arrived.

We greeted each other, then went upstairs to my room.

"Sid just moved in," I told her happily. "Today."

"Sid, as in 'future husband' Sid?" she asked.

"Yes."

"Do I get to meet him?"

"He went to the city. If he's back before 6:30, you'll meet him. If not, you'll definitely get another chance."

"I'd better. We wouldn't want you marrying without my approval."

"You probably would stamp his forehead. 'TAYLOR APPROVED.'"

"I carry that stamp with me at all times."

We talked a while in the living room, with sandwiches and Bill, who was still Prot.

Taylor looked at me seriously. "What do you think I should do about Hawk?"

"Don't let him bother you. That's probably what he wants."

"Good advice."

"Never run from your problems, Taylor," Prot said.

"Yeah, they just keep chasing you around if you do, I guess." Taylor paused. "Isn't that how 'The Birds' ended? They just drove away?"

I laughed. "I think so. We'll have to change it to 'Never run from your problems unless an evil flock of birds are after you.'"

Taylor giggled. "Or Hannibal." Her favorite fictional psychopath.

"Or Michael Myers." The killer, not the comedian.

Soon Taylor's mom came to pick us up.

We found Key and Dan and some people they knew in the theatre's arcade.

"Hey Taylor, hey Phyllis," Key greeted us.

"Hi Key."

Key motioned to the others. "This is Liz, this is Steve, this is Jake. You know Helen." Key peered around the group, to the claw machine. "And that's Tony over there."

Taylor's jaw dropped.

Tony was very tall and wiry, and had blonde hair just past his shoulders.

"Hi Taylor," he said smoothly. "I remember you."

Taylor acted as if she was just now realizing it was him. "Oh yeah! Last year you were in some of my classes."

He nodded. "How've you been?"

And that's how I lost Taylor for the night.

It didn't matter though, because through the movie and the car ride home, I was thinking about Sid. Going over his dark thick hair, his deep brown eyes. And his strong, low voice.

But he hadn't told me when his birthday was, damn it.

Maybe he just didn't want you to get him anything, the voice suggested.

I must have fallen asleep, because when we stopped in front of my house I'd been dreaming.

"Thank you Taylor, thank you Mrs. Venchak."

"Anytime Phyllis." Taylor had probably been thinking of Tony the whole time.

"You know you're always welcome, Phyllis," said Mrs. Venchak.

"Thanks. Bye," I said, closing the car door. I went inside.

"How was it Phyllis?" asked Aunt Chasey, on the couch with a book. "French Women Don't Get Fat," one of her favorites.

"It was all right." I yawned. "I'm going to bed."

"All right dear. Good night."

"Night," I replied, and went upstairs."

As I passed Sid's room (right across from mine), I heard the clink of something metal hitting the floor.

"Hmm," I murmured. I closed the door, got ready for bed, lay down. I fell asleep with Sid on my mind.

Supporting Waffles.

I woke up and looked around. Sun was streaming into my room.

Ah, Saturday. Ah, ten hours of sleep instead of six.

And then I remembered that Sid had moved in with us.

Ah, Sid. And his room was right across from mine.

What a lovely day, I thought.

Phyllis dear, said the voice, you're sixteen. You've never had a real boyfriend. Except for Toby Rutledge last year for two weeks, and Tommy Ivanson when you were six for a day. And now you're attracted to a handsome, older man *you* don't have a chance with.

He lives with me, I informed the voice. It's gonna go one way or the other.

Whatever you say.

I got up, out of bed, and looked in the mirror. I brushed my mane until it looked like human hair again. Then I went into the bathroom to wash my face. There were five bathrooms in the house — one in the basement, one downstairs, one in the other section of the upstairs, one in ours for the tenants, and the one I shared with the Aunts.

Now Sid was the only one using that other bathroom. Bill and Quincy had theirs in the other section, and Anna would dominate the basement. She'd kept several pets while here; Dexter the hamster, Spike the iguana, Charlie the gerbil, and Gonzo the snake. Dexter had had a stroke, Spike had been lost in the backyard, Charlie had been discovered by Wonder Woman. Gonzo had survived—now he was traveling with Anna.

Anyway, I washed my face and headed out into the hallway.

I almost bumped into Sid going down the stairs.

"Hey Philly." He looked at his watch. "That was a good idea."

"What?"

"Sleeping til eleven. I stayed up talking to Quincy and Bill."

"You mean Quincy and Prot?"

Sid smirked. "Actually, he decided to watch part of 'Indiana Jones' last night..."

I groaned. "Oh, no."

"He's been Indiana Jones before?"

I nodded. "He was Indiana Jones for a long time. I was ten or eleven, I think, and Anna bought him a whip. A lotta things broke, and he was always trying to swing across the front hallway." I put a hand to my forehead.

Sid chuckled. He studied me. I, of course, was doing the same to him.

"Your hair used to be lighter. Did you dye it?"

"No. But that happens to a lot of people when they grow."

Sid nodded. "Yeah, but when you were five your hair was practically blonde. Now it's almost black."

I shrugged. "Is that bad?"

Sid shook his head. "Nope," he said, moving a loose strand of my hair back. "Black's sexier."

I could have melted. It was all I could do not to breathe out smoke. "I wish I remembered what you looked like."

Sid half-smiled. "Exactly the same."

I smiled. "Did you find what you were looking for yesterday?"

Sid nodded. "Took a little while, but yeah, I did."

"What was it?" I asked, remembering the metallic sound.

"You really want to know?"

"Yeah."

He grinned. "A robe."

"A robe?" A metal robe.

"Yep." They're all the rage.

"Oh." I paused. "You have everything else you need, right?"

"As far as I know."

"You have a house, don't you?"

He nodded again.

"Is it far away?"

"It's up north, about five hours if you know the right way."

"Wow."

"You should eat. Chasey made waffles."

Of course she did.

"Well, it's an occasional morning, I s'pose," I told him. "You're here." I headed down.

"Watch out for Bill, he might've found that whip," Sid called.

"Will do," I called.

Next I almost bumped into Quincy, who was dressed for work, and smelled very good.

He gave me a kiss on the cheek. "See ya Phyllis, I gotta go to work."

"What are you wearing?" I asked, sniffing the air.

"It's 'Flame,' the new cologne and perfume line from the makers of Crimson. You like?"

"I do."

"I'll buy some perfume up for you. Bye Phyllis!" Quincy sped out the front door.

"Sounds like Quincy had an eventful night," said Bill, coming up behind me.

I turned. "Nice hat."

Bill did that Harrison Ford half-smile—watch just about any Harrison Ford movie, he'll do it. "Thanks Phyllis."

"What happened?"

"I'm just not sure about this Damien guy."

"That's just because you've been unlucky in love, Indie."

"Okay, so the last girl fell off a cliff when we were getting the Holy Grail. That doesn't mean I'm unlucky."

I went into the kitchen.

"Phyllis! You're up!" said Aunt Chasey happily. "I'm glad to have your company. Kippie's at the hospital, Quincy went to work, Bill...I mean, Indie probably has some archaeological mission. And only God knows what Sid is up to."

I looked at her. "You think Bill could ever find someone?"

"I do wonder about that. Could he settle into one personality long enough to have a relationship, or even get married...what kind of children he might have! It's so wonderful to have children in the house. I do hope you'll consider having some of your own. When you're older, of course." She gave me a look. "And *married*."

I nodded quickly. Married, of course. "Do you wish you'd done things differently?"

Aunt Chasey shook her head. "Never. I consider what it might be like, from time to time, but I'm happy with my life. I'm glad that I can provide a home to everyone here."

"What about what happened with Sarah and Ben?"

Aunt Chasey tsked. "That was awful. I wish I could have helped her."

"She was never around to help." I paused. "Aunt Chasey, do you think Sid came back to be with Anna?"

Aunt Chasey laughed. "Oh no. That would be the *last* reason he would ever come back."

"Why's he here?"

Aunt Chasey hesitated. "Do you feel uncomfortable with him here?"

"No. No, not at all." I said the words quickly, shaking my head. Oops. I hadn't meant to give *that* impression.

"You're okay with him then?"

"Mmhmm." I smiled. "I'm just curious, that's all. I mean, if he's rich and everything else..I'm starting to get the impression that he's got some kind of big secret or something."

"We all have secrets Phyllis. You know that life very well yourself. Sid's may just be a bit...in need of better hiding."

"So he *does* have a secret."

"That he does. But I'm afraid I can't tell it to you."

"Why not? I'm a Sorin—we know how to keep a secret."

Aunt Chasey chuckled. "Yes, but we also know to respect the wishes of others." She gave me a look.

"He doesn't want me to know?" Ouch.

"I don't know for sure Phyllis. He hasn't said whether he does or doesn't. That's why I can't tell you. You'll just have to wait until Sid tells you." She poked my arm. "And don't you go prying about, either. It's Sid's business."

I sighed. "All right."

What a good girl, said the voice.

Shut up, I told it.

I now had a mission. Something had made Sid come here, and I was going to find out what it was.

But first, I needed some breakfast.

I took my waffles into the living room, and Aunt Chasey said she'd join me in moment.

I found Abe sitting on the couch, flipping channels.

"Hey Phyllis," he greeted me.

"Hi Abe." I sat next to him. I had quit asking why Abe randomly showed up. It had become a simple fact of life.

"Those waffles look good," he told me.

"Want some?" I offered.

"Sure."

I cut a waffle in half, and Abe grabbed it and shoved it into his mouth.

"Are you all right?" I asked, taking a bite myself.

"Yeah. I just didn't have any breakfast."

"Go tell Aunt Chasey to make you some waffles."

"Nah."

"Well eat *something*!"

"You sound like the woman yourself."

I shrugged. "What do you expect?"

Abe sort of nodded. He switched the channel to Cartoon Network.

"So," he asked me, "have *you* met Damien yet?"

"No. I figure I will eventually."

"Aw man. I was hoping we could swap opinions on him."

"What's your opinion of him?"

"He's a nice guy."

"You don't seem comfortable with it."

Abe sighed. "It's just that Quincy seems *too* comfortable with Damien. They've only been an official couple for like two weeks, and they act like they've been going on and off through...past lives!"

I held up a hand helplessly (the other was supporting waffles). "Maybe they have been. What about you and Butch?"

Abe gave me a look. "What about us?"

"You love each other."

Abe shook his head, his blonde hair swishing. "Don't start that bullshit."

"Abraham!" I mimicked Chasey.

"Seriously man. Quincy used to tell us that all the time. I knew Butch a while before he introduced me to Quincy. If it were meant to happen, it already would have."

"It's not true about you two, then?"

Abe hesitated. "It's a different kind of thing, Sparks. It's like...you *are* straight, correct?"

"Correct."

"You have male friends, right?"

Uhh.. "Yeah."

"It's like if you went out with one of them..or just, any close friend. We've been friends too long to turn it into love. It would ruin what we have. We know too much about each other."

"But...isn't that good, sometimes? You know exactly what you're getting into?" I stopped him before he replied. "I understand. But I still think the two of you should consider...uhh...coupling up."

"Puh!" Abe took the rest of my waffle.

I rolled my eyes.

* * *

I went for a walk that afternoon. There were still piles of snow lining the streets, but the roads were quite clear, and it wasn't very cold. It hadn't been that cold of a winter, come to think of it.

I wound up at Taylor's, knocking softly on the door. If I had called first, I would have just walked in. We were past that whole knocking thing.

Taylor's sister answered the door. I knew it was her from pictures around the Venchaks' house. She looked different then Taylor did, with long, brown curly hair and mahogany eyes hidden by black-framed glasses. Freckles dotted her cheeks.

"Hi," I said. "Is Taylor here?"

She looked at me. "Phyllis?" Her voice was lower than Taylor's, powerful like a politician's.

I nodded. In the flesh, Taylor would have said.

"Yes."

"I thought so. Come on in, Tay's on the phone."

"Oh, well I—"

"No, please. Any excuse to bother my sister is a good excuse." She grinned, and then I saw Taylor shine through.

"So you're Whitney?" I inquired. I don't know why I did; who else would she be?

"I'm Whitney," she confirmed. "I'm very glad to meet you Phyllis." She shook my hand.

"You too," I told her.

We went to Taylor's room. Whitney banged on the closed door. "Taylor! Phyllis is here!" she bellowed.

"Hold on!" Taylor screeched.

After taking her time hanging up, Taylor opened the door.

"Hi Phyllis. Sorry."

"No, I'm sorry I interrupted."

"Don't be, I'm glad you're here. We have things to discuss." Taylor looked at Whitney. "Should I introduce you two?"

"Already done, hon. And I have to go."

"Now?"

Whitney nodded. "Yep. Long drive."

Taylor shook her head. "I can't believe you."

Whitney shrugged. "Some things in life are just worth it."

So then we went to the door with Whitney because apparently she was going back to college.

After her shiny blue car disappeared around the bend, Taylor turned to me. "Only my sister would come back from college, for like, less than an hour, just to get her 'Sex and the City' DVDs. I can't believe she forgot them in the first place."

"She should meet Quincy," I told her. "And *you* should meet *Sid*."

"Oh, I have things to tell you first!" Taylor closed the door, and we went to sit in the living room. "I gave Tony my number and he called me! He actually called me, Phyllis!" Taylor was one of those annoying people who didn't realize how fun and pretty she really was. And thin, for that matter. I myself had developed a decent chest, but I was still working on the slender part.

"He called you Phyllis?" I grinned.

Taylor rolled her eyes.

I smirked. "Sorry. So are you going out then?"

Taylor shook her head. "Nope. But he's really fun to talk to. And he likes Batman."

"All guys like Batman. The question is, does he love Batman to your level?"

Taylor nodded. "He has all these Batman videos, Phyllis. He has season one of the TV series!"

Taylor had every season of the Batman TV show, the one on Cartoon Network. (But she'd made it clear to me that it was Batman: The Animated Series, not The Batman. For some reason, the fact that they'd added "the" in front of "Batman" pissed her off.)

"Wow," I said, impressed. "Well I hope he has a car."

Taylor grinned. "I don't know yet. But he's great Phyllis, he's *so* great."

I smiled. "I'm glad, Taylor."

After a pause, Taylor spoke. "You want me to come over?"

I nodded. "Assuming you want to meet Sid."

She nodded. "You're marrying him, aren't you? Of course I want to meet him."

We departed.

Quincy and the guys were pulling out when we returned.

"What are you doing here?" I called. It was past the lunch hour.

Quincy rolled down the window. "I forgot my wallet!" They drove off.

I looked at Taylor. "He's getting absent-minded. Damien's really gotten to him."

"Have you met Damien?"

I shook my head. "He always comes over when I'm in school, or gone. Not on purpose, I'm just never there."

We entered the house.

"Where's Bill?" Taylor asked, eyeing the TV.

"Donuts."

Taylor giggled. "Who is he today?"

"I'm not sure, I think a hit man from 'Pulp Fiction.'"

Aunt Chasey came out.

I looked to her. "Where's Sid?"

Aunt Chasey shrugged. "I'm not sure. Upstairs would be most likely. His coat is still here." She smiled at Taylor. "Hello Taylor. You girls don't mind if I go to the grocery store right now, do you?"

"Nope."

She nodded. "All right, I'll be back in an hour or so then. Goodbye."

"Love you Aunt Chasey."

"Bye Chasey."

Just as we were sitting down, Sid came down the stairs. "Did Chasey just leave?"

"Yeah," I replied.

"Damn," he murmured. He saw Taylor. "Sorry," he apologized. "I kind of erupted at your Aunt," he told me, "and I think I drove her out."

I raised an eyebrow. "You got mad at *Aunt Chasey*?"

"Not mad. I just...used a harsh tone."

"What happened?"

He waved the question away. "Aah, it doesn't matter now." He nodded to Taylor. "Hello."

Taylor was staring. She blinked. "Hi, I'm Taylor."

Sid walked over. "I'm Sid." He sat across from us, in his Chair.

"*She* said she wasn't sure where you were," Taylor told him.

One eyebrow slanted slightly. Ah..Sid's eyebrows were in the same league as Johnny Depp's cheek bones and Angelina Jolie's lips. "Who, Chasey?"

Taylor nodded.

"She was in the kitchen when I left her, so she may not have heard me go up the stairs."

Taylor considered. "Good point."

"You sound like a detective."

I looked to Sid. "Taylor wants to be a prosecutor."

Sid chuckled. "You'll be good," he told her.

Taylor half-smiled. "Thanks. Why's that?"

"You're not shy."

Taylor blushed.

"I heard you dated a guy named Hawk," Sid continued.

Taylor nodded. "Big mistake." She looked at me. "But we stole his Gatorade. And Key took his shoelaces."

"She what?" I hadn't heard this story.

"She took his *shoelaces*?" Sid questioned.

Taylor nodded again. "That she did. He left his sneakers in the boys' locker room while he was swimming, and she snuck in and took his shoestrings right out of his shoes."

"How'd she get in?" I asked.

"She's Key, that's how."

I shook my head. "But Key only does it for the thrill."

"Is there a better reason?" Sid wanted to know. I looked at him. I wondered if he'd do me for the thrill.

You didn't just say that, said the voice.

"Not really. Taylor does it for the sake of being evil, but I guess that's not exactly a *better* reason." Taylor and I grinned at each other.

Sid's mouth curved upward at one end. "I don't think stealing Gatorade or shoelaces really falls into the evil category."

Just then, the phone rang.

I hopped up. "I've got it." I answered it.

"Hello?"

"Hello, Miss," said a male voice on the other end. The sound of his voice was like nothing I'd ever heard, and at the same time it sounded familiar. Kind of like Riff Raff from "The Rocky Horror Picture Show." He definitely had an accent, maybe some British variation. He just sounded...weird. "How are you?"

I held back a shudder. I felt like I had been called by Count Dracula. I hoped he didn't want a room. "Good, you?" was my reflexive reply. I noticed Sid looking at me attentively.

He spoke slowly. "Fine, thank you very much. Do you happen to know if a man by the name of...*Evan Garmon* is available for me to speak to?"

I processed the name. "I think you have the wrong number." I tried to say it politely.

"You don't recognize the name? *Evan Garmon*?"

"No, there's no one by that name here."

"Dear me. Well, I'm terribly sorry to have bothered you Miss. Have a wonderful day." (Click!)

I hung up. "I think Dr. Lecter just called." I shook my head. "That was very, very weird."

"Who was it?" they said in unison.

"He didn't say his name. I should have asked. But he was looking for someone named Evan Garmon. When I told him he had the wrong number, he acted like I was lying at first. He was creepy. He sounded like..like Nosferatu."

"I wouldn't be surprised at all if Nosferatu called this house," Sid said.

Taylor had an odd look on her face. "What was the dude's name that he was looking for again?"

"Evan Garmon?" I held up my hands cluelessly.

She giggled. "That's funny. There's a name like that in 'Red Dragon.' Garmon Evans. I don't think he's even mentioned more than once, but it's in there." She grinned. "I've read all those books about three thousand times."

"Taylor, you have too many obsessions. Superheroes, Hannibal Lecter, Johnny Depp..." I noticed Sid was looking at Taylor in such an interested way that it made me feel a pang of jealousy.

"*Be* a detective," he told her.

She raised an eyebrow. "Why?"

"You have a good memory for details."

"It's just because I love the book. Phyllis's memory is better than mine, I think."

I snorted. "I'm the one who can't remember half her life."

"Yeah, but you can *breathe fire*," she protested.

Sid looked at Taylor and grinned. "Isn't it awesome?"

I laughed. Taylor nodded. "I want to learn how."

"The first thing she asked me after I told her the story was whether or not we still had the stuff I was injected with," I told him with a grin.

"You can't blame her, can you?" He looked into my eyes.

I shook my head, automatically agreeing.

He stood up.

"I've got to go out for a while. Tell Chasey I won't be here for dinner." He grabbed his keys and jacket. He opened the door, then turned back to us and pointed. "But *not* because I'm mad at her. Make sure she knows that."

"Where are you going?" I asked.

"Out on the town." He shut the door.

"Won't tell me a damn thing," I muttered.

"Do you know what there is to tell?" Taylor questioned.

I shrugged. "I only know he has a secret."

"Well yeah. Do you have any idea what it is?"

I leaned back. "So far I've considered a few things. He's a fugitive, he's in the Mob, he's a secret agent."

"What about being a prosecutor?"

"He doesn't seem to have a job, but he seems to have money and experience. And Tay, he has a house up north."

"So why the hell is he *here*?"

"He said it gets lonely." I tried to remember back to our conversation on my fifteenth birthday. "But when I think of it now, that doesn't really make sense. You'd think he'd have...I don't know, flocks of people around him, like a celebrity."

"He definitely looks like a celebrity."

"Mmmhm."

"Do you have a plan?"

"A plan?"

"As to how you're going to entice him into committing the rest of his life to you," she explained.

I shook my head. "None whatsoever. It's just going to happen."

"You'd better find out what his secret is before it happens."

She had a point.

Taylor didn't stay much longer, saying her mom would want her home for dinner, but my suspicion was that she just wanted to call Tony.

Dinner was the next big event. Nobody showed up. Just Chasey and me. And the cats.

"Let's see," she said. "Quincy is with Damien, I'll wager. Kippie's working late, poor thing."

"Oh," I said as if I'd forgotten, "Sid left. He didn't say where or why, but he wanted me to tell you that it wasn't because he's mad at you. He was sorry," I added. I wondered what on earth they could have quarreled about.

Chasey waved it all away. "Oh, I know. The man just has that animal temper inside of him, like a wolf."

A wolf. Where had I heard Sid associated with a wolf before?

"Sid's got some wolf to him." Quincy had said it the night of my fifteenth birthday. All events including Sid so far were inscribed in my mind.

"What makes him like a wolf?"

Aunt Chasey put a bunch of napkins in the napkin holder on the table, and laughed. "Well— " She stopped suddenly. "Nothing." She smiled. "Though you should ask him to howl for you, it's quite convincing."

I raised an eyebrow. "Right."

Later that evening, Key called. Only Aunt Kippie had returned, and I waved to her before taking the cordless phone into the sitting room.

"Hey," I said.

"Hey. Any idea who Taylor's on the phone with? I must have called her ten times today and she's either been gone, or it's busy. And she sure as hell isn't calling *me* back."

"She's a bit taken with this Tony character."

"Tony's a good guy. Wait—she got his number already?"

"I guess so."

"Weren't you hanging out with her last night?"

"Well yeah, but my mind was on other matters."

"The girl needs call waiting. And to tone it down. I mean, she overdid it with Hawk, and now she's definitely overdoing it with Tony. And they're not even fucking dating!"

"Key, calm down."

Key took a breath. "Sorry. I'm not used to having trouble reaching people. And uh.." she stifled a chuckle "..Dan decided today that he's not in the mood for a girlfriend."

I sighed. "Oh Key...I'm sorry." I hardly knew Dan.

Key snorted. "Well I'm not." She paused. "You're lucky, you know that Phyllis?"

"Why?"

"You seem to be holding out for a worthy guy. Keep holding out. They're all sons of bitches."

"Key dear, you know what Taylor would say?"

"What?"

"You're going to have found another guy by next week, and have completely forgotten who Dan is. You know it's true."

Key laughed. "Thanks Phyllis. You're great, you know."

I know, said the voice.

"Whatever you say, Key." I couldn't give relationship advice from my own experience; only from what I had observed at school and in my own house.

"You know, Rick's cute."

"Rick?"

"He hangs out with Cannon or whatever that kid's name is. The one who does terrible freestyle at lunch."

"Gunner, you mean." There were odd people in my school.

"Yeah, that one."

"Yeah, but Gunner hangs out with Rita Stokes."

"So?"

"Rita Stokes hangs out with Tiffany Mcbriston, and uh, I do believe she is dating Hawk."

Key sighed. "Godammit, why can't we all just freakin' get along?"

Tiffany seemed to be pure evil, with an army of girl clones that obeyed her every bidding. And Rita Stokes was her friend. I'd talked to her once or twice. Her hair was stick straight, overly perfect, and she was completely self-absorbed. What I hated most about her was that her face was always scrunched up as if she was trying not to laugh. And that she was the older half-sister of Jeremy Heron. Basically, what was really behind my protest was that Jeremy might have told Rita what I did to him and if we were to become acquaintances, somehow it would come up. What if he got a bunch of people together to jump me?

"Because I said so," I said, answering Key.

"You sound like Taylor."

"Can't help it."

"Okay well, I'll go then."

"All right. Good luck calling Taylor."

"Yeah, thanks, I'll need it."

"Most likely. Dan's a loser."

"He definitely is."

"Keep saying it."

"Okay. Talk to you Monday."

"Yup. Bye."

"Bye Phyllis."

I pressed the OFF button and started to open the door to go into the kitchen, but stopped when I heard Aunt Kippie mention Sid.

"What were you two arguing about? He started it, didn't he?"

"It wasn't an argument Kippie, just an outburst. I told him a few of my concerns and he told me sternly not to be...concerned."

"You'll just have to forgive him Chasey. His temper's always set on high around this time."

"Yes, I know. But Kippie, I worry."

"Stop it. Don't be ridiculous. He has better self-control than anyone we know. Imagine what he has to go through."

"It's not ridiculous Kippie. That's not what I'm worried about! We're not going to be able to keep this from Phyllis. She's our niece! She walks around the house! Suppose one evening she happens to stay up late on the computer writing something, or talking on the phone, and—"

"Chasey. She's not going to sneak out in the middle of the night. Phyllis is the most trustworthy girl I've ever met. Sid will tell her when he decides she should know. He already knows she can keep a secret."

"Yes well, Sid's always been one who subscribes to the 'two can keep a secret if one doesn't know it' policy."

The Batman policy, I thought.

"That's why he's so alone." Kippie sighed. "You know, I really thought, all those years ago, that he and Anna would stay together."

"The whole thing was volatile, I'm afraid."

"I worry about Sid though. He thinks that if he falls in love, he'll ruin someone's life."

"Well I presume that when he finds the right girl, she'll either be one of his kind or she'll gladly become one."

Become what?

"I hope he doesn't wait long. Women aren't going to find that 'giving up your life for the man you love' idea so appealing as time progresses." She paused. "Of course, I can't think of many who'd pass up an eternity with Sid, with or without his temper."

"I just hate keeping this from Phyllis. Oh Kippie, hand me that bowl, will you?"

"Of course." Aunt Kippie sighed. Then she changed the subject. "You know Jane Deering is having a baby?"

"Oh! How wonderful!"

At that point, I walked silently back through the living room and up the stairs.

I lay on my bed, breathing fire, and tried to analyze what I'd heard.

Okay, Sid had a BIG secret, that everyone seemed to know but me. He had a bad temper.

Maybe he murdered someone who deserved it, mused the voice.

Could be, I considered. But what else is there..Kippie said "he's so alone" and Aunt Chasey had said he would find "one of his kind." What the hell did that mean? Obviously Sid was a very unique person, but the way she worded it...as if Sid were a species.

A species of *wolf,* said the voice.

Yeah, I thought, but I don't think there's anything to that. Maybe he has a disease. Maybe it's terminal.

"He thinks that if he falls in love he'll ruin someone's life."

Maybe Sid was going to die. Maybe that was why he didn't have a job. Maybe he wanted to be with us for his last days.

And what was all that about me sneaking out?

I couldn't quite figure anything out that made sense. And in the midst of it all, I fell asleep.

Prying.

I didn't see all that much of Sid for the rest of the week, except for hellos and goodbyes. He only came to dinner on Sunday night, very quickly. But I guess it was okay, as I had other things to think about.

For one thing, Quincy's cat, poor Enrique the Spaniard, was being ignored by Quincy, who was gone even more often than Sid.

"Poor thing," I whispered, holding him. He purred, forgetting about Quincy's neglect. Wonder Woman and Johnny curled up together, keeping warm next to us on the couch. Xerxes was still alive but I hadn't seen him since December. Sightings had been reported by Bill and the Aunts.

Luckily Quincy arrived home early on Saturday night and I was able to explain the problem.

"Oh my poor baby!" He picked up Enrique in the careful way that he had. "I'm so sorry sweetums! I'll start bringing Damien over more often okay, 'cause he loves you." He kissed Enrique on the top of his white little head.

I went to my room to sleep, hoping that was the end of it.

And then there was the matter of Key.

"Mary was telling me today that she could find me someone right away," Key told me in the bathroom on Monday as she put on her eyeliner. "But the truth is, Phyllis, I don't want someone else. I want Dan back."

"What happened to Rick?" I asked her, smoothing my hair back. I never wore my hair in a ponytail unless I was swimming, and though it was hardly past my shoulders, it was constantly getting in my face. I thought about how Sid had called it sexy. I wondered if anyone else shared his opinion.

Key sighed, getting out her eyebrow ring and putting it in. Her parents had yet to find out about it. Key's eyebrows were thin black lines that she waxed strictly, and I often wondered how her parents didn't notice the little hole. Her bottle-black hair, gelled back into small pigtails, was never in her face. There was no shield.

And the fact that I'm thinking of hair as a shield says just how antisocial I really am.

"I don't know Phyllis. He might be too loud. Dan was the dark, quiet type, and I *loved* that." She went on, saying how they'd been going out since November, he had been her longest relationship, and when I finally got a chance to speak and ask her if she'd gotten in touch with Taylor, Taylor walked in.

"Key darling, can I borrow some mascara?"

"Taylor, you'd still use it if I said no."

"Yes, but I am polite."

"She's got a point," I told Key.

Key handed her the mascara. "Do you want to use anything, Phyllis?"

I was virtually make-upless. I only wore faint lipstick and a teeny bit of sparkly eyeshadow.

"Nope. Thanks, though."

Key folded her arms and studied Taylor.

"You know you're the only person I've ever met, including guys, who puts on her mascara with her mouth shut?"

"Key, I think that's just a stereotype."

"So are you and Tony dating yet?"

"Why?" Taylor raised an eyebrow.

"Because I couldn't reach you this weekend. Your line was bus-ay."

"Sorry."

"Dan dumped me."

"What?!"

I left, deciding to let Key tell Taylor the story, whatever it was, alone.

In the hall, I found a flyer advertising the school musical, Grease.

"Jesus," I muttered, remembering what had happened after Bill watched that movie.

The auditions were that week, and the poster said specifically to freshmen not to expect large parts.

I'd done plays at my old school, my tiny school, in sixth and seventh grade. They were among the only experiences there where I recall having fun.

So, before first period, I went to the music room and signed up for auditions, which were on Wednesday.

Classes went on as usual, and at lunch I asked everyone at our table if they were trying out for the play.

"No, why, are you?" Key asked.

I nodded. "Yeah. It sounds like fun and music's my thing."

Taylor looked thoughtful. "I don't think I could do the musical. Have you ever heard my singing?"

I smiled. "You'd be fine."

Taylor grinned. "I'd prove you wrong but I don't think you want to hear it."

Key sipped her juice. "I was in the musical last year. They did one in the summer too, but I decided to stop."

"Why?"

"I have better things to do with my time than sing songs with all the annoying people in our school who all want to be the center of attention. There's so many of those skinny, dancing drama queens and they're all in love with themselves."

Mary rolled her eyes. "Key, *you* are skinny."

"What's wrong now, Key?" Taylor asked.

"Key covered here eyes." "Look behind you."

We all turned to see Dan sitting at the table behind us. It wasn't just any table. It was the same table where Hawk, Tiffany Mcbriston, and the girl clones sat.

"He dumped me for *them*."

"Then he's not worth crying over, trust me," said Helen.

"How do you think I would look with dark hair? Like, Key's shade?" Mary asked.

"You mean pitch black? Pale," said Helen.

"What about Phyllis's shade?"

"It might be a little more natural but you'd still look pale. It works for Phyllis because she's just a little bit dark."

"Why would you want to dye *your* hair anyway?" Taylor wanted to know.

Mary had long, wavy white-blonde hair that shone like the sun. A color I could never pull off in a zillion years.

"For a change. I'm starting to get tired of my hair. I'm starting to get tired of *everything*."

"When that happened to me, I pierced my eyebrow," Key informed her.

"I'm not into self-mutilation."

Taylor ate a chip. "Self-mutilation is cutting yourself. Piercing your eyebrow is for the purpose of jewelry and a fashion statement; it's cool."

"Whatever." Mary studied a strand of her hair. She was wearing a fuzzy pink sweater that made me itch just to look at it. "Key, you know my friend Jesse? Curly red hair? Plays bass? Leather?"

"He beat up Gunner last year," Helen added.

I looked at Key. "No connections then."

"What do you mean?"

"He's not friends with Gunner or Tiffany or Rita or Hawk...or Dan."

Key nodded sadly.

Mary looked at me, then back at Key. "He thinks you're the cat's pajamas. And yes, that is how he phrased it."

"Doesn't he have a motorcycle?" Key asked.

"Yeah."

"Does he have this lunch period?"

"Nope."

"Damn."

"Wanna meet him after school?"

"Yeah, I do."

By Tuesday, the Key problem was solved by Jesse.

Tuesday night, Taylor called. I answered it in the living room.

"I think Tony and I should just be friends."

What the hell? "Why?"

"Because I would never want to break up with him."

I rolled my eyes. "Well I wouldn't ever want to break up with S—"

The stairs creaked. I looked up to see Sid. He smiled at me.

Ahh.

"— Johnny, but I'd still go out with him."

"You don't *know* Johnny."

"Well, I can't...you know what I mean."

Taylor sighed.

"Isn't love supposed to mean taking risks anyway?" I was turned away from Sid, but I could almost hear the expression on his face.

"Who are you talking to?" he asked. He was putting on his coat.

"Taylor," I told him.

"What?" said Taylor.

"Sid asked me who I was talking to."

"Tell him hi."

I looked at him. "Taylor says hi."

He smiled. "Hey Taylor."

"Did you hear that?" I asked Taylor.

"Yup."

"Hold on," I told her. I looked to Sid. "Where are you going?"

"Out. See ya Philly." And then he left.

"But Phyllis..." Taylor said.

"What?"

"What do you *really* think of Tony?"

"I like him."

"Is there anything you *don't* like about him?"

"He's too tall. It's going to look ridiculous when you make out."

Taylor laughed. "You really think so?"

"No Tay, I'm kidding! Go out with him. At least you have a *chance* with the guy you like."

"Keep trying."

"I plan to."

Taylor giggled. "That's my girl." She paused. "So you really think I should go out with him? I mean if he asks me?"

"Yes."

"Okay."

I laughed. "What if I'd said no? You don't usually let anyone change your mind, Taylor."

"Indeed, you're right. Well, I'm gonna go now."

"Okay. Bye. Good luck."

"Thanks. Bye."

I sighed.

Don't think about Sid, said the voice.

Easier said than done, I told it.

Think about auditions.

Aw crap.

I hated auditions. The first time I'd auditioned for a school musical, I'd had to do it in front of a group of girls and the director. The director jotted things down and the girls kept looking at me and talking, giggling. But I'd gotten the role of Pepper, one of the orphans in the musical "Annie." So I figured I'd keep going.

The nice thing about high school auditions was that we would find out our roles the following day. Plus you were alone with the director and no giggling girls were involved. Except for the reading, when there were two or three other people reading with you.

Singing, however, was still difficult. I went up on the stage in our very large auditorium and was supposed to sing part of "Summer Nights" loud enough so that my voice could be heard throughout. That wasn't hard; being able to breathe fire keeps my throat clear, except for when I'm extremely sick. The difficult thing to do was keep my voice at scream-volume without letting any smoke or fire come out.

"Phyllis," said Mrs. Reygor (music teacher, director, and piano player), "I want you to sing the verse on the sheet. Don't think about whose part you're singing; think about singing *loud* and *clear*. Okay?"

And don't set anything on fire. "Okay." I swallowed.

Fire-wise, I did okay, at first. I faced the nonexistent audience and tried my best to make every word understandable and distinct. And on key.

But those damned high notes.

When I got to "summer days, drifting away," some smoke came out. Still singing, I glanced at Mrs. Reygor to see if she'd noticed. Luckily she'd picked that moment to look down at her fingers. When I'd finished the verse, however, there was a small cloud in front of me.

As she turned, I quickly inhaled it all back in so that she wouldn't notice.

She blinked, as if questioning her own eyes, then said, "That was very nice. Thank you. Roles will be posted on the auditorium doors tomorrow morning."

"Okay, thanks," I said, hoping she hadn't seen anything.

Aunt Kippie came to pick me up. I sighed, wishing it was Sid, but at the same time glad that it wasn't.

"How did it go dear?" she asked.

"Good, I hope. I don't think I'll get a big part, I'm not a senior."

"Yes well, maybe they'll remember in the future that you're talented."

I rolled my eyes. "I just hope she doesn't remember that smoke came out of my mouth."

"What?!"

"It was just a little bit of smoke that came out towards the end of the audition. I think I inhaled it back in before she saw it."

"You *think* you inhaled it back in? Phyllis, you have to be more careful!"

"I can't help it!"

"Well someday you might have a big solo on stage! What are people going to do when you start spouting fire and brimstone?!"

I giggled.

"Honestly Phyllis. You've done such a good job hiding it. But you have to *keep* it hidden. People can't be trusted. Secrets are best when they *stay* a secret."

I looked at her. "Are you in a bad mood?"

Aunt Kippie sighed. "I'm sorry Phyllis. Chasey and I were just discussing changing some of our renting policies."

I raised an eyebrow. At least half the rooms were empty. "Why?"

"Sid.."

"Sid what?" I wanted to know.

"He..." Aunt Kippie paused. "We told him about what happened to us when Sarah was making trouble...he got a little bit angry. He told us we shouldn't be letting just anyone into our home."

"Yeah, but when you took Sarah in you probably thought she just needed a little help."

"Oh Phyllis, Sid knows we have good intentions. He just doesn't want us to get hurt." Aunt Kippie put a hand to her forehead. "Plus we just got another letter from Anna and I realized we never told her that Sid was back."

"So tell her."

"Phyllis, you know as well as the rest of us that anything the slightest bit touchy becomes explosive around Anna." Aunt Kippie was pale. "I'm worried about having those two together again. Something is bound to go wrong."

I touched her shoulder. "It'd probably be best to write and tell her now, when she's not actually with you."

Aunt Kippie laughed. "Yes, you're right. Being on the receiving end of Anna's wrath will be better if she's miles away."

Once we reached home, I was sent upstairs to do my homework "immediately" because it was almost dinner time.

Nobody was in the house. It was odd. Sid was "out," or at least, I assumed that he was, Bill was working, Quincy was with Damien and the guys, and I was shut up in my room while my Aunts bustled about the kitchen.

I was in the middle of my math (big surprise) when my mind left me.

She didn't see the smoke. Jeremy didn't tell Rita what I did. And my parents are crazies. No one's found out that I can breathe fire.

What would happen if someone did? said the voice. I mean really. They're not going to come into the house carrying huge fire extinguishers ready to subdue you and take you to a lab.

I wouldn't let them, I told it. I wouldn't let them get a hold of how to make other people like me.

I did sometimes wonder what my respiratory system looked like, what it consisted of. But maybe that was something I wouldn't want to know.

I started to get frustrated. I had a secret, I was okay with it. I trusted the people I had told, including Sid. Didn't he trust me? What was Sid's secret? How bad could it be? Why wouldn't he tell me?

Think, I told myself. He had a "kind." He wanted someone of his own "kind." And for some reason, the Aunts don't want me out at night. He did something at night.

I couldn't think of anything.

God damn it! I thought.

I looked down at my homework and sighed.

Just doesn't get any better, remarked the voice.

Whatever you say, I thought.

* * *

I couldn't sleep that night; there was too much on my mind. Luckily this happened often and I had a remedy.

I had a small lamp next to my keyboard, which was by the window. The window looked out into the backyard, or rather the side yard where the garage was. We had a little room back there, where there was an ancient green couch, a table, a dart board, and shelves of the various junk one finds in a garage.

I turned on my lamp, turned the volume on my keyboard way down, and played. My eyes began to close, my fingers slowed. My head bent and my elbow pressed the power-button as I rested my arms and head on the keyboard.

I don't recall much of my dreams that night, but I'm pretty sure that Sid was in them, and I swear there was a howling wolf.

I woke up an hour earlier than usual, when the sun was barely up, and birds were singing. I blinked, got up, turned off my lamp and headed back to my bed. Mind you, I would've tried to get back to sleep even if I'd only had 2 minutes.

I rolled over when I heard the back door of the garage shut, and went back to the window. Sid had come out, and was walking back into the house carrying a chain in one hand.

"All righty then," I muttered sleepily, and, deciding to think about it later, went back to my bed and fell asleep.

* * *

By Friday, Taylor and Tony were an item, but they didn't smother each other with "I love you" and kisses. It was almost as if they were above that. There would be subtle gestures like holding hands or inconspicuously wrapping an arm about a waist, but it was nothing like it had been with Hawk. And that made us all happy. Another plus was that Tony was cool, in every circle. Which meant he'd be taking Taylor to a lot of places.

Now everyone I knew seemed to have a significant other. Key, Taylor, Quincy.

I started to wonder if Sid *did* have a girlfriend, and that was where he was always going. Maybe he wanted to hide it; obviously he had a secretive nature.

And then of course, all week I'd been wondering why he'd been out in the garage, at such an un-Godly hour.

I thought a lot about this, and I couldn't come up with much. Maybe he was building something in the garage.

Thursday night I went in and looked around, but found everything as it should have been. That was out.

Friday night, he was gone, and I was home.

"Aunt Chasey," I asked after dinner, "where's Sid?"

"Darling I wish I knew."

"Think he'll be back soon?"

"I don't know dear, why?"

"Aren't you going to the movies with Taylor?" Aunt Kippie had entered the room.

"No."

"Why not?"

"She's somewhere with Tony. They're going out now."

"Oh Taylor has a new boyfriend? How exciting!" Aunt Chasey shut the dishwasher and sat at the table.

"Well, Bill's watching 'Sabrina' downstairs with Butch and Abe, if you'd like to join them," said Aunt Kippie.

"Where's Quincy?"

"With Damien. And I'm going to give him a good talking-to when he gets home. I just let the boys in and they said he was supposed to be here! Of course I told them they were welcome to stay, Quincy or no Quincy. But Damien or no *Damien*, Quincy's going to need his friends."

I sighed. "First Enrique, now Abe and Butch." I stood. "Is it the old 'Sabrina' or the new one?"

"I believe it's the new one."

I grimaced. "I'm going upstairs. No one can replace Audrey Hepburn." I loved Audrey Hepburn, a trait passed to me from Quincy. We had all of her movies.

The plan was, of course, to go into Sid's room and see what I could find.

I stood in the upstairs hall, at the closed door. I'd have to make sure I closed it before I left. And I couldn't take too long. One never knew when (or if) Sid was coming back.

I knocked on the door, just in case, and upon hearing nothing, I opened it. It wasn't locked, to my surprise. Almost every door in our house was lockable, and every tenant got a key to his or her room. Judging by his previous actions, I'd expected to have to use my keys. I had seen the room before, obviously; it was big, but dim, the only window being a skylight. Wait a minute, there was another window. Small, but there. I looked around and saw that it had been covered by dark grey-blue curtains. There was a desk with a lamp and book on it below the window. I turned to make sure no one was coming up the stairs, then turned on the lamp and opened the book. It was a sketchbook. There was a sketch of a forest, then a house. It wasn't just a house; it was a mansion. I wondered if it was his, or even someplace he'd been. Most of the things I drew myself were from my own mind.

I turned the page. It was *our* house on that page, I recognized it instantly. Sid was good, but he still didn't seem like the artist type to me. I mean a prosecutor who sketched? Or what? When could he have been a prosecutor if he was only 30, or whatever he was, and didn't have a job? How was it that he had a rich family? And why were they all dead?

I stopped mid-thought, realizing that Taylor's brother had been 8 or 9. And I'd almost died once, too. It's a lot easier to die than people think.

I sighed, turned the page again. It looked as though one had been ripped out.

But behind it was a picture of a wolf.

The wolf thing was getting weird. Was he an animorph or a werewolf or what? Maybe they were his obsession...maybe he was in some sort of wolf-worshipping cult, and that was what Aunt Chasey had meant by "one of his kind." Hell, I'd worship wolves for Sid.

Turning *that* page, I saw a picture of a family. No one I knew, perhaps one Sid had seen or just imagined. A couple next to three kids and a dog.

No, not a dog.

It was another wolf. It wasn't with the family; it was *watching* them.

I turned again, hoping none of his sketches would become violent.

Hardly; the next one was another forest scene, a lake under a full moon. I flipped through the rest, most of the pages were blank. I closed it and turned.

The bed was made, albeit a little wrinkled. I went to the closet and opened it up. Some shirts, some pants, his red bathrobe hanging on the inside of the door. I stood on my tiptoes to see what was on the top shelf. It was a metal box. I reached up and turned it to the front, to see if it was locked. It wasn't, so I grabbed it and pulled it out. It was heavy. Glancing out into the hall again, my heart beating a little bit faster, I set the box down on the floor, lightly so that it didn't clink or bang. If my Aunts caught me, I was dead. If Sid caught me, well, I wasn't sure what he'd do.

I exhaled a bit of smoke out of nervousness as I undid the latches on the box, then breathed it back in quickly. I opened it.

Inside was a chain, a shiny metal chain curled up like a snake, and a big lock and the key to the lock. The chain from the garage.

"Okay," I muttered. Hmm..maybe Sid *was* a fugitive in hiding. I shut the box, lifted it up, and put it back on the shelf, making sure to turn it so that the back faced outward as it had before.

I kneeled down to see what was on the floor of the closet. Three pairs of shoes, and a shoebox. I slid the shoebox out toward me, and opened it.

Ibuprofen and an orange bottle of pills I didn't recognize. I put the top back on the box and pushed it back into the closet. It hit against something metal, and I looked down there again. It was a safe, with a combination lock. I knew I wouldn't be able to open it. I decided to assume that it contained money.

I peered under the bed, but all that was there were what appeared to be socks.

There was a bookshelf next to the closet with another lamp on top of it, and a square of black carpet in front of it (the rest of the floor was hardwood). Some of the books were law books, mystery novels, and intellectual things that I had no interest in at that time in my life. A pile of magazines, some CDs, a small CD player. I glanced at them. Among others, there were Frank Sinatra, Nat King Cole, Led Zeppelin (even Sid knew they made you cool), Aerosmith, Beethoven, Alice Cooper, Rob Zombie, Iron Maiden, Marilyn Manson..Cannibal Corpse? What the hell?

So Sid listened to Frank Sinatra and heavy metal..interesting. Next to the shelf was a mini-fridge.

Hmm. I opened it.

It wasn't a fridge; it was a freezer, and it only contained meat.

Maybe Sid *owned* a wolf. I mean, the chain, the meat, the sketches...

"Maybe he just really really likes meat?" offered the voice.

Could be, I considered.

I moved on to the the bureau. In the top drawer, there was underwear. Boxers. I shut it.

The next one had T-shirts and some sheets, all folded. Some were wrapped in plastic, unopened. I shut it.

The third had socks, a pair of black sandals, an envelope, and a black leather book.

I picked up the envelope and felt keys. I put it down and took the book. Upon opening it, I discovered that it was an address book. The first page had our address and phone number and Aunt Kippie's cell phone and hospital number. Under that it said "Stacia" and under the name were a couple of different phone numbers.

The next page was dedicated to someone called "Vance Frobisher" and had a long list of different places and numbers that took up the two pages after it as well. The next few pages after that were places in Illinois and Massachusetts, names and numbers in places around the world, then the names of some clubs and stores in the city. The last address was for a pizza place. I closed the book, wondering who "Stacia" and "Vance Frobisher" were, and why they had been placed ahead of all of the other names...what was the significance of any of it? I replaced it in the drawer.

In the last drawer was a pair of black sneakers, boots, some socks, and another shoebox.

I turned around again, praying I hadn't missed the sound of the stairs creaking and that someone wasn't in the hall. I gave a sigh of relief when I saw that it was empty. I opened the shoebox.

It was a muzzle. A muzzle!

I put the top back on it and quickly closed the drawer.

It wasn't a mask like Dr. Lecter's or anything, it was clearly meant for a dog. Or a wolf.

Deciding I'd seen everything there was to see, I walked out of Sid's room, closing the door softly behind me. I almost expected to bump into the man himself and find he'd been watching me in amusement the whole time, but I didn't. Thank God.

I went into my room. There were a great many possibilities; the first one being that Sid owned a wolf or a dog somewhere. But what would be so horribly secret about that? Was he using it for something illegal? Did he kidnap it from the wild or a zoo and use it to eat people he didn't like?

I just didn't know. But I knew there was definitely something *to* know.

* * *

The next morning, I actually saw Sid for the first time since Wednesday night...er, Thursday morning. He was drinking coffee with the Aunts when I came down (my hair sticking up every which way and my attire consisting of a Superman T-shirt and a pair of pants with snowmen on them) for breakfast. It was, of course, Saturday, so I, of course, had slept a little later and had expected Sid to be gone.

"Good morning, Phyllis," Aunt Kippie greeted me.

"Oh.." I stopped a second when Sid's eyes met mine. "Hi. Good morning," I said, looking back to the Aunts.

"What would you like for breakfast? I'll slice an apple for you while you decide."

I sat. "Thanks Aunt Chasey, I'll just get myself some cereal."

"Oh, well maybe I can make you some oatmeal," Aunt Kippie suggested.

Aunt Chasey and I looked at each other cautiously. Letting Aunt Kippie cook *anything* was dangerous.

Kippie folded her arms. "Oh *fine*." She took a section of the newspaper in a huff and began to read.

I looked at Aunt Chasey and shrugged. She did the same and began slicing an apple into a bowl.

"Hey Philly," Sid said, giving me a smile.

"Hi Sid. How've you been?" He didn't know, he didn't know, he couldn't have known, he didn't know.

"Fine. What did you do yesterday?" he asked, taking a sip of his coffee, keeping his eyes locked with mine.

I went through your room. So, what's with the chain and the muzzle anyway? "Ah, just school and stuff." I paused. "Taylor's got a new boyfriend."

"Really?" Sid set down his mug. "Tony?"

One of my eyebrows rose. "Yeah." I searched my mind but couldn't quite recall mentioning Tony in front of Sid. "I told you about Tony?" I half-smiled. "It sounds like I'm talking about the kid's friend in 'The Shining.'"

Aunt Kippie's finger came up above the top of the newspaper like a periscope. "Danny isn't here Mrs. Torrance." Bill had seen the movie one too many times, and so had the rest of us.

Aunt Chasey set the apple slices in front of me. "Oh Kippie don't do that, that movie was so *odd*."

"Chasey you never learned how to have fun."

"I learned how to have fun, Kippie, *and* I learned to cook."

Aunt Kippie went back to the paper.

I looked to Sid. He was setting down his mug again, amused.

"When did that start?" he asked, meaning Taylor and Tony.

"Just yesterday," I told him.

"How long you think it'll last?"

"I'm not sure," I said. Before he could say anything else, I asked him, "What'd *you* do yesterday?"

Aunt Chasey turned from the sink. "Phyllis, that's—"

Sid held up a hand. "It's fine Chasey, I asked her." He looked at me. "I went to see a friend in the city."

"How did that go?"

"Very well." He kept his eyes solely on me, looking me up and down the way detectives on "Law and Order" would. "I might've stayed gone a little too long though."

What did *that* mean? Did he know? He couldn't have! He didn't!

"Well *I* certainly would like to see more of you, Sid." Kippie put her paper down and looked at him.

He kissed her on the cheek. "Okay Kippie, I'll try to spend more time around here."

Kippie raised her eyebrows as Sid stood. "That was easy," she remarked.

Sid patted her shoulder. He went to the cupboard in which the bowls were kept and pulled out two.

"What kind of cereal do you want Philly?"

"Oh Sid don't worry about it, I can get it."

"No, I'm up, *I* can get it."

"Don't Sid, I'll do it in a minute."

He laughed. "Philly I *want* to get it, okay?"

"Are you sure?"

"Yes."

"Fruit Loops." I grinned.

"Nice choice. I think I'll have the same." Sid poured two bowls of Fruit Loops, put in the milk, grabbed the spoons and put it all on the table. "Here you go Philly."

I smiled. "Thank you Sid."

"Anytime."

I ate a spoonful. "You know you're allowed to have friends over here, right?"

Sid nodded. "Maybe I should bring some guys over and have Quincy give them makeovers, like that show..."

"'Queer Eye For the Straight Guy.' Love it! Where's Quincy?" Butch was standing in the doorway of our kitchen. Or, um, that is to say, Beatrix was, complete with dress, heels, wig, make-up, and feather boa. He looked surprisingly womanly. Except for a few subtle differences. It was still a bit startling for me.

"Beatrix! How nice to see you," Aunt Chasey greeted him with a hug.

"Thank you Chasey. Do you know where I can find Quincy?"

Aunt Chasey frowned. "He hasn't come home yet."

"All right, that is *it!*" Abe came stomping through. "He stands us up and then he *never* calls *anyone*? At all? He gave no effing explanations?!"

"Watch it Abraham," said Aunt Kippie. "No, Quincy didn't call any of us. But we can all stay here and wait for him to come home and tell us just what is going on, and you may tell him *your* feelings."

"I don't feel too happy about it either," I told them. "*I've* been feeding Enrique! And I already told Quincy the cat needs attention."

"Oh! Poor Enrique! I'm going to go see him *right now*!" cried Beatrix, rushing into the sitting room and up the back stairway.

Abe sighed. "I'll be on the couch. As usual. I *knew* this would happen." He left the room.

"The poor dears," murmured Aunt Chasey.

Sid looked at me. "That...was Butch."

I nodded. "Yes, yes it was."

Sid blinked. "He was never..uh..Beatrix when I lived here before."

"I've only seen Beatrix once before myself," I told him.

Sid lifted another spoonful of cereal into his mouth. "We should've offered them some Fruit Loops."

"I haven't even met Damien yet," I complained.

Kippie smiled. "Oh, you will."

I winced. "Do I *want* to?"

"I do," said Sid.

"He's very nice..." began Aunt Chasey.

"But what?" I wanted to know.

"You'll find out when you meet him," said Aunt Kippie.

I understood. Damien was one of those unexplainable people. I knew lots of those. I was sitting across from one now.

"He can't breathe fire, can he?" Sid winked at me.

Aunt Chasey laughed. "No, and he's not a—" She stopped mid-sentence as if catching herself.

"Not a what?" I asked eagerly.

"Nothing." Aunt Chasey turned to the dishes.

Sid stood. "I'll be upstairs in my room if anyone needs me." He brought the bowl to the sink and began to rinse it out.

"No no Sid, you go, I'll get it," Aunt Chasey insisted, brushing his hands away.

"Thanks Chase. See you later Philly." He nodded to Aunt Kippie. She nodded back.

I figured I'd wait a little while and then go upstairs and find a reason to talk to Sid. Some sort of advice I needed, maybe? Obviously there were billions of things I wanted to tell him, to ask him, but was there any conversational path I could take to get to them naturally? And if we did, would he tell me?

I never got the chance to do this, however, because after I finished my cereal, Aunt Kippie looked to me and asked, "Phyllis, did you have plans today?"

Oh no. I raised an eyebrow. "Nope, why?"

"I wanted to take you out to get some new sneakers, and some *nice* shoes."

I sighed. "All right."

So, instead of conversing with the man of my dreams and attempting to find out something, anything about him, I went into the city with Aunt Kippie.

The tall blonde girl working in the shoe store reminded me of a Barbie doll I'd set on fire once when I was twelve and realized I wouldn't ever be tall or blonde. I wasn't in incredible shape either; I'd gained some weight since September.

And next to this shoestore woman, I felt like I had no chance at getting Sid with such people about.

"Is there anything I can help you with?" she asked brightly.

"Not at the moment thank you, but we'll let you know." Aunt Kippie smiled. She'd been beautiful in her day, still was in an older-woman kind of way. She turned to me. "I think we should get you some nice heels, Phyllis. They'll give you some height *and* your legs will look great!" Aunt Kippie was clearly excited.

I rolled my eyes. Quincy had already gotten annoyed with me for not having as many shoes as I was "supposed to." He'd asked why I only had sneakers and the boots he gave me, and when I'd said, "Because they're comfortable," he'd folded his arms and shaken his head, saying, "You certainly ain't no Carrie Bradshaw."

She found a pair of dark red heels. "Now these are your color!"

Red had been forced on me since the Aunts found out I could breathe fire, and even more so now that it had its own clothing line. My favorite color was actually blue.

"Okay," I agreed, and tried them on.

In the end, we wound up with a pair of navy heels and green flats that I knew I wouldn't wear, but Kippie was so enthused that she let me get a pair of red, comfy sneakers and a pair of white fuzzy slippers. They were on sale.

I felt guilty that we were buying shoes that would've been better off with someone else, but Aunt Kippie was happy.

As long as I got the fuzzy slippers.

The cashier, a honey-brown haired girl with no-rim glasses, handled our purchases. She looked vaguely familiar. And peering out from under the sleeve of her turtle neck, I saw part of a green tattoo.

Sarah.

Our eyes met as she piled up the boxes and put them into bags. We were both fearful. She knew my secret. And my secret was dangerous.

I wondered what had happened to Ben. I wondered if Sarah had changed; this look was one I had never seen before on her. And she had had a different look each time I'd seen her. I said nothing, though.

We said quiet, "Thank you"s and "Have a nice day"s and then left.

But as we walked across the way to the parking lot, she rushed out.

"Kippie, Phyllis!" she called.

We turned.

"I...just wanted to apologize. I broke up with Ben. I'm through with all that bad stuff I used to do. I'll never, ever bother you again. Please tell everyone in your household that I'm more sorry than you know for what happened." She looked to me. "Okay?"

I nodded. "Don't go back to it Sarah." I let some smoke escape my lips.

"N-no, I won't."

"We're very happy for you Sarah, we wish you good luck," Aunt Kippie told her. "You're welcome to come for dinner sometime."

"Thank you. Come back anytime!" Sarah called, going back into the store.

Aunt Kippie and I walked to the car.

"Phyllis," she said as we got in with the shoes, "I think you just may have scared that poor girl into a better life."

I smiled. Either way, Sarah wasn't going to tell. That was all I needed to know.

We stopped to eat, and got home in the evening around five or six o'clock. We walked right into an eruption. An eruption of gay men.

"Quincy you don't *think!*" Beatrix was shouting as we entered. Quincy, too, had apparently just returned.

"Look B, I'm *sorry*! I *said* I was *sorry*!" Quincy cried.

"Boys please! *Do lower your voices*!" Aunt Chasey yelled.

Aunt Kippie looked at me. "I think I'm going to go find my old megaphone." She hurried up the stairs.

"You've been spending *all* your time with Damien!" Abe told Quincy, loudly. "We were waiting for you here last night and you never showed up! You haven't even fed your goddam cat! Phyllis had to feed him!"

"Yeah Quincy, it was one thing to ditch us, but when you don't take care of your *pet*?" Beatrix folded his arms. "You're lucky you have Phyllis, who *cares*!"

"Do *not* bring me into this," I said, trying to keep even volume.

"But everyone is in this!" Abe said. "You've hardly even *brought* Damien here, and now *you* are hardly ever here."

"Well I'm *sorry* that I'm having a good time! I'm *sorry* that you're mad at me for having a successful relationship for once. I'm sorry you're *jealous*!"

Abe folded his arms. "Jealous? *Jealous*? Of you and Damien? *As if!* You know what, I don't even care. You can just go on and ignore us, 'cause we'll just be ignoring you right back! I'm leaving!"

"Hold it!" Aunt Kippie's voice came through the room like the voice of some almighty power (with really big speakers). She had the megaphone. I would have to ask her about that later.

We all looked up at her. She stood at the top of the stairs with the big white megaphone.

"All of you, sit!" she ordered.

We did. At least we still knew when to do what the Aunts said: always.

She came down, held the megaphone at her side. "Sorry about that. Now listen to me." She came into the middle of the living room. "Quincy, there is no question that your friends deserve some heads-up before you change your plans with them. We are all happy for you, but this *must* end. You have to make sure you keep half a mind on the *rest* of your life, the part that *doesn't* include Damien." She turned to Abe and Butch. "As I've said, you are Quincy's best friends. I'm sure he wants your support and understanding. You'll have to cut him some slack when he does stupid things. Because we've *all* been in love, haven't we?"

Beatrix sighed. "I *suppose* so."

Aunt Kippie went back to Quincy. "Apologize to your friends. I know you already have, but I'm afraid you'll have to do it again."

Quincy sighed too. "I'm sorry guys. I didn't mean to leave y'all waiting last night. It's just...Damien....Damien's the closest thing I've had to true love so far. Besides you guys. I still love you guys with *all* of my heart, I promise you. And yeah, I know you'll be the ones who'll have to hear me bitch about all this if something goes wrong."

"Damn straight!" Abe put in.

Aunt Chasey shook her head.

Quincy looked to Abe. "And for that, I thank you."

Beatrix smiled. "Oh! Hug!" he gushed.

The three of them hugged.

"We forgive you," Abe told him.

"Love keeps no record of wrongs!" Beatrix quoted.

"Thank you guys. I promise I'll be better from now on."

Abe looked at Quincy. "Even to Enrique?"

"*Especially* to that poor Spaniard."

"Isn't that nice?" remarked Aunt Chasey.

"I say we watch 'Breakfast at Tiffany's' to celebrate!" Beatrix decided.

"I agree!" said Quincy.

"We need snacks," Abe announced.

"I'm coming too," I told them.

"Phyllis, do you have homework?" Aunt Chasey gave me a look that said, "You'd better fuckin' do it." I sighed.

"Yes." Grabbing the bags of shoes, I trudged up the stairs, hearing Aunt Chasey mention to the guys that Bill and a friend were in the basement so they ought to use the living room.

Sid's door was opened when I got to the top of the stairs. I peered silently into the room.

"Hey Philly," he said.

I went to the doorway. "Hi Sid." He was lying on his bed, fully clothed unfortunately, looking at me.

"I uh, know you were in suspense so I figured I'd let you know that the guys made up."

Sid nodded. "Good. Maybe Butch'll come back to us."

"Yeah."

Sid eyed the large bags I held. "Anything good?" He sat up.

"Are you a shoe guy?"

Sid grinned. "I can be for now."

I involuntarily lit up as I entered the room. "Want to see?"

"Sure."

I showed him the heels first.

He looked at them. "Ouch."

I laughed a little. "Yeah, I don't think you'll ever see these again." I got out the flats.

"I think you might be able to walk in those," he told me. "Honestly, I can't believe the shoes women wear nowadays."

"Nowadays?"

He looked at me. "Yeah. What else did you get?"

I showed him the sneakers. "That's better," he said. "They even match your breath."

I smirked. "Should I dye my hair red too?"

He shook his head. "I like your hair; don't dye it." He paused. "But then, maybe you should ask Quince for that kind of advice."

He likes my hair, I gushed.

Shut up already, said the voice.

I looked at him. "The Aunts told you about Sarah Lagano, right?"

"Yeah. You saved them from her, didn't you?"

I shook my head. "Not really. You sound like Taylor—when I told her

I could breathe fire she said, 'You have superpowers!' But um...we saw Sarah at the shoestore."

"Jesus. What happened?"

"She..she said she was trying to turn her life around. She looked a lot different from how she used to."

Sid half-smiled. "Your Aunts believe so much in good that it must have rubbed off a little."

"Yeah. I hope so. It..made me feel better, like what happened with her had a real purpose."

"Yeah, you'd be surprised how many things in life have a purpose." He smiled. Ahh.

"Phyllis, are you doing your homework?" came my Aunt's voice up the stairs.

I stood up, taking the bags. "Yes!" I called. I looked to Sid. "I'd better go do that."

Sid nodded. "See ya Philly."

It took me til midnight to finish everything. But now I could dedicate Sunday to trying to talk to Sid.

* * *

Sunday morning I came down a little after ten, determined to talk to Sid. However, he was not at the breakfast table.

I had a big glass of orange juice, alone in the kitchen, and sighed.

Bill entered, wearing sunglasses. "I brought you some donuts for breakfast." He held up a bag.

I looked at him. "Aren't you off this weekend?"

"Yes, but I get a discount."

"That's cool, Prot." I took a glazed donut out and it helped me sound happier.

Bill went to distribute the goods. Aunt Chasey came in as I was finishing the donut.

"Did you sleep well dear?"

"Yes, you?" I got up to rinse out my glass.

"Mmhmm. And you finished everything? *All* of your homework?"

"Yes, Aunt Chasey."

"Good, good."

"Where's Sid?" I asked, putting my glass in the sink.

"In his room, I believe."

Yes!

I nodded again. "All right," I said in a final tone, ready to bid her farewell and go up to find Sid.

"Oh, Phyllis?" But Aunt Chasey, the lovely woman, stopped me. "Could you take these down to wash and dry?" She gestured to a basket of clothes by the basement door.

I sighed. "Of course Aunt Chasey."

With a great big smile on her face, she handed me the basket. "Thank you Phyllis."

"Mhmm." I took it and headed down.

The basement had four rooms; the laundry room came first. It was the largest room in the basement—there wasn't really much in it though. Three washing machines on one wall and two driers on the wall adjacent to it. Pipes, furnace, basement-type things, I suppose. If it had been night and I had been all alone, I might've gotten creeped out. But I was too worried about making sure I did the laundry correctly. I couldn't cook *or* sew, not like my Aunts, so I'd made myself learn to do laundry.

I opened up the washing machine *we* used—the Aunts and I—and put the clothes in. Then I turned it on.

As it filled, I realized I'd forgotten the soap. No! I looked around, but it just wasn't there.

I'm a failure, I thought. I can't wash clothes.

The voice was peppy. Yup, it agreed.

Phyllis, the poor dear, my Aunts would say. She's the sweetest girl, but she can't do a thing around the house.

I was saved, though, when I found it in the cupboard under the sink, wedged tightly between a large pipe and someone else's bottle of detergent.

I grabbed it and pulled.

Stuck, the voice said observantly.

I pulled harder.

"AH!" I cried, flying backward. The soapbox was in my hand, but the loosely capped bottle of detergent had gone flying, spilling all over the floor.

"Grrrrraaaaaa," I grumbled. After putting the soap in the machine, closing it and such, I cleaned the detergent up as best I could and put the bottle back in the cupboard.

Just as Quincy came down.

"Hey Ph— Whoa!" He wrinkled his nose as he opened one of the driers. "What happened?" He gave me a look. "Phyllis, are you trying to get high?"

I put a hand to my forehead and laughed. "Nooo. I spilled detergent."

He began scooping his clothes out into his basket. "Well it smells like you're trying to get high off inhalants. You know kids die from that all the time?"

"Quincy. Don't worry."

He sneezed. "Whose detergent was it anyway?"

I shrugged. "I don't know." I gave him a look. "Did you feed Enrique the Spaniard?"

Quincy hugged me. "Yes Miss Phyllis, I did. Thanks for doin' it for me. I'm sorry if I was an ass." He flinched. "Don't tell Aunt Chasey I said that."

"Did you apologize to Enrique?"

"Yes I did."

I grinned. "I won't tell her then. And you weren't *that* bad." I leaned away and folded my arms. "So when do I meet Damien?"

"I'll bring him for dinner, next weekend, I promise!"

"All right. I'm glad you found someone."

He shook out a shirt. "*You* find any 'someones' yet, Phyllis?"

I shook my head. "Not yet."

Quincy smiled. "No rush honey, you got your whole life in fronta you." He patted me on the head.

"Quincy." I ducked.

He put the last of his clothes in the basket, closed the drier, and pulled a bottle out of his pocket.

It was Flame, his cologne.

"Quincy!" I wrinkled my nose as he sprayed it around.

"At least now it smells stylish." He picked up the basket and headed back upstairs.

I opened the small basement window as best I could, and went into the TV room to watch something until the clothes were done washing.

I found Xerxes, the vanishing cat, lying on the couch.

"Mowrr," I greeted him. I meowed rather convincingly, if I do say so myself.

Xerxes looked up at me like I was nuts.

"Hello cat." I rubbed behind his ears. "Where you been?" He purred. "I love you Xerxes, you're such a good kitty." I baby-talk all cats. He let me scratch his chin, and closed his eyes.

"Wish I was a cat," I muttered. I picked up the remote and turned on the TV. I settled on a loud Nickelodeon cartoon and started watching it.

"I should have a cartoon," I told Xerxes, who continued to sleep. I yawned, accidentally letting some fire go with it. "That's a good idea," I said. I closed my eyes.

I didn't actually think I was going to fall asleep. That usually didn't work for me, not instantly, even if I *had* stayed up late the previous night. However, I fell into a deep sleep and dreamed about the cartoon I was watching. At least, I'm pretty sure I did, because everything was high-pitched and colorful.

It was nice to nap. I highly recommend it.

I don't know how long I slept, but it was long enough for Spongebob Squarepants to come on, because I woke up to a fish screaming, "CHOCOLATE!!"

I turned to find that Xerxes had, once again, disappeared. Like Batman. Xerxes was Batcat.

I stood and stretched, and after I'd turned off the TV, went back into the laundry room.

It didn't smell any better. I mean, it smelled clean. But much *too* clean.

Should've been more careful, said the voice.

I try, I told it. That's what matters.

You're just an idiot, said the voice as I opened the washing machine. You can't even do laundry without spilling something.

"Bitch," I whispered.

"Who?"

I whirled around so fast that I might have gone around twice and not realized it. Sid was coming down the basement stairs.

My face turned red. "How did you hear that?"

He pointed to his left ear. "Good ears."

"Really good ears," I agreed, hoping he couldn't hear my very thoughts. "I'm sorry."

He waved my apology away. "Don't worry about it Philly. You can swear, I don't give a shit. Just watch out for your Aunts."

He opened one of the washing machines. I waited for him to say "Where's my detergent?" but he didn't. It must've been Bill's. I heard him sniff. "Jesus, it smells like you tried to sterilize the air."

"I spilled a bottle of detergent."

"Is that why you swore?"

"Yeah."

He started putting clothes in the machine. "Well, just don't exhale any fire in case it's flammable, because it sure smells like it is."

I laughed slightly. "I won't."

"You don't ever play with propane and that kind of stuff, do you?"

"No." I don't need it, I thought.

I finished unloading my clothes and put them in the drier. When I stood up and turned it on, he was behind me.

"Why'd you say bitch?"

I turned. He was close; my face came up to where his neck began.

You're making him sound like a giraffe, said the voice.

Go away, I told it.

"What?" I said, hoping he might say, "Never mind" and I wouldn't have to explain myself.

Sid didn't make things easy though; he wasn't that kind of man. "Why did you choose that particular word? As opposed to damn? Or better yet, fuck?"

Sid swore well; that is, bad words sounded good when he said them, and I know how that sounds, but it's true. Everybody knows someone who can't swear, and everybody knows someone who does it better than most.

How was I supposed to answer that question, though? "I got mad at the voice in my head—she called me an idiot, so I called her a bitch"? Yeah, that'd go *real* well.

"I guess I was sort of referring to myself," I told him. "I was....mad at myself."

Yeah, that was much better, said the voice, giggling at me.

"You're not a bitch," he told me.

I half-smiled.

"Whose clothes are you drying?"

"The Aunts' and mine."

He looked at me. "You can still blow smoke rings?"

I nodded.

"Do it."

I did, blowing one, then another, and another, and another.

"I love that."

I love you. "Do you smoke, Sid?"

Sid shook his head. "I *have* smoked, but I get too..preoccupied to go out and buy cigarettes. And too cheap. But you, you'll never have to smoke."

"I didn't plan on it."

He smiled. "I wonder if it would hurt anything."

"I don't know."

"Ever been x-rayed?"

I shook my head. "I've never had any respiratory problems."

He chuckled.

"I'm glad you moved in," I said suddenly.

He smiled again. "Me too."

"How long do you think you'll stay?"

Sid shrugged. "As long as I need to."

"*Why* do you need to?"

He paused. "Do you *want* me here?"

I nodded.

"Well there you go."

"Does that mean you're staying for as long as I want you to?"

"Maybe."

"How will you know if I want you to or not?"

"I'll ask you. You seem honest enough."

"I suppose that's a good thing." I looked at him. "Are *you* honest?"

He nodded. "I only lie when I absolutely have to."

"When's that?"

"Can't tell you."

"Were you lying when you said you thought my hair was sexy?"

Sid laughed. I liked his laugh, even when he was laughing at me. "No Philly. I never lie about my opinions. Unless I'm discussing certain issues with your Aunts." He grinned.

"That applies to everyone, I think."

"True."

True. Taylor said that a lot. "What'd you think of Taylor?"

"She's nice. Observant."

"Did you like her?"

"I saw no reason not to."

I smiled. "She comes here a lot."

"Well we all want to be part of your family, Philly."

I shrugged. "I feel more related to people I'm not related to. I haven't seen my parents since...whenever. My grandparents are dead, my uncle disappeared off the face of the earth, I never had brothers or sisters. Quincy and Bill and Anna are my family."

"Where do I stand?"

I grinned. "You're facing me."

"Smart aleck."

"Taylor liked you."

"Did she?"

"She said you looked like a celebrity."

"Did she say which one?"

I shook my head. "I think she meant you should *be* one."

Sid gave a laugh. One "ha." As if it was the most absurd thing anyone could ever insinuate. Then he looked at me. "What do *you* think?" he asked with half a smile.

"I agree," I told him.

"Really?"

"Really."

"Why?"

Didn't the man ever get *tired* of being told he was good-looking?

"You have a good face."

He looked surprised. "Thank you Philly."

I'd just told him the world's biggest understatement.

"May I ask you a question?" I asked.

"Anything."

"Where were you all week?"

"Out on the town."

"With friends?"

"Sure."

"So why *didn't* you bring them back to the house?"

"Didn't want to."

"You didn't want to, or they didn't?"

"Both. I'm not going to bring strangers back to your home, Philly. All I have is a room, and it's right next to yours."

"Thank you for being considerate, Sid."

"Anytime."

"So you have a girlfriend?"

"No, I don't."

"Really?"

"Really. Why, Philly?"

Avoid that question. "How come you call me Philly?"

"Do you dislike it?"

"Not at all."

"There you have it."

"Sid?" I looked up at him.

"Hmm?"

"Can you read my mind?"

He grinned. "Maybe."

"What am I thinking now?"

He studied me.

I want you to kiss me, I thought.

"You want me to kiss you," he said. Then he kissed me softly on the lips.

No, that didn't really happen.

Actually, he said, "You're wondering how much longer the clothes are going to take."

I shook my head. "Nope."

"What, then?"

"I can't tell you."

He smiled slightly again, his eyes flitting around my face for a moment. Then he said, "Your hair *is* sexy, Philly. But don't think I'm hitting on you."

I shrugged. "I don't care," I said quietly, under my breath so that even if he heard me, he could pretend that he hadn't.

Sid went over and got his own soap and put it on the floor next to the machine.

"How's school going?"

I said "Bleh," or some sound of scorn and disgust, and he laughed.

"It's almost half over."

I sighed. "It's still taking too long."

"I never liked school either. But you'd be surprised at how fast time goes by."

"That's what everybody says. I haven't seen any proof of it yet though."

Sid held up his hands and gestured to himself. "You're looking at proof, babes."

I smiled. "What do you mean?"

"It feels like I was just here and you were turning six."

I raised an eyebrow. "You don't still think of me as six, do you?"

He chuckled. "No Philly. You're almost a different person now."

"How's that?"

"Taller. Darker. You talk more."

"I talk more?"

"You didn't talk all that much. You were a shy kid."

I folded my arms. "How'd you end up here, Sid?"

"It was a combination of things. Location. Anna. And you, when you came along. I didn't want to leave and come back to a burned down house and an innocent little girl who had no idea what happened."

"Did my Aunts pay you to help me?"

"I volunteered, Philly. I knew there were advantages to knowing someone who could breathe fire. And I like kids."

"Why don't you have any?"

"Easier said than done, I'm afraid."

"Seriously. You can't be having trouble finding someone, can you?"

He tilted his head. "What if I am?"

"Are you?"

"Why wouldn't I be?"

"Because..." Because why? I could think of a whole bunch of Quincyisms I could've told him (your features suggest GQ; you couldn't be more delicious if they'd carved you out of dark chocolate; you don't have an ugly bone in your body), but instead I said, "Because..you're..." I searched. "You..." Uhhh..

He grinned. "Have a good face?"

"That works." I couldn't stop my face from turning red.

"There's more to it than just finding *someone*. It has to be the *right* someone."

Hey, what'd I have to lose? "What makes her the *right* someone?"

"I'm not sure. I haven't found her yet."

She's standing right in front of you, chief. But I didn't say that; I just smiled sympathetically. Empathetically. Maybe just pathetically.

Somewhere upstairs a phone rang.

"Did Quincy leave?" I asked.

"I don't think so."

"Then that's probably Damien."

Sid nodded. "What about you, Phyllis? Any guys?"

"Phyllis!" Aunt Chasey called down the stairs. "Taylor's on the phone."

I looked to Sid. "Um.."

"Go ahead Philly. Tell her I said hi." He smiled.

"Okay," I said, hiding my reluctance to leave. I went up the stairs and took the phone in the sewing room.

"Hey," I said.

"Hi Phyllis. Wanna come over?" No.

"Sure, unless you want to come over here."

"It doesn't matter."

"I was just talking to Sid."

"Ohmigod! Did I interrupt your conversation?"

"Actually you kind of saved it. He was asking me if there were any guys in my life."

"Key'll set you up any time you want."

"I'll remember that."

"Tony can drive a standard."

"Really?" Any driving was a big deal to me.

"Yeah!"

"I didn't know he could drive at all."

"Not legally."

"Who taught him?"

"His brother. He said he'd teach me too."

"Awesome." I'd always pictured Quincy teaching me how to drive, but now that Sid was around..

I blinked. "Wait, so he drove you somewhere?"

"Yeah! We drove all over. I *love* him Phyllis. I can just talk to him, about anything, for like...ever. He's nothing like Hawk. He's nothing like...any guy I've ever met." She sighed. "And I bet he would've been good with my brother."

Every time Taylor mentioned her brother, I got the most uncomfortable feeling. The thing was, I'd never suffered a real loss, except for when I myself almost died, if that counted for anything. Everyone I loved was still alive.

"Then you've probably found the right guy, Tay."

Her voice brightened. "I do believe I have, Phyllis."

I smiled. "You sound like Aunt Chasey."

"Your Aunts should meet Tony! When I have their approval, I'll *know* he's the right guy."

"Well keep in mind that my Aunts approve of a lot of different kinds of people, and I wouldn't call all of them 'right'."

Taylor laughed. "I think I'll come to your house."

"You need a ride?"

"I'll walk. I need the exercise."

"Taylor." Taylor was strong but slender. She needed exercise like I needed a hole through my head.

"I'll be there in like," Taylor paused, probably checking the time, "A half an hour."

"Okay, see you then!"

"Bye."

"Bye Taylor." I hung up. "Taylor's coming over," I told Kippie as I entered the living room.

"That's nice dear. How was her date with Tony?"

Recalling bringing up driving "prematurely" in the past with my Aunts and recalling their reactions, I simply said, "Good. She really likes him."

"Well I just hope she doesn't take it too seriously. You girls are much too young to make the same mistakes I made. *Much* too young."

"What mistakes were those?"

"If I don't tell you, you might not make them."

"Indeed, I'll make worse ones."

Aunt Kippie whacked my leg. "When's she coming?"

"Half-hour."

"All right."

I went upstairs. The door to Sid's room was open. He was writing something, sitting on the edge of his bed with a small notebook and pen.

"Hey Philly," he said without looking up. "How was Taylor?"

"Good, she's coming over." I stood in the doorway.

He grinned, still looking at his writing hand. "Gonna tell you all about her date with Tony?"

"Yeah, apparently he can drive."

He looked up. "Can you drive?"

I shook my head. "Not yet."

"You'll like it."

"Whatcha writing?"

"A list of things I need."

"You don't seem the type who would need to rely on a list."

"You'd be surprised."

He said that a lot, I'd noticed, and I told him so.

"Well, it's true. Things aren't always what they seem." He smiled. "But then, you know that better than most, don't you?"

"I suppose I do," I agreed.

Are you what you seem, Sid?

"So when's she comin'?"

"About 20 minutes or so."

"You think you'll hang out in your room?"

"Yep."

He smiled again. "Do you tell her everything?"

I half-smiled. "Kind of."

He nodded. "Never take your friends for granted."

"I never will."

He stood, shoving the list into his pocket.

"Leaving?" I questioned.

"Yup."

"Umm..do you want me to put your clothes in the drier or anything when they're done?" If you really are gonna have to serve somebody, it might as well be a someone with a face like Sid's.

He looked surprised. "No Philly, don't worry about them." He grinned. "You're not *my* niece; I can't have you do my chores."

"What am I?"

He looked at me.

"I mean, what do you consider me?"

He walked over to me and patted my shoulder. "A good friend." He passed me, and went to the edge of the stairway. "Why, what do you consider me?"

I consider you the *real* sexiest man alive.

"The same," I said.

"Thanks Philly. See ya later." He headed down.

I went into my bedroom. I'd check the drier after Taylor arrived.

* * *

The rest of the day consisted of "Everything You Always Wanted to Know About Tony Whether or Not You Were Afraid to Ask." Tony this,

Tony that, I love Tony, Tony's re*ally* close to his brother, isn't that great, most siblings want to kill each other, his dad's like seven feet tall, his mom owns a bar, he has huge grey eyes, isn't that the coolest thing, he's only had one girlfriend before me, he says he doesn't want to make out right away, he wants to take it slow, he wants to be a DJ, he plays bass, he goes to church on Saturdays. I found out just about everything except his social security number.

"I already feel like I've known him forever, like I've been with him forever. It's like...he's a part of me." Taylor said as I shut the drier.

"You're a part of me, but you don't even know it. I'm what you need, but I'm so afraid to show it," I sang. Gladys Knight and The Pips; but the version I could play was from an Alicia Keys CD. I explained this to Taylor.

She nodded. "You're good."

"At singing?"

"Yeah."

"Yeah right."

She nodded again. "Yeah, you really are."

I smiled quickly. "Thanks."

"It's just a fact. Anyway I was thinking about how people give celebrity couples names, and I couldn't figure out one for Tony and me."

"What do you mean?"

"You know, like Bennifer."

"Oh yeah."

"I can't make one; our names both start with T, so it would have to be something stupid like Tonaylor. Or Tonlor." She giggled. "But I did figure out what you and Sid would be."

"What?"

"Syphilis!" She chortled maniacally.

"That's great," I said sarcastically. "Wonderful. I am *so* getting you back for that."

"You have to admit it's funny."

I was grumpy. "Well we're not *anywhere* near being a couple so you can't name us."

Taylor stopped laughing. "Is something else wrong?"

I sighed, sitting on the basement floor. I rested my elbows on my knees and my chin on my fists. "I've been trying to find out about Sid. Nobody would tell me anything, so I went through his room. All I could figure out was that he has some sort of connection with wolves."

"Connection with wolves?"

"Yeah, I know it sounds weird. But I just can't figure out anything that makes sense! And that just makes me angrier that he won't tell me! I mean, why wouldn't he trust *me*? I tell him things. He knows *my* secret." I blinked. "This is so stupid. I don't know what I'm even *thinking*!"

"Maybe he's waiting, to see if he can really *really* trust you. Or perhaps it's a really long story that he can't tell you in the time you usually have together. Maybe he's waiting for *just* the *right* moment."

I sighed. "I hope so."

"Don't give up though, I want to know his secret too." She grinned.

I smiled again. "I don't think I could give up now if I tried."

Taylor nodded. "Good." She paused. "Do you think Mary's been acting a little...*different* lately?"

I tilted my head to the side, pondering. "What do you mean?"

"She's all gloomy. Asking us how she would look with black hair, saying she's tired of everything. And the other day she was talking about Ouija boards."

"So?"

"Have you seen 'The Exorcist'?!"

I grinned, quoting, "'Captain Howdy, that isn't very nice.'"

"Exactly! If Mary starts messing with those things.."

"I don't think Mary's going to get possessed. I've always wanted a Ouija board myself," I told her. "But I'd *never* ask Aunt Chasey for one. She'd be positively horrified."

"Is she really really religious?"

"Not *extremely*, but religious enough. She uses the golden rule and what not. But I don't think she's still a virgin."

"I'd hope not."

"Do you believe in God, Taylor?"

"Someone's there. Why not God?" She grinned. Then she stopped. "He'd better be there. My brother died too soon for there to be nothing."

I nodded. "I can't imagine that there's nothing at all. That would be horrible."

"Whoever it is, it must be male. Look at how fucked up the world is."

I laughed. "You can't be sexist, you were just raving about your boyfriend."

Taylor sighed. "There must be a God because Tony is an *angel*."

I raised my eyebrows. "Taylor."

"Well he *is*."

"Then I hope Sid's a demon."

* * *

After putting the basket of clothes upstairs, we came back to the living room and watched "Ghostbusters" with Bill.

"Quincy's with Damien?" Taylor questioned.

I nodded. "They're introducing Damien to Maria. Maria has met Damien. And yet I still haven't."

"Saving the best for last," Taylor assured me. "Speaking of the best, where's Sid?"

That's why I loved Taylor. "He went to buy some stuff, it seems. Whatever that means." I looked at her. "You know he listens to Marilyn Manson?"

Taylor's eyebrows rose. "Well, that's interesting."

"I've heard him but if I brought one of his CDs home Chasey would probably burn it."

"Where *are* your Aunts?"

"Aunt Kippie's at the hospital. Aunt Chasey is probably in the kitchen but she could be upstairs cleaning."

"Does Sid tell *them* where he goes?"

"Not in front of me. But they know what his secret is."

"Well think about it Phyllis. You waited a little while to tell me *your* secret. Maybe it's that kind of thing."

"Yeah, yeah I know, and if I really care for him I'll respect his wishes. I can't help being human."

"It ain't easy bein' human." She smiled. "Bob Dylan."

"I'll take your word for it."

"That it's not easy being human?" Her eyes widened. "You are human, aren't you?"

I laughed. "Yes Taylor, I meant about Bob Dylan."

"Oh." Taylor burst out laughing. "Well," she sputtered, giggling, "how was I supposed to know? You don't expect your best friend to be able to breathe fire either. I think after that, I'll accept just about anything as a possibility."

"I think that's a good way of thinking." I looked at her. "See if you can think of something possible that could be Sid's secret."

Just then, and thank God that it was just then, the front door opened and Sid entered, holding bags.

"Hey Philly, hey Taylor," he greeted us.

Bill, enthralled in the movie, didn't look up.

"Hi Sid," said Taylor. "Go shopping?"

He grinned. "Oh yeah."

"What'd you buy?" I wanted to know.

"Just a bunch of CDs. And some groceries for your Aunts." He headed up the stairs. "I'll be down later."

"Sid shops for your Aunts?"

I hadn't told Taylor about the freezer full of meat. There were certain things I wasn't sure if I should disclose to anyone, even Taylor, if I myself was disturbed by them.

"I guess," I replied.

Wait. Maybe that was what the freezer was for; cooking. Maybe Sid liked to cook, or just liked being helpful to Chasey in her cooking.

Yeah, right.

While Taylor's attempts to reassure me had worked briefly, they were beginning to wear off. Still, somehow I just felt my will to discover Sid's secret strengthening, even though my crush on him was useless.

Taylor stayed and ate dinner with us, and soon afterward, her mother picked her up. Sid never came back downstairs.

* * *

On Monday, the first rehearsal for "Grease" was held. To my surprise (and delight) I had gotten a small role. I was one of the teachers. I had about two lines, but they were, in Taylor's words, "quite humorous." Other than that, all I did was dance and sing in the chorus, but I knew that would be work enough. The first rehearsal was simply a reading of the script.

Quincy picked me up on his way home from work.

"Snow's melting," he pointed out.

"Thank God." I was partial to the warmer months, though I'd never been one of those people who became cold easily.

He gave me a sideways glance. "The hell do you care, Phyllis? *You* could just *melt* the damn stuff."

I shrugged. "Yeah but then it just turns to water. I want it to be *all* gone."

"You just want it to get hot so you can see Sid with his shirt off. I don't blame you girl, God knows I do."

I snorted. "What makes you say that?"

"The fact that he's the sexiest man either of us have laid eyes on!" Quincy eyes suddenly grew wide and he put a finger to his lips in a shushing motion. "Don't you tell Damien I said that. I don't wanna lose him."

"Yeah well, I don't have any reason not to think that Damien is a sexier man than Sid. I've kind of never met him."

"I'm sorry baby, I'll have him over as soon as I can when you're around. I've just been busy, and so has he." He winked at me. "Valentine's Day's comin' up, you know." He gave me a look. "You got anyone special Phyllis? I won't tell your Aunts if you don't want me to." He glared at me. "But you'd better not be screwing around. That ain't right, not at your age."

"Not that I'm eager to do that, but there's no one for me to screw anyway, Quincy, so you don't need to worry."

"Aw, poor Phyllis. You'll meet someone, sweetie. You're pretty."

"Do you have to be pretty to meet someone?" I questioned.

"It does help, I'm not gonna lie to you. But it's not a must. It depends on who you wanna meet." He grinned.

I nodded. "I know what you mean." I'd already met Sid, I just couldn't get him to fall in love with me. Yet.

Hahahahahaha, cackled the voice.

I made a dissatisfied, groaning sound.

"What's wrong with you? You worried about Valentine's Day?"

"No, it's not anything serious." I exhaled smoke through my nostrils. "I'm just *so tired*."

"I hear you."

I sat quietly for a moment, then sat up quickly, trying to seem as if an idea had just come to me.

"Where does Sid go all the time? Do you know?"

"Honey if I knew, I'd go with him. But Sid's a man of mystery and he's gonna stay that way. It suits him."

"Why is he staying with us?"

"Ask him. It's none of *my* business."

"Quincy..are you serious?"

"What do you mean, 'am I serious'?"

"I don't think I've ever heard you say that." I didn't think that Quincy had ever even *thought* anything close to that statement. Quincy's mouth was bigger and poured out more than the Mississippi River.

"Hey, what's that supposed to mean?" Quincy whacked me in the shoulder.

"I already asked Sid, Quincy." I paused. "He wouldn't tell me. He answered questions with questions or...distracting statements."

"'Distracting statements'? Nothing illegal, I hope."

"Quincy. Sid was a lawyer. You don't really think he'd do something..like that." Though I wish he would.

"You never know. Sid has a very sizable soft spot for you."

I raised an eyebrow. "What do you mean?"

"He's loved you since you came to live with us. You were like...the daughter he could never have."

"Never have?"

Quincy flinched slightly. "I kind of consider Sid a hopeless cause when it comes to his love life."

But I didn't want to be like Sid's daughter!

"Do you think he still thinks of me as a daughter?" Please, please, please say no.

"Nah, I think you're more like a pal."

Pal could be good, pal could be very good, I thought.

He gave me another sideways glance. "What is he to you?"

"Definitely not a father figure." Perhaps I made too much a declaration of that sentence.

Quincy grinned widely, but made no remarks. I knew that couldn't be good. Quincy always had remarks, even if he didn't say them out loud. It was his way of life. And if he didn't make them to me, he might make them to someone else.

Who are you trying to kid? the voice demanded.

Fine.

If he didn't make them to me, he would definitely make them to someone else.

* * *

When we arrived home, I was internally ecstatic to see that Sid was in his chair. Bill was on the couch, this time watching Ghostbusters 2. He'd been Dr. Venkmen since the previous day, and it looked as if that was to continue.

"Hey Philly," Sid greeted me.

"Hey Sid."

"Our little star is back from rehearsal!" Quincy announced.

"Oh Phyllis, you haven't eaten a *thing*!" Aunt Chasey hopped up from the rocking chair and hugged me. "Let me go make you something, dear."

"Hi..ummm..." She was off to the kitchen before I could say anything more.

"You look exhausted," Sid informed me.

My eyebrows rose. "I do?"

He nodded. "Sit on the couch. You probably haven't relaxed all day."

Quincy came up behind the recliner and embraced Sid. "How's it goin' Mr. Siddons?"

"Quince, you've gotta decide on one man. How can I commit to you with someone else in the picture?" Sid said this quite seriously, and it frightened me.

Quincy patted Sid on the shoulder. "I just can't let go."

Sid waved the remark away. "It wouldn't have worked out anyway."

"Aw Sid, you're so fun. Can I give you a kiss?"

I giggled.

"No," Sid replied.

"Please? One little kiss for your friend?"

"No."

"Fine, I'll give Bill a kiss then!" Quincy went over to Bill and kissed him on the cheek.

"Oowhoa!" Bill was quite startled by this indeed. "Hello Quincy."

"And Phyllis gets one too!" Quincy kissed my cheek as well.

"Aw thank you Quincy," I said sweetly.

Quincy gave Sid a big toothy smile. "Don't you want to kiss Phyllis too, Sid?"

Sid shrugged. "Sure, why not?"

Yay! A kiss a kiss a kiss! I danced around inside my head.

Cough pathetic cough said the voice.

I was too happy to notice.

Sid rose from his chair, came to the couch, and kissed me on the cheek.

I smiled. "Thank you Sid."

"If Phyllis gets one, I get one too!" Quincy declared.

Sid sighed. "Fine dammit. C'mere." He kissed Quincy (doing so faster than lightning) on the cheek.

I cringed. Sid saw my face and laughed.

Quincy shook his head sadly. "Nope, the feeling just isn't there for me and you, Sid."

"Yeah Quincy, I *know*."

"I don't think it was meant to be, Quincy," I told him.

Quincy shrugged and sighed. Then he perked up. "Time to call Damien!"

"You broke my heart Quincy!" Bill called. Dr. Venkmen, I mean. Oh never mind, I'm not even going to try.

Quincy had disappeared up the stairs.

Sid sat back down. "I've learned it's good to be open-minded, but I'll only go so far."

"I still haven't met Damien," I told Sid.

"Don't worry about it Philly. They could break up within three days and Quincy won't want anyone to remember who Damien was. Of course," Sid smirked, "that doesn't seem to be likely."

"I'd better meet him before they get married. Or at least before he moves in."

"He's sure made Quince a happy man; he's running around acting like a 13-year-old girl who just got her first boyfriend."

"I'm afraid I can't relate myself to that situation, but I have to agree," I told him.

"You were 14 the first time I came here, weren't you? After I left?"

"Yeah."

"Have you remembered anything more from when you were 6?"

"Nope." Believe me, I tried.

"It's probably a good thing, anyway. Most of the time I was arguing with Anna."

"What do you plan on doing when she finds out that you're here."

Sid's eyes widened. Then he began to laugh.

"What is it?"

"I can't wait to see the look on her face." He stopped laughing. "But then she'll try to start a fight and break my neck."

"Maybe she'll explode and then you won't have to worry."

Sid half-smiled. "At least I don't have to worry about her burning down the house."

I was alarmed. "That never happened, did it?!"

Sid grinned. "No."

The phone rang. (Quincy now used his cell phone permanently for all calls because, being that most of them were made to Damien, they were so damned long.)

"You want me get that Philly?"

I sighed. "Sure." I didn't want to get up.

Sid answered it. "Hello?" I felt a tap on my shoulder. "Hi Taylor, yeah she's back." He looked to me. "Here Philly." He handed me the phone.

"Hey, Tay."

"Hi, Phyllis. How's the play going?"

I shrugged. "It'll be fun once I know some people. I talked to a couple of them, they seem nice." Sid was in the recliner again, watching me.

"Any annoying skinny people?" We'd since made fun of Key for complaining about skinny people.

"Yeah, but they're only annoying to me because I'm not skinny."

"No, you're curvalicious. You're a babe, and I envy you greatly my darling Phyllis."

"Oh Taylor, you're not allowed to have body-envy."

"Says who? If Mary Kate Olsen thought she had to be thinner, so can I."

I rolled my eyes. "I hope Bill never watches them."

Taylor giggled. "Has he ever gone transvestite on you?"

"No. Butch has, though."

"Nice."

"Yeah."

"How's Sid?"

Staring at me. "Good, everyone's good as far as I know."

"I've decided to move in."

"You'd probably get the room next to Quincy."

"Ah yes, Sid sleeps next to you." Taylor giggled.

I looked to Sid. He didn't look as if he'd heard. "That's a nice way to put it."

"I thought you would enjoy it." She paused. "I went to the library with Tony today."

"Did you manage to turn that into something fun?"

"Oh yeah, Tony loves books. They had this whole display dedicated solely to vampire books. Novels mostly. Phyllis there are so many freaking vampire books. Promise me you will *never ever* write one."

"Yes, because you know I am an aspiring author."

"Indeed."

"Could I call you back later tonight? I've still got to do my math. If I don't do it, my Aunts will somehow find out. No matter what, they always do."

"It's not so bad tonight."

"Taylor, if it's math, it's bad, okay? That's just the way it works."

"Aren't musicians supposed to be good at math?" Taylor stopped. "Hey, wait, you *are* good at math!"

"That doesn't mean I like it. Or understand it. You can't like a subject you don't understand."

"Ah, but does the same go for people?"

At this, my eyes went to Sid's face. "No."

* * *

The week moved by uneventfully; Sid, to my dismay, kept to himself, staying in his room.

On Saturday night, however, a shipment of boxes arrived at the house. It was Anna's precursor to moving in, things she was sending before she arrived in April.

I was doing horrible evil terrible global homework, up in my room. I had finally found the answer to a question that was giving me considerably more trouble than usual, but I couldn't find my pen. I searched frantically, realizing finally that I was sitting on it.

"Phyllis," Aunt Kippie called up the stairs, "could you please come downstairs for a moment? We're having trouble carrying some of Anna's things into the house."

I threw the stupid pen down and went downstairs.

I was stopped in the middle of the stairway by the sight of Sid in a T-shirt. Those lovely, lovely arms.

"What the hell's in this box anyway?" Quincy demanded. He and Bill were supporting a big cardboard box on either side. Bill didn't seem to be having any difficulties. He'd watched Justice League with Taylor and I the previous evening, and he was now Martian Manhunter.

"I suppose it is what someone from Earth would call a 'large contraption'."

Sid laughed.

"You wanna take this 'large' effing 'contraption,' Sid?"

"Quincy," Aunt Kippie said in a low, dangerous tone.

"Sorry Kippie."

"Yeah sure," said Sid. He looked to me. "Have any muscles, Philly?"

I nodded. "Yeah."

"Help me lift this."

"Okay."

Sid took one side, and I took the other, trying not to only focus on his arms, and to pay attention to the boxed large contraption I had to carry. It didn't feel as though Sid was struggling to lift it at all, but I was glad to be helping him.

"Didn't Anna send you a message about this sh-stuff, Kippie?" snapped Quincy.

Kippie nodded and read from a small sheet of paper. "I'm sorry to inconvenience you all— "

"But better you than me," Quincy muttered. Sid chuckled.

Kippie cleared her throat. "But thank you so much for your help. I can't wait to move in again, I'll see you soon!" Kippie glared at Quincy and Sid. "She wishes us all the very best and gives us her love."

Sid gave me glance and bounced his eyebrows once. I half-smiled and shrugged.

Suddenly Quincy's phone rang. He rapidly answered. "Hi baby, how are you? Aw don't worry, I ain't gonna forget about you on Valentine's Day. Mhmm. Yeah we're just movin' some stuff in. Aw honey you don't have to do that but it's so sweet of you to offer!"

Sid nodded to me. "You wanna take this down to her room with me, Philly?"

I nodded, a bit burdened by the weight of the contraption. "Yeah."

We went down into the basement.

"Sorry Philly, I just can't take too much of that."

"Why not?" I was unsure as to whether he meant the thought of Anna or Quincy on the phone.

"I've never been a smotherer."

"I beg your pardon?"

"Where love is concerned," Sid inched down the stairs, looking behind him so that he didn't trip, "I don't like to smother people with my feelings."

"Oh," I said, understanding him. "Is that what Anna wanted from you?" Oops.

Nosy nosy, chided the voice.

Sid's mouth tilted, not a smile or half of one, just an unintelligible tilt.

"Anna always thought we could be something that," Sid looked behind him again as we carefully descended, "we never could."

"What was that?"

Sid smiled sadly. "I *abhor* this cliché, but 'happily ever after'."

"Why couldn't you?"

"Because of the way I am."

"Which way are you?" My voice was strained.

Sid grinned. "You gonna make it Philly?"

"I don't think I'll be able to carry this much longer," I admitted reluctantly.

"One more step," he assured me. His tone made me want to kiss him. "Have any Valentine's Day plans?" he asked suddenly.

"Why, are you interested?" I really just wanted to put the damned box down.

Sid grinned. "I don't do Valentine's Day Philly, but if I did, you'd be the first I'd go to."

I beamed. I couldn't help myself. Luckily, Sid didn't seem to notice.

Finally, we put the box in the middle of Anna's room, careful not to block her way to the bed or closet.

"I bet it's her weapons collection," Sid remarked.

I nodded. "Most likely. Or it could be her extreme manicure set."

"Could be an organ."

"Maybe it's for another, bigger pet."

Sid tapped the box. Nothing happened.

"We know it's nothing alive," I told him.

"Jesus Philly. Maybe these are bodies she needs to dispose of." He grinned again. "You could incinerate them for her."

I grinned back at him. "Incinerating can be quite enjoyable."

Had Taylor been about, she would have said, "That should be on a T-shirt."

Sid chuckled. Then he looked into my eyes. "Blow smoke rings again."

I did so.

He pointed to me. "Someday, Philly, that's going to make a man fall in love with you."

I hope it'll be you, I wanted to say.

Sid turned and left the room. "She's probably got some more large contraptions."

We nearly collided with Bill and Quincy as they brought two more boxes down the stairs. Kippie, behind them, carried a suitcase and a remote control.

"What's that for?" I asked her.

"A stereo, I imagine."

Quincy huffed and puffed. "Girlfriend sure don't travel light."

Sid and I exchanged looks as we passed them by.

"You think she'll want you back?" I asked Sid.

"What? Anna? Jesus Philly, I don't know. I hope not." He grunted. "God knows what she needs so much shit for." He nodded to me. "What is it with you and other people's lives?"

"What do you mean?"

"You're nosy, Philly."

"Only about those I live with."

"Aren't your Aunts' attitudes toward everyone *here* about accepting them no matter who they are?"

"Yes, but I have to *know* who they are before I accept them."

"You don't accept *me*, Philly?"

"Is there something I don't know about you?"

"Plenty, Philly." He came a bit closer. "But I don't know everything about *you* either."

"Do you want to?" I asked without thinking, and his grin broadened.

"Now that wouldn't be fair."

"Why not?"

"Because I'm not telling you a damn thing."

Valentine's Day.

"Look at this!"

Taylor was in a state I had only once seen her in, when she'd gotten a Justice League T-shirt. Now it was because she had gotten a valentine from Tony. Presently she was showing me a card that said "I Love You" in big capital letters, but when one looked closer, it was apparent that each letter was made out of smaller "I love you"s.

It was a little...well...extreme.

"Look at this Harley Quinn doll!" Taylor held up a large stuffed doll.

"Did you get candy, too?" Key asked. "That's what I got from Jesse."

Taylor nodded. Then she turned to me. "Phyllis, I know you haven't..um.. arranged things with your special someone yet, so I got you this." Taylor pulled, from her backpack—we were gathered in the hall around her locker—a heart-shaped box of candy.

"Aw, Taylor." I gave her a hug. "Thank you."

My classes went by as slowly as ever, every minute dragging on. Finally it was lunchtime. I struggled to recall something interesting that had happened, and told everyone that Mr. Hamil, my English teacher, had written "Happy Valentine's Day!" on the board at the front of the room.

"He must have gotten laid," Mary said with a certain air. She had streaked her platinum hair black, and, sad to say, it looked like she was wearing a long black-and-white striped hat. I could tell everyone was trying to avoid the subject, even Mary herself.

"I still say he's gay," said Helen.

Key came to the table, and, upon catching sight of Mary's hair, feigned a faint.

"Mary...Mary no!"

"Shut up Key. It's not your hair."

"If I had hair that..superior to every other head of hair in this damn school, I wouldn't *ruin* it by making it look so.." Key shook her head in despair.

"So *what*?" Mary dared her.

"*Common,* dammit."

Mary looked to Helen. "Helen, what do you think?"

"Don't get me involved."

"Mary, you've gone psycho," Liz told her.

Mary stood. "I thought I could at least depend on my *friends,* but I guess not!" She stalked off into the crowd.

Key sat down and lay her head on the table, her arms carelessly tugging at her pigtails. "Soon she's going to be trying to raise the devil!" she whined.

"Calm down, Key," Helen told her.

"How the fuck are you supposed to calm down when one of your best friends starts engaging in the fucking worship of *Satan*?!"

"I want the old Mary back," said Liz.

"What exactly happened?" I wanted to know.

Key's pigtails, for the first time ever, were becoming loose as she pulled at them. "Phyllis, that's the scary part. There was no cause. She just showed up one day and was like this. In her room, she has all these candles, a Ouija board, all these damn books on black magic and voodoo and the devil!"

"It's probably just a phase," said Taylor. "She probably just saw 'Rosemary's Baby'. Or 'The Ninth Gate'. *There's* a movie that could have gotten me into Satan-worship." Taylor gave me a high-five. "The Ninth Gate" stars Johnny Depp.

"Oh Jesus." Key shook her head.

"Can't one of you talk to her?" I asked.

"I tried," Liz said.

There was a pause. Key looked at Liz. "What happened to your arm?"

Suddenly we all noticed that Liz had a bruise on her upper left arm.

Taylor and I exchanged looks.

"Oh dear," said Taylor.

Liz rolled her eyes. "I got in a fight with my brother."

"Oh," we all said, bored with the logical explanation.

"What, you thought I'd been harassed by Lucifer?" Liz looked at Key, who folded her arms.

"Key looks kind of like a devil, doesn't she?" Taylor teased. "Those two pointy pigtails could be horns."

"Roar!" Key curved her fingers into claws and snapped at us.

"The devil doesn't eat people, Key," Taylor told her.

I laughed. "Or else *you'd* be obsessed with him, Tay."

"Actually, there's a level of hell where he does," said Key.

I looked at Taylor. "Uh oh."

After lunch, things were, again, deadly dull. In art class, we were supposed to draw a heart in a surrealistic style. How unexpected on Valentine's Day.

But something interesting happened in study hall.

I sat at the piano (very exciting) and began to play. I'd brought a bunch of stuff, mainly photocopies of books I had or had borrowed from Mrs. Reygor, but I ended up running through "Piano Man." I wanted to memorize it for Taylor.

I was startled in the middle of "now John at the bar is a friend of mine" when the door opened.

It was a boy. He looked strong, and had the lightest shade of messy brown hair.

His hair was really all I saw at that moment because after he walked in and we exchanged smiles of acknowledgment, I went back to playing.

"Piano Man," he knew.

"Yeah," I replied, having trouble with talking while playing.

"That's cool."

"Thanks."

"They let you practice in here?"

"Mmhmm."

"Are you a prodigy?"

I stopped and smiled. "No, I'm just friends with Mrs. Reygor."

"Cool. I'm sorry I'm in here, I just have to get these guitars." He lifted two acoustic guitars off the wall they were hanging from.

"What're they for?"

"Chorus. I'm Mrs. T's errand boy." He sat and began tuning the guitars.

I paused.

"You can keep playing, I'll be able to hear the guitars."

"You don't want to use the piano to tune them?"

He shook his head. "Don't need to."

"You've played a while?"

He nodded rapidly. "Forever. What's your name?"

"Huh?"

"Your name."

"Phyllis."

"I'm Eric."

"Nice to meet you."

"You too."

I began to play again.

"Don't you know Tony Rhodes?"

Everybody does, I thought, looking up. "Yeah, he's my best friend's boyfriend."

"Oh yeah...uh, the one with the Batman shirt."

"Taylor Venchak."

"Yeah! She's your best friend?"

"Yep."

"That's weird. I see her all the time, but I've never seen you."

I smirked. "Not that many people seem to."

"No, I remember people."

"You didn't remember Taylor."

He held up a defensive hand. "I remembered her face." He smiled. "I'll remember your name, Phyllis, I promise."

"Thanks."

He stood, finished. "I hope I see you later Phyllis. Are you gonna be here a lot?"

I nodded. "Yeah, have fun with your guitars." Have fun was a Key phrase I had stolen.

"Have fun with your piano." He left.

I smiled to myself. He wanted to see me again.

Whoa, wait a minute, said the voice. That wasn't Sid. How can you *speak* to him?

Shut up, I told it.

He had been cute. But no one compared to the dark mysterious man who lurked in the upper corner of the house.

* * *

"Eric! I remember him!" Taylor exclaimed when I told her about him. She chuckled.

"What?"

"He broke one of Tony's guitar strings."

"Oh."

"You think he really liked you?"

"No. He was nice though."

"Phyllis! His name is Eric! Like the prince in 'The Little Mermaid'!"

I rolled my eyes. "I'm the polar opposite of a mermaid."

"You love to swim, Phyllis."

"Yeah, but I breathe fire."

"Oh my God."

I looked at her, alarmed. "Did you forget?"

Taylor covered her mouth. "Phyllis. What if you kiss a guy and you accidentally burn his mouth?!" She burst into giggles.

I laughed. "I should do that to guys I don't like."

"Yeah but could you even control it?!"

"I think so." I half-smiled. "I used to singe my bedroom ceiling at night."

"How did you stop?"

"I never told my Aunts. I started taping my mouth shut at night, and I'd wake up when I exhaled fire. Eventually it stopped."

"You were quite the resourceful child."

"I was used to solving problems on my own."

"Well, now you don't have to." Taylor gave my shoulder an affectionate pat.

"Thanks Tay."

"You're welcome Phil."

We grinned at each other.

"You're staying after for rehearsal?"

I nodded. "Yeah."

"All right, I'll see you later. And I'll let you know if Eric mentions you!"

"Well, don't *you* mention me."

She made a cross on her chest. "I promise."

Rehearsal, as usual, was tiring but fun. Still, when it came to an end, I was relieved. My feet can only take so much dancing. And my hands can only take so much hand-jive.

"Great job enunciating your words, guys!" said Miss Kaye, a young, hyped-up teaching assistant. "Terry, try not to overdo your laughing on that last line. Frenchie, are we gonna be able to get some bubble gum for the performance?"

"Definitely."

On the way out, as I struggled into my coat, I bumped into Mary. Her makeup was smeared by tears.

"Mary! Are you okay?!"

"What did they tell you? That I'm a Satanist?"

"Mary *what's wrong*?!"

"Key thinks I'm a freak."

"Key's just worried about you, Mary." I touched her shoulder. "Do you need a ride home?"

Mary blinked, keeping her eyes shut for a few seconds. Then she nodded. "Yes, please."

I nodded. "Okay."

What I wasn't expecting was Sid waiting for me in the parking lot.

"Oh my God, who is that? Your uncle?!"

I shook my head. "That's Sid, he rents a room in my house."

"Wow." Her hands went to her face. "Oh no, my mascara."

"Mary, maybe you should talk to Key. Or just talk to *someone*," I told her as she searched her pockets for something to wipe her face with.

Mary shook her head. "She's too good for me now."

"Mary dammit she's really worried about you! And I am too! Please talk to her."

"It's just a matter of acceptance, Phyllis. Accepting me for my calling."

"What calling is that?"

"Magic."

Uh huh. "I'll accept you as long as I don't get poked."

"Huh?"

"With a needle. Like a voodoo doll."

She smiled a bit. "Phyllis, I don't hurt people. I've just found a new way to get what I want."

Suddenly Sid was with us. "You coming Philly?"

"Can we give Mary a ride?"

Sid smiled at Mary. "Sure." He looked at her. "Are you okay?"

She nodded rapidly. "I just need to get home. I can get a ride with someone else—"

"No, that's fine."

"Thank you so much."

"Actually.." Sid looked to me. "We're supposed to meet Quincy and the guys for dinner. You want to invite Mary?"

I looked to Mary, feeling a slight, okay, a rather large pang of jealousy . "Do you want to go out to dinner with us?"

"Oh I couldn't, I'll probably already be in enough trouble when I get home. But thank you."

"No problem," I said.

Mary didn't live far from the Italian restaurant Sid and I ended up in.

"She's got some problems," Sid said as we walked in.

"How did you know?"

He smiled. "Her hair was one thing. But I've known people with similar ones. It's all in the aura."

"You see auras?

"When I say aura, I mean vibes. She gives off real bad vibes but not..not in the way that a bad *person* would. It has to do with confusion."

"What do you think she's confused about?"

"Everything." He pointed. "There's Quince."

Quincy was waving to us from a large booth in a corner. The seat was like a rectangle missing one of the shorter sides. We headed over.

"Hey Quince."

Quincy was with Butch, who wore a feather boa, Abe, and a brightly dressed man with brown hair and blonde highlights.

"Phyllis, Sid, *this* is Damien."

Damien was very cute, very colorful, and very Quincy. He gave me a big smile. "Hi Phyllis, I have heard so much about you."

"Damien, this girl's so hot she *breathes* fire!" Quincy winked at me as I sat down. I rolled my eyes.

Damien touched Quincy's shoulder playfully. "You're so articulate, I never would have thought of a metaphor like that." He looked at Sid. "And *you*!" He turned to Quincy. "You *live with this* man and you're dating *me*? I must have done something right."

"You sure did baby!" Quincy hugged Damien.

I held back giggles, and looked to Abe at my left.

He patted my thigh. "Phyllis, this is only the *tip* of the iceberg."

"I'm glad I'm finally meeting you," I told Damien.

"Ditto. Quincy sings nothing but your praises."

"Well what do you think he says about *you*?" Butch wanted to know. He and Damien laughed.

"What the hell?" said Abe.

"What?" we all said, with the exception of Sid.

"Is that a hat or her *hair*?"

A woman with spikey pink hair had walked in.

"Butchie that reminds me of the time you dyed your eyebrows blue!" Quincy told him.

Damien laughed. "Oh my *God* what a 'don't'!"

I looked at Sid, hoping he could make this dinner a little less gay. There was only so much I could take of fashion criticism.

He leaned down. "I'm glad I'm sitting next to *you*," he whispered. I knew he meant he was glad because otherwise he'd have to endure the four gay men harassing him about his looks and oozing fashion magazine minutia into his ear. (And probably hitting on him too.) But the utterance had made me quite happy nonetheless.

"Likewise," I told him. "I promise not to make fun of your clothes. Ever."

He chuckled.

"Did I tell you Phyllis is in 'Grease'?" Quincy said enthusiastically. "We *all* have to go and see her on opening night!"

I sighed. Sid put a comforting hand on my arm.

"That is *the* coolest thing. I love plays, I've seen *so many*." Damien said. "I'll have to take you all to one. We can go to a Broadway musical."

"Aw Damien. Did you know Damien owns a *dance club*? He's been letting me use it to promote the store!" Quincy exclaimed.

I nodded. "Wow."

The waitress came and we ordered our drinks.

"God, even her *walk* was peppy," Abe whispered as she left.

"Yeah, but you need that in a waitress," Damien said.

"So Philly, how was your day?" Sid asked suddenly.

"It was..okay."

"Any valentines?" Quincy asked excitedly.

"Yeah, did all the cuties give you flowers?" Butch clasped his hands together.

I shrugged. "Taylor gave me some candy, and this guy told me my piano playing was cool." Oh, no. I had pulled the trigger.

Simultaneously, the gay quartet chorused, "Ooooh."

"A *boy*," Quincy said with a giggle.

"A *guy*," Abe corrected.

"Was he hot?" Damien asked.

"What's his name?" Butch inquired, propping his chin on his hands.

I sighed again. Saints preserve us.

"He was decent," I told them. "His name was Eric." I suppose, being brought up in part by Quincy, I should be the type that gets excited about gossip. Well, I do. Just not my own.

"Like the prince in 'The Little Mermaid'!" Butch gushed.

I stared at him.

"What?" he wanted to know.

"Phyllis found her handsome prince!" said Abe.

"Abe," I remonstrated in vain.

"What'd he look like? How'd you meet him?"

"Was he hot?"

"Was he nice?"

"Obviously he was *nice*, silly."

"Yeah, but was he hot?"

"Guys! Let her be!" Sid put a protective hand on my shoulder. "Relax!"

"Aw Sid," Butch fussed. "You're no fun."

"Yeah, I wanted to know about the boy." Quincy folded his arms and gave a mock whine.

"Aw, it's okay," Damien comforted him with a squeeze.

"When are *you* going to meet someone, *Sid*?" Abe interrogated.

"He's got me an' Phyllis, what else could a man *want*?" Quincy broadcasted.

"We should buy the girl with the pink spikes a drink," Butch said suddenly.

"Mm-mm! I can't afford that!" Quincy cried.

"Quincy, this dinner's dutch," Damien reminded him.

"Yeah Quince, nobody's paying for *me*," Sid promised. "And I'm paying for Philly."

"Well.." Quincy shrugged. "Hey, I'm not the type who refuses the opportunity to save a little money, honey."

"Thanks Sid," I said.

"No problem Philly."

"Quincy," I inquired, "why aren't we having dinner at home with the Aunts?"

"They got dates, sweetie." Quincy grinned.

My eyebrows shot up. "Really?"

Quincy nodded, his eyes and smile wide. "Yeah. Kippie's with some guy from the hospital, and Chasey's with some guy from the church."

"Why didn't *I* know about this?" I demanded.

"They didn't know until today, while *you* were in school."

"Wow," was all I could manage.

"All I have to say is, it's about time," said Butch. "Both of them deserve someone good, and I know how hard that is to find, but Jesus! You *gotta browse* a little."

"Hear hear," said Damien.

"*Quite* right," agreed Abe.

"Well sometimes, a man just walks into your life." Quincy rested his head on Damien's shoulder. Then he looked at me. "Oh, Phyllis, guess who else has a date?"

I shook my head cluelessly.

"Bill! Apparently he met some girl who thinks she's an alien!"

Damien choked on his water. "Does she have more than one head?"

"Probably has three tongues or something."

Our server came back and took our orders. Once she had gone, the guys chattered on amongst themselves. Abe pulled out an issue of GQ and Quincy took Glamour out of his bag, and they all began to pour over those. There was also some conversation about financial matters, and as soon as I heard math becoming involved, I became uninvolved.

That left me to talk to Sid.

"That was interesting," I said in reference to Bill's alien friend.

"Wonder what planet she's from."

"Maybe she's like Bill and she's a klingon or something?"

"A what?"

"Alien from Star Trek?"

"Movie?"

"TV show. Well, both."

Where've you been? said the voice.

Don't question Sid! I ordered it.

You're the one who wants his life story. Shouldn't he have grown up with that stuff?

"Ah. I'm sure it won't matter to Bill. I'm more concerned about your Aunts. It's hard for them to find guys, especially in Chasey's church circle, who can deal with everything they do and everyone they live with." Sid nodded subtly to the men around us.

"You mean because they're tight-ass conservatives?" This was a term I heard frequently spit out of Quincy's mouth, usually in reference to people who told him he was going to hell.

"Somebody should smack you for saying that."

"You?"

"Of course not. I couldn't go up against a girl who breathes fire." He paused. "You can't make flames shoot from your fingers or anything, can you?"

"Let me see." I grinned and lifted my hands up. I focused on my fingertips. "Anything?" I asked.

He half-smiled and shook his head. "Nope."

I set my hands on the table and immediately felt the wood begin to sink beneath my fingers.

Sid instinctively (or at least, it was fast enough to be instinctively) grabbed my wrists and lifted them off of it. "Jesus Christ Philly," he said in a tense but quiet tone. He subtly touched my fingertips. "They're hot," he told me. He took my hand. "Do it again."

My eyes widened. "No!"

"Why not?"

"Sid, I'll burn you!"

He shook his head. "Don't worry about it Philly."

I shook mine. "No."

Sid was exasperated. He grabbed his glass of water and set it on the wooden seat of the booth, between us.

"Put your fingers in here."

"It won't work underwater."

"Philly, please."

"Okay." I put the fingers of one hand in the glass and, seeing the small black burn marks on the table (hardly noticeable thanks to Sid's quick action), focused the heat into that hand. This time I felt small vibrations in my fingers.

The water began to bubble, and I pulled my hand out, startled.

"Hot," remarked Sid, wiping a drop I had splashed onto his face off.

"Oh my God!" I whispered. "Are you okay?"

"Yeah Philly I'm fine," he said. He touched my arm briefly. "I told you not to worry."

"You're not fireproof too, are you?"

"I don't get hurt easily."

"Oh, don't let me get sauce on your tie!" The waitress was passing out our orders (Quincy's was first; ironically his tie was red).

"You do and I'll sue!" Quincy exclaimed.

Our server was alarmed.

Quincy laughed. "Oh honey, I'm just joshin' you."

"Thank you *so* much," Damien said to the waitress as she gave him his lasagna. I had ordered that, too. Sid had manicotti.

"Did you know you could do that?" Sid asked me quietly as he received his dinner.

"No," I whispered, lifting my fork. "I may never have found out if it weren't for you."

Sid smiled slightly. "I don't know if that's good or bad, Philly."

Disagreements.

In the days that followed the dinner, I practiced my new found talent. I used mugs of water, and found that I could use my hands like a stove or microwave; I could heat things up from the outside. Over the next week I ate lots of spaghetti-os and hot chocolate milk.

"Phyllis did you use the stove?" Aunt Chasey asked on Saturday upon seeing me with a bowl of ravioli. She usually oversaw my every move in the kitchen.

I shook my head. "Aunt Chasey, I found something out. I— you're wearing earrings!" Aunt Chasey didn't usually go out with much make-up or jewelry, a trait I'd inherited.

Chasey blushed. "I have a date with Mr. Meneses."

Aunt Kippie and Aunt Chasey had both had good experiences on their Valentine's Day dates. Aunt Kippie hadn't seen her guy again. Mr. Meneses, however, had been by the house once since.

"That's awesome Aunt Chasey! Where are you going?"

"We're going to a greenhouse in the city and then out to eat at a little restaurant he enjoys." Aunt Chasey was clearly happy. Her voice had taken on a slightly dreamy tone.

"Chasey honey, you'd better wait a while before you cook for that man. Once he tastes your cooking he'll propose." Quincy was coming down the stairs. He adjusted his tie and then hugged my Aunt. "You have fun. I'll make dinner for everyone."

Aunt Chasey was shocked. "Really?"

"Oh yeah. I'm just goin' to pick up Damien and the guys." He waved, told us he'd be back soon, and was gone.

"Now Aunt Chasey, don't feel pressure to do anything you're not comfortable with." I grinned, stood and gave my Aunt a hug.

She laughed. "Very funny, Phyllis." She then became serious. "That better not be any implication of what *you've* done with boys."

I rolled my eyes. "Of course not, Aunt Chasey."

She nodded. "Can I trust you to watch the house until Quincy returns? Sid's here too, if anything happens."

"All right. I'll just hang out here with my ravioli."

"Oh, what was it you were going to tell me about dear?"

"I'll tell you when you get back from your date, it's not that important."

"Everything in your life is important to me," Chasey said sincerely.

"Thanks Aunt Chasey."

There was a knock at the door.

"Oh! That's him!" She rushed to put on her coat.

"Bye Aunt Chasey."

"Good-bye Phyllis, I love you!" Aunt Chasey blew me a kiss as she went out the door.

"Love you too."

And then I was again alone with my ravioli. But not for long.

"Did you heat that up yourself?" Sid had come down. Which room he came from I failed to see. He had a sketchbook, but not the one I had looked through in his room.

"Yeah." I shrugged. "I had a bad experience with the stove."

"It's a good thing we found your new power then."

I half-smiled. "How did you think of that?"

"At the time I was joking. But I've always wondered about your potential. The most damage you could possibly cause." He grinned. Then he was serious. "Thank God you turned out the way you have."

I raised an eyebrow. "Why?"

"Imagine if someone fucked up had the power you have. You could destroy cities, Philly." And schools.

My eyes brightened. "Hey, you're right.."

"Don't even think about it Philly."

I gave him a mischievous look. "I can't even *think* about it?"

Sid smirked. "So have you seen any more of that guy?"

Guy? What guy? was my attitude, but I knew he meant Eric.

"The one who liked your playing."

"Oh, Eric? Nope." And it was for the best. I couldn't be distracted from my pursuit of Sid by trivial matters like a cute boy who played guitar and had wanted to see me again.

"Do you *want* to see him?"

I shrugged. "Doesn't matter to me."

"Why not?"

"Um..I'm not incredibly interested in him." I paused. "Why do you ask?"

"Wanted to know."

I decided it would be useless to ask why he wanted to know because it was basically the same question, and he'd be able to find some way to evade it.

"Yeah, there's another guy I've been hoping for," I said boldly. Perhaps a little too boldly.

"Sometimes you have to make the first move." He chuckled a bit. "We're not always sure of ourselves."

"We?"

"Men."

"Oh. Well, I can't."

He wore a pondering expression. "Why not?"

"It's a difficult..it's..if he didn't feel the same way, it'd be a really awkward situation."

He nodded. "You see him a lot?"

"Yeah."

"Who is he?"

I shrugged. "Just a guy."

"What kind of guy?"

"A great one."

Sid grinned. "Is he as great as I am?"

I laughed. "I hope so."

Sid's smile was surprised. "Thanks, Philly."

"Anytime, Sid."

He took a moment before he spoke again. "So you'll never be cold again will you?"

I half-smiled. "Cold hasn't ever been a big issue for me."

"You'll come in handy in the winter." He grinned.

"I'll take that as a compliment."

"Good."

I ate my last piece of ravioli. "Sid?"

"Hmm?"

"What did you think of Mary?"

He raised an eyebrow. "Just what I said."

"She hasn't been in school."

"Did she ever talk to her friend?"

"Key? I don't know. Key's been kind of quiet. How did you know about that?"

He shrugged. "Things I remember hearing. When I was a lawyer I had to be able to draw fast conclusions."

"So you *were* a lawyer?"

His eyes flashed; it was quick and if I hadn't been staring at him I would have missed it. "Yes, but only for a short time."

"Wow. Why aren't you doing that now?"

"Various reasons."

"Such as?"

"I vaguely remember suggesting that I wasn't going to share my personal life with you."

"You've shared parts of it."

"My life gets a little more personal than that."

"Sid, *I'm* a part of your personal life."

"I'll tell you Philly, sometime. But for now it's none of your business."

"But I live with you."

"Your Aunts are the ones I pay, babes."

I smiled a little. He certainly could make a point.

"Maybe you should call her." Sid said suddenly.

Huh? Think Phyllis, think. "Mary?"

"Yeah."

"Don't have her number."

"Get it."

"Her problem isn't with me, though."

"Maybe you could convince her to call Key." He squinted. "How'd she end up with the name Key?"

"Who knows. But Taylor's working on getting Key to phone Mary."

As if it had heard its name, the phone rang.

I got up and answered it.

"Phyllis? This is Debbie Kaye."

"Hi, Miss Kaye."

"Do you think you could come at six tonight to rehearse?"

"I thought tonight was leads only."

"Yeah, but there are leads in your scene and we still need to get you a costume."

"Um, I don't know..nobody's really here who could give me a ride.."

"Philly." Sid pointed to himself with both index fingers, drawing another fast conclusion.

"Oh wait." I covered the receiver. "She wants me to go to rehearsal tonight at six."

Sid nodded. "I'll bring you."

"It's until nine."

"And I'll pick you up."

"Thank you!" I went back to Miss Kaye. "I can be there."

"Oh great! Well then I'll see you at six."

"Yup."

"Bye Phyllis."

"Bye." I hung up. "Thanks Sid."

"No problem Philly."

"You're not going anywhere today?"

He shook his head. "Nope. Blank schedule."

"What time is it?"

"Four."

"I think I'll take a shower." Want to join me?

"Just let me know when you're ready to leave." Guess not.

"Okay." I went upstairs.

As I combed my hair, which I did several times a day, I noticed it was almost down to the middle of my back. One of the guys usually trimmed my hair. I wondered if I could do it myself. My bangs were messy too, uneven and in my eyes.

I shut the bathroom door and looked in the mirror. I looked at my eyes. While studying my face meticulously one day, as I often did, being sixteen, I had discovered something.

I breathed out smoke and watched the reddish orange tint briefly come into my eyes around the outside of the irises. I grinned and looked over my teeth. Then I showered.

When I emerged, dried and dressed, I sat at my keyboard.

I could make up a song about Sid, I thought.

Bwahahahahahahahahaha, chortled the voice.

I decided against it.

Instead, I decided to play "How Come You Don't Call Me" by Alicia Keys. It was the first song I'd ever heard by her, thanks to Quincy. It had a broad range of notes in the vocals (if I tried to sing it like she did) and helped me warm up for rehearsals. Plus it was fun to sing. What was most fun to sing for me was what the Aunts called "angry music," the rock and heavy metal with screaming and such. But when I scream I tend to exhale fire. So I stuck with my nice soft, happy piano music and only sang along with the louder stuff when I really needed to scream.

Maybe Sid has anger management problems, said the voice. He has a lot of heavy metal. Maybe he *always* really needs to scream.

We all have our moments, I admitted.

Sid must have a lot of them, the voice concluded.

It did have a point. Many of the bands on his CD shelf I had never heard of and could only presume were heavy metal. But they hadn't looked like easy listening.

I realized then that I wasn't singing, so I began to. Once I was finished with "Call Me" I played "Fallin'".

I ceased abruptly when I heard my bedroom door open.

"Sorry Philly. Are you ready?"

"You didn't knock."

"Element of surprise."

I turned off the keyboard and stood. "Yeah, let's go."

We went downstairs. I left a note for the Aunts, and then we left.

"Sorry, I lose track of time when I'm playing."

"That's all right Philly." Sid and I got into his car, and he turned it on and pulled out of the nearly empty driveway. "You have a pretty voice."

"Thank you."

"Anytime."

"What are you going to do while I'm in school?"

"I could stay and watch." He gave me a hint of his brilliant white smile.

"Um.."

"Or I might visit a friend."

"Wow! You actually told me."

"Yeah I did. But don't expect too much of that."

* * *

"That's fabulous, wonderful!" Mrs. Reygor exclaimed when she saw me in my terrible costume. The wig was grey curls piled on top of each other, and the dress was brown. I think it was tweed.

"Is this really how you want to personify yourselves? I mean you're teachers, too!" I cried.

"No, but the play is mainly about teens and how *they* see things," Mrs. Reygor told me.

"Now when you say those lines I want you to think of Mrs. Highman, okay Phyllis?" Miss Kaye told me

I giggled.

She grinned. "Seriously. You've gotta just be this mean, burnt out, bitchy teacher. You're tired of all these damn kids."

I nodded. "I can do that. But do I really have to wear the wig? You can be burnt out when you're young."

"The wig is *great*," Mrs. Reygor asserted sternly. "We are *definitely not* getting rid of the wig. You'll be able to change out of it when you're in the chorus."

"Okay." Oh well. All part of being an actress I suppose.

After my scene, I didn't do much else for a while, so I went out in the hall to get a soda from a machine. My pockets were always full of change.

"Hey Phyllis." Eric was sitting in the hall, catching me off guard.

"Hi." Are you stalking me?

"You're in the play?"

"Yeah. I'm a teacher."

"Cool."

"Oh yeah, real cool. Especially my costume." I grabbed the orange soda from the bottom of the machine.

"I can't wait to see that."

"What are you doing?" I inquired.

"Guitar lesson."

"Really?"

"Yeah." He smiled. "I teach."

"Whoa."

"Yeah, so if you ever decide you want to learn to play..."

"You should give Taylor some tips, I know she plays."

"She's got Tony."

"Is he as good as you are?"

Eric grinned. "Almost." He stood. "Really though, let me know if you want to learn to play."

I nodded. "I'll do that."

"See you later Phyllis." He walked toward one of the rooms.

"See ya." I want back into the auditorium, sat in the audience, and drank my soda.

Guitar *would* expand your musical horizons, commented the voice.

I'm happy with the present length of my musical horizons, thank you very much, I told it.

"Phyllis, do think you could change quickly enough to be in the chorus for 'Summer Nights'?" Mrs. Reygor called to me.

"Definitely!" I set down my soda and ran to the stage, and spent the rest of the rehearsal learning the choreography for the song with the leads.

Sid was waiting for me by the doors when I left the school.

"How'd it go?" he asked as we walked to his car.

"Good, we got a lot done. I saw Eric," I blurted out.

He was intrigued. "How was *Eric*?"

"He teaches guitar lessons, apparently."

"He might have just said that to impress you," Sid warned. We got into his car.

"I don't think so."

"Ask him to come over and play for everyone at the house."

"I hardly know him."

"You have to take chances."

"I'll leave that to you."

"My days of taking chances are over."

"You make it sound like you're really old."

"I *am* really old."

"No you're not."

He smiled, almost nostalgically, though I couldn't imagine what he was remembering. Then he stopped, suddenly.

"How old *are* you?" I asked.

"Old enough." He reached into his pocket. "Bought a phone." He handed the small silver phone to me.

"I don't get a phone until I start driving." I looked at him. "You bought this while I was rehearsing?"

"Nah, I bought it a few days ago."

"What'd you do just now?"

"Visited my friend."

"What's his name?"

"Van. He lives in the city."

I blinked. Vance Frobisher, from Sid's address book.

"What's he do?"

"He does a lot of things. I don't really know, he's hard to keep track of. We haven't seen each other in a few years."

"How do you know him?"

"He helped me get a job after I finished law school."

"Oh." I couldn't fathom Sid ever needing help. "What's your number?" I asked, studying the phone.

"It's on there."

"Where?"

He grinned. "See if you can find it."

By the time we returned, I had Sid's cell number.

"I can call you for dinner from the living room now," I told him.

"That you can."

We got out of the car and went inside.

Abe, Beatrix, and Quincy were on the couch, the first two on either side of the latter.

"You'll find someone else," Abe reassured him.

Uh oh.

"Maybe you can work this out." Beatrix patted Quincy's shoulder.

"He just doesn't understand," sobbed Quincy. "Why can't he just leave it alone?"

"Quincy what happened?" I went to the couch immediately.

"He broke up with Damien just a little while ago," Abe told me. At that, Quincy burst into tears.

"Damien and Maria don't get along. They've gotten into some arguments, and Quincy of course never takes sides, so they both get mad at him. Damien and Quincy had a fight about it and it ended badly," Beatrix informed us.

"He stormed right out," Abe added.

"Oh!" Quincy buried his face in Beatrix's shoulder.

"You'll get over him. You're strong Quincy, be strong!" Abe squeezed Quincy's arm.

"No I'm not!" Quincy sobbed.

I hugged him. "You'll get through this Quincy."

"Quincy why don't you cry it out, then call Damien and see if you can just patch up things and kiss and make up?" offered Beatrix.

"It's just not that s-s-simple!" Quincy cried.

"I'm sorry," I told him, giving him a squeeze before I stopped hugging.

"I should just forget him!"

"Quince don't think about it now. Wait until you're more rational," Sid told him wisely.

"Oh where's Anna when I need her?"

"Merciless Anna," Beatrix muttered.

"Oh Jesus, time for me to go," said Sid. He headed upstairs.

"I have to go to my room," Quincy said. "I just..I need to be alone. Thank you guys for being here, but I've got to go be alone."

Abe nodded. "That's fine Quincy."

"We'll be down here if you need us," Beatrix told him.

"All right." Quincy wiped his eyes (with a tissue, never his sleeve) and headed to the back stairway.

"Maria doesn't like Damien?" I wanted to know. I hadn't heard about this before.

"She thinks he is 'a pompous little idiot'," said Abe, making air quotes.

"What did he say to her?"

"He probably insulted her Manolos or something."

"I think he may actually have told her that they were overrated," said Beatrix, putting a hand to his lips in shock.

"Well, I agree that you need to explore more than one brand, but really!"

"So unnecessary," Beatrix said.

"I'm..gonna go finish my homework," I lied. I went up the stairs to my room. Wonder Woman was sleeping on my bed.

"Hi honey." I scratched under her chin, then got her comb and started combing her fur. Lucky cats didn't have such complicated relationships. I bet two cats never ignored each other over a damn shoe. Cats don't shy away from people they're interested in, no matter how old they are. Cats aren't always timid. They don't have laws.

Just then I remembered my Aunts. After apologizing to Wonder Woman, who ended up running down the stairs with me, I went to the kitchen where Chasey was.

"Isn't it a shame Phyllis? Did you hear about Quincy and Damien?" She paused, looking a bit confused. "When did you come home?"

"About fifteen minutes ago. I just abandoned Wonder Woman to hear about your date."

"Oh Phyllis it was wonderful! Such a sweet man." Chasey handed me a carton of eggs. "Would you take three of those out please?"

I nodded, removing the eggs and replacing the carton in its place in the fridge. "What are you doing?"

"Making a cake."

"It's almost 9:30."

"I know." She sighed. "But Kippie won't be home until eleven and if there's a cake waiting for her I'll be able to get her to sit and talk with me."

"Ah. Are you going to tell *me* about your date?"

"It's not a big story or anything. There are other things I need to talk to her about." She smiled. "But I did have fun."

"What happened?"

"He is such a gentleman. And we agree on so many levels. We don't agree on *everything* of course, but we had *such* conversations. He's the kind of man I can simply *talk* to, Phyllis. And that's very difficult to find...should you find a man like that, you should hold onto him, so to speak."

Chasey went on and on. She was happier than I'd ever seen her, giggling and advising and repeating herself a lot. She said some exciting things, I'm sure, but I ended up zoning out. Sid, the play, Eric. I snapped out of it when Chasey said my name.

"Phyllis, why don't you go keep Quincy's friends company. I need to find the frostings."

I told my Aunt I would, and I did.

I ended up falling asleep in Sid's Chair, not even awakened by the guys' banter. I woke up to Sid standing over me.

"Hi," I greeted him, my voice cracking as I looked up.

"Tired?"

I nodded. "I am."

He sat on the couch, the end nearest to his chair.

"Aunt Chasey's making a cake," I told him.

"Yeah, I smelled it as soon as I walked in."

I inhaled, and could hardly detect the scent of the cake. "Good nose."

"You're the one who said I have a good face."

"You do."

He smiled. "She said it's almost done."

"What?"

"Chasey. The cake."

"Oh. Good." I stretched. Abe and Butch were gone.

"Where'd the guys go?"

"Kitchen, fussing over your Aunt. They couldn't fuss over you because you were asleep." Sid grinned.

"Is Kippie back yet?"

"She should be soon."

I noticed a sketchbook next to Sid's lap. "May I ask what you're drawing?"

Sid held it up. Surprise; it was a wolf.

"That looks real," I told him, because it did. Alarmingly.

"Thanks."

"Why a wolf?"

"I like wolves. I can't get this one out of my head."

"Have you ever seen one in person? Er..face to face?"

He chuckled. "Yeah, once or twice."

The door opened. "Oh boy. Hello Phyllis, Sid. How are you?" Aunt Kippie trudged in.

"Good," I told her. "I had rehearsal today, I'm in another scene, in the chorus."

"That's very nice dear. When should the performance be?"

"Three weeks or so."

"I can't wait. Ohh, I'm tired." She sank into the couch beside Sid.

He squeezed her shoulder. "Chasey made a cake."

"I knew she was good for something."

I giggled. "I'm telling her you said that."

"You go right ahead. But wait until I've had a piece of cake please."

"And now, the lady of the hour," Beatrix announced. He and Abe had emerged from the kitchen with plates and forks, followed by Aunt Chasey, who was carrying her luscious chocolate cake.

She set it on the card table. "Everyone, help yourselves."

We did, of course.

"I'm gonna go get Quincy. Cake'll cheer him up," said Beatrix.

Sid stopped him. "He won't want any."

Abe shrugged. "More for us."

Beatrix tapped Abe on the shoulder. "What's with you? You're not mourning this breakup at all."

"It's not *my* breakup. Quincy has to figure his own sh..stuff out. I feel bad. But we've done all we can, dude."

Beatrix sighed. "I guess you're right."

"You wanna watch a movie downstairs?"

"Yeah sure. Yeah. We'd better stay here in case he needs to talk," Beatrix decided.

So, the guys took their cake and headed for the basement.

Aunt Kippie sat down with her cake. "Chasey, why on earth were you baking at eleven o'clock? Did your date go *that* well?"

"It went quite well."

"I'm so glad you've found someone. It's been so long."

"Yes, I am too. Which brings—"

"Is that cake? *Chocolate* cake? Y'all made chocolate cake an' didn't tell me?" Quincy had come back down.

"Oh Quincy, I'm so sorry." Chasey put a regretful hand to her lips.

He smiled. "I'm just funnin' Chasey. You mind if I have a piece?"

"Go right ahead." Chasey smiled warmly.

"You were saying?" Aunt Kippie reminded Chasey, after she'd swallowed a bite of cake, of course. Aunt Chasey despised people who talked with their mouths full.

"Kippie, it's been years. Years upon years. You'll be ever so much happier if you start dating again."

Kippie set down her plate. Her eyes were serious.

"I'm too old to date."

"Pish tosh. *I'm* older than *you* are." Chasey folded her arms.

"By less than a year."

"Still."

"I don't want to date right now."

"Kippie, love is *worth* taking risks."

Peer pressure.

"I don't think like a teenager anymore." She held up a defensive hand. "Not that that's a bad way of thinking. Don't let this conversation influence you, Phyllis."

"See Kippie, you just encouraged the exploration of love! You *still believe*!" pushed Quincy.

"I'm *not saying* love shouldn't be explored. I'm saying *I'm* not ready to explore it again."

"Kippie you might *never* be ready!" Quincy cried.

"I know, Quincy."

"Don't you wanna get some Kippie? Even *Chasey's* gettin' some, girl!"

"Quincy!" Chasey scolded.

"I'm joking sweetie, I'm joking! Seriously though Kippie, you can't *hide* from love. Even Sid kept on dating, for a while. At least *he* has an excuse to stop." I recorded those words in my mind.

"*Quincy.*" Sid hissed.

"What excuse is that?" I asked.

"Phyllis please don't interrupt," Aunt Chasey requested.

"Honestly Chasey, why are you worried about *me*? Everyone I love is here," Aunt Kippie told her.

"Yeah Chasey, Sid's the only one any of *us* want to sleep with." Quincy giggled.

"Sexual harassment," Sid warned him.

"You can harass me anytime."

Aunt Chasey sighed and said to Kippie, "I just want you to remember how nice it can be."

Aunt Kippie nodded. "Yes, at first it's nice."

"This is hopeless, ain't it?" Quincy asked.

Kippie nodded.

Sid stood. "I'm gonna get a piece of cake and go upstairs." He got his cake and stopped in front of Kippie. "But Kippie, you have a chance to fall in love, take it, because you can. Trust me."

"Better to have loved and lost," Quincy added.

"Thank you boys," was all Kippie said. Sid went upstairs.

"What did he mean?" I demanded.

"Where're Abe and B.?" Quincy asked nearly simultaneously.

"Downstairs," the Aunts chorused.

"*What* were you talking about?" I asked again.

"I'm sorry to have bothered you about that, Kippie."

"It's fine Chasey, you're my sister."

"Aunt Kippie—" I began.

"I'll help you clean the kitchen, Chasey."

"Thank you Kippie. We ought to save the rest of the cake for Bill and his extra-terrestrial friend."

They were ignoring me!

The Aunts went to the kitchen. I purposely left my plate on the coffee table so that my poor Aunts would have to pick it up. Served them right for ignoring me.

I was angry with Sid, too. I rushed up the stairs. The door to his room was closed.

I knocked on it.

"What is it, Philly?"

I opened the door. "How did you know it was me?"

Sid turned, he'd been at his desk. "Who else?"

"Why don't you trust me, Sid?"

"You have enough to worry about, babes."

"So just tell me and I won't have to worry about you anymore!"

"If it were that simple, I would. *Why* are you worried about me?"

"Why shouldn't I be?"

"Nothing to worry about. It's *not your business,* Philly." Sid sighed. "You should go to sleep."

"I know. But—"

"Go Philly."

I did as Sid said. But I would not be defeated.

Reconciliation and Discovery.

Sid didn't pay much attention to me in the following weeks. He was home more often, but seemed to purposely avoid me.

Luckily, I hardly had time to daydream. Rehearsals were longer and more frequent. Then there were my friends. Mary was back in school. She wouldn't tell us why she'd been out, and she wouldn't even speak to Key, though Key apologized repeatedly, sincerely. She was talking to everyone else, though. One day, at the very beginning of March, she approached me in the hall before lunch. Taylor was talking to Tony, and Mary pulled me aside.

"Phyllis, how old is Sid?"

"What?"

"The man who picked you up on Valentine's Day," she said as if I didn't know him. "How old is he?"

"I don't know, somewhere in his 30s? I don't know."

"Oh." She sounded disappointed.

"Why?"

"I think I..thought he was someone else."

"Who?"

"Don't worry about it." She waved to Helen as we entered the cafeteria and walked ahead of me.

"Hey." Key tapped me on the shoulder. "I found out why she's not talking to me."

"From?"

"This guy told Tony people are calling her 'Scary Mary' and she thinks I started it."

"Oh wow."

"Liz started it."

"I thought they were friends."

"Not behind Mary's back, apparently. People really suck these days."

"Yeah," I agreed.

"I'm gonna talk to her. I've got to."

I watched as Key bravely marched up to Mary, who sat at the table with Helen.

"Mary, you need to talk to me."

Mary sipped her milk.

"Mary you need to talk to me *right now!*" Key yelled.

Mary stood up and began to walk away.

"I am *not* calling you names behind your back, damn it!"

Mary turned. "Well, then *who* is?!"

"I don't know! Why would you think *I* would *do* that?!"

"Why should I believe you? *You're* the one who told everyone I worship *Satan*!"

Key tugged at her pigtails. "Maybe you could *explain* to me what the hell you're doing so that I don't have to draw my own stupid conclusions. I miss you Mary."

Mary sighed. Then she went over and hugged Key.

Someone started clapping. I looked over and saw that it was Taylor who stood in one of the doorways of the cafeteria. I began clapping too. Soon our whole table was, and a couple others. But most of the people in the room just looked confused.

Taylor came and sat next to me. "Promise we won't have a huge fight?"

I considered. "I can't think of anything we could have a huge fight over."

She smiled. "True." She touched my shoulder. "Hey, I was talking to Eric."

I raised an eyebrow. "Cool?"

"He asked me about you."

"Uh oh."

"He asked how you were. He asked if you had said anything about him."

"What'd you tell him?"

"That you'd said you'd talked to him once or twice."

"And?"

"He said, 'Oh.'" She grinned. "He wants you bad Phyllis."

I rolled my eyes. "I'm sure he does." I'd talked to Eric once since the time at rehearsal. We weren't discussing anything deep. "How's Tony?"

"Good."

"That's good."

"Yeah. How's Sid?"

"Still not speaking to me."

"Are you still nosing about?"

I giggled. "I would be, but I'm having trouble figuring out where to nose. Nobody'll tell me anything. Not even Quincy."

"Sid must really not want you to know, and he must be really scary when he's angry. That's the only way I can see Quincy keeping whatever Sid's secret is." She took a bite of her sandwich. "Maybe you can trick him into telling you."

"Sid?" I gave her a look.

"No silly. Quincy."

"I don't think so. He'd recognize any attempt to draw out a secret; that's what *he* does."

"Has he talked to Damien?"

"He won't even talk *about* Damien."

"Maybe they need divine intervention."

"Sid and I need divine intervention."

"I think that's just a matter of luck. But you really should consider Eric."

"Why?"

"Because *he's* talking to you and *he* likes you."

"Sid likes me. He's just not in a friendly mood these days."

"Maybe you should burn him. Not like, horribly. Just a little mark on his hand. He'll get the message."

I laughed. "I don't think it would do much good, but I appreciate your input my dear Taylor."

"You are quite welcome my dear Phyllis." She paused. "Can I come to your house on Friday night? I want to see everybody."

"Yeah, definitely," I assured her. "Maybe you can be Quincy and Damien's divine intervention."

So, on Friday evening, I came home from rehearsal and cleaned my room and told my Aunts that Taylor was coming at 8.

"That's fine dear," Aunt Chasey told me.

"It's been much too long since she's been here," Aunt Kippie added.

"Yes," I said. "Where's everyone else?" I asked, because the Aunts were the only people I'd seen. But there were several cars in our driveway, including Sid's.

"Quincy's having a small party in the basement," Aunt Chasey told me.

"I don't think you girls should go down there at all, all right?" Kippie gave me a look.

I nodded. This meant they were drinking. A lot. "Taylor said she was bringing movies anyway, we can watch 'em in the living room."

It wasn't long before Taylor arrived. "I brought 'Underworld' and 'Casablanca.' And 'House of Wax.' I thought it'd cheer us up to see a skinny blonde die."

"You *are* a skinny blonde," I said.

Taylor shrugged. "I'm not rich."

"True. Let's watch that one first."

Taylor and I watched movies long into the night. It wasn't until the beginning of "Underworld" that Taylor asked where Quincy and Sid were and what was going on in the basement.

"Party."

"Ah. We weren't invited?"

"They are apparently engaging in heavy drink."

Taylor tsked. "Indeed!" Then she giggled. "I'd like to see Quincy drunk."

I leaned over and whispered, "I'd like to get Sid drunk."

"Date rape." Taylor approved.

"Whoa," I breathed as one of the men fighting the great Kate Beckinsale turned into a werewolf. "Ick."

Taylor grimaced, but not at the wolf. "I don't know why you'd want to fight in a sexy outfit."

Suddenly the basement door opened.

"Hey, a party up here too," Sid remarked. He stood behind the couch where we sat. "What the hell is that?" He squinted.

"'Underworld,'" Taylor informed him.

"What the hell's it about?"

"Had a few, Sid?" Taylor asked him.

"Nope, had a bunch."

"It's about the apparent war between vampires and werewolves," I told him matter-of-factly.

Sid's eyebrows went toward each other, as if the idea were absurd. He came around and stood next to the couch, his eyes on the screen. "*Hhwhat?*"

"An ancient feud between sanguinaires and lycanthropes," Taylor told him, waving her arms around crazily.

Sid chuckled. "That *thing* is supposed to be a werewolf?"

"Yep."

He shook his head. "I'm sure werewolves and vampires get along fine. There're too many movies like this one." Then he turned and went upstairs.

Taylor and I looked at each other.

"What, like he knows from experience?" Taylor raised an eyebrow.

"Maybe he's a vampire."

"Maybe he's a werewolf. Or both!"

A werewolf.

The possibility didn't exist, but it seemed almost probable. He had a fridge full of raw meat, pictures of wolves, a skylight in his room. And he lived in my house, where the strange roam freely.

"He was also intoxicated," Taylor said smartly.

I didn't pay much attention to the rest of the movie; I was busy zoning out. Or maybe I was subconsciously rejecting the film because Sid had scorned it.

Sid. Maybe he had a thing for werewolves. Maybe his obsession went a little too far. Maybe he was slightly crazy, like Bill, and thought he *was* one. A beautiful crazy man. People could be nuts without seeming it, couldn't they?

I mean, look at Taylor.

At this thought, I giggled.

"You think all of this pointless carnage is funny?" Taylor said with mock disapproval.

"Taylor. You have laughed at every decapitation scene in every violent movie we've ever watched."

She grinned and made the slurping sound that Anthony Hopkins makes in "The Silence of the Lambs."

We didn't go upstairs until sometime after one. Once we were in my room, I confessed my suspicions to Taylor.

"You think Sid's a werewolf?" Taylor was, at the very least, doubtful.

"No! As many weird things as I've seen, I'm still *pretty* convinced that there's no such thing as a werewolf."

"No one's been eaten. He can't be a werewolf."

"What I was thinking was that maybe he *thinks* he's one."

"Huh. Well, anything's possible in *this* house. And I wouldn't put it past Sid to be a werewolf. He's hot enough to be one." She held up a defensive hand. "But *I* have a boyfriend." She grinned.

"My point exactly." I yawned. "I need to sleep."

"Whoa, Phyllis, watch it!" Taylor ducked as flames streamed out of my mouth.

I inhaled it back in. "Sorry Tay."

"Let's sleep, but please don't burn me!"

"Are you okay?" I bit my lip.

"Yeah, I'm fine. Of all the things to worry about, I have to worry about my best friend incinerating my head while I'm sleeping." She patted my shoulder. "But then, if I had to choose someone to incinerate my head, it would be you."

* * *

We slept so late that as soon as Taylor woke up, she had to leave. (But not without breakfast of course.)

Not having anything urgent to do, I sat with Quincy on the couch in the living room. Bill was on the floor near the TV.

"Hey Phyllis, you're just in time. There's a 'Law and Order' marathon on today," Quincy said. Quincy, Bill, and Anna had been "Law and Order" buddies since I was little.

There was a crash of thunder outside.

"Did Taylor *walk* home?" Quincy asked, worried.

I shook my head. "Her mom."

"Good. Power better not go out."

"That'd be terrible. In the middle of a marathon!"

Quincy nodded. "It'd be an omen of somethin' bad to come."

I giggled. The theme song was just ending. "I love this show," I said, knowing that I had his approval.

"Yeah, me too," Quincy agreed as I'd known he would. "You know," he said, pointing to Jerry Orbach's character, "he played the candlestick in 'Beauty and the Beast'."

"He was in one of the 'Aladdin' sequels too."

"You're good." Quincy gave me five.

We watched a little more.

"You're under arrest," Bill muttered along with the detective. "You have the right to remain silent.."

"Has he said much about the alien girl?" I murmured to Quincy.

Quincy shook his head. "I think they're just friends. God knows how he found her, though."

"Sid didn't know what klingons were."

"They broke the mold after that man, and that is for sure."

"Isn't that weird?"

Quincy shrugged. "Yeah, but Sid's a little weird baby."

I looked at the TV and saw that they were in the court room. "He used to be a prosecutor, right?" I asked.

Quincy smiled a little and nodded.

"Did you ever see him in action?" If I used the right techniques, it was possible to get Quincy to let something go.

"Yeah, he was great. Women already wanted to tell him all their secrets, and men were afraid of him. Sid's pretty scary ."

"Mmm." I took care in plotting my next move, pretending I was enthralled with McCoy's merciless drilling of the witness.

I never actually carried out any more moves because Quincy said, "You're in love with him, aren't you?"

It took me a moment to realize just what he'd said.

"What?" With McCoy? No. Don't get me wrong, he's great, but...

"With Sid." He gave my shoulder a nudge with his. "You're in love with Sid."

I tried my hardest to find something *really good* to say. How would I react if I *wasn't* in love with Sid?

Quincy grinned a wide grin. The man knew about love. "You're *definitely* in love with him."

I shrugged helplessly. You couldn't lie to Quincy.

"I don't blame you one bit, Phyllis." Quincy giggled. "But honey, he's too old for you."

I nodded. "I know."

"But..?"

"I can't help it."

"Mm-hmm."

"Yeah."

"Why don't you try lookin' at guys your own age?"

"After you see Sid, no one else looks as good."

Quincy burst out laughing. "I'm gonna tell him you said that."

"Quincy! No! If you tell him, I might as well be the typical teenage girl with the typical teenage crush."

He giggled some more.

"Don't tell him Quincy," I pleaded.

Quincy sighed. "Oh, *fine*."

"Thank you."

He's not gonna keep his mouth shut for long, said the voice.

Neither do you, I told it.

The voice didn't say anything else.

I decided to change the subject. "Have you talked with Damien yet?"

Quincy turned and looked at the TV, and left my question unanswered.

"Quincy..."

"Wait, I gotta see this part!"

This was Quincy's way of avoiding the subject. I knew better than to try to get him to talk about heartbreak.

* * *

It was still raining the next day. It was Sunday, but everyone was working. Aunt Chasey was volunteering at church.

I was left alone with Sid. Obviously he knew this, because he didn't leave his room, so I decided to stay downstairs. I wouldn't get any closer to Sid by bothering him.

I sat in his chair upside down, my head on the foot rest, my feet hanging off the reclined back, and listened to the rain falling outside. Maybe I should've been working on something too, but I was perfectly content as I was.

I had dozed off when the door opened.

"Hell-oo?" It was Butch.

I hopped up. "Hey!"

"Hey Sparks! Is Quincy here?"

"He's at the store."

Butch flinched. "Oh *damn*."

My eyebrows went up. "What is it?"

Butch bit his lip. "Damien called me and asked if Quincy was working today, and I told him no! He wanted to go 'cause they're having a sale on scarves." He proceeded to nibble his nails. "Shitshitshit. This could be *baaad*." Then he shrugged. "Oh well. They have to work this out sometime, don't they?" He looked around. "Is anyone else here?"

I gestured to the staircase. "Sid's in his room."

"Ahh." Butch plopped down on the couch. "What are you up to?"

"Lyin' around."

He nodded. "It's that kind of day." He snapped his fingers. "But! After the rain's over, it's going to be *sunshine* for the rest of the week. Thank *God* all this blah weather will end."

"It's about time," I agreed.

"Oh I *know.*" He winked. "*And* there's a full moon on Wednesday and we might be able to see through clear bright skies!"

A full moon, eh. Perhaps I would watch Sid carefully on that day. Werewolf or not, I might as well investigate. "So where's Abe?" I wanted to know.

"He wanted to see a movie. I think he went with Maria. So cliché, the straight woman and her gay best friend. It's in all the romantic comedies. What I don't like is that there's never been a movie about a gay man with his straight best friend." Butch sighed and shook his head. Then he looked at his watch. "You know, I think I'll go. I don't want to be here when Quincy gets back for lunch, not if he and Damien didn't patch it all up. It's such a damn shame Phyllis." Butch stood and put on his cap. Then he pointed at me. "Don't *you ever* let true love run out on you. We only get one chance." He started to go.

"Butch.."

Butch turned.

"What about you and Abe?"

"Honey I really have to go." Butch rushed up and gave me a quick peck on the cheek. "Buh-bye!"

It had almost been worth the try.

A little before one o'clock, Sid appeared.

"Hungry?" I asked him as he came down the stairs.

"Yeah, I'm gonna' get a sandwich." About ten minutes later he came back into the living room with a half-eaten sandwich in his hand.

"How are you?" I asked politely. "Or is that asking too much?" I cringed. Shit. "Sorry."

Sid grinned, surprisingly. "It's okay, Philly." He sat next to me on the couch. "I'm all right. How are *you*?" Sid took another bite.

I couldn't keep from breathing out the very slightest bit of smoke. "Fine. Quincy's going to be back soon." I eyed the door. "He may have had a run in with Damien." I stood, using this as an excuse. "So I'll be back later."

Sid nodded. "Understood."

That wasn't why I left. I'd left because it was getting difficult to talk to Sid. I didn't know everything I felt I should have about him, but I would voluntarily tell him anything he wanted to know about me. How humiliating it was to be in love.

You're definitely *in love with him.*

Damn Quincy. I hoped it wasn't that obvious to *everyone*. God, that would positively suck, I thought. My Aunts would twitter at me, Sid would..I don't know what Sid would do, but he probably wouldn't talk to me anymore.

Not that he was talking to me that much now.

I shouldn't pester, I thought. But then, maybe I should. I had a right, didn't I? We lived in the same house. Sid was the one who'd said I had every right to question someone I'm living with! Ooh, was I going to use that against him...

Quincy had come home.

I lay on my bed in thought for some time longer, before it dawned on me.

Quincy was terrible at keeping secrets. He knew one of mine. And he was alone with person who it concerned.

"Huh," Taylor would have said, "well, that's probably not good."

Fuck.

I lifted myself up again and went down to the living room, praying I wasn't too late.

Sid was drawing, sitting on the couch with a notebook of some sort.

Quincy was in front of the mirror to the right of the front door. He was trying on three scarves.

He turned. "Hey Phyllis, look at these! Three scarves for fucking fourteen ninety-nine! Do you *know* how good a deal that is? And they're Crimson scarves, too!" He swished the scarves, all three around his neck.

"How was work?" I questioned carefully. He probably wouldn't say anything even if he had seen Damien.

"Oh fine, fine." He was clearly deep in thought. "Hmm." He turned back to me. "Which one should I keep, Phyllis? And which ones should I give to Abe and Butchie?"

I studied them carefully, then came to a decision. "Give Abe the blue one," I said, pointing to a blue, purple, and white-striped one. "Give Butch the red." I pointed to a red one with several tiny black polka dots. "And you keep the gold one."

Without looking up, Sid said, "I agree with Philly."

Quincy stared at his reflection. "Hmm. Hm-hm-hm...I'ma keep the red one, give the gold one to Abe, and give the blue one to Butch."

Hmm. "That works too," I said, feeling a bit offended.

Sid made an exasperated "Tshh" sound.

Quincy, putting the scarves on the card table, sat beside Sid. "Whatcha drawin'?" he asked, taking the pad.

Sid grabbed it back. Or, rather, snatched it back. "Damn it Quincy, mind your own goddamn business for once!" He got up and went upstairs.

Quincy held his hands up in a surrendering gesture. "That time of the month again," he said, heading for the kitchen.

"What?" I looked at him.

Quincy suddenly looked alarmed. Then he laughed hysterically. "No, no honey, I was jokin'."

I looked at him, still a bit perplexed. "Oh. Okay."

"Sorry, Phyllis, I didn't mean to insult your *man*," Quincy teased.

I stuck my tongue out at him.

"You know what? I'ma grab Subway for lunch today." Quincy gave me a hug. "Love you Phyllis."

And with that, he left.

"Thanks Quincy," I muttered. "Now Sid won't come out of his room for the rest of the day."

Then it struck me. Full moon. That time of the month.

Sid would indeed be under close observation on Wednesday.

Quincy and Damien were back together by the evening. The breakup and make-up would turn out to be the first of a bijillion.

They sat on the couch holding hands. Chasey had made a delicious casserole, composed of numerous delicious casserole items, and we all ate it as we listened to their story.

"I was walkin' in and Damien was walkin' out," Quincy said.

"Quincy was just gonna walk right by me, I knew. So right then, in front of the whole store—"

"He told me how sad he was without me." Quincy nuzzled his head in Damien's shoulder.

"Well, I do hope this bodes well for the future," said Aunt Chasey.

"Yeah *Damien,* you should've seen what *we* had to go through when *you* weren't around," said Abe.

"God I hope that never happens again," Butch muttered. Poor Butch.

"So uh..what're you gonna do about Maria?" I risked.

Damien put out a hand, as if he were showing me his manicure. "Listen Phyllis, me and Maria are *fine.* We have all made peace."

"Isn't the world much nicer when we all get along," Aunt Kippie remarked.

"Speaking of nice things, *where* is Sid?" Abe asked.

Aunt Chasey shrugged. "In his room I suppose. He's going through a lot at the moment."

Aunt Kippie locked eyes with Aunt Chasey, gave me a very quick, sharp glance, then looked back at Chasey. "But we can discuss that later. It's best that we all *mind our own business.*"

"Aw Kippie, that's no fun!" Abe protested. I could have hugged him.

"Phyllis dear, have you finished your homework?" Chasey wondered.

"Yes Aunt Chasey."

"Well." Aunt Chasey's eyes moved about the floor uncomfortably, her lips pursed and her face unsure. "Per..perhaps you should go up in your room and practice your singing, so that Sid isn't *all* alone up there. I *do* feel so terrible for him."

But why, dammit?!

I sighed and did as she said.

"Hey Phyllis wait! Come back and play us a song before you go! I didn't know you could sing!" Damien cried.

I knew this wasn't what my Aunts wanted, for some reason or another. I smiled politely.

"I'd rather not just yet, but you can come see my play. It's.." Oh God. "It's this weekend."

"Oh my," said Aunt Chasey.

"Well, we'll *all* be there to see it," Abe informed me.

"So don't get nervous!" Butch added.

"We'll bring a big sign with your name on it," Quincy said with a giggle.

"All right. I'm going upstairs." I really did have to practice now. I had a crowd to please.

* * *

Monday went by quickly. Rehearsals that week were from the end of the school day to 6 or 7 o'clock, and when we got breaks, it was only while other people were practicing. Needless to say, from all of the dancing, singing, retrying, editing, and improvising, I was freaking exhausted.

On Tuesday I decided I needed to think through my plans for the next night. How in the world could I figure Sid out if my theory was incorrect? I'd have to knock on his door after it got dark and see what he was doing in his room. If he was growling and tearing up his bed sheets, I'd know. A part of me kept saying what idiotic suspicions mine were. But I had to try each and every possible idea I had until someone told me what the hell Sid's problem was.

That's when the voice would say, Why am I wondering if Sid's really the one with the problem?

It was warm outside now. I needed my mind to settle. I took one of my drawing pads and headed to the back porch. I recalled talking to Sid here. Why didn't he trust me?

Suddenly the back door opened. Speak of the devil.

"Hey Philly." He sat in the chair across from me as he had that night. "You've got stamina."

"Huh?" The word stamina always made me think of sex.

"All these damn rehearsals. I hardly see you."

"You don't seem to be around during the same times I am," I told him.

He didn't say anything for a moment. Then, "I'm not avoiding you, Philly. But I don't know if I can keep up my friendship with you without personal questions being asked."

"Can't you just answer them?"

"What if I started asking intimate aspects of *your* life, Philly?"

"Go right ahead."

Sid took his lighter, which I hadn't seen in at least a year, and turned it in his hands, remembering, "You did say I could ask you anything."

Uh oh. "When?"

"After your fifteenth birthday, Philly. We were out here." He grinned. "I told you I'd remember."

"Well then...you can." My mistake.

"You going out with that musician kid yet?"

"I hardly know him. I've seen him like twice."

"Have you had a boyfriend?"

I shrugged. "Sorta'."

"What's 'sorta''?"

I didn't want to talk about anything that brought me back to my middle school experience. I just shrugged again.

"I see."

"Yeah, it's quite a complex matter," I told him, drawing a small snowflake in my drawing pad for no reason.

"So have you ever kissed anyone?" Sid fingered his lighter.

My eyes shot up at his face. "Why?" I obviously hadn't, and if asked I would automatically get defensive.

Sid smiled a little. "I wanted to know what happened. Did you burn the guy's tongue out?"

"No."

"So you *have* kissed someone."

I shook my head. "No." But you're welcome to change that.

He looked surprised. "Really?"

"Really."

"Were you afraid to?"

I shook my head again. "I uh.." I remembered what he'd said to me once. "I haven't found the right someone."

"Hmm." The ends of his mouth twitched upward.

"Why, don't you think I'd be able to control it?"

"I have no idea."

"I've kissed my Aunts and Quincy and Bill on the cheek before," I offered pathetically.

Sid leaned forward a bit. "There's a big difference between cheeks and *really* kissing."

"True." I paused. "So what brought this on? You found a girlfriend or you just decided to give me a taste of my own medicine?"

"The latter."

"Oh, I remember. You can't get a girlfriend. But you won't tell me why." Oops. "Sorry."

Sid leaned back a little and sighed. Then he looked at me. "What'd you care, Philly?"

I was quiet. Eventually I looked away.

Sid's head tilted upward, toward the sky.

"Damn. Look at that moon."

"Full tomorrow," I said, wanting to keep talking to him. He wanted to give me more of my own medicine? Fine. I'd swallow down every spoonful.

"I know."

"Do you have a moon thing as well as a wolf thing?"

"Maybe. I've always liked the sky."

"Gonna ask me any more questions?"

"Will it prevent you from asking *me* questions?"

"No."

"Probably not."

I sighed. "Why'd you come here Sid?"

Sid glared at me. "Do you *not* want me to be here?"

"No! No, not at all. I ..like you here. But I—"

Sid smirked. "Quincy said you had a crush on me."

The man was gossiping like a high school studen—wait, what? Damn Quincy.

I tried to seem unphased. My face wasn't flooding red, which helped. "You...never answered my question."

Sid leaned forward again. Closer to me. "Come here Philly."

"Why?"

"I want to be sure of something."

I leaned in. "What?"

He grabbed my chin and kissed me. His lips felt like..better than anything. I felt the inside of my body relax and melt. The flame was there, in my throat, but I didn't feel it come up.

I wasn't really sure of what I was doing, but he definitely was. My brain crumbled into oblivion. In a good way.

He stopped and stood. I just stared at him, out of breath.

"Well, you didn't burn my tongue. It was pretty hot in there, though. But you're safe."

"Huh?" I was confused and worried and in love.

"To kiss."

"It was just a test?"

"Philly...you're a great girl. You're beautiful and incredible and you've always been a wonderful person. I care for you with all my heart babes...but I'm *way* too old for you."

I wanted to cry. "You never answered me," was all I stupidly got out.

"That's because it's none of your business. Night Philly." He went inside.

"Sid!" I called. This is bullshit! But I didn't say that. My strike would be subtle.

He peeked out the door. "Yeah?"

"How old are you again?"

"29."

I raised an eyebrow. He'd been 30 last year. Hadn't he? "When's your birthday?"

Sid laughed slightly. "It doesn't matter."

Sid didn't know how old he was.

* * *

"The full moon is today," I told Taylor after school the next day.

"Is Quincy proposing or something?"

I giggled and shook my head. "No. It's just..going to be an interesting day." Then I remembered that venomous tone in Sid's voice, the way he told me to mind my own business, and I sighed.

"What's the matter?" Taylor asked, concerned.

"Sid just hasn't been open yet. We almost had a nice conversation."

And a nice kiss, but I couldn't tell her that.

"And?"

"It just ended with him telling me to mind my own business. Again."

"Did it ever occur to you that maybe he'll tell you once you *do* mind your own business?"

I shook my head. "No. And my entire life, I've known when not to ask." I considered. "But then again, I always thought I'd be told eventually. I should just stop, I know. But Taylor I just can't."

Taylor pondered. "In romance novels, when the woman gets scorned or whatever, it's always because the man is afraid. Maybe Sid is trying not to need you."

"Need me?"

She nodded. "He does seem like the type who tries not to need people too much."

Can't disagree with her there, said the voice.

"Hey!" Tony sprang out from behind a corner and hugged Taylor quickly. "Hi Phyllis," he said to me.

"Hi Tony."

"We're going to see 'Grease' on Saturday," Tay informed me for the 14th time since Monday. "Did I tell you?"

"Nope."

"So is it the same as the movie with all the make-out scenes?" Tony wanted to know.

I shook my head. "A lot of it has been changed or edited out. But it's not too bad."

"You should be *really, obviously* imitating Mrs. Highman," Taylor told me.

"I want to *pass* history, not become a part of it."

Taylor cringed. "That was bad."

I nodded. "Gotta work on my improvisation."

On the ride home, after rehearsal, all I could think of was Sid. I had to find him as soon as I got home.

As soon as I *did* get home, however, my Aunts made me do my homework in the sewing room, because Chasey was bustling about in the kitchen, I'd get distracted in the living room, and they wanted to be able to check on me. Boot camp, I tell you.

I finished the work quickly, sloppily. I quickly headed up the stairs.

"You done, Phyllis?" I looked down to see Quincy.

"Close enough."

"Come down in the basement with me an' help take Anna's stuff out of the boxes."

"Where's the rest of your crew?" I asked, absent-mindedly pressing the B-flat key in the middle of the piano.

"Butch and Abe are busy. Damien's workin' real late. It's just you and me, Phyllis." He motioned with his hands. "C'mon! She *called* me and asked me to do it, and I really want to see what she's got!"

Dammit. Couldn't Quincy be nosy a different night? Tonight was supposed to be my night.

"All right," I decided. "I'll be right there. I have to go talk to Sid about something."

"Gonna tell him how you feel?"

I folded my arms. Oh yeah. Quincy was the one who'd told Sid how I felt. I hadn't told Taylor that yet either. If I didn't say it, it was kind of like it hadn't happened.

"Think *you* took care of that for me, Quince," I told him sternly.

Quincy winced. "Aw Phyllis, I'm sorry. I really am. I didn't *mean* to tell him, it just sorta' came out and it sounded so good!"

"Yeah, well, don't expect to be confided in again any time soon." I walked out and up the stairs.

"Aw Phyllis wait! Just come with me. You don't have to tell me anything at all! Not one damn thing!"

"What was that, Quincy?" came Chasey's voice from the kitchen.

"Sorry!" he called back. "He ain't there Phyllis."

I turned. "Where is he?"

Quincy shrugged frustratedly. "How the f...how in goodness's name should I know? He never tells anybody!"

I sighed again. "Okay."

"Now c'mon, let's go up the back stairs."

Shit, where was Sid?

Quincy didn't give me much time to ponder this. We went down to the basement, and the first thing he wanted to open was the biggest, heaviest box.

"Hasn't gotten any fuckin' lighter," Quincy noticed as we hauled it into a more open part of the room.

"Brilliant deduction," I grunted.

We untaped the box and found a large keyboard, nearly the size of a small piano.

Quincy shook his head. "We already *have* a piano."

I sighed.

He ran a hand through his hair. "She's comin' back with all *kinds* of unnecessary baggage, Phyllis." He opened the next box, rummaged through, and looked at me significantly. He tossed out a photo album. "You think she still has pictures of Sid?"

I groaned. "Quincy, what exactly did she want you to do with her stuff?"

Quincy shrugged. "You wanna eat, Phyllis?" Quincy asked. I did.

That was quick, I thought as we went back upstairs.

A little too quick, the voice agreed for once.

Like a quick diversion.

We went down and ate dinner with my Aunts. I noticed Aunt Kippie's eyes constantly sliding in the direction of the backyard, and as soon as I'd finished, she said in a quick, nervous-sounding voice, "Phyllis, I'd like you to go to bed early. You look *exhausted*."

I raised an eyebrow. "I'm fine."

Aunt Chasey smiled understandingly, playing the good cop. "You'd better do as Kippie says, Phyllis. We've been a bit worried you'll tire yourself out this week. If you're not doing this for yourself, could you please do it for your poor old Aunts?"

"Hey, who's old?" Kippie wanted to know, nudging her sister in the arm.

I gave in, offering a small smile. "Okay. Goodnight Quincy, goodnight Aunt Kippie, goodnight Aunt Chasey. Love you all."

"Thank you Phyllis," said Aunt Kippie.

"We appreciate it, and so does your poor, tired body, dear," said Aunt Chasey.

"We all love you too!" Quincy chimed.

I blew Quincy a kiss, agreed with my Aunts, and went upstairs. I checked Sid's room with a glance. The door was shut. I knocked on it. He hadn't yet returned.

God damn it, I thought.

I went into my room and sat on my bed. I left the door a crack open, so that I'd hear when Sid came back. I turned off the light.

I heard my Aunts go to bed after a while, and I heard Bill come home. But not Sid. Eventually I fell asleep, tilting over in the fetal position.

Then I woke up. It was the middle of the night and I was freezing, having fallen asleep above the covers. I got up, pulled on a sweatshirt, and stared out the window.

I heard a crash. Something in the garage.

Sid hadn't come back.

I'd seen him come out of the garage in the morning before. Had it been a full moon?

I crept out of my room, and, glancing behind me to make sure the doors to the Aunts' rooms were closed, I gently knocked on Sid's door and then I opened it. The bed was bare.

I went down the stairs very slowly, very carefully, constantly watchful of the stairs in front of and behind me.

The living room was empty and dark, a state even I hardly ever saw it in. It must have been two or three o'clock.

You're going to be sorry tomorrow, said the voice.

I know, I told it. But I have to do this.

The kitchen, unlike the living room, had an occupant.

Bill sat at the table, asleep.

I tiptoed. As I neared the back door, the floor beneath my foot gave a loud creak.

"Uh oh," I whispered.

Bill shook awake.

"You can't go out there," he told me.

"Who are you?" I demanded. If I could figure out what movie he was from, I could figure out how to get by him.

"That doesn't matter. *You* can't *go* there."

Damn, he could've been anyone.

"Just watch me," I threatened.

He came close to me. "Listen *Phyllis*—" he said my name as though I should be surprised that he knew it "—I *can't let* anyone through here."

"Why not?"

"They might be killed."

"Who are you guarding it for?" I tried.

"That doesn't matter either!"

"What if I paid you to let me by?" I had an old crumpled dollar in my sweatshirt pocket, which I handed to him. "I bet they aren't paying you this much."

He glanced about. "I never saw you here." He patted me on the shoulder. "You're a brave one."

"You're a good fellow," I told him.

I opened the back door quietly. I felt like there were people hiding who would shoot me if I was heard. I was tempted to crawl across the yard, but then I remembered I was in my pajamas. I'd have to make sure I put socks on my feet before my Aunts saw them; I was barefoot, and it was muddy.

I followed the stone path through the backyard to the side door of the garage, to go into the room in the back.

I turned the doorknob as slowly as possible, and stepped in.

And couldn't move further.

In the corner of the garage, next to a shelf of various garage items (old toys, paint, the dart board, jars) that had been knocked to the floor, was a furry, growling animal. It was staring at me, with angry brown eyes. The growling sound it made had to be the scariest sound I'd ever heard. It was a deep, grinding, furious noise.

Behind it was a disheveled pile of clothes.

"Sid?" I whispered, my voice cracking.

It stopped growling.

Holy shit.

I took a step toward it. A small step.

It backed away, sat on the clothes, and resumed growling. I began to back away again.

The animal licked its chops and lunged at me.

It was definitely a wolf, and, judging by its actions, it was very possibly

Sid.

Its mouth, or moreover, its teeth, went for my arm. I exhaled with as much force as I could, which unfortunately came with fire. I propelled myself back against the door. The wolf wasn't phased; it was like the fire had just blown by it like air. It had chomped into my sweatshirt, trying for my arm. It struggled now to get me, but it couldn't. It was chained to the shelf that had been knocked over, as well as a pole in the very corner of the garage.

Probably for a reason, the voice said.

Staring at me, the wolf backed away. It was no longer growling. It looked as if it was in pain. It was the darkest, blackest thing I'd ever seen. It made the night look light. Except for its teeth, which were pure white. They also looked quite sharp.

Now it was looking right into my eyes.

"What's wrong?" I whispered. "I didn't burn you."

At that it started growling, and crouched to lunge again.

I opened the door and stepped out.

The wolf. The image of that wolf would never leave my mind. So ferocious, and yet I'd wanted to caress it and help it.

"Oh my God," I whispered. "Oh my God." A wolf in our garage. Could that really have been Sid? I swallowed and blinked. Sid? *Sid* had tried to eat me? Sid was a wolf?

I looked around the yard and tugged at my hair, searching for signs that this was a dream. I looked up at the moon. It glowed brightly down on me.

The moon was real. Maybe I was the figment.

But that couldn't be right either.

A werewolf?

That was impossible.

Werewolves didn't actually exist. They were rabid dogs someone had made up stories about, right?

Mythical creatures didn't exist. Werewolves were mythical. They didn't *really* exist.

Though, at the moment, it certainly felt that way.

I went back in through the kitchen. Bill was awake but feigned slumber as soon as I walked in.

I never found out who he'd been that night.

As I slipped back into my room. I knew I'd never get to sleep. I looked at my sweatshirt to reassure myself I wasn't somehow imagining everything. It was pretty well shredded on the right arm.

It was old anyway, the voice assured me.

I pulled the covers up over me, the wolf clouding my mind's eye. Maybe I hadn't wanted to know Sid's secret after all.

Nah.

Part Two

In the Car.

"You're mean, Sid." Sometimes I wished to God that Sid had never found out about my feelings for him.

"Really Philly. I wanna know."

But he *did* know, and a girl might as well be honest with the man she loves. "Yeah," I answered.

Sid grinned.

My throat was on fire, almost literally, with embarrassment.

"Do I bother you?" I asked, trying to hold flames back.

He shook his head. "Of course not."

I was silent a moment, going over our conversation in my mind. "That's a strong way to put it."

Sid's eyebrows assumed a confused configuration. "'Of course not'?"

"'In love with'."

"Are you?"

I stared out the car window and didn't say anything. If I did, the flames would come up.

"It's amazing Quincy survived betraying your confidence. You didn't want him to tell me, did you?

I shook my head. "It didn't really do any good."

"It upped my self-esteem," Sid offered.

"Because you're *so* lacking in that area," I said sarcastically, rolling my eyes because he most definitely was not. And I loved him for it.

The Talk.

The next day I was quite tired. And quite shocked.

When Aunt Chasey came to wake me, she found me already up. I asked her if I could stay home.

"Why dear? You really shouldn't miss school. Remember how much extra work it takes to make up one day?"

"I know Aunt Chasey. I don't feel well, and I really didn't get enough sleep last night." I added in a yawn for dramatic effect. Or maybe I just yawned because I was tired. "I can call Taylor and get the work after school."

"What's going on?" Aunt Kippie peeked in.

"Phyllis isn't feeling well, Kippie. She'd like to stay home."

Aunt Kippie raised an eyebrow. "Do you have a fever?"

"I don't think so."

Aunt Chasey felt my forehead. "No."

"You just aren't feeling well?" Aunt Kippie said.

I nodded.

"Maybe she needs a day off to relax," said Aunt Kippie. "*I* can relate to *that*. It's fine with me, Phyllis, but you get some rest now." Kippie went downstairs.

Chasey frowned. "You have *no* tests today?"

"No tests." I think.

"And your homework is finished? You're not staying home because you procrastinated?"

"It's all done and in my backpack, Aunt Chasey."

She sighed. "Good."

"I'm past that stage now," I said.

"Good." She sat on the edge of my bed. "Are you okay dear? Just tired?"

"Yeah, I really am. I need to rest for a day. I need to catch up on my sleep. I *promise* I'll make up everything I'm missing in school."

She smiled at that, and embraced me. "I'm so proud of you Phyllis. Your parents may not have been as wonderful as you are, but they *were very* smart. And I'm glad you're like them in that way."

I would have laughed at that if I hadn't been so tired. The voice certainly did. I thanked her anyway.

She stood. "You get some sleep. I'll make you breakfast if you decide to come down."

"Thank you Aunt Chasey."

Surprisingly, I fell asleep soon after she left the room.

My dreams were only variations of what I'd seen during the night. In some the wolf was bigger. Once it turned back into Sid and he said he was just kidding. In another dream there were several wolves circling me, and they followed me from the garage up to my room, and shrank, becoming mice. And then the dream morphed into the one with all of my parents' lab mice crawling all over the floor.

Finally I made myself wake up.

The first thing I did was shower. Then I went downstairs in hopes that *everything* had been a dream. I didn't look at my sweatshirt, but threw it in the back of my closet.

"Phyllis!" Aunt Chasey greeted me with a hug. The kitchen clock read 12:36 and I knew I hadn't dreamt the wolf. Quincy was home for lunch.

"I made brownies." Chasey gestured to a plate on the table. "You certainly slept a while. Do you feel better?"

"I feel a little better, thanks Aunt Chasey."

"Well you will feel *loads* better once you have one a' these brownies, Phyllis. They're de-*lish*!" Quincy peered over an issue of The New Yorker.

"Do try one, Phyllis," Aunt Chasey coaxed.

I picked one up and took a bite. "Mmm." I looked around. "Where is everybody?"

"I for one hafta' go back to work soon," Quincy informed me, taking another brownie and a sip of milk.

"Bill and Sid are watching a movie in the basement," said Chasey.

"They're down there 'cause Kippie's tapin' something on the living room TV," Quincy added.

Chasey elaborated. "She's taping a special on cooking. Though I don't think it'll do her any good, the poor dear," she said softly. "Some just aren't blessed in the kitchen."

"Well, *you* certainly are," Quincy told her, his mouth full.

"What are they watching?" I asked. Hopefully it was a movie I could use as an excuse to join them.

"'Batman'." Aunt Chasey put some brownies onto another plate and handed it to me. "Here, bring them some."

"How'd you know I was going to go down?"

Chasey smiled. "You just told me." I gave her a kiss on the cheek.

"Chasey you're gonna make us all obese," Quincy told her.

I headed down into the basement with the brownies and found Sid and Bill in the TV room where they were, indeed, watching "Batman." Sid was on the couch. Bill was in a folding chair.

"Hi," I greeted them.

"Hey Philly," Sid said, turning. "Heard you're sick."

"Yeah, I'm pretty tired. But I brought you guys brownies."

"I'm a little tired myself. Sit down." Sid seemed mellow. Not in the cool way he usually was, though. But then, I could understand why, if..if my suspicions were correct.

"Have one," I said, sitting and holding out to him the plate of brownies.

He did. "I'm starving."

So...how's the weather? God, what could I say? So uh... how was your evening? I saw that there was a wolf in the garage. I think your clothes were next to it. I uh..hope you didn't miss them.

Instead I opted for, "Hey Bill, you want another brownie?"

Bill turned. "It's Jack, Phyllis, it's Jack." Jack was apparently the Joker's name before he became the Joker, though it does depend on what you're watching. In most comics and cartoons, his previous identity is unknown. This is all according to Taylor of course, and Taylor's comics, and Taylor's DVDs.

"Hey," he said, taking a brownie, "j'ever dance with the devil in the pale moonlight?"

"Yes, yes I have."

Jack turned back around.

We all watched the movie for a while. I kept *almost* talking to Sid and then stopping myself. I couldn't really think of anything to say.

Dear Abby: How do you ask someone if they're a werewolf without being offensive?

Suddenly he spoke.

"Philly...do you remember what you saw last night?"

I turned and looked at him. "I don't..I don't know..."

"Philly. In the garage. Do you remember?"

I nodded.

"Did I hurt you?"

My eyes involuntarily widened. "Sid. What?"

"Philly that was me. I know you were there. But you *have* to *tell* me *now.* Did I hurt you?"

I shook my head.

"You weren't bitten?"

"You...you got my shirt but I didn't feel anything."

Sid grabbed me in a hug. "Oh thank God. Thank God."

Taking advantage of the opportunity, I hugged him back.

He stroked my hair hanging down my neck. "Damn it Philly what the hell were you doing in the garage?" His breaths were unsteady. "I could've killed you, I could've ripped you apart."

"I didn't know, Sid. Nobody told me, Sid."

He leaned away from me. "Jesus, Philly. I've never met anyone as relentless as you. And I've been alive a long time."

I swallowed. "You..you're a werewolf?"

"I'm a werewolf."

"That was you last night. You chained yourself up in the garage."

"Yeah."

"Why? You saw me, didn't you? Aren't you aware of yourself?"

Sid exasperatedly smoothed one of his eyebrows. "It's a lot to explain. I didn't know when to tell you or how. You weren't supposed to know yet, babes."

"I'm sorry. I had to."

"It's okay Philly. It wasn't my smartest move, keeping it from you. I can't change it now." He looked at me. "You're not afraid of me now, are you?"

"No."

"Good. I'm not dangerous as a man." He paused. "It's like this Philly; I'm half wolf. At this moment as I sit here talking, it's in me. It knows what I'm doing, but it can't overpower me while I'm in human form. It can only let me know what it wants and lend me its instincts. It's the same way for me when my body is in wolf form. When I saw you come into the garage, I tried my hardest to overpower it and tell it not to bite you. But it couldn't resist. That's why I was chained up, Philly. If I don't do that, I'll attack people. I'll tear them to shreds, I'll eat them alive. Or I'll just bite them, and they'll become like me."

I put a hand on his shoulder, maybe to subconsciously assure myself that he was still Sid.

Sid nodded. "I was lucky not to have been killed when it happened to me."

"Is that why you can't remember your age? Is it that you can't remember anything before you were bitten and you ended up here with my Aunts?"

Sid smiled sadly. "No Philly, I know how old I am, I just need to keep better track of how old I *say* I am. Physically I'm 26, the same age I was when I was bitten. But if you're going by years, well..I'm about 160 now."

My eyes grew impossibly wider. The man I loved was 145 years older than I was. 15 years suddenly seemed like zero difference whatsoever.

"Oh my God."

"You would've ended up 16 forever if you'd been bitten, Philly."

"You're.."

"Old."

"No, you're immortal." Maybe I could just grow into him!

Sid grinned. "I'm not a god, Philly. But yeah, that's how it looks from here."

"So..werewolves really do exist."

"I'm afraid so. I'm sorry you found out this way. Why did you go out there in the first place?"

"I heard you knock the shelf over. And..I'd seen you come out of the garage in the morning before."

"Well now you know. Don't *ever* go out there again on the full moon, Philly. You already have your own interesting quality. You don't need two."

"You'll live forever?"

"Yes."

"And that's why you can't fall in love," I realized.

Sid laughed. Really laughed. I waited for him to stop.

When he did, he looked at me, a small smile still on his lips. But his tone was grave. "I can't think of a better way to put it."

I squeezed his wrist. "How did it happen Sid?"

"I was in Boston. I was a lawyer. I'd stayed late at work and was walking home in the middle of the night. It never did seem safe to be out on the full moon, but no one then actually thought anything like *this* could happen." He shook his head. "Just around the corner from my apartment, Philly, a big black dog with huge teeth charged at me. Bit my leg. Then it ran off, growling and barking, down the street." He absent-mindedly reached down and touched his shin. "The worst pain I've ever been in. The wound heals itself like that," he told me with a snap of his fingers. "But it felt like my leg was crumbling. I had no idea until the next full moon."

"What did you do?"

Sid sighed helplessly. "I tore around the city attacking everyone I saw. Someone shot me. It didn't do any good. When I realized I couldn't stop myself *and* that I couldn't *be* stopped, I panicked. My mind shut down and there was only the wolf. The next morning, I packed up and started to leave the city. On my way out I bumped into a man who told me everything I'd felt that night. He took me out of the city and into a place where I'd be safe and everyone around me would be, too."

I squinted. "What happened?"

"His name was Van Frobisher. His sister, Stacia, has a mansion. Creatures like me live there. It's hidden. We're brought away so we're not discovered."

"Sid. I'm extremely confused."

"There aren't just werewolves, Philly. There are psychics, hypersensitives, vampires, witches, warlocks, mermaids, shapeshifters, changers, illusionists, psychic vampires. This place is like your Aunts' house for monsters, in a way. I'm not sure how else to convey it to you."

"This is crazy. There aren't *vampires* or *mermaids*."

"And there aren't werewolves."

"Point taken. So..there are..*vampires*? Vampires that can sneak into the house and drink my blood?"

Sid chuckled. "They're a little different. But they exist." He continued his story. "I learned what I was, how I'd become what I was, and what other things were involved now that I *was* what I was. It was horrible. But I knew why I was suddenly craving all this meat and wanting to bite things and other animalistic shit."

"How'd you end up here?"

"The mansion wasn't a good place, babes. I'd always thought humans were screwed up but with immortals it only gets worse. Van helped me get a job back in the regular world in the 20s. Went back to the mansion during the Depression. Afterwards I had an apartment Van owned in Chicago until the 50s. Settled here in the 60s, met your Aunts in the 70s. I met them when I was prosecuting a man named Joseph Tell. They'd turned him in for selling drugs. He was their friend though, it was a hard decision for them. At that point they were pretty damn young. I moved in with them in the 80s. After I told them." Sid looked at me. "I'm living here now, Philly, because every few years, I have to hide out. People can't notice that I don't age. I can't work at the same law office for too long, or colleagues will start asking me when I'm going to start a family, how I stay so young-looking, how I keep my physique. Why I have such a good memory of historic details since the mid 1800s." Sid grinned.

I didn't care how old Sid was. Obviously he would always be hot.

"How did you get so close to my Aunts?"

"I had to spend a lot of time with them, getting evidence and testimonies and court shit. Once it was over we just kept getting together."

"Oh. I thought maybe you dated one of them."

Sid shook his head. "Nope. My relationship with your Aunts has never come close to being that way. Plus, when I met them Kippie was with the man she would marry. The one who left her before you showed up."

"So, you dated Anna."

Sid nodded. "That was a while after I'd moved in here, babes."

"I don't understand why you can't fall in love when you had a relationship with Anna. Are you waiting for another werewolf?"

"Anna was different."

"How?"

"She already knew I was a werewolf so we decided to give it a shot."

"Did you dump her *because* you loved her?"

"No. Anna and I just didn't get along. We were constantly trying to kill each other. I've never been more stressed. Our feelings just dissolved. We were too different or too similar or whatever the hell you want to say."

"Oh." I paused. "What's it like?"

"It's a fucking nuisance, babes. The wolf causes all those urges in me. If I couldn't resist them we'd all be in big trouble." He pointed to my arm. "Like right now. I'm dying to bite your arm."

I moved away a little, instinctively.

He laughed at me. "Don't worry Philly. I've been resisting the wolf for over a century and I'll resist it for centuries to come, if I'm not killed."

"How would that happen?" I asked, worried.

Sid shrugged. "Mainly suffocation. My skin can't be penetrated by most metals. Or burned."

"That's why you—"

"Yeah. I was the only one who could help you without getting hurt. And damn straight I would have if I'd been human." He paused. "I can't be poisoned either. Silver doesn't work, wolf's bane doesn't work."

"Can you feel pain?"

"Yes. I can feel everything."

"If you were to bite me in human form, would I became a werewolf?" Man this was great. It was the most exciting moment of life. And I could just ask and ask and ask.

"I don't know." His face was suddenly pained. "Please don't talk about it, Philly. Don't mention it."

"Why?"

"First of all, I don't want you to think I'm a one-way ticket to living forever. Living forever means that everyone else dies, Philly. Secondly, sinking my teeth into you is exactly what I want to do now. The less I'm reminded of it, the better." He grinned at my expression. "Nothing personal babes. I would never want to hurt you. You just look delicious."

I giggled in spite of myself. "I'll take that as a compliment." Flames were at the back of my throat but I held them in. God, Sid was just the person I wanted to hear tell me I looked delicious, but I wasn't sure I wanted him to mean it literally.

Suddenly Sid grabbed my chin. "So don't *ever* mess around on the full moon again. You understand?"

"Yes." Please don't eat me.

"And you *cannot* tell *anyone*. Not even Taylor. Do you understand that? No one can know. Can I trust you?"

Can I trust you?

Nope, said the voice.

I already had a voice. I guessed I'd have three if I became a werewolf.

"Yes," I told Sid sincerely. "You'll always be able to trust me, Sid. No matter what."

He released me. "Good." He looked into my eyes. "Now that you've found out my secrets—all of them, babes—it's your turn. What the hell were you doing in my room?!"

"What?" Uh oh.

"My room, Philly. You went through my room."

"H-how do you know?"

"Your scent was all over the place. My floor, my closet, my drawers. What the hell were you doing?"

"My scent?"

"Your scent. I have a *very* sensitive nose."

"Is it a bad scent?" I should've apologized first, I know, but I was so afraid of seeming flawed in that way to Sid.

"You couldn't have been brought up by Chasey and Kippie and smell bad, Philly. Why were you in my room?"

I sighed. "I...was trying to find what you were hiding. But all I found were clothes and heavy metal CDs and a mini freezer stashed with meat."

Sid chuckled. "Jesus Philly."

"I'm not a nosy person. Okay, yeah I am. But I'm not usually this extreme. You just seem to be a person whose secrets are very...worth knowing."

He looked at me. "Are they?"

"Definitely. So uh..the heavy metal and meat?"

"I get cravings. I keep lots of spare sets of of sheets, too, because I like to rip things. And I have anger issues."

My eyes flashed. "Is the meat what keeps you from eating *people*?"

He looked at me seriously, darkly. "The meat is *from* people."

My eyebrows lowered and my mouth made an "o" and Sid burst into laughter.

"I'm *kidding,* babes. The meat helps but I don't need it to keep from turning to cannibalism. I just need it, almost 4 pounds of it a day. Loud music calms me down."

"And ripping your bed sheets?" I couldn't help but giggle.

"That's one way to put it."

I'd like to help him rip his bed sheets, I thought.

Sin! Sin! Sin! said the voice. I couldn't tell if that was a scolding alert or a command. Later I decided it was a command.

"Are you angry?" I asked him.

Sid shook his head. "As risky as it seems to trust a 16-year-old girl, nope."

"Sid."

"Phyllis."

"You know I'm not like most girls."

Sid grinned. "You think I've never met anyone else who can breathe fire?"

"I...have you?"

"Nope, you're the only one, Philly." He smoothed his eyebrows again. "Which just goes to show how smart your parents were. Not even the world I..benefitted from..has firebreathers."

"I don't think they meant to make me able to breathe fire."

"They sure didn't tell your Aunts that."

"Do you think they would have fought as hard for me if they'd known?"

Sid looked into my eyes. "They may have fought even harder, babes, if it'd been possible. I've never seen anyone as determined to get anything as your Aunts were to get you. And once they had you, they were no longer Kippie and Chasey. They were *Aunt* Kippie and *Aunt* Chasey." He touched my shoulder. "You have two people who love you thousands of times more than life itself."

"Have you ever loved someone that much?"

"Yes."

"Did she die?"

"It's not just that the people I love will die, Philly. It's that I'll live. Every time I look back on the lives of the people I loved it just gets more and more painful. The more people I love, the more pain I feel."

"Jesus Sid." Almost reflexively, I hugged him. Then I looked at him. "Isn't that from a song?"

He smiled. "Everything's from a song."

I wouldn't die if you decided to love me, I thought. I let go of him. "So are you going to be nicer to me?"

"Philly the only reason I wasn't as nice to you was because I thought it might discourage you from trying to figure out what my secret was." He paused, then quickly added, "But you're still too young for me."

"You don't even *have* an age."

"I do, and it's about 150 years older than yours."

"144."

"Philly."

"Well, you look about 25."

"That'd still be too old."

At least he's not saying you're too young, the voice pointed out.

That might be better, I told it. It might imply that I could grow into his age range.

"Will you always be too old for me?"

"Stop it Philly."

"So what do I smell like?"

Sid looked at me. "You smell good. Kind of sweet." He grinned. "Like honey-barbecue sauce. Sorry, the wolf's still a little strong the day after, even though I'm tired as hell."

I raised an eyebrow. "I smell like *barbecue sauce?*"

"You smell like something delicious. Your mouth tasted a little like grilled meat."

I bit my lip. "Sorry."

"No, it was good." He looked at me and then away from me. "I sound hungry, don't I?"

"Yep." I gestured to the brownies. "Have another."

"I need meat right now, babes." His eyes flashed. "Maybe you." He snapped at me and I jolted back, nearly falling off the couch. But Sid grabbed my arm, and pulled me back up to him. "Sorry Philly," he apologized. His lips were close to mine.

"You could do another routine check-up to see if I'm okay to kiss," I suggested brazenly.

"You don't give up on anything."

"You said you were hungry and I tasted good."

He let go of my arm. "You're fucking sixteen, Philly," he whispered. He sighed. "But, since I scared you.." He gave me a kiss on the lips. His lips pushed gently on mine and I wished to God I was eighteen or twenty-one. At least seventeen.

Then he stood. "I'm gonna make some steak. Want to join me?"

"Sure." I looked at Bill. "You mind, Jack?"

"Call me the Joker."

"You'd think he would've added something witty after that," I said softly to Sid as we headed up.

"Maybe he's not getting enough sleep to be witty."

"Are you implying something?"

"Relationship success." He grinned.

Ooh, he's implying sex, the voice said.

He implies it well, I told it.

We entered the kitchen.

Aunt Chasey looked at us.

"Philly knows," Sid said in a low voice.

She only nodded.

AAAHH!

So I knew. I stopped stressing about Sid, and suddenly a multitude of other problems reared their ugly heads. Grades. Homework. Mary. Eric. And the wig. The terrible, horrible wig.

And everyone was going to see me in it, including Sid.

So, Thursday morning I headed into school ready to inform Taylor that Sid and I were on good terms again, complain about the damn wig, and thank her for giving me the homework assignments I'd missed.

But in the lobby, I didn't find Taylor. I found Eric and Tony sitting on a bench with a guitar.

"Hey Phyllis," Tony greeted me.

"Phyllis!" Eric looked up at me. "I'm comin' to see the play tonight."

"We're going Saturday," Tony added.

I nodded. "I know." I smiled. "I'm glad you guys are coming. I'm supposed to be promoting it but I'm so *nervous*." I could hear Mrs. Reygor in my mind saying, "That only means you care."

"I think I perform better when I'm nervous. And you don't make mistakes when you play the piano," Eric said.

Hahahahahahahaha! The voice was cracking up.

"Oh yeah, that's how you guys met, isn't it?" Tony said, as if Eric and I were old friends from forever ago. Or a married couple.

"Yeah," Eric said with the same tone of voice.

"Where's Taylor?" I asked, slightly creeped out.

"She went to her locker. She's been gone a while, though. I'm gonna go find her. I'll be back."

"Oh. Okay," I said as Tony rose and left.

"You wanna sit?" Eric offered. I sat next to him and thanked him.

"How's teaching?" I asked him politely.

"It's not bad. It's not what I'd want to do forever."

"What'll you do?" Crap, he'd probably return the question and I had no idea what I would do.

Eric grinned. "Rock star."

I smiled. "Why aren't you in the pit band?"

"I have lessons five nights a week, no time to practice. But I'll definitely come watch the show tonight."

"I'm glad. I hope you won't hate me if I screw up," I said awkwardly with a small laugh.

He laughed a little too. "I don't think so." He looked at me. "You're a freshman, aren't you?"

"Yeah." Somehow I hated to admit it.

"I never realized it. I guess you'd have to be." He shrugged. "You seem a little older."

"Good. What grade are you in?"

"Oh I'm just a sophomore. But uh..I have my license. I'm driving to the play tonight."

I nodded. "Cool."

He paused. "I was wondering if you'd want to get something to eat after the play." He grinned. "You'll be hungry and you won't be nervous anymore."

Whoa, said the voice.

Oh my God. He was asking me out. I hadn't had a real guy friend for years and now I was being asked out by a boy I hardly knew. Even the guy I'd "gone out with" for two weeks in eighth grade had been kind of like a friend. Till I dumped him.

Well. Eric didn't seem so bad. And it wasn't like we were going steady. It was just a thing. That's what Quincy would have called it. And if I told Aunt Chasey, she wouldn't tell Quincy if I asked her not to. But would she let me ride in a car with a strange boy? That was the question.

Yeah, she would, the voice knew. She's in love now.

"Um..that sounds like fun. Is anyone else going?"

Eric shook his head. "I thought we could just hang out."

The first bell rang.

"Okay, well that sounds good," I babbled. "Want to give me your phone number real quick?"

And I went off to my locker, suddenly with a date.

* * *

The great thing about Taylor was her pep talks. Playing the piano before school ended, seeing all the flyers for "Grease" all around me had only reminded me of the wig. When I found Taylor at my locker later, she wanted to talk about Eric and Sid (I'd told her that morning), but I needed to bitch about the wig.

"You don't understand just how horrible this wig is," I told her. "I'll always be 'that girl who wore the stupid wig'!"

"Oh don't worry about the wig," Taylor said.

I pouted.

"Don't think like you'll be remembered as Ms. Whoever in the play with the stupid wig. Think like you'll be remembered in general, and for being entertaining at that," said Taylor. "This could be the beginning of a promising acting career."

"Tay, if this has any effect on or involvement with a promising acting career, it's going to be a little photo in a magazine saying, 'Guess who this wannabe became?' or something."

"Well, it'll still be entertaining," she said with a big smile. "And you'll have fun, Phil. This is what you love."

"Thanks Taylor, you're sweet."

"You know it."

We walked down the hallway before lunch.

"Of course Mr. Hamil gave us an essay to do the week of the performance," I told her.

"50 bucks and I'll write it for you," she said with a grin.

I held up my hand in a stop-motion. "I'll be okay, thanks." Taylor was a good writer, probably because of all she had read, and well worth $50, but I didn't have the money. At least the essay wasn't math.

You know what, never mind. I don't like either of those subjects.

That's when another problem walked up to us.

Mary, who now had added white streaks to her blonde and black hair, suddenly came out of a classroom.

"Hey Taylor, hey Phyllis," she said. Her attire, which had once consisted of light polo shirts and khakis, was getting darker every day. Today it was a long, evergreen velvet dress, which was actually very pretty. But her personality seemed to be darkening, too. And not in a pretty way.

"Hi Mary," I greeted her. "You should get blue streaks in your hair," I suggested, hoping to distract her. Every time she spoke to me it was about how Key wouldn't tell her who'd started the Scary Mary thing. Even when Key told Mary she didn't know, Mary insisted she did. Which was true, but that's beside the point. Key couldn't give out the names of her friends, and Mary should have tried someone else.

"Or dye your eyebrows blue," Taylor said with a giggle. She'd heard the story of Butch's eyebrows.

But Mary didn't seem to hear us. "I found out that Liz was the one who started those rumors about me, that whole 'Scary Mary' thing."

Taylor's eyebrows shot up, along with mine. We knew Mary would only have asked Key. Key's policy was, very strongly, never to give in unless forced.

"How'd you find out?" Taylor asked.

"Key. I made her tell me. Because I can. And I need to make Liz stop because more and more people are staring at me."

"Your hair does kind of leap out at people, just because of the dramatic changes in color," Taylor told her.

"No. They're staring at me because Liz told them I was a freak. Even Key thought I was, for a little while."

"How'd you get Key to tell you?" Taylor asked again.

"Neither of them ever said *that*," I told Mary. "You're not a freak. People see anything different and they automatically draw away from it." Believe you me. I knew that side of people.

Mary nodded. "You're right, you're right. You know what that's like. You've been there, you're seen how different people are treated."

"Weirdly cool people live in her house," Taylor said quickly to get our ears, "but how'd you get Key to tell you?"

Mary smiled wickedly. "Like this." She grabbed Taylor's face with both hands and stared at her.

"Intimidation?" Taylor wanted to know. She looked a little weirded out.

"What's something you've never told anyone?" Mary asked.

"My mom had to sleep next to me every night for almost a year after Davy died." Taylor's eyes grew wide.

Mary let go of Taylor's face.

"I..I went through a lot when that happened.." Taylor said. "But..you.."

"I have power now."

Now I was seriously freaked out. If I stayed any longer, Mary might grab my face and make me tell her I breathed fire and that Sid was a werewolf.

"I have to go," I said, and rushed down the hall to the auditorium, where our very last dress rehearsal was.

I could hardly think about Taylor as we changed in the backstage dressing rooms.

"I am *so nervous*," one of the girls murmured to me as we all climbed into our costumes.

"Me too, and embarrassed," I said, gesturing to the terrible tweed.

"Oh my God sweetie, you have a really fun part! Play it up!" Sandy insisted. Sandy was a blonde, beautiful, loud girl named Sharissa.

"Yeah, this is our chance to make the teachers look bad. We're depending on you, girl," said Rizzo, giggling. Rizzo was a mulatto ballerina with a mini-afro and a voice that made you listen. Her real name was Mika.

I sighed as I put on the wig. "If I can feel good doing anything for my school, it's that."

"You okay Phyllis?" asked a girl named Amber.

"Yeah I'm fine. Just..one of my friends might be in trouble."

"Aren't you friends with Mary? Is she who you're worried about?"

"Maybe her, too," I muttered. I hadn't even said anything to Taylor, just walked off.

As we were herded out onto the stage and the nervous rush hit me, the realization that I'd be doing all this in front of an audience in less then 24 hours, I only had a second to make a decision about the Mary. So I decided— as soon as I got home, I'd call Taylor and make sure this wasn't some weird joke. Then I'd talk to Sid. He'd mentioned witches.

We sang and danced and gossiped and provided comic relief. Over. And over. And over.

Finally it was 7. And I should have been dead, but I wasn't.

"You've all worked really hard, everyone has," Mrs. Reygor told us. "We'd like to thank you for your dedication. But it's not over yet."

"That's right!" Miss Kaye chimed in. "We've got a great show. I'm expecting a full house and standing ovation, people. Your every move should be in character, your every *thought* should be in character. If you, or one of your castmates screws up, improvise something. Don't be ashamed if you mess up, either. I know you can all do it. We've taught you well. Now get home and get a good night's sleep. See you tomorrow for opening night!"

Everyone cheered and screamed.

"I am *so excited*," one of the girls murmured to me as we all climbed out of our costumes.

"Me too. I can't wait!" I told her, nearly breathing out an enthusiastic flame. I held it back, of course.

As I rushed down the hall from the auditorium, my makeup was splotchy and sticky, and my muscles were aching. But I felt great.

Driving home was like returning to the real world, the normal one. Switching dimensions. But I didn't mind all that much, for as real as my dimension was, it was far from normal.

"We're all very proud of you, dear," said Aunt Kippie as we pulled into our driveway. "Get a good night's rest, now."

"That's what Miss Kaye said," I told her.

Aunt Kippie gave me a look. "That's because she's the reason you've hardly *gotten* any sleep."

When I walked into the house I expected Aunt Chasey to pop out of the kitchen and say, "Be sure you've gotten your homework done, dear." Instead, she popped out and said, "Would you like some tea, dear?"

I must've looked tired.

I went into the sewing room with my backpack and called Taylor. Her mother answered and quickly gave her the phone.

"Hello?"

"Hey Taylor. Are you okay?"

"Um..yeah."

"Taylor that wasn't a joke, was it? What happened with Mary?"

"No, it wasn't. It was the most incomprehensible thing. I..I just spoke. I didn't even know I was speaking until after I'd said it."

"Jesus Taylor. What the hell did she do?"

"I really don't know. I really don't know, Phyllis. It wasn't something she warned me about, it was just talk and my mouth moved and it freaked me the hell out." She paused. "It was completely against my control. I can't stand it, I can't stand not being able to control what I'm doing. It's like falling, when you know you're falling and there's nothing you can do. It's bad enough that I can't control the people around me, if I could Davy wouldn't even be dead.." Taylor stopped, taking a deep breath.

"Do you need me to come over Tay? Do you need to talk about it?"

"No, no thanks. I can't right now. I need to just be alone, I think. I don't know, maybe I subconsciously made myself say it. Maybe I need to think about it."

"Are you going to be okay, Taylor? Do you think she did something to your mind?"

"No, nothing besides forcing me to say that. It wasn't really *that* terrible a secret. It's a hell of a good thing she didn't ask you, I was more worried for you once I realized what she was doing. Don't worry about me, okay? Just don't expect me to always be around when Mary's there." She paused. "Phyllis I'm thinking there may just possibly be a tad more to this phase our dear Mary is going through than meets the eye."

"Yeah, me too. I think I'm going to look it up online or ask Key or something. Because it must have happened to Key, too."

"Oh my God, you're right! Phyllis I've got to call her!"

"Okay, I'll see what I can find out elsewhere, okay? You sure you're all right?"

"I think so. I just have to call Key and affirm my sanity."

"All right," I said with a small laugh. "Good luck."

"Thanks. Thank you for calling me to see if I was okay."

"No! I'm sorry I just walked away."

Taylor laughed through her nose. "I did the same thing once she'd let me go. *You're* the one with a *real* secret, anyway. I was more relieved that she didn't do it to you than I was scared of her. Thank *God* you walked away."

"Oh Taylor."

"Really Phyllis. Mary's gotten weird. Who knows what she could or would have done if she'd found out." She was serious all of a sudden. "You'd better be careful, Phyllis. Promise me you'll be careful. It would really suck if scientists locked you in a lab. You know, I'd have to conjure up a rescue plan, tell Tony you breathe fire so that he'd know why we were busting you out, and Key..it'd just be totally inconvenient for me." She paused. "It'd make a great movie, though."

"Taylor, I'm glad we're friends."

"Me too, Phyllis. I'll talk to you in the morning."

"Okay. And you're gonna be okay? Emotionally, I mean."

"Yeah, I'll recover."

After I hung up, I was still worried.

Now it was time to do research.

Leaving my stupid backpack with my stupid essay in it downstairs, I headed up to Sid's room.

I hesitated, then knocked on his door.

"You don't have to knock, babes. I can hear you coming, remember?"

I opened the door. "Sid, something weird happened today, I thought you might be able to..I thought you might know something about it." I spoke quickly and nervously.

Sid raised an eyebrow. "What happened, Philly?" Sid was at his desk, on a laptop that I'd never seen before. He turned to speak to me.

I nodded to the computer. "When'd you get that?"

"At a point in time *after* you went through my room. What happened?"

It was then that I realized how weird my relationship with Sid was.

"My friend Mary, she's the one that—"

"I remember Mary. Is she okay?"

"I don't think so. She did something strange today. To Taylor."

Sid straightened in his seat. "Is Taylor all right?"

"She's okay, I called her. She was a little shaken up."

"Tell me what happened."

"Taylor's little brother, Davy, died, three or four years ago."

Sid nodded. "Ouch. Strong girl."

"Yeah, Taylor's tough." I continued on to tell him about Mary and Key, and finally about the exchange between Mary, Taylor and me. I sat on the bed when I'd finished, the story tiring me.

Sid's face was pensive and serious, his eyes burning a hole into the floor. "I think Mary's a witch."

"Don't witches need *spells*?"

Sid shook his head. "I don't know much about witches, Philly, but they have a lot of power and capabilities. They're different from most people who have the energy—"

"The energy?"

"It's what I call whatever makes people like me the way they are. I guess it could be magic, but it's really more than that."

"Oh, got it."

"Nobody really understands them. But they're extremely rare and they're very in touch with their energy. Some of them are psychics and illusionists in addition to being witches."

"Wait wait wait. What's an illusionist?"

"Someone who can make you think you're seeing one thing when it's really another." Sid grinned. "Kind of like a lawyer. Only the illusion leaves your mind if you get a certain distance away from the illusionist. They can only get into your mind if they're near you, and can't read it."

"Sid how did you survive that world?"

Sid shrugged. "Immortality, Philly."

"Do you know what Mary did, exactly?"

"No. But she may not have done it just because she dislikes Taylor. Having so much of the energy in them is supposed to give witches all kinds of problems. Hypersensitivity, vulnerability to possession—"

"Possession?! You can really get *possessed* too?!"

"Not by the devil," Sid said, raising a defensive hand. "By spirits. And they can't get into people who don't have the energy."

"Ghosts?"

"Not just aimless dead souls floating around. I don't know much about spirits either, Philly. I spent most of my time with vampires, werewolves, changers. People like me who knew what it was like to *have* to submit to this stuff unwillingly. Witches have a choice. I knew *some* witches but wasn't close to them. The only one I remotely spent time with started trying to kill me."

"What?!"

Sid quickly waved the remark away. "It's a story I'll tell you later, when you don't have all this other trouble."

I'd have to remember that part of the conversation for another time, I had to know why someone would try to kill Sid. But for now I had to find out about Taylor's safety. And mine.

"Could Mary do anything *worse* than forcing people to say things they don't want to say?"

"I'm not sure, she seemed like a beginner—"

"Seemed? You mean from what I told you?" I paused. "Did you *know* she was a witch when you met her?"

Sid shook his head. "No, but people with the energy can feel it in each other. And they're often attracted to each other without knowing it, the way Van was to me after I became a werewolf. It's for a purpose Philly. I needed help. Mary is going to need help. Witches don't just show up in anyone's life. She's in yours for a reason."

"I don't have the energy."

"No, but you definitely have something."

I raised an eyebrow. "She can't know anything about *me,* can she?"

"No. As I was saying, I'd think it takes more than a few months to learn all the tricks. But she should be with Stacia. If she stays here she could be, without knowing it, exposing a world she never realized existed."

I paused. "Is there a possibility that you're wrong?"

Sid nodded. "Yes, but not a very large one." He paused, thinking, then he looked back at me. "Don't let her touch you, Philly. But keep an eye on her if you can. If you see anything else, let me know. If you don't see anything else for a while, invite her over."

"Why?"

"Because I'll know if I talk to her."

"You sounded sure a second ago."

"I am. Pretty sure. But I feel I should be more than pretty sure before I convince this girl to leave her home forever."

"Forever?"

Sid quickly added, "It's her choice. There aren't many who choose not to go the first time they're asked. And there aren't any who live in the normal world without being connected with Stacia or Van somehow."

"How are you connected?"

"Van's got an office in the city. That day I brought you to your rehearsal he gave me a job." He nodded to the laptop. "That's what this is for." He turned and closed the computer. "You sure Taylor's okay?"

"Yeah, I just talked to her about it. She said she was going to call Key, since Mary must have done the same thing to her. But I think she'll be fine."

"Good." Sid stood, walked to his bed and sat next to me. "She's got a good memory."

"What do you mean?"

"You remember the call we got? A guy who called and asked for Evan Garmon?"

"Mmhmm." I wasn't sure, but I'd go along with it.

"That was Van asking for me. I told him that was what I was changing my name to the last time I saw him. Which was right after you turned six. I chose it at random out of 'Red Dragon'."

I thought.

You don't recognize the name? Evan Garmon?

Nosferatu! "He's got a creepy voice."

"He's a creepy guy. He lives up to the vampire stereotype. Most of them don't."

"Which vampire is he? You said there was more than one kind."

"He's a rare mix of both. He feeds on blood and energy. He can see into minds."

Just lovely. I paused. "Why'd you change your name?"

"I didn't want them to find me again. I wanted to start over, by myself."

"Why'd you come back?"

He gave me a small smile. "Missed everybody here. Knew no one would look for me here." He looked at me. "And I wanted to know how you were. I wanted to see if you were still okay with your fire-breathing and if you'd been trying to contact me." He grinned. "And you didn't even remember me."

"I'm sorry S—"

He cut me off. "Don't b—"

I cut him off. "I liked you though, right away."

He laughed. “I liked you right away too, Philly. As soon as you walked in I knew you’d be interesting.”

“Interesting?”

“That’s the only way I can put it, babes. You walked into a house full of strangers. You weren’t scared, and you were only five.”

“What’d I do?” Like I said, my first memory is of my sixth birthday or slightly before. I missed out on a lot.

“You smiled. You were a little shy but you shook our hands and said, ‘Hi, I’m Phyllis.’”

“Whoa.” I was a brave kid. I could hardly shake hands with people at 16.

Sid nodded. “Then you showed us all your bandages. You didn’t seem to remember how you’d gotten them, though.”

I shook my head. “I don’t remember the fire. Sometimes I have flashes of stuff but that could be anything.”

Sid leaned forward. He was close to me and I was painfully aware of it. “What do you remember?”

“Sometimes..” I tried to make coherent words form in my brain. “Sometimes I have dreams where nothing bad is happening but I feel this awful, horrible feeling, like I’m alone and scared, abandoned and there’s nobody. It’s just..it’s the worst thing I’ve ever felt, and it’s only in a dream.”

“That’s probably why you’ve blocked it out, babes. What’s your first memory here?”

I considered. I told him they were all jumbled together in my mind but it seemed to be my Aunts putting me to bed. Aunt Chasey had taught me the Lord’s Prayer soon after my arrival in the Sorin house, and before bed the Aunts and I would all say it together. Once Anna the Opera Singer, who was faithful but not churchgoing, had compared praying in unison to Satanic chanting. But, before I’d heard all of the faithlessness, cynical, scientific, forcing points of view about religion, or that God was strict and unforgiving and a feared ruler rather than a loving guide, my first taste of religious praying, with my Aunts, had always made me feel safe and warm. Nothing I could remember of my parents made me feel as though I had been loved.

Growing up with Kippie, Quincy, and Anna, however, I was keen to know others' opinions of religion.

"Do you believe in God, Sid?" Could he?

Sid shrugged. "I don't know Philly. I've seen a lot. I've never seen an angel though." Sid gestured to me. "But that could mean nothing. Look at you. You're a walking miracle."

Sweet, said the voice.

"Maybe I'm here for a reason," I remarked.

Sid half-smiled. "Could be."

"Maybe we both are," I suggested. And maybe that reason is to fall in love. And attempt to reproduce!

"I'm not sure about that. I think I might've missed my reason, unless it was helping you hone your talent." Sid's eyes glittered suddenly, as much as dark eyes can glitter. "Do you remember that at all? Me, I mean."

"I think seeing you again helped me remember certain things." I told him. "But before I turned six, everything is fuzzy. And if I try to remember before when it gets fuzzy, it gets completely black. Or I get that awful feeling." I'd never told anyone about the terrible, deserted feeling inside when I tried to remember the fire. I didn't feel it often; I didn't want to, so I didn't try to remember. "My parents' faces show up sometimes, but they've gotten different over the years, I think. I'm losing any memory of them."

"Do you think that's bad?"

I shrugged. "I don't know. Sometimes I think people started treating me differently when they found out I didn't have..conventional parents. In school I never had a ton of friends. So once in a while I'd wish I had a Mom and Dad. But not the ones I *did* have."

"It's a good thing Philly."

"What?"

"What they did to you. Look how different you would be if your parents hadn't done that horrible shit. You wouldn't be here, you wouldn't breathe fire, you would never have even *met* your Aunts, Quincy or Bill. And you wouldn't know me." He grinned.

"You're right." Oh my God. No Sid. "If they hadn't been crazy I wouldn't exist, as I am now. It's sad that they left me. But I got the Aunts because they did." I stared out into nothing, feeling the impact of my mini revelation, when a vision came to me.

I whirled my head back to Sid. "I *hurt* you!"

Sid shook his head. "You never hurt me babes."

"Yes I did, Sid. I burned you! We were in the backyard and you told me I couldn't breathe fire on people because it would hurt them. And then I did it to you." I stopped.

"Remember the rest?" Sid asked.

"Someone screamed your name...one of the Aunts yelled at me that I could have burned you and I might have hurt you and I started crying. But you were smiling, you forgave me."

"And you apologized to me," Sid recalled.

"Good," I said. "That's a relief."

Sid chuckled. "What else?"

"You were always telling me to concentrate and control it and things like that...you and Anna fought a lot, but you'd always kiss and then Aunt Chasey would take me to another room.

Sid grinned. "She didn't want you to witness sin."

A lot of good that did, said the voice.

I held back a giggle, and said, "Sid..how did you teach a five-year-old to breathe fire?"

"You were a smart kid, Philly. You've always seemed older than you are."

"Thanks."

"It's true. Your mind always seemed way ahead of the rest of us."

Unwillingly —I swear—

Bullshit, coughed the voice.

Ahem. Without meaning to, my hand touched Sid's. Or his hand touched mine. In any case, our hands touched.

I know it doesn't sound like a big deal, but I didn't know what to do. Would it offend him if I pulled my hand away? It wasn't like we were holding hands. But if I didn't pull away, would he think that was bad, too?

Sid's the experienced one in the field, let him take care of it, said the voice.

He did.

He squeezed my hand and said, "You'd better get some sleep, babes. You have opening night tomorrow. And a witch to watch." Sid smiled.

My eyebrows shot up. "Opening night, oh my God." And Eric, too. I stood. I shook my head. "Everything happens at the same time, Sid."

"It's called life."

As I walked back to my room, my stomach began to turn. Why had I said yes to Eric? I must have been thinking of the food he'd offered, because I certainly hadn't considered how awkward it would be.

Maybe you said yes because you've never been on a real date in your life? the voice offered.

Who needs teenage boys? I retorted, thinking of Sid.

Of course, it did feel a little lonely when my friends spoke of past boyfriends. I could tell stories of nearly every kind of person. Except the boyfriend kind. And as much as Quincy and the Aunts and the adults around me said it was better not to have to worry about relationships during high school anyway, well...that wasn't how I felt when I strolled past the couples holding hands and making out in the hall.

I didn't want to hold hands and make out with just anyone. But if I at least did this one thing with Eric, maybe I wouldn't feel as left out.

Assuming I survived opening night.

Grease.

Quincy drove me to school an hour and a half before the show started. Quincy was cheap and gas prices were high. He and I needed to talk.

"Heard Kippie and Chasey're letting you go out with a boy tonight, girl."

I looked at Quincy. Why'd he have to find out everything?

He whacked me on the shoulder. "Phyllis why didn't you tell me? I heard about the boy but I didn't know *you liked him*!"

"I don't like him *that* much, Quincy. But he's nice."

"How'd you convince the Aunts to let you go out with him? You know how *relieved* they've been by your lack of a boyfriend?"

"Thanks, Quincy." I wasn't sure if I believed him. They might become more relieved to know I might *have* one.

I'd asked my Aunts about Eric that morning, almost hoping they'd say no. Why hadn't I realized that I *hardly knew* Eric?

"Oh, this is the boy who plays guitar?" Kippie had questioned.

"Yeah. You can meet him first or something if you want."

"Do you think he's a decent young man, Phyllis?" Chasey'd inquired.

"Yes. I've never driven with him though."

"Hm." At that I'd expected, "Maybe another time, dear. We've never met the boy!"

However, Kippie's final reply was, "Well Phyllis, I think I can trust you not to do some of the things *I* did when I was your age." She'd paused. "Just make sure you're back by 1 am."

"Yes indeed!" Chasey chimed. "If you're not, I'll call the police and you'll be in enormous trouble."

"And you'll never go out again." Kippie gave me a sweet smile.

And I'd returned it. "Thank you. I'll be sure I'm home by then."

So now I was stuck in a sort of mess, sort of "Yay I have a social life!" thing.

"He *is* cute, right?" Quincy made sure.

I nodded. "He's not bad."

"*You* shouldn't settle for less than gorgeous, sweetie."

I smiled a little but rolled my eyes.

"Hey, they can say all they want about inner beauty. I want *both*," Quincy said.

"You're terrible."

"And proud of it. If vanity sends me to hell, I'm happy to go, girl. Just don't tell Chasey I said that." Quincy grinned. "I'm bringin' *everybody* to your show tonight and we gon sit in the *front row*."

"Thanks for reminding me."

"Anytime, sugar. Plus I gotta meet this guy to see if he's perfect or not."

"What if he is?"

"Then we could *possibly* keep him." Quincy winked.

"I don't think I want a perfect guy."

"Why you lustin' for Sid then? No wait, I'll take that back. Sid's got some inner, emotional issues I wouldn't want to deal with. Not to mention a zillion *past girlfriends*. I think Anna was like number 3 thousand 64!"

"*Quincy.*"

"But then, Sid's system must be invincible to STDs. But I mean Jesus, the *man* has a temper. And probably some inner perversions we don't even *want* to know about."

"Everybody has inner perversions."

"*You should know*," the voice told me.

"Yeah, baby, but think of the people Sid's known. People that mess with your mind and your body, all your systems. Sid's built up a strong defense but think how much they could have fucked up before he built it up. He got used to things that most of us aren't even capable of." Quincy tapped my shoulder. "You ever find them out, you tell me."

"Like I'm ever going to tell you anything else about Sid."

"Aw, baby, forgive and forget."

"It's gonna take a while, Quince. But it'll help if you don't tell anyone else about Sid." My eyes grew wide. "You didn't tell my Aunts, did you?"

"No, I didn't. Only Sid."

"Good." I gave him a look. "You're lucky I put up with you."

"I know, Phyllis. How about we say I owe you big, and the next time you need a favor I won't even think about refusing."

"Okay," I agreed. Despite his big mouth, in most cases—most—Quincy was good for his word.

"But datin' Sid...that'd be some dangerous business. Sometimes you can't tell if it's him or the wolf talking."

I raised an eyebrow. "What do you mean?"

"You haven't known about it that long. You'll see."

Soon after I was dropped off in front of my school, and that's when I started to get nervous. I hated that we had so much time before the performance began. With each moment I became more and more anxious. I told myself I'd better not forget my lines. I only had about two.

* * *

Waiting behind the curtain (the opening scene between Danny and Sandy was decidedly staged outside the curtain, to make us all the more nervous), a bunch of us all squeezed each other's hands and for the last time mouthed "good luck". The curtain rose and the show began.

I waited in the wings until my part arrived. I swallowed and marched out on stage with a huge figurative stick up my ass. I exchanged words with the greasers, then marched away with the stick lodged up even further. I could hear the audience laughing but didn't beam until I was gone.

I was funny!

After that, each song and dance routine flew by, and before I knew it, we were doing curtain call. All those long, sweaty, grueling rehearsals, and the actual performance of the show seemed to last only an instant. An instant that earned standing ovation, baby!

After we all bowed, we ran to the dressing rooms bouncing up and down, and gushed over each other. I changed quickly, hearing everyone happily spouting opinions of the performance, and contributing my own as well.

"That was so much fun!"

"Everyone was so GOOD!"

"Phyllis you were awesome!"

"Oh my god, *I* almost laughed on stage."

"Amber I was looking at you for dance steps the *whole* time. You were totally great."

"You guys are so talented!"

"Oh my God, I almost forgot my lines."

"Did I sound angry enough?"

"Did I sound happy enough?"

"Did I sound ditzy enough?"

"Guys you all did a great job. Let's make sure our other performances go this well," Ms. Reygor told us, sticking her head into the girls' dressing room. We had performances on Saturday and Sunday night as well.

"Are you going to the cast party?"

"I'm so exhausted now, I don't know if I could do it Saturday night!"

"I was *so* nervous, and *nothing bad* happened."

"We rocked."

But now I was more nervous than ever. Now I, all by myself, one-woman show, had to face Eric.

We'd decided to meet in the lobby. So after I changed and wiped my face off, I headed out, my stomach filled with butterflies. But not the love kind. The stage fright kind.

I should have known then it was a lost cause. Why should a date feel like a show?

"Hey," he greeted me. Then he hugged me, very, very unexpectedly. "You were the best part of the show."

I laughed and rolled my eyes. "Great. It was that stupid wig."

"No, you've got talent. Man, you can sing and act and play the piano. All I can do is play guitar."

I smiled. "But you do that better than I can do all of those things. And you don't have to wear a wig."

"It just showed that you were willing to make sacrifices for your audience. You stole your scene."

"Hey girl!"

Uh oh.

The gays were coming.

There was nowhere to hide, but then, if Eric and I became anything, he'd meet them eventually.

As promised, Quincy had brought everyone.

Quincy, Damien, Butch, Maria, and Abe all rushed over. "Phyllis you were *amazing*." Quincy.

"Was that *tweed*?" Damien.

"Who's *this*?" Abe. Interestedly.

Obviously the fact that I had a date was going to surmount anything else I'd ever done. Any attempts I made to protect Eric from gay interrogation might only make it worse.

"This is Eric," I introduced, waiting for the embarrassing "Oh, *this* is Eric! I've heard about you!"

But it didn't come. It was like the guys understood.

"It's nice to meet you, Eric. Did you enjoy the show?" Quincy asked, firmly shaking Eric's hand.

"This is Quincy," I said quickly. "And Abe, Butch, Damien, and Maria," I introduced, gesturing to each of them.

"Hi," Eric greeted with a small smile.

"You must be thrilled to be dining with such *talent*," Butch told him.

Good grief.

"Were you in the show?" Maria asked him.

Eric laughed. "Oh no, I can't act. I'm a musician."

"Oh! What do you play?"

"The guitar."

"That is *so* cool," Damien told him.

"You are also very cute," Abe added.

"We should get going," I cut in. "So that I'm back before the Aunts call the police." The Aunts! I looked around. "Where are they? Did they like the show?"

"Of course they did!"

"Of course we did!"

The Aunts pushed through the crowd and gave me a giant hug.

"Our talented little girl. I couldn't believe it, Phyllis!" Kippie chirped.

"You were phenomenal. You should've been a lead. And the dancing..!" Chasey put her hand to her heart.

Gotta love the Aunts.

"This is Eric?" Kippie questioned.

"I'm Eric," Eric confirmed.

"Oh how nice to meet you. Thank you so much for taking our Phyllis out to dinner. Heaven knows she deserves it after that performance!" Chasey said, smiling.

"Oh yeah," Eric agreed.

"Have you been driving long? I trust you're responsible if Phyllis likes you," said Aunt Kippie.

"I've been driving for a little over a year, Ms. Sorin. I promise she'll be fine."

He sounded so mature. I could tell they loved it.

"All right, you two may go," Aunt Kippie informed us, as though we'd been waiting for her to do so.

"Sid didn't make it?" I inquired.

"Oh, sweetie he told me to apologize for him and tell you that he'll be coming tomorrow night," Quincy let me know.

"All right." I nodded. "See you later everybody, thank you so much for coming. I'm glad you liked the show!"

"It was nice meeting you guys!" Eric called. That was all we got out before they disappeared into the crowd behind us.

"I heard your Aunts rent out your house. Do all of those people live in it?" Eric asked, unlocking his car.

"Oh no, Quincy does, but the rest besides my Aunts were all his friends. They visit a lot, but they don't live with us."

He started it. "Were all of the guys gay?"

"Oh yeah."

"Good, I was afraid you'd glare at me and say, 'No, why the hell would you think *that?!*'" We pulled out.

I laughed. "Because they didn't say *anything* that made them sound gay. At all," I said sarcastically.

It took him a moment to tell I wasn't serious and then he laughed too.

"I just live with my mom and brother," he told me.

"They both play guitar?"

"Just my brother, Terry. He and Tony taught me. Now I'm better than the both of them."

"I never got better than my piano teacher, I just wanted to play stuff on my own. Taylor gave me a book of Billy Joel songs," I told him.

"Taylor doesn't seem that musical."

"She plays a ton of instruments! Why not?"

Eric shrugged. "She never talks about it." He looked at me. "Friendly's?"

What? Oh! "Sure. I'm paying for myself."

"Phyllis, I can pay for you."

"No. You can't."

"You sure? I have a job and the money would be going toward a good cause."

I guess I was a good cause. "I'm sure."

"Okay."

The date didn't go too badly. One could almost say it went well. First we spoke about my house.

"So how many people live in your house?"

"Hm." The Aunts, me, Bill, Sid, Quincy... "Six. Soon to be seven."

"You're not related to all of them?"

"Only the Aunts. They're *like* my family, though. A really odd family."

"Because one is gay?"

"Oh no." I looked at him. "Do gays bother you?"

"Only if they hit on me or smack my ass." He grinned. "No not really. My brother has a gay friend. He's an awesome singer."

I told him about Anna and that she was playing Carlotta on the tour.

"Isn't that the one who croaks?...Like a toad?"

I laughed. "Yeah."

"Cool."

"She's coming back soon. It'll be interesting."

"Why?"

"She's got a temper is all." And an ex.

"Does she break windows with her voice when she gets angry?"

"She's never done it when I was around, but I don't think she would break anything that belongs to my Aunts. She has broken other things, though."

"My mom kicked my dad out because he broke some dish she liked. She told us it was because he was a jerk. But I think she just didn't want her stuff broken."

"Was he a jerk?"

"Yeah, he was. But I still don't think that's why she kicked him out. Do you ever have to kick people out of your house?"

"Most of the people have always lived there, but when we do get new ones, they're usually fine. We did have to kick a woman out last summer."

"Why?"

"She threatened Quincy."

"Whoa. Did he bother her or something?"

"No. He didn't like her though. She *was* a little scary."

"Why'd your Aunts give her a room?"

"She was very polite, even though she had a different look. And they probably thought they'd be able to help her out. My Aunts are big on kindness."

"There's definitely a shortage of *that*."

"I don't know why people won't get along. Everyone in my house is completely different and *they* all get along."

"A lot of it had to do with money. But I'm not interested in that. I want to play music, but whether I make a ton of money or not isn't a huge deal. Not that I'd mind." He smiled.

We got onto the subject on music then, piano, guitar, learning to play, etc. We got our food.

Before ordering dessert (Eric had without question decided to get dessert, and I liked him even more) things were going extremely well, I couldn't believe it. Then he asked me a question.

"So do you usually find yourself attracted to musical people?"

I shrugged. "Musical people are usually cool, but I like all kinds of people. Or, I try to."

"Do you go out with a lot of guys?"

"Not remotely."

"Really?"

"Yeah, why?" I didn't like this discussion.

"You're just really cool, Phyllis." Or maybe I did. "Do you think you'd ever want to hang out again?"

"Sure." Another hasty decision. But he was really nice, and funny, and he seemed to like to talk as well as listen, and about interesting things too.

I noticed his face brighten a bit, but then he caught himself. "Maybe you could come to my house. I could just drive you there after school."

"Yeah, that'd be nice. I'll have a lot more time now that the play's over."

Eric nodded. "I figured."

Then the waitress came and got our dessert orders.

"How long have you been friends with Tony?" I asked Eric afterwards.

"Almost twelve years. His parents are friends with my mom. He's a year younger than me, so I don't think we would've met otherwise."

"Do you turn seventeen soon?"

He shrugged. "In October. When's your birthday?"

"November, coincidentally." I paused. "I'll be seventeen, too."

"Cool." He paused. "Do you like cherries?"

I nodded, relieved he hadn't asked if I'd failed a grade. As for his question, I liked all food. "Why?" I asked.

"I don't, and they come with the sundae. Want mine?"

"Sure."

Later, Taylor would taunt me for eating Eric's cherry. It was a good thing it hadn't been the other way around, she would've had a field day with that. ("Eric took Phyllis's cherry!")

We left after we finished our sundaes.

"You don't know the way to my house, do you?" I realized as we got to the car.

"Not really." He smiled at me. I decided it was a very pleasant smile indeed. Charming, even. "You can give me directions though, right?"

"Oh yeah, all you have to do is get out of the city and then it isn't far."

So I directed Eric back to my house. He stopped in the front.

"You want me to walk you in?" he asked.

I shook my head. "No thanks, I should just run in."

"Okay. Thanks for coming out with me."

"Thank you for taking me. It was fun."

He nodded. "Yeah." Then he leaned over and, with a gentle grip on the side of my face, kissed me. It didn't involve tongue, but it was no peck just the same. It was nice. Very very nice.

We leaned away from each other. I smiled awkwardly.

"Thanks Eric. Good night." I got out. I hadn't seen any smoke clouds around my head so I figured I was good to go.

When I got to the door and looked back, he waved and turned around. I hoped he knew the way home.

Your first and only date and the guy gets lost, said the voice.

"Shut up," I whispered, opening the door.

"Hello Clarice." Sid was on the couch.

"Can you do the slurp?" I asked him. Having become Taylor's best friend, I was now very familiar with "The Silence of the Lambs."

Sid grinned. Then he did a very precise imitation of the slurping sound Anthony Hopkins makes in the film. Sid would have made the sexiest cannibal. No offense to Sir Hopkins, of course.

"Why're you up?"

"To make sure I didn't have to attack your guy." He paused. "Don't tell me about the play. I'm seeing it tomorrow."

"You want to go in without previous impressions?"

"I know you'll be good. I just don't know what kind of part you have. I want to be surprised. I don't get a lot of those anymore."

I can think of some surprises to give you, I thought.

"Do you *want* more surprises?" I asked innocently.

"Don't get any ideas, Philly." He nodded to the end of the couch. "You wanna sit down or do you need to sleep?" He shook his head. "Do people still *say* 40 winks? Jesus I'm old."

Well then you're the sexiest old man I've ever seen, the voice muttered.

Ha! I told it. Even *you* can't resist him!

"You're not old, Sid." I sat near him.

"How was your date?"

"Good."

"Are we gonna meet him?"

I shrugged. "I don't know. I'm not sure...I guess I didn't really think of it as something that could become something until he kissed me." Oops. That should have been caught.

"Ohhh, he kissed you. He didn't walk you to the door. Did you guys park?"

"No Sid, people don't really park anymore. And I've hardly talked to him before this!"

He leaned forward a bit. "What kind of kiss was it?"

I wanted to say, "I could show you." Instead, I shrugged again (I had shrugged a great deal this night) and said "A goodnight kiss, I guess. I can't really compare it to a ton of others."

"Was it quick?"

"No."

"Tongue?"

"No."

"Smoke?"

"Not that I noticed."

"Good. Better than mine?"

I yawned, and, feeling daring as some smoke escaped, declared, "Hell no."

Sid grinned. I reconsidered.

"But then, I can't really judge. You never gave me an actual *real* kiss. They were just tests."

"Good. I shouldn't be giving you kisses at all, babes. Stick to guys your own age. Unless you can't find a good one." He gave me a look. "Is *Eric* a good one?"

"He seems to be. He asked if I'd like to come to his house. He was nice to talk to."

Sid nodded. "That's the important thing. Until you start having sex." He held up a defensive hand. "That was a joke, and if I hear about you having sex I'll bite the guy's arm off."

"I um...wasn't planning on it. But I'll definitely take that into consideration." I looked at him. "Do you remember your first girlfriend?"

"Philly, it was in the 1860s. She wasn't exactly a girlfriend...but yes, I remember her."

I blinked. "Jesus Christ."

"Don't tell me you didn't think of that babes. You're good at math."

"It's just..you're just.." You'd be rotting. I hugged him, I had to. "I'm glad you're here, Sid."

Sid was probably confused, but after a second he hugged me back. "I'm glad I am too, babes."

I leaned away. "What was her name?" I said, after waiting a bit.

"Rachel. I don't remember her last name."

"Did people call you Dominick then?"

"Yeah. Van Frobisher started 'Sid'."

"Really?"

"Yeah...he's into nicknames."

"You think I'll ever meet him?"

"I hope not."

"Why not?"

"Van's not a good guy. Especially not around pretty young girls such as yourself."

"I'm pretty?"

"Yeah. I guess you just haven't accepted it yet."

"Why not?"

"You're a teenage girl."

"How would you know about teenage girls?"

He nodded to me. "I know you," he offered.

"I don't think I'm like most of them."

"Sorry Philly." He grinned. "You're a good kind of girl either way."

Whatever that meant. I rolled my eyes. "Are you speaking in terms of how much I taste like barbecue sauce?"

He laughed. "Maybe."

"Have you ever had a family, Sid? Before you became a werewolf or something?"

"I had the family I was born into. I never had a wife or children." He thought. "There were kids in the mansion, but most of them were really decades old."

"Did you ever meet anyone you wanted to settle down with?"

"If I'd been human, yes. For the rest of eternity, no. I couldn't ever force that on anyone." He gave me a look. "Why are you interrogating me?"

Oops. I wanted to know everything about Sid; it was my first instinct to ask him questions. "You've had an interesting life."

"It's not that interesting. It's just long."

"You just don't want to tell me about it."

"Not all in one night," he agreed.

"You should write your autobiography. You could always make it a series."

"I can't write, Philly. I can talk my way out of anything, I've had a lot of practice. But I could never write a book and *enjoy* it. Plus, I can't expose an entire, separate kind of people, even if I call it fiction."

"They probably wouldn't find out about it, if they're all isolated from the rest of the world."

"Oh, they're not. They know everything that's going on. They can leave the house, but most of them don't do it for good."

Mary. "How would you get Mary there?"

Sid paused. "I'd take her to Van."

"I thought he's not good with girls."

"He isn't. But he's good to people who need his help."

"Well then what's his problem?"

"Hopefully you'll never find out." Sid got up, his body unfolding carefully as he rose. "It's just a life you should never have to lead, babes. I'm going to bed."

"Oh. Okay. Where are the Aunts?"

"In their rooms. I'm supposed to report to them if you're not home on time."

"Would you have, if I hadn't been?"

"It would've depended on how late you were. I'm not big on getting people into trouble who don't deserve it. Especially with your Aunts."

"What if I'd been in trouble?"

"Philly, I've never, ever had the faintest doubt about your self-defense capabilities." Sid grinned. "I've experienced them, remember?"

I smiled. "Yeah. Thanks Sid."

"Night Philly." He smiled at me, turned and went upstairs.

I sat on the couch for a bit, reflecting on my date and my conversation with Sid. Should I keep going with Eric? Would it be right, when I was so smitten with someone else?

I decided I was too tired to figure it out, and went to bed.

* * *

I only saw Sid briefly after the next show. Taylor found me and we had important things to deal with.

"Philly you were great," Sid told me, a wonderful beautiful smile on his face. He gave me a hug.

I beamed. "Thank you Sid. Thanks for coming to watch."

"Phyllis! Oh my god, you were so funny!" Taylor rushed up to us. "And not one nervous puff of smoke."

I smiled a little. "I've had practice holding it back."

Tony followed. "That was a good show."

Taylor smiled at him, then at Sid. "Sid, this is my boyfriend, Tony. Tony, this is Sid, he lives with Phyllis."

Tony was confused for a moment, then remembered the conditions of the Sorin house. "Oh, hi, Sid."

They shook hands. "Nice to meet you Tony," Sid said. He looked at me. "Hey, I've gotta head back. You have a ride home, don't you?"

"Oh yeah. Thank you Sid."

"My pleasure babes. See you later." Sid disappeared.

"Gorgeous," Taylor whispered to me.

I decided our conversation would require more time. "Did you want to come over tonight, Taylor? Sorry Tony, I don't mean to like, steal her."

Tony held up a hand. "It's no problem Phyllis. I think I can spare some Taylor. But only for you."

"Indeed," Taylor agreed, giving him a look.

Tony grinned at me. "I heard you went out with Eric."

"Oh my God, yeah! How was it?" Taylor wanted to know.

"It was good," I said, suddenly reluctant to speak.

"He said different."

Tony reminded me of a pirate sometimes. Not as hot as Johnny, but I mean, Johnny was hot as a bald druggie.

"What did he say?" I asked, petrified. I was a bad kisser! I talked about stupid stuff! My house was ugly.

Hey, my house wasn't ugly! How could he say that? I would kick Eric's ass.

"He said it was *very* good."

Oh.

Taylor looked at me. "Did you screw him?"

I laughed. "Yes Taylor, right in the middle of Friendly's."

"Really?"

"No."

"Oh. I'd do it. Not to Eric, though." Taylor grinned.

"You dirty dirty girl," Tony accused her. He gave her a kiss. "I've gotta go home. You leaving with Phyllis?"

"Yup."

"All right. Call me tomorrow."

"Sure thing puddin'."

I gave her a look. "Puddin'?"

"It's what Harley Quinn calls the Joker!"

"She's in an abusive relationship, Taylor."

"Plenty of things don't make sense in the comic book world. Not that a lot of things make sense in this world." She grinned. "Like how you can even begin to compare Eric to Sid. Sid gets better looking every second!"

"I'm telling Tony you said that."

"That'll just make him want to prove he's better. Somehow."

"Somehow? Did you guys have sex?"

Taylor shook her head rapidly. "No. We talk about it, once in a while." She paused. "More than that. But we're not ready. It's not just sex, you know? I don't mean the emotional commitment. I'm sure I'd feel the same about Tony no matter what. But I don't know.." She lowered her voice, glanced around us. People surrounded us, but they were making enough noise so that we could hardly even hear each other. "I don't know if I'm comfortable enough with myself, let alone comfortable enough with other people."

I nodded. "I understand."

"Plus I don't think it'd be a good idea to do it right now. Maybe in a few years." She looked at me. "We're overdue for a long conversation, aren't we?"

I nodded. "It is so, my dear Taylor. Let us find the Aunts."

Taylor stopped me. "You find the Aunts, I'll call my mom."

Soon we were in the living room at my house. Kippie was "always happy to have you, Taylor."

"We haven't had a sleepover in such a long time," Taylor said.

"I know. T—"

"Tell me about your date with Eric!"

"Taylor—"

Just then Bill came through, wearing sunglasses. "I'm getting so sick of pastries. I don't know why you humans desire them so when you have fruit. Especially apples. Red delicious has always been my favorite." He'd been various aliens all week, and I suspected he was getting more involved with the alien girl, whoever she was.

Taylor watched him as she left. "What's with the sunglasses?"

I explained the situation. "He has this friend who's an alien, some girl he sees once in a while. Met her at the donut shop."

Taylor brightened. "Aw that's so sweet! Has he watched 'Invader Zim'?"

"Uh.."

"Maybe they'll fall in love."

I nodded. "That seems to be the trend this year. You, Quincy, Aunt Chasey—"

"With that church guy?"

"Yeah, Mr. Meneses. They're out right now."

"Whoa." Taylor grinned again. "I wonder if they make out. Those churchgoers..."

"Change of subject. No talk of my Aunt making out with anyone."

I had to get to other business, business I'd been trying not to contemplate or fear. Mary. Would Taylor shy away if I asked about Mary?

Only one away to find out, the voice urged.

"Taylor..did you..you talked to Key about Mary, didn't you?"

Taylor's face went instantly grim. "She wouldn't go into it that much Phyllis. You know Key, Phyllis. Blunt, honest, loud. She said Mary was forceful and that she had to tell her. But she didn't..she *wouldn't* go into detail at all. I know why, Phyllis. She's afraid. Key is afraid of Mary, Phyllis. Do you know what that means?"

"What?"

"That she's worth being afraid of. She's worth staying away from. She really *can* make you tell secrets."

"Well, I mean, Taylor, did you really doubt *yourself*?"

Taylor smiled sadly. "Phyllis, I was so prepared to handle being crazy. I wouldn't have *too* much of a problem with that. I've never really been that sane anyway. Having someone who can suck your secrets out of your mind...I don't know if I can handle that."

"Why didn't you say anything?" I asked. "To me, I mean?"

"First of all, I didn't want to talk about it. I'm sorry Phyllis. I...was also kind of afraid you'd ask me questions about Davy, and the car accident."

"Oh no! No Taylor, I would never..force you to talk about it. You can when you're ready, even if that is never."

She looked relieved. "Thank you Phil." She paused. "But I also didn't mention it because I thought it might put you some sort of danger."

My eyebrows creased over wide eyes. "Why?!"

"Because you still talk to Mary. I don't know, she might look inside your head or something."

"She can't see inside your head," I told her. I knew this because of Sid.

I couldn't tell Taylor that, though. "How do you know?" she demanded.

Think Phyllis, quick now... "Why would she ask you for a secret if she could read your mind?"

Taylor nodded. "Oh...good point. But what if she just doesn't want us to know?"

"She'd want to show it off."

Taylor sighed. "Remember when she was just a plain, nice, friendly girl? She still had all her friends and invited people to sit with us?"

"Yeah, she helped us lowly freshmen out."

"No no no. Sophomores are lowly. Freshmen are annoying," she explained.

"What about juniors and seniors?"

"Juniors are stuck-up. Seniors are awesome."

"You have decided this for the world?"

She shrugged. "I think it's just the way things are."

"The structure of life," I agreed sarcastically.

She smiled. "At least we can avoid it here."

Just then, Damien came out of the kitchen, moonwalking on the hardwood. He gave us a mischievous smile and a wave, and danced out the front door.

Taylor and I exchanged looks as we heard a loud, "Bye baby!" from Quincy's window on the side of the house, and the beeping of Damien's car horn as he drove off.

"Yes, there is certainly no structure here," I told her.

"Damien?"

"Mmhmm."

"He's cute. Very..brightly colored."

I nodded. "Yes he is. On both counts."

"So, speaking of cuties. Date with Eric?"

I nodded. "Yeah...we went to Friendly's last night."

"What'd you eat? I can never decide there."

"Grilled cheese."

"Boring."

"I didn't want a huge complicated meal, Tay. I was nervous enough."

"So you like him?"

I sighed. "Taylor, I don't know. I mean...yeah, I like him a lot. But I don't know how much like that is. I've hardly had any male friends, let alone a boyfriend."

"You'll figure it out, Phyllis. I stopped having *any* friends for like two years. Death can make you such a basketcase." She pointed at me. "*You* could have died once. Maybe you had some divine knowledge and guys could sense it. And they were all intimidated."

"Taylor, I think you have a better excuse for lack of a social life."

"Neither of us lack it anymore. You have the potential to have a lot more friends than you do, Phyllis. You just choose not to."

"You don't think I have enough friends."

Taylor shook her head. "No no, I mean there's no such thing as too many friends, but you have a whole house of people to be friends with. Plus, I'm really the only person in our school worth being friends with anyway," she joked.

I laughed. "It's probably true."

"Yeah right. But, seriously. Tell me everything. What'd you talk about? What'd he say?"

I summarized the date, trying to make it sound interesting.

Taylor only interrupted once. "Wait..he said he's a better guitar player than Tony? Yeah right, in his *dreams*!"

I didn't mention Eric's saying that she didn't seem the musical type.

Then I got to the kiss.

"Oh God, were you okay? Could you hold back your firebreath?"

I nodded. "Yeah."

"Was it a good kiss?"

"Yeah."

"Your first."

"My first official kiss," I agreed. It wasn't really a lie.

"Nice."

"Yeah."

"And you like him?"

"I think I do. He's really nice to talk to, he seems like he actually cares about my life."

"Yeah. Tony says he's a pretty caring guy. He also says Eric really, really likes you."

I snorted. "God only knows why."

Taylor rolled her eyes. "Because you're awesome. Duh!"

"Aw Tay, what would I do without you?"

"What indeed."

I sighed. "So..now I don't know what to do." I glanced up at the stairs to make sure Sid wasn't standing there. The man could pop up as unexpectedly as Batman and catch you in the act. "I like Eric," I whispered. "And he'd probably be a good boyfriend. But I don't know if it would be fair."

"Because you'd only be going out with him to have a boyfriend?"

"No! I wouldn't do *that*, I'd at least have to think the person was nice and what not. No. Because I'm in love with Sid. You can't date one guy while you love another. So to speak."

Taylor pursed her lips. "Okay..well..don't feel pressured to have a boyfriend...but I think you should go on some more dates or whatever with Eric."

"Why?"

"He's nice, he's funny..he's cute and plays guitar. And he..he's realistic. Maybe he could make the whole Sid thing go away," she said cautiously.

And cautiously with good reason. Had I been Quincy, I would have said, "Say *what*?"

"What do you mean, 'go away'? It's not just some fleeting thing, Taylor. He's always in my head."

"C'mon Phyllis. He's sexy. He's like a model. It's like being in love with a movie star. It's understandable, enviable but it isn't likely that anything would ever come of it."

Well, duh! "Do you think I don't realize this?! Taylor, I tell myself every day what a stupidly impossible goal Sid is. Do you think it's helped at all? And the worst part is, we're friends. We talk all the time. Oh, and guess what? He knows I like him. He *also* thinks it's hilarious. But God Taylor. I can't imagine not having him in my life. I almost want to tell him exactly how I feel. He teases me about it. Do you think it makes me love him any less? No. It's hopeless, Tay. There's nothing I can do. I'm in love with Sid. That's how it is, and I can't help it."

Taylor took it all in, and nodded. Then her eyebrows shot up. "He *knows?!*"

"Yeah. Quincy found out and told him."

"Wow. I am never telling Quincy anything again."

"Yeah, that's what I said."

"How did Sid take it?"

"Oh, he loves it. It's like he thinks it's cute."

"I'm sorry, Phyllis."

"He does tell me more stuff. I've noticed that."

"Really? Anything good?"

Uh... "Just stuff about his past. His first girlfriend, how he came to want to prosecute. Nothing *too* detailed, but more than before."

"You'll tell me if he says anything important."

"Of course. Unless it's like, some deep dark secret involving an unknown civilization or species or something." I grinned innocently.

"Because we all know Sid's from another planet." She sighed. "The planet of gorgeous men." Then she got serious. "But Phyllis, I still think you should try going out with Eric. Even if you still love Sid..it won't be a serious relationship, it can just be a nice experience."

"You just want to go on double dates together."

"I think you'll be happy." Taylor's eyes widened. "Oh no. Oh no, Phyllis, did you see what I just did?"

"You...tried to convince me to go out with Eric?"

"I was trying to tell you you needed a boy to be happy." Taylor closed her eyes and sank. "Don't listen to me anymore Phyllis. I don't know what I'm talking about. I sound like a stupid tween romance novel or something."

I patted her on the shoulder. "It's okay Taylor, you meant well. You just want me to stop being stressed about Sid."

"But I didn't put the words correctly. Intentions are immaterial, action is what counts. Sucks for people who commit manslaughter."

"Still. I understand," I told her. "I have to think about it, I guess." In my mind though, I had already decided to give Eric a try. Maybe it would turn out to be more worthwhile a pursuit.

More worthwhile than Sid?

Taylor nodded. "Well it's obvious why. Sid's so.." she searched.

"Speechless-leaving."

"Yeah, that's it."

"Heyyy, Taylor. Thank *God* you're here." Quincy came from the back stairway.

"Hello to you too," I greeted him.

"Sorry baby, but I made a big mistake," Quincy told me.

"You told someone else she likes Sid?" Taylor gave him an evil look.

"Okay, I made *another* big mistake. And FYI, Jesus says forgiveness, Taylor!"

"That's between me and Jesus." Taylor smiled. "What was your mistake?"

"I let Damien leave, and I still have the whole night ahead of me."

"Get Bill and we'll watch a movie," I suggested.

Quincy nodded. "I'm sure Bill'd love to see Taylor."

"What about Sid and the Aunts?" Taylor suggested.

Quincy shook his head. "The Aunts are asleep—"

"Chasey's out on a date," I reminded him.

"Oh, yeah. Kippie's asleep. You can try Sid, though."

So, I sent Taylor to ask Bill (they got along especially well when he was a superhero or an extra terrestrial), and I sent myself to fetch Sid.

His door was closed. I knocked on it, and, listened. Faintly I could hear his voice, so I stuck my head in. He was on his cell.

"Yeah I know, hold on a minute Van." He put his phone down on his bed, and walked across the room to me.

"Do you need something Philly?"

"We're all watching a movie in the living room. Do you want to join us?"

Sid looked at his watch. "At quarter to midnight?"

"Quincy's idea."

Sid smiled a little. "I'll come down babes, but let me finish my phone call."

"Want me to wait and you can escort me down?" I asked a little too hopefully.

"Sure Philly."

I watched him and listened to what he told Van.

"Yeah, we're all set. I don't even know for sure. I wanted to clear it with you just in case." Sid snorted. "Yeah, I'm sure you do. Night Van. Mhm. Bye."

"What was that, if I may ask?"

"It was half of a conversation."

"About what?"

"I just asked him if he'd mind if we brought him Mary. *If* she turns out to be a witch."

"What did he say?"

"He said it'd be fine." He widened his eyes, blinked and sighed. "Always willing to help out an old friend was how he put it. And I think he thinks it means he'll meet you."

"How does he know about me?"

Sid grinned. "He asked who the charming young girl who answered the telephone was. Plus, Mary's your friend. I don't want him to think I'm having random affairs with strange teenage girls."

"Huh. Well, I'm not strange or random."

"Philly." Sid gave me a look.

I tried to look innocent.

"You won't have to meet Van, though."

"He can read minds, right?"

"Only if you look into his eyes."

I looked into Sid's eyes and swallowed. "I don't think I want to meet him."

"At least if you *were* to meet him, you'd know exactly what he is."

I thought of "The Silence of the Lambs," the doomed Dr. Chilton saying, "Oh, he's a monster."

"I *really* hope I never run into one the street."

Sid's eyes flashed. "Why Philly? What's on your mind?"

"That's why I don't want it to be read. So no one *knows*."

Sid grinned. "You made a great teacher, Philly."

I made an attempt at a growl. I only scratched my throat. He laughed at me.

I sighed and ran a hand through my hair. "It's still flat from the wig."

"So pull it back. It doesn't matter if it's flat it if it's in a ponytail."

"I don't like the way looks when it's back." My hair was, as of now, just past my shoulders. I didn't think there was enough of it anymore for a decent ponytail.

Sid got up and came close to me. Aah! close. And ahhh close.

It turned out to be aah! close, because he grabbed my hair and pulled it back. It felt kind of good, but I knew it didn't look good.

Sid studied me. "You don't look bad."

"But I don't look good, either."

"You always look good." He gave me another look. "But don't get any ideas."

"Thanks Sid."

"You don't have to thank me for telling you the truth."

I smiled. "So can you growl at will or does it just happen when you get angry?"

Sid looked at me and I heard the low growl from his throat. His face didn't change.

Smoke rose in my throat and just a little bit escaped from my lips. It was just the most irresistible thing I'd ever seen.

Sid grinned. "It's cool, isn't it."

I nodded.

"Wait til you hear me howl."

"I think I did, once. I didn't know it was you, though."

Sid touched my shoulder. "I'm sorry I kept that from you."

"It's okay, Sid. I can understand wanting to keep a secret." I'm not sorry I found out, though.

"Thanks Philly."

He grabbed my hand and headed out into the hallway. He led me down the stairs until we were in view of everyone. Then he let go of my hand.

"Good choice," he murmured as he noticed what was on.

I hardly had to hear the movie let alone look to know it was "The Silence of the Lambs." Déja vu, man.

Taylor, looking very pleased with herself, was in Sid's Chair. Bill was on the couch.

She patted my arm. "This movie is a work of art. Even the Academy saw that it deserved awards. They even gave them to it." Taylor shook her head. "I'll never trust them again after they gave half of the awards to 'Lord of the Rings'. Love the books, but they weren't meant for film."

I shrugged, never having read or remained awake through any version of the stories. "I just don't trust them because they never gave Johnny best actor."

"I know right."

"I mean, sure he didn't actually want it, but—"

"That's too damn bad for him," Taylor finished. "Don't tell Tony I was singing another man's praises, though." She squeezed my arm. "I love this scene!"

I shook my head. Just because Taylor hadn't imagined Mary making her tell a secret didn't mean she wasn't crazy.

I instinctively looked around the room when Buffalo Bill was preparing for his naked dance. Sid caught my eye.

"You hungry Philly?"

I nodded. I looked at Taylor.

"Taylor."

She stared at the screen, wide-eyed.

"Taylor!"

She blinked and turned.

"You want to get a snack or something?"

"I can't, I'll miss the 'don't you MAKE me hurt your DOG!' scene!"

"You hungry Quince?" Sid said.

Quincy nodded and rose. "I'll getch'all some food."

I stood. "I'll help."

Sid hopped up. "Yeah me too."

We went into the kitchen, leaving Bill and Taylor.

"Why didn't we ask Bill?" I wanted to know.

"Personally I was worried he'd become Buffalo Bill," said Quincy.

Sid shook his head. "Still wearing the sunglasses."

Quincy grabbed a pan.

Sid squinted. "I was thinking more of a snack."

"Well I want some chicken. You can go grab a pheasant or whatever you wolf people eat."

Sid chuckled.

Something occurred to me. I turned to Quincy. "Did you get me to start going through Anna's room with you because you were trying to keep me away from Sid?"

Quincy coughed.

"Anna's room, huh?" Sid said. "What *was* that large contraption?"

"A big keyboard piano," I said.

"I'd like to see *your* large contraption, Sid," said Quincy.

"You can get jailtime for sexual harassment," Sid reminded him.

"You guys want chicken?" Quincy said quickly.

I shook my head. "I'll find something else."

Sid gave me a look. "You *are* good at searching things."

I coughed.

"I'm surprised you haven't had your key taken away yet. Going through all these rooms like—"

"Wait—"

"I told him about Sarah," said Quincy.

I sighed.

"What went through your head when you saw some of the things in my room?"

"None of them really make sense now."

"Philly honey, I'm sure my being a werewolf wouldn't have made sense either."

"Okay, well...I thought you might have some sort of wolf obsession. Or you *had* a wolf."

"Those are both pretty spot-on if you ask me," said Quincy, flipping a piece of chicken.

"I'm going to check the pantry," I said. The pantry was a small room on the side of the kitchen. I went in, looking for something reminiscent of chips.

Sid came up behind me. "You're lucky I don't go through *your* room."

"It's not that interesting," I said, debating hand-heating some Chef Boyardee.

He took my shoulders firmly and turned me around. "That isn't the point, Philly. It's that you invaded a personal place. And continued to do so after I told you not to." He brought up my chin gently with two fingers.

"I'm sorry I didn't tell you, Philly. And I'm sorry I kissed you. I didn't mean to fuck with your feelings. I just suffer a loss of self-control around the full moon."

I took a breath, caught off-guard by his blunt contact. "Does the wolf...come out? Is there any time you're not there at all, in human form?"

Sid shook his head. "No. But it's a constant fight around that time."

"So when you kissed me—"

"Mainly the wolf."

"I like the wolf."

Sid grinned. "He likes you back."

"Is that a problem?"

Sid cocked an eyebrow. "If I let it have its way babes, you'd end up either raped or in pieces." His voice got low and serious.

But I couldn't take him seriously or I'd get scared. "The wolf wants to have sex with me?" I raised an eyebrow. Maybe I could get the wolf to try and convince Sid of some things...

Sid cringed. "I meant if it took me over. Basically it'd just do as much damage as possible." He touched my arm. "But don't think about it, Philly. I would never let anyone, myself included, hurt you."

"Likewise," I told him. "Apparently you're a little easier to protect though."

Sid laughed. "It helps to be immortal. But you're still a good person to have on my side."

I took the can down and went into the kitchen, where Quincy was leaving with his chicken. "Taylor might want some of that," I said quickly.

"I have a little for Bill and her." He went into the living room.

"She'll be in the mood for meat after this movie," I muttered.

Sid chuckled. Oh yeah. Wolf hearing.

"Hey Sid," I asked, pouring the raviolis into a bowl, "why'd you pick that room? For the skylight?"

Sid smiled. "No, I know the moon schedule by heart, babes. I picked that room because it's dark, and because I paid extra to get it completely soundproofed." He sighed. "All except for the door."

"Your hearing really is that good?"

"Philly, if those were normal walls, I'd be able to hear every single breath you took in your room."

I raised my eyebrows. Creepy.

He laughed at my expression. "Yeah." He paused. "When I lived here ten years ago, I realized how nice it was to have the room furthest from Anna and the room closest to you."

I looked at him curiously.

"In case you lost control of the fire."

"Thanks, Sid."

We stood silent for a moment as I held the bowl in my hands and it began to steam.

"Sid, you said there were psychics...are there people who can tell the future?"

"Why do you ask?"

"It would be nice in a lot of situations."

Sid nodded. "Yes, there are people who know the future. There are only 2 or 3 in existence. Most of them commit suicide."

My mouth formed an "oh."

"Yeah. Some are powerful enough to control when they get their visions or whatever they are. As you can probably tell, I've never been able to tell the future."

"Did you meet any fortunetellers?"

Sid smiled. "Usually they're referred to as connections."

I raised an eyebrow. "Why?"

"They're considered a connection to the direct source of the energy."

"You make them sound like telephones."

"The name was around long before phones were."

"So have you met any 'connections'?"

"Yes."

"Will you tell me about it?"

"*Her*. Maybe, but not now." He gave me a small smile and turned to leave.

Damn.

We went back into the living room and the credits were rolling.

Bill turned. "Oh, chicken. Lovely."

"Why don't you take your sunglasses off, Prot? It's *been* dark for a while," Quincy said gingerly.

"I see your point. I've become so accustomed to having them on that sometimes they feel as if they're not there." Bill/Prot removed his shades.

"Look at that attractive fellow. You give Sid a run for his money, Prot," Quincy told him.

"So much focus on appearance on your planet. That's one thing that's set you far behind in the universe," said Bill, setting his shades aside.

"New movie," Taylor announced. "What'll it be?"

"Brokeback Mountain!" yelled Quincy. "Just kidding," he quickly added. "I'm thinkin'..."

"Nothing too long," I requested. "I'm not sure how much later I can stay awake."

"On that note, as they say here, I'm going to retire. Goodnight everyone." Bill left.

Quincy went on. "Let's watch something funny. But not funny in that it makes Taylor laugh. Because those movies are just disturbing."

"Hey!" Taylor glared at him.

"Disturbing isn't necessarily bad. But he has a point." I had to agree.

"Marx Brothers," Sid suggested. "I used to..watch those all the time."

"Do we even own the Marx Brothers, man? We ain't all old like you." Quincy winked.

"The Aunts definitely have 'Duck Soup,'" I remembered. The Marx Brothers were from the 1930s, yes. But they still made me laugh.

We all settled into our spots. Quincy and Taylor on the couch, me in a rocker, and Sid in his Chair.

Just then, the front door opened.

"Good heavens. I should have known not to trust Kippie with the household. Look at how late you all are up!" Aunt Chasey was home.

"Look how late YOU'VE been out!" Quincy retorted.

"Sorry, Chase, we had a movie to watch," said Sid.

"And me to entertain!" said Taylor.

"And you'd better tell US what Mr. Meneses did to keep you up past midnight!" Quincy practically screeched.

"For your information, we looked at the stars together. Mr. Meneses is an honorable man."

"Do you at least call him by his first name when you're with him?" Sid wanted to know.

"Of course, Sid." Aunt Chasey rolled her eyes. "Now let me go get my tea and we can all have our fill of idle gossip."

She left the room, and it was quiet for a few moments.

Then Taylor spoke. "So do men really think of sex every five seconds?"

I looked at her and blinked. "I think it was every seven."

Quincy and Sid were laughing.

"More than that, honey," Quincy giggled.

"Women think about it JUST as MUCH," Sid said strongly.

If not more, said the voice.

"I just can't believe it could literally be every 5..er..7 seconds."

I giggled. "It must be an average."

"Really though, how is that? It's like..I mean, in the middle of like, math class, how do you suddenly start thinking about sex?"

"It doesn't take much," Sid confessed.

"In math class I can REALLY understand because in that class I'm trying to think of ANYTHING else," I said.

"Or you might get reminded if your teacher writes a big 'one' on the board," Quincy snickered. "Or a zero, if that's your preference."

"Only YOU would associate numbers with genitals," I said.

"That's a little too basic for me," said Taylor.

"Or the infinity symbol," Sid remarked.

"Sid likes his women curvy," Quincy purred.

Taylor shook her head. "This is the best place ever. No one ever thinks my questions are weird here."

"Sex isn't weird," Sid told her.

Taylor rolled her eyes. "Especially at my age when we teens are curious about these things, right? EVERYONE says that."

Sid shook his head. "I don't think how much you think about sex depends on your age. I'm pretty old."

"Are you admitting to something?" I wanted to know.

"It depends on your libido, not how old you are!" gushed Quincy. "And how hot your partner is. Like, if it were Sid—"

"Harassment," Sid growled.

"Holy crap! That was awesome!" Taylor exclaimed.

He looked at her. "What?"

"You growled. It sounded so real."

"Thanks. I think," said Sid.

"Okay, I'm here. Sorry boys, no more X-rated conversations." Aunt Chasey entered, kettle and cups on a tray for us. When Chasey did tea, she did tea right. Honey, sugar, milk, lemon, cinnamon, and all kinds of tea. Usually.

"I've brought out green and chamomile, for health and a good night's rest."

"It's a little late for that, Chase."

"I always keep up hope, Dominick. You know that."

"My mom used to always read me Peter Rabbit, and he had to drink chamomile tea at the end of the story because he felt sick and needed to sleep," Taylor remembered.

"Aw man! We used to read that to Phyllis! 'Stay out of Mr. McGregor's garden!' Aw Chasey, can we get another little kid in the house? That was the greatest." Quincy held up a defensive hand. "Not that I undermine The Shopping Years. Thirteen until you DIE, baby."

"Thanks Quincy." I rolled my eyes.

"Did she ever burn any of the books?" Taylor wanted to know.

"She set the couch on fire once," Sid shared.

"Dominick has always loved that memory," Aunt Chasey told her.

"Philly was a great kid. But I can't say I regret she's grown," said Sid.

I looked at him. "What do you mean?"

"You're someone I wouldn't have liked to miss out on knowing, Philly."

"I agree," said Aunt Chasey. She looked at me lovingly.

Taylor looked at me. "You little devil you."

I looked to the floor. When I wanted everyone's attention, it was near impossible to obtain it. But when it was the last thing I wanted, everyone gave it to me.

"I do wish we'd met you before, Taylor. Phyllis had such a hard time in elementary school," Chasey began.

"Aunt Chasey," I muttered.

"I have an excellent idea. Let's change the subject," announced Taylor.

Chasey waved her hand. "It's just as well girls, I need to get to sleep."

"But what about your big date?" Quincy demanded.

"I will most certainly tell you all about it tomorrow." She left quickly.

We all sat for a moment.

Sid yawned quietly. "Shuteye," he murmured. "I need to sleep, guys."

"Who gets to clean up the tea?" I wanted to know.

Sid looked at the tray. "I say we take care of it in the morning."

Taylor yawned now. "I agree. Sleep sounds very good."

"It was the damn chamomile," Quincy muttered. "I'll get the tray guys, go on up."

"Thank you SO MUCH, Quincy," I said, already on the stairs.

Sid looked up at us. "Night you two."

A bit later, Taylor and I settled down and got into my bed.

"Oh my God, I'm tired," I whispered, because even my voice was exhausted.

"Uh huh," Taylor yawned. Then, "So you're gonna go out with Eric?"

"I guess, if he decides to make it an official thing."

"Do you like him enough?"

"I like him a lot."

"Ah."

I looked up at the ceiling.

"I have to tell you something." Taylor's tone became serious out of nowhere. "I'm really scared of Mary, Phyllis. People who can get into your mind aren't supposed to exist, they're really not, and I don't ever want to see one again." Taylor's voice shook and I could tell she was struggling to speak without crying.

"It'll be all right, Tay. No one is going to force you to ever even *stand* near her again, okay?" As unawkwardly as possible, I squeezed her shoulder. (I was very careful to make sure it was her shoulder.) "If she does anything really terrible, we can get her some sort of help."

"What kind of help?! I could never get her help, Phyllis. I never want to deal with her again."

"You won't ever have to, Taylor. I promise. I won't let her come near you. Neither will Tony." I paused. "Did you tell Tony?"

"Y-yeah."

"What'd he say?"

"He said it was creepy and told me I should stay away from her. I was like, 'Well duh!'"

"Just don't tell him about the fire thing."

She sighed exasperatedly. "*Fine,*" she said, as if it were a terrible thing to have to do.

I laughed just a little, and paused to yawn again. "Let's go to bed, Taylor. The Aunts say everything looks better after nine hours of sleep."

"So we're shooting for noonish?"

"Probably later by now."

"Think we can do it?"

"I don't know."

"Yeah, sleep's pretty strenuous."

"Start on go?"

"How about on stop?"

"Okay." I reached up to turn off the light. "One, two, three, stop!" I turned it off.

* * *

I could hear the phone ringing in one of the Aunts' rooms from my bed in my sleep, but I was hardly awake so the sound melded into my dream. In the dream, Sid and Eric and Zorro from art class were all in my living room.

"Someone's ringing the doorbell," Zorro told me.

"I think she can hear it too," Eric said coolly.

I realized later that I should have known it was a dream; we don't have a doorbell.

"I'll get it, it's hurting my ears." Sid rose and opened the door.

"I killed. Take the blood off of my hands, Sid." The woman at the door was unfamiliar to me, but her hands were red.

"What the hell did you do now?" Zorro yelled at the girl.

"I killed you," she told him. She was pretty, with black hair and green eyes that had catlike pupils. Diamond-shaped rather than circular.

Zorro fell to the floor. Sid slammed the door in the girl's face.

Eric took my hand. "Let's go."

But whoever she was kept ringing the doorbell.

Until Aunt Kippie woke me up and handed me the phone, which I'd been hearing as a doorbell in my sleep.

"It's Key, dear. You should be up by now anyway."

I took it. "Hello?"

"Hey Phyllis. You wanna go to the mall with me and Jesse?"

"Taylor's here."

"Good, I was gonna call her too."

"When do you want to go?"

"Like in an hourish?"

Like in an hourish. I looked at the clock. It was 12:45.

"So at like 2?"

"Yeah."

"Lemme' run it by the Aunts." I set down the phone. "Aunt Kippie?"

"What?"

I asked about the mall, then went back to Key.

"As long as we're back before six. I have to be at school at 6:30."

"Bring your stuff and we'll drop you off on the way."

Sounded good to me. "Okay. See you soon."

"Without a doubt." She hung up.

Taylor stretched and cleared her throat. She looked over at me, her hair sticking up in all directions. "What just happened?"

"Want to go to the mall with Key?"

"Sure." Taylor lay back down.

"Not gonna get up?"

"It's Key. She'll be late."

I laughed a little, and lay back down as well. "One more show."

"Yeah. Aw, are you gonna be sad?"

"Yeah." I paused. "I'm not sure how to treat Eric in school, now."

"You said last night you'd go out with him."

"If he really asks me. I mean, what if he decides he doesn't want a girlfriend?"

"Oh! Oh my God, I totally forgot." Taylor dove over the side of the bed and rummaged through the backpack her mom had dropped off the previous evening. She pulled out a CD.

"I made this yesterday. It's a mix of some old pop and R&B stuff. It's all mushy, sappy music that makes you fall in love," Taylor told me, handing me the CD.

I laughed a little. "So that I'll fall in love with Eric?"

"Yup. Think how convenient *that* would be."

"I don't think I can do it, Tay."

"I know, I know, and it might just make the Sid thing worse. But I figured it was worth a try and felt like listening to old pop songs. I can only get away with it if I say it's for someone else." Taylor smiled.

"You didn't put any Billy Joel songs on there, did you?" I asked.

"No, why?"

"He tends to make love sound like a problem to solve."

"Love *is* a problem."

"Since when has it been a problem for you?" I demanded, stretching. "You're pretty happy with Tony."

She shrugged. "It's just so unpredictable, Phyllis. There's no way to tell what'll happen. It's easy to say you'll be with someone forever, and it's easy to say you'll never be with the person you want most. But you don't know for sure. Death happens, other people come into the picture, and *you* may only want someone until you can actually have them."

"You sound so experienced."

"No, I've just had my share of unpredicted events."

I nodded and gave her a hug. "How about some breakfast?"

"Oh yeah!" I'd known that that would cheer her up.

The kitchen was empty when we entered. Aunt Chasey must have been doing something churchly. But...I knew where Quincy kept his Heath Bar Cookies.

"How about cookies and hot chocolate and strawberries?" I'd been raised to incorporate something somewhat healthy into every meal.

"Mmm, sounds good to me."

I took out two mugs and poured in some milk, then put in the chocolate.

"Do you microwave those, then?" Taylor asked, tilting her head to one side.

I smiled and shook my head. “Nope, watch.” I cupped each mug, and after about 30 seconds the water began to bubble.

“Holy *ish*!” Taylor exclaimed. “Since when can you do *that*?”

“I just found out in February, thanks to Sid.”

“Isn’t it awesome?” Sid came in from the living room.

“Your hearing is uncanny,” Taylor told him. “But yeah, it is.”

“Sorry.” He looked us over. “Wow. You guys just woke up.”

We both smiled. “Yep.”

He grinned. “That’s talent.”

After breakfast, Taylor and I got ready to go to the mall. Key and Jesse arrived at 2:15. Ish.

Jesse played his music loud (nothing wrong with that) so that we had to yell to each other.

“Can we go to the bookstore first?” Taylor shouted.

“Which one?” Jesse yelled.

“The bigger one!”

“Barnes and Nobles!” Key told him loudly.

“There’s only *one* Noble! It’s Barnes and Noble!” Taylor screeched.

“Whatever!” Key yelled.

“She’s right though,” Jesse told her. He had to tell her twice, practically shrieking the second time.

“So can we go there?” Taylor demanded.

“Yes!” Jesse shouted.

“Thank you!” Taylor screamed.

So, upon arrival, the four of us headed straight for Barnes and Noble. Jesse and Key went to look at CDs and DVDs. Taylor and I wandered about aimlessly.

Looking over the books, I didn’t spy anything tempting. I usually get books at the library or for Christmas, a habit started long ago when I was saving money for a keyboard. Now I was saving for a car.

First I just had to learn to drive.

Unlike me, Taylor was a book addict, and had something to say about every book she saw. She picked one off a shelf. “Phyllis, this author calls himself F. Paul Wilson. What do you think his friends call him. F? or F. Paul?”

"F. Paul, time for dinner!" I giggled.

"I wonder what the F. stands for." Taylor put the book back.

"You know," she said, "there are certain books I can't buy. It's not that the books are bad; some of them are probably really good. I'm just a bigot."

I raised an eyebrow. "Bigot?"

"About books."

"I thought you'd read anything."

"Oh I would. I just don't buy anything." She looked around and pointed to a book on a bestseller table. It looked like one of those action/romance/murder type deals. "Look at this author. *She's* the reason I can't buy her book."

"She looks like your mom."

"Yes she does. And my mom would never—" Taylor scanned the book info "—never *ever* write a book like this." She replaced the book, looked around for another. "And this one," she said after she'd read the back. "This one is about a girl, narrated by a girl. But a man wrote it."

"Doesn't Stephen King do that? And Harry Potter?" God forgive me, but I'd never read a Stephen King or Harry Potter book. I don't have enough patience and energy for all the pages. And I've decided my life is weird enough as it is.

"They're different."

"How's that?"

"Stephen King switches." She grinned. "And my mother abhors him. I just bought his books in the first place to piss her off." She held up a defensive hand. "But I *do* read them. And Harry Potter is too good to apply stupid rules to."

I pulled out a Janet Evanovich book. "What about her?"

"Her main character's hilarious. But I get pissed because she eats donuts and cake all throughout the books, and she's still being...sought after by guys."

"She probably works out."

"It never says she does."

"Well I don't tell everyone whenever I go for a walk or eat something less fattening than usual, but I still do."

Taylor snorted. "If you got fat it'd probably just go to your chest."

"You're lucky I don't say anything bad about you skinny people."

She laughed. Taylor and I understood each other.

Taylor didn't buy any books in the end, but Jesse got another loud CD.

We decided to eat after we left the bookstore. After much debate, we settled on fast food.

"Man. I missed cheeseburgers," Taylor said, biting into hers.

"Maybe you should *eat* them more often," Jesse suggested.

"No, it would take away their charm."

Key smiled at Taylor, then fed Jesse a chicken nugget immersed in barbecue sauce. "Phyllis is dating Eric, did you hear?"

"Do you know Eric?" Taylor asked Jesse.

"I'm not—" I started to say.

"Yeah, I know Eric, he's that guy who plays with Tony." (Taylor giggled at that.) "Yeah, he's cool." Jesse laughed a little. "He kicked Tony's ass at Guitar Hero."

Taylor and I looked at him blankly.

"Video game," Key explained.

We nodded. "Oh."

I paused. "I'm not his girlfriend, at the moment."

"He'll ask you out. Tony said he's crazy about you," Taylor said.

"But will *she* accept?" Jesse reminded her.

"Most likely," I said.

"He must have mad skill with his hands if he beat *Tony* at Guitar Hero," Key pointed out.

"Is that what you look for in a boyfriend, Key?" Taylor teased.

Key laughed. "No, Jesse's a butterfingers."

"No I'm not!"

We all laughed because Jesse's voice went up high when he argued.

"Seriously. He must have a good connection between his brain and his body."

"Do you have to make *everything* sound dirty? It's called hand-eye coordination!" Jesse insisted.

"It only sounds dirty because that's the way you think," Key told him.

"He must be smart, right? Smart guys are deeply appreciated," said Taylor.

The connection between his body and his brain. The connection between the present and the future. My connection of everything to Sid. He had to tell me about the connections *he* knew. After Grease was over.

"Are you guys coming to the play tonight?" I asked.

"Aah, sure why not?" Jesse took a sip of his Dr. Pepper.

"I've hardly had any time to think about it," I realized with disappointment. "I can't believe it's over."

"Yeah, you dedicate like half your life to these things for two months and then you perform it three times," Key remarked. "But, you will now have more time to dedicate to your wonderful friends. Except maybe Mary."

"What's going on with her anyway?" I asked.

"She told me she's not coming to school anymore. She keeps saying she can't find people who 'know' and 'understand' her and shit. I was like, 'Duh!' It's not just the way she looks, it's the way she acts! She's not nice. She's really quiet and condescending. She gets *annoyed* with everyone." She shook her head. "But her parents told her they'd kick her out if she dropped out. Basically they were just like, 'Cut this shit out or you're gone.' I asked her if she wanted help, but she's so damn stubborn! I don't know what's going to happen."

"She's ripping her life apart." Taylor sighed.

"She's trying to change into someone else, but she's in the wrong environment to do so," I thought aloud.

"Well where do *you* suggest she do it?" Jesse wanted to know.

I looked at him blankly. "Well I mean, I don't know where exactly but I'm sure there's an appropriate place."

"Yeah. Like a coven," Taylor agreed.

"Don't go there," Key warned.

* * *

I was surprised that night by Sid waiting for me in the school's lobby after the show, not far from Key and Jesse.

"You were a bitch. High-five!" Jesse congratulated me.

I laughed. "Thanks." I slapped his hand.

Key rolled her eyes. "As always you were great, Phyllis. I'm sorry about him." She gestured to Jesse with her thumb.

I patted him on the shoulder. "I think he's all right."

"See?" Jesse gave Key an I-Told-You-So look.

Key hugged him, then me, and while she did, she whispered, "There's an incredibly hunky fellow standing by the door staring at you, Phyllis."

"Dark hair?" I whispered.

"Yuh-huh."

"Leather jacket?" I whispered hopefully.

"Yuh-huh."

"Looks like he might be able to hear us?"

"Yeah, actually. He kinda' looks like he's trying not to smile."

"That's Sid." My face—my entire being, truthfully—lit up.

"Holy fuckin' shit," she whispered. "You lucky ho."

"Such obscenity!" I gasped.

She giggled. "I swear a lot when overwhelmed by cuteness, as Taylor puts it."

"He must be giving me a ride home."

"You're lucky I'm with Jesse or I'd steal him."

"What about me?" Jesse demanded loudly.

Key looked at him. "I told her she can't have you." She gave him a kiss. "Thanks for taking me to the play tonight."

Key knew how to work the system.

"Thanks for coming guys, I'll see you later!" I waved to them.

"See ya!" they said.

"Hey Philly," Sid said as I approached. "Your friend has good taste."

"You're so humble."

"I'm just joking, babes. I've never found myself attractive. You, on the other hand..." He winked at me.

"Yes, I do find you attractive." I rolled my eyes.

"No, I meant I found *you* attractive, Philly. But don't get any ideas."

"You're just being nice."

"I'm just being honest."

We walked to the car.

"Wasn't there some sort of cast party?" Sid asked.

"Yeah, it was Saturday night." Obviously I had not attended.

"Why didn't you go?"

I sighed. "It was at the girl who plays Frenchie's house. So there was probably alcohol."

Sid nodded.

"Not that I planned to drink, but I mean, I guess...things happen, and I don't know how my system would react to alcohol," I explained.

"Usually drinks go down your esophagus, babes. Not your respiratory system."

I rolled my eyes. "I know, but I don't know what my system looks like, or what might intersect or just...I don't want something to go wrong and spontaneously combust."

He chuckled. "Understood." He glanced at me. "You ever worry that you'll get x-rayed someday and they'll find something?"

I shrugged. "Not really. Not yet."

"You handle yourself well, Philly."

"Thanks." Whatever he meant by that.

"You ever worry about how your system's gonna be affected if you start fooling around with guys in cars?"

"He only gave me a goodnight kiss, Sid."

"I know. That's why I ask beforehand."

"How old were you when you started 'fooling around'?"

He sighed, and admitted, "Probably about fifteen."

"You can't remember?"

He glared at me. "Can *you* remember 145 years ago?"

"I wasn't alive!"

"I was a different person."

"Wish I could've met your fifteen-year-old self. You must've been interesting."

He shrugged. "Not at all." He paused. "You seemed especially angry at the students tonight, Philly."

"I'm tired. It helps."

"You were up pretty late. Later than I recommend to mortals." Sid grinned.

"Do you sleep, Sid?" I raised an eyebrow.

His grin grew wider. "I don't have much else to do at night, babes. But I can go for a while without it, if needed."

We were silent for a moment.

Then a thought sprang into my mind. "Can you change into the wolf at will?"

He didn't answer for a few seconds. Then, "Yes. But I don't do it often because it's tiring to change back."

"I can imagine," I murmured, yawning at the mention of tiredness.

"Philly honey, you're gonna be dead tomorrow."

"What else is new?"

Sid smiled.

Suddenly, I remembered my dream. "I had a funny dream last night."

He glanced at me. "What happened?"

"I can't remember much. But a girl came to our door and I think she wanted something bad to happen to you."

"Who was it?"

"She never said her name. Just a girl, I guess."

"Not Anna?"

"No. She was white."

"What'd she look like?"

"She had blood on her hands."

"Was she drinking it?"

"No. She didn't look unhappy about it though."

"Well what did she look like?"

"She had black hair and green eyes. Her eyes were weird though."

Sid looked expectant.

"They were like...Johnny's eyes."

"Your cat?"

"Yeah."

"Jesus. What'd she say?"

"Um..I'm not sure."

"Anything?"

"Well..she asked you to take the blood off her hands and you slammed the door in her face."

"She does sound familiar." Sid looked at me. "I never told you what Stacia Frobisher looks like."

"No, I don't think so. Why?"

"She's got cat eyes."

"What about black hair?"

"She's a blonde. Maybe your mind was incorporating details you know about my other failed endeavors of love."

"You poor man." I rolled my eyes.

"Did she have pointed nails?"

I laughed. "No, she definitely wasn't Anna."

Sid sighed. "Anna's probably the next person whose face I'll have to slam a door in."

"She's supposed to come next month. And why are you slamming a door in her face?"

"Not literally, I hope. But Anna sets me off. And I have a hard enough time staying out of arguments. With the wolf, it's almost impossible."

"That's why people run away when you're angry?"

Sid grinned. "I suppose so. I blame the wolf."

"Is the *wolf* still in love with her?"

Sid chuckled. "The wolf wants to eat her alive."

I raised my eyebrows.

"Just kidding." He took two heavy breaths. "You mind if I put on some music?" He waved the question away. "Never mind, I don't have to ask a girl like you, do I?" He reached into a small compartment and pulled out a CD to put in.

I braced myself for screaming music. I could appreciate almost any kind of music, but after all the 50s sounds I'd just been smothered in, the change might trigger an aneurism. Instead my ears received the light fluttery yet soothing sounds of Stardust.

"A girl like me?"

"Yes. A girl like you, who's into music."

"You're into music too. I saw your CD collection."

Sid nodded. "Music helps with my mood swings."

"What do you mean?"

"If I need to satisfy the wolf when it's angry, the loud music helps. This stuff," he gestured to the radio, "helps me calm down."

"You need to calm down?"

Sid nodded.

"Why?"

"Several reasons."

"Can you tell me?"

Sid grinned. "Anna's one."

"What else?"

His grin grew wider. "Can't tell you."

I sighed. "Why is Anna one?"

"I'm prepared to argue with her. It's inevitable, we're going to have some yelling matches."

"If you've prepared yourself, why are you stressed about it?"

Sid glanced at me. "Anna never makes things easy. And she'll never admit to mistakes." He paused. "I have your deepest confidence, right babes?"

My breath caught. "Of course."

He paused, then said, "I'm afraid she's going to ask me to come back to her again."

"Hard to resist?" I inquired, discouraged.

Sid shook his head. "Hell no. But even at my age it's very difficult to sidestep awkward situations. She knows it won't ever work again, right now as we speak. But when she sees me, she'll think of me as proof she made a mistake."

"How?"

Sid paused. "I think she thought we'd last. She thought I was *it*. And when she found out what a monster I can be, she knew I wasn't the one for her. So now she thinks of us as a failure."

"Why should that bother her so much? She didn't know."

Sid sighed. "I told her everything, babes. She said she could handle it, even though she hadn't experienced it yet. Once she realized what it was really like, she realized she couldn't stay. I would never hold that against her, but I think she holds it against herself."

"I'm sorry, Sid."

"Don't be Philly. I didn't regret it until I realized I'd have to see her again. But she's *always* regretted it. She blamed me for our split." He paused. "Obviously a god damn lot of it *was* my fault. But not all of it. She might try to get me back so that she can show that she was right, that it was just that I got scared and left, but she knew I'd come back." He shook his head. "Or some shit. Maybe she just wants to be irresistible. But women can be just as afraid of love as men can."

"I think it depends on the situation. I can see being afraid to be with someone for a lifetime. But your lifetime...that must be terrifying to some people."

He gave me a sidelong glance. "Can't disagree with that," he muttered.

"But it must be even worse to have times when you think you'll be alone for eternity."

Sid was surprised. He gaped at me for an uncomfortably long time, considering he was driving. Then he turned back to the road quickly.

"It's hard to know what'll happen in life," he said. "You're sure you know what's going on, and it turns out to be completely different."

Witches.

Upon my arrival back to school, I was showered with unexpected compliments from unexpected people. My friends all told me I'd been great, which reassured me that I'd picked the right friends. But random people in the halls on my way to class congratulated me on pulling off my impression of Mrs. Highman, asked me if I'd been "the teacher in Grease," told me I was hilarious. Even Mr. Hamil told me I'd given quite a performance.

When I reported this later to Mrs. Reygor, she told me, "No matter how small your part is, someone will always notice you. Someone will always be looking. You did a very good job, Phyllis."

In lunch we all noticed that Mary wasn't in school again, or, at least, in lunch or swim class. Taylor sat with us (I had a feeling she'd go elsewhere when Mary returned) and so did Liz.

"Has she done anything to you?" I asked her, thinking of Sid's with theory. Or, probably, fact.

Liz raised an eyebrow. "Done anything? What could she do? All she does is give me dirty looks."

"So why don't you sit with us anymore? There's more to it than that you two just aren't talking," Key deduced.

"Liz is moping. She knows what she did was wrong and that she has to eventually apologize," said Helen.

"Like I can apologize. Like I *will* apologize. Mary's the one who should apologize. It's like she just decided one day, 'Hey, I think I'll be a freak.' I swear, she was herself one second, and then she wasn't!"

"Maybe this is who she's always been," I suggested.

They all looked at me like I had just grown a new nose, squinting the way I had at so many terribly confusing math problems.

"Phyllis, this might sound offensive, and I'm really really sorry if it does, but you haven't known Mary as long as we have. She's never been *this* weird," said Helen.

"Though that doesn't justify what Liz did," Key added.

Liz sighed loudly.

"She's been weird before?" Taylor asked. Always the little detective.

"Yeah, but everyone has their weird moments," Key said.

"What'd she do that was weird?"

"She'd say stuff like, 'Religious people are stupid' and then tell us later how we needed to accept Jesus," Liz recalled.

"She'd overblow things. So to speak," said Key. "She'd get extremely mad at people. But she never got mad at any of us until Liz decided to be an idiot!"

"She got that mad at me once," Helen said.

"Really? Why?" asked Key.

"It wasn't ever...I'm not even sure. But I think it was because I called her normal. Or average. Same thing."

I shook my head quickly. "No they're not."

Helen frowned. "Why not?"

I had been insulted a great deal in my time and had pondered everything everyone could ever call you. I knew about average and normal.

"Well...normal's kind of safe-sounding. It makes it sound like nothing's wrong with you and you don't change much. It doesn't usually have a bad tone to it."

"But it also might imply that you're predictable," Tay quipped.

"Yeah," I said, "but it's a level above average. Average insinuates, like, dullness, kind of. You know, you're average. Nothing great or special or exciting or anything. Okay, maybe good, but in no way awesome or amazing."

"Average is like when a guy you really like tells you he just wants to be friends," Key said with a sad sigh.

Apparently everyone could relate to that.

"So what'd she do when she was mad?" Taylor got us back to Helen's story.

"She got all obsessed with her family, she started looking up her name on the internet and shit. She said she found stuff that was strange and cool, but she didn't show it to me."

"Mary's like that. She never wants to show you the evidence," Key said. "She got mad at me when I was 5—she was 7 or 8—and I told her Santa wasn't real."

"SANTA ISN'T REAL?!" Taylor cried, rising up from her seat dramatically.

Some people turned and looked, but mostly it was just our table that looked at her, almost laughing, almost sure she was kidding. But with Taylor, you could never be sure.

She grinned and sat back down.

I wondered if Mary had found out she was a witch from a website.

"I wonder if we'll ever see her again," Taylor said.

"Why wouldn't we?" Liz snapped.

"She might make herself disappear."

"Why do you keep making witch references?" I demanded. I would never have mentioned the witch thing to Taylor; then I'd have to tell her about Sid. I wanted to know how she'd come up with it on her own.

"Who else could force you to just say something? There was no knife to my throat or gun to my head. And it happened to Key, too."

"Taylor.." Key's voice was reminiscent of a growl.

"You know it happened Key. There's more to this than anyone's saying, and I am not going to ask her. One of you has to know something."

"That didn't happen, Taylor," said Key.

"You're in denial."

"I don't know anything about Mary being a witch or whatever, Taylor," said Helen, "but—"

"We wouldn't put it past her," Liz grumbled.

I knew something. But I said nothing.

Felt-Tipped Pens.

There was a huge bouquet of flowers resting on my disturbingly perfectly made bed (an Aunt must've delivered the flowers) along with a card. It read:

These roses are red
These violets are blue
Meryl Streep won the Academy Award
And so should you!
Love,
Quincy and Damien (authors of the beautiful poem)
Sid Aunt Chasey We love you Phyllis!
Aunt Kippie
Great job honey!

I giggled.

"I didn't write the poem," Sid called from his room.

"I know," I called back.

"I picked out the tiger lilies though."

I laughed. "Thank you Sid."

There were blue lilies, tiger lilies, roses, tulips. They were all beautiful.

I went to Sid's doorway. "Thanks Sid. When did you guys get this? Where are the Aunts?"

He was at his desk. He turned and smiled. "We got it today. Your Aunts are at a funeral."

My face fell. Great. "Whose?"

"A man from the hospital where Kippie works. One of her retired colleagues. His sister just called to tell her this morning." He paused. "I heard the phone conversation."

"Are they okay? Was it anyone they knew?"

"Not well. But you know your Aunts. They want to help everyone. They probably brought a casserole and a sympathy card signed by the entire hospital."

"She probably brought lasagna, a salad, and fudge. And a really nice personal note with a funny story about the man that died in it, plus the card."

Sid nodded. "You know your Aunts."

I smiled. "They're good at ...goodness." I shrugged, unable to come up with a better word.

"Yeah." Sid rolled his eyes. "That must be the sole reason they took Quincy in."

Uh oh. "What'd he do?"

"Started bugging me about being single again."

I was about to point out that Quincy only thought being single was a problem for others when he was with someone, when it dawned on me.

"Did Quincy set you up with Anna?"

Sid grinned. "No Philly, I walked into that mess myself."

"I guess he's lucky he didn't."

"She did tell Quincy a lot of things about us though. He was always trying to give me advice I didn't ask for. He was only in his early 20s then."

Hmm. I wondered if Quincy would remember any of the things Anna told him.

Sid sighed. "I shouldn't be telling you this. You're just like Quincy."

My eyebrows shot up. "Really?" I didn't want Sid to see me as a gay man.

He smiled. "Only in that you feel no shame in searching other people's rooms."

"What did he say to you?"

"He'd tell me everything Anna complained about. But it was never anything she hadn't told me herself. One thing about Anna, she never lied. She was never indirect."

There were so many other things I had to ask Sid about. Magical creatures and what he knew about them and what dangers they put the rest of us in. But I had learned that with Sid, it was wisest to ask questions when he was already on the topic. And when I married Sid—

You poor deluded girl, said the voice.

—I would want to know about his past relationships. Especially Anna, who was exceptionally skilled at stealing men away.

"Did Anna initiate your relationship?" I asked him.

He shook his head. "No, that was me. She flirted and I fueled it." He paused. "You look disappointed in me."

"Oh...no," I lied.

"I learned from my mistake, babes," he promised.

"Why was it such a mistake?"

"Because we held onto it for so long. We couldn't accept that it wasn't working. And we came out hating each other." He sighed. "Don't ever stick with someone if all of your conversations turn to arguments."

"Thanks."

Then Sid brightened. "How's Eric?"

"I didn't see him today." I felt a drop inside as I realized it. He must not have wanted to date me after all.

Sid frowned. "Really?"

I nodded.

"Did you want to see him?"

Come to think of it, Eric had been the first thing on my mind when I walked into school. But I'd forgotten once I'd started getting complimented, and then after lunch I'd been thinking about Mary and Sid.

I shrugged. "I don't know."

"You gonna go out with him if he asks?"

First of all, how many people were going to ask me this?! And what the hell did Sid care? I wanted to yell at him. How could he be so irresistible and annoying at the same time? It was painful; he'd kissed me, "oh that was just a test," and then he tried to be my close friend, but, "I'm too old for you, Philly."

"What's it matter?"

"I just want to know if I'm gonna have to stay here and keep an eye on you."

I rolled my eyes. "You won't have to either way."

"I doubt that. Once you've gotten into physical stuff for the first time, you don't want to stop."

"You can't even remember your first girlfriend, Sid," I reminded him.

"It was literally a lifetime ago! And I wasn't in love with her."

"What were you?"

Sid grinned. "Sinful."

"Well why would I do the same things you did?"

"You're an intense person, especially because of that fire. You won't be able to stop easily."

I sighed. "Isn't that how it is for everybody?"

"Yes. Which means with you, it'll be even worse."

I folded my arms. "How do you know?"

"Because the fire is affected by your emotions. When you physically desire a release, it's going to be amplified by the need to release the fire. So, you'll want it twice as much."

He was very clearly talking about sex. I felt extremely awkward, mainly because that was what I constantly thought about doing with him.

"That was very...scientific," I said.

He smiled. "It's just an educated guess. But the chance is all the more reason for everyone to watch out."

I sighed. "Sid, how old were you when you lost your virginity?"

"Men are different. We can't bear children."

"What about the girl you lost it too?" I gave him a look. I wasn't going to back down.

Sid sighed. "She didn't get pregnant."

"I'm not even Eric's girlfriend!" I protested. "I don't even feel that much for him!"

"Cut me some slack, babes."

"Well then I'm going to do the same thing when you have a girlfriend."

Sid smiled sadly. "I won't."

I folded my arms. "Why not?"

"Because as of now I'm having trouble finding my bearings in that area."

"Finding your bearings? Why don't you date another werewolf?"

Why the fuck was I encouraging him to date?!

"It doesn't feel—" He sighed. "Philly, what do you care?"

"Why shouldn't I?"

"I shouldn't be having this type of conversation with you."

"Yes you should."

He grinned. "Why's that?"

A lot of whys were in this conversation.

"You said I was your friend."

"And?"

"And you should be able to tell your friend...stuff."

"I don't want you getting any ideas. You might start thinking it's okay to have sex at 16."

"I'm not going to have sex with Eric, Sid."

"You don't know that, babes."

"Neither do you." I folded my arms. "When would you recommend that I have sex, anyway?!"

"When you're 18."

I raised an eyebrow. Being raised by two somewhat God-fearing women, it'd been drilled into my mind that I should not have premarital sex. I'd never had the nerve to inquire about the fact that neither of them were married. "What about marriage?"

"I've never been married in my life, babes. If sex without marriage is a sin, then I'm way past going to hell by now." Sid held up a defensive hand. "It's a good idea, though, I presume, and if that's what you believe, then it's probably the best thing to do."

"I don't think I do," I confessed. It was a terrible thing. But the fact was, if right at that moment Sid had offered to screw me, no way was I going to say, "You have to marry me first."

I didn't tell that to Sid, though.

"Really?" He was surprised.

"Yeah."

"I can't believe it."

My eyes widened. "Are you going to tell the Aunts?"

He gave me a look. "Philly. If I told them about all the talks we've had and what they contained, they'd have thrown me out."

"What for?" I knew perfectly well what for.

"For kissing you."

"You're welcome to do it again."

"No, I'm not." He looked into my eyes. "You need someone your own age. Think about if I looked my age. I'm an old man." He blinked. "I'm a dead man."

"Sid. You know you're nothing like an old man. You're young no matter what."

"That may be. But even at 26, I'd still be too old for you." He paused. "What is it you like about me so much?"

I didn't know what to say. It took a minute. Finally I just said, "What's not to like?"

He grinned. "You're good for building up my confidence."

"Why did you kiss me?" I blurted out.

It took him a few seconds to answer and I stared at him as he assembled the words in his mind. Or whatever the hell he was doing that delayed his response.

But, of course, he stared right back.

"Because I don't have enough self-control, babes. The wolf wants flesh. Yours was the closest. And the preferred." He grinned again. "You're young and you smell good and you taste good." He paused. "It won't happen again, Philly. Next time I'll be smart enough not to get so close to you when the wolf is strong. I'm sorry."

I nodded. Great. "Thanks for the flowers," I said, and left.

An hour later, Eric called, and said he'd missed school because of a music competition. He asked me if I wanted to keep going out with him.

"Definitely," I said.

Eric paused. "Phyllis...I really want to be your boyfriend."

* * *

"You should have said no, since it was what Sid wanted," Taylor told me on the phone later.

I'd just told her some fragments of the conversation with Sid. I had brought the phone into an empty room in section 2 of the upstairs so that Sid would have no chance of hearing my conversation, accident or not.

She was telling me I should have said no to Eric, since Sid had told me to say yes.

"Wait a minute. You just told me, like, a night ago, to go out with Eric."

"I didn't know Sid and you had such deep conversations about your feelings for him."

"Deep?! We hardly touched the surface! He thinks it's a childish crush."

"And you think it's everlasting love."

I flinched out of habit.

"Phyllis?"

"Sorry, I always expect Quincy to start singing if I hear a line from a song he likes." I paused. "So I'm Eric's girlfriend."

"Did you do it because you like him, or did you do it for Sid?"

I sighed. "I..I don't know. I really like Eric."

Taylor cackled. "Plus, he offered you his CHERRY!"

* * *

"Oh Phyllis, that's wonderful!" Aunt Chasey paused. "I presume he is a gentleman and everything you deserve?"

"Aw Chasey they ain't gettin' married!" Quincy was eating strawberry ice cream out of the carton. I'd just told the Aunts, Quincy, and Damien that I was going out with Eric.

"I certainly hope not. Not now, anyway," Kippie added that last part in quickly.

Aunt Chasey frowned. "I'd like to make sure this young man is worthy of my little girl."

"You sound like a father," Damien told her.

"Father, mother, guardian, aunt. No matter what I am, Phyllis is my child. I helped raise her and I'm proud of her. And she'll always be a little girl to me."

"Don't try for applause, Chasey, you're not going to get any," Kippie quipped.

Chasey tapped her very lightly on the head with her rolling pin. She was making the crust of a pie. Yes, she was making an entire pie from scratch.

"It's a good idea, though," Kippie admitted.

"What is?" I wanted to know.

"Finding out about Eric."

"We'll have him over for dinner Wednesday night!" Chasey said excitedly.

"Oooh, can I be there?" Damien wanted to know.

"You know you're always welcome, Damien dear," Chasey reassured.

"After all, we did the same thing to you!" Kippie chortled.

"Who else is going to be there?" I demanded.

"Whoever shows up, Phyllis, as always. You just make sure Eric can come."

I should have expected this. That any time I had a boyfriend, he would be integrated into our little house family.

I'd never thought I'd have to deal with any issues related to having a boyfriend. If I'd been asked on a date last year, I would have known it was a prank. I'd been the shunned girl that so many parenting books and Lifetime movies talk about. Somehow I was starting to become the normal teenage girl with friends that I'd envied but known I could never be.

Of course, now that werewolves were real, I realized that anything could happen.

* * *

"Felt-tipped pens are my new favorite thing," Key announced after she finished putting on her make-up in the school bathroom Tuesday morning. She lifted her pant leg to reveal an elaborate design she'd drawn on her ankle.

"That'll come right off," Helen told her.

"You'll get fuckin' ink poisoning," said Liz.

"They're my favorite thing, too," said Taylor. She pulled one from her pocket and clicked the cap on and off.

"Oh my God, I love doing that!" Key squealed, pulling her own pen out of her cargo pants.

"The Aunts are making me invite Eric over for dinner," I said solemnly.

"What's wrong with that?" Taylor wondered.

"How can you look at Eric's mug with Sid living in your house?" Key gushed. She was very, very hyper. According to Jesse, it was his fault for giving her Espresso early that morning.

"Eric's a hottie," Liz shot back.

"Sid's pretty good-lookin', Liz," Taylor told her.

But I was happy that Liz was defending my boyfriend.

"I'm rather happy with Eric's appearance," I informed them. "but I don't want to sit there while they interrogate him."

"I want to have dinner at your house," said Taylor. "They can interrogate me. And when did you see Sid, Key?"

"Sunday night. He picked Phyllis up after the play. What is he, like, 22?"

"26."

"I can never keep track of his age," Taylor muttered.

"Ahhhhhh wow. I want to eat dinner at your house, too," said Key.

"This guy can't be that gorgeous," said Helen.

"He's beyond gorgeous," I admitted.

"I'm telling Eric."

"Oh shut up Helen," Liz told her.

"You better watch out Liz, Mary's here today."

Liz frowned. "Is not."

"She is," Key confirmed sadly.

"I've got to go," Liz said.

Taylor slumped down on the floor of the bathroom. "I was hoping she'd dropped out," she whispered to me.

"I wasn't thinking about her," I confessed. Since seeing my wonderful beautiful awesomerriffic bouquet, I hadn't had a single thought about Mary.

"Lucky you," said Taylor.

"I don't see her being here much longer," said Key honestly as Liz departed. "She's just a different person. Her eyes aren't even the same color."

"It's called contacts," said Helen.

Key shook her head. "No. Her eyes are black. I'll bet she's taking some drug that makes her pupils amazingly huge."

Taylor rolled her eyes. "Key, that is not what she's doing."

"What do you think she's doing?" Helen demanded.

"Maybe she's possessed," I suggested.

"Who's possessed?" Frenchie (the girl who played her in "Grease") stepped out of a stall and strode to a sink to wash her hands. She looked at Taylor. "The most germs are on the floor," she told her.

"I know, beauty school dropout," said Taylor.

Frenchie grinned. "Was I okay?"

Tay nodded. "You were perfect."

Frenchie finished washing her hands. "Thanks." She patted my arm. "Phyllis here was the only other person who had to wear an awful wig. We bonded."

We did? I smiled and gave a quick agreeable laugh. "At least yours was pink." I didn't even know her real name.

She nodded. "So who are you guys talking about?"

"Do you really need to know, Sophia?" Helen asked. Apparently they knew each other.

"What if I catch it?"

Key coughed. "Ditz!" She coughed again with no word hidden in it, then said, "Sorry, sore throat."

"Scary Mary," Taylor told her.

"Oh wow. Yeah, that girl is pretty weird. But didn't she used to wear cute stuff?" Sophia asked.

"Yeah."

"Ew, why would you ever ruin yourself like that? See you girls later." She opened the door and bumped into Mary herself.

Mary glared at her.

"Watch it." Sophia hissed the words and stalked off. But I noticed, though she did it quickly, that Mary ran a hand through her hair and then touched Sophia's shoulder.

"Hi," Key said to her.

Mary walked in. "Talking about me?"

"What the fuck do you expect?!" Helen demanded. "Look at yourself!"

Mary was wearing a long dark blue duster that reached her ankles. Under it she wore a long black skirt and a white blouse. On her neck there was a splotch of ink that, coincidentally, looked as if written with a felt-tipped pen. It didn't look like Key's, though, it almost looked like a letter. She wore flesh lipstick and heavy black eyeliner. Her hair was pulled up and then fell directly down in white and black strands, almost like dreadlocks.

Mary looked very angry for a moment. She glared at Helen, then turned and stormed out of the bathroom.

I followed her, opening the door and saying, "Mary, wait." I caught up with her. She turned and looked at me.

"There's no point in being around anyone anymore," she said.

"Helen just doesn't understand, Mary."

Mary looked into my eyes.

Her eyes were, indeed, black.

Oh shit. Oh shit, could she see my thoughts? Aah Sid had told me not to go near her what was I doing could she hear me thinking all this?

"She won't care about anything I say. Not unless I make her." Mary sighed. "I remember when she was my best friend. She seemed different from other people. But she's really just the same." She paused. "You aren't, though."

I took a deep breath. "You really scared Taylor."

"Good. See you at lunch." She turned away and walked off.

* * *

"Hey." Eric found me on my way to second period.

"Hi," I said. "I have to tell you something."

He hugged me. "Go ahead."

"I told my family we were going out. They want you to come over for dinner on Wednesday."

Eric considered. "I have two lessons at four."

"It wouldn't be until about six."

"Sounds good," he said amenably.

I smiled. "Do you remember the way to my house?"

"How could I forget your house? Especially since I first kissed you outside of it." He leaned over and gave me another quick kiss. "Will you be in the practice room today?"

Still not quite used to being kissed, it took me a moment to tell him I would be there.

* * *

We all tried not to look at Mary as we ate. I was scared she'd steal my thoughts or something. Key, for once, didn't know what to say. And Helen was just being a bitch. Taylor and Liz were nowhere to be found, understandably.

"So...are you going to stay here, Mary?" I asked finally, not looking into her eyes but at her hairline.

"Where?" She looked at me.

"In school."

"I...don't know. There's...stuff going on. I need time to practice."

"Practice what?" Helen demanded.

"What I do, Helen. You wouldn't understand. You don't want to understand."

Suddenly there was a loud noise that sounded like what I would imagine spontaneous combustion to sound like. It was a commotion of people getting up and away from a table and screaming and going, "Ew!" and "Oh my God."

Frenchie had thrown up all over her lunch table. Some had even managed to land on Tiffany McBriston. When I looked back at my lunch I heard her vomit again. I took my bag and left. Later I was told that she couldn't stop for ten minutes and when she was hurriedly offered a bucket, she missed it.

"Serves her right," said Mary.

"I won't eat for the rest of my life," said Key.

"Why were you watching?!" cried Helen.

Key shrugged. "Vomit turns me on, Helen."

"You asked for that," I told Helen.

"Everyone is so blind," said Mary.

* * *

I couldn't help looking forward to seeing Eric in the practice room. I felt that there was still so much I didn't know about him—because there was—and I couldn't wait to know it. And I wanted to kiss him again.

But there was Sid in the back of my mind.

Okay, the middle. Kind of really close to the front.

But I had to get over him. I had decided. All I was to him was some sort of wolf-pacifier. He was 100+ years older than me. I had a life I had to live, and he wasn't interested anyway. There was Eric. There were millions of guys in the world, I bet I could even find one BETTER than Sid. I mean, really. Even Taylor had told me how unrealistic my feelings were. Sid was probably right; I just had a crush. How could I possibly know what love really was at 16? It was so stupid; once I realized how stupid I was being, getting over Sid would be a snap. I could focus on Eric. He was the window opening after Sid's door had closed.

Of course, I didn't actually believe any of this yet. Maybe it would come with time, and with help from Eric.

As if on cue, Eric entered.

He shut the door. "Hi."

He sat next to me at the piano bench.

"Hi," I said.

"Play something," he told me. "After I met you, I thought of you every time I saw a piano. I wanted to see you again."

I smiled at him. "Just after you met me, you thought about me that much?" I had to bask in his flattery, it didn't happen often.

He nodded. "Yeah. You wanna know what happened?"

"Sure."

"This girl had just asked me out and I'd told her I'd think about it. I was gonna go out with her because I hadn't had a girlfriend in a while." He paused. "And then I saw you in here and decided not to."

I raised an eyebrow. "Why?"

"You reminded me that I didn't have a girlfriend for a reason." He winced. "That is, you reminded me that I'd been waiting for someone I really really wanted."

Oh wow. Oh wow, he was so sweet. Was he going to dump me in three days?

I smiled. "Thank you. I really..I really didn't think you'd give me a second look."

He looked at me, confused. "Of course I would. You're a musician. And you're gorgeous."

I laughed. "You're gorgeous too, Eric."

He smiled, and leaned in.

We kissed. And kissed. And kissed. I didn't want to stop. His lips felt so good, and it didn't feel like he'd pull away any time soon.

But then he did. "Sorry," he said.

I looked at him incredulously, and leaned over to him and we began to kiss again.

He laughed a little into the kiss. "Never mind, I'm not sorry."

"Will anyone walk in?" I asked him, worried to keep kissing.

He looked at me. "They could. I did." He smiled.

"Would you get in trouble?"

He shrugged. "I don't know." He paused. "Want to see?"

I grinned. "Yes."

Just like that our heads were back together, our lips locked, and every once in a while one of us would come up for air. But then we dove right back into a sea of kisses.

And no, I don't care how corny that sounds.

He held my head and gently ran his lips over mine, then he bent his head and began kissing my neck. While that occupied him, I realized I was exhaling smoke. I don't know why he hadn't noticed yet, but I was lucky. I inhaled it all back in.

"Can you breathe okay?" he whispered.

I sighed happily. "Yes, why?"

"You just breathed in really fast."

"It just..felt really good."

He kissed my throat. "You're really warm," he whispered.

I ran a hand through his hair. "Do you mind?"

He kissed my lips again. "No, you feel really good."

I paused. "I've never made out with anybody before."

"Really?"

I nodded.

He grinned. "Well I'm really glad you are with me." He leaned to my ear. "Do you like it?" he asked softly.

"Yes," I replied. I did, very much. But I could also feel myself trying not to think of Sid. And every time I stopped thinking about Sid, I started thinking, "Hey, I'm not thinking about Sid, that's good." Then he'd come back and I'd have to try not to think of him again.

This wasn't to say that I wasn't enjoying what I was doing, however. I kissed Eric's neck and tugged gently on his hair and ran my hands through it. And inside I was hot. My organs were flaming in a way that felt good, but it was hard to hold back the fire.

When we finally both stopped, we looked at each other for long, silent minutes. Finally I said, "You'll come on Wednesday?"

Eric nodded. "Definitely."

"Eric..." I wasn't sure what to say.

He looked at me expectantly.

"There's a lot of stuff I don't know about you yet. But...I.." am not sure what the hell I'm trying to say.

He came forward and kissed me, and in between kisses, he said, "My birthday is October 24, I live with my mom and my brother, I have a car that I bought with my own money, I make money teaching kids to play guitar, I have no allergies." He grinned. "And I have no STDs."

I giggled.

He looked at me. "I'm a virgin."

I nodded. I'd just assumed we'd be going slow, but I supposed this was a good thing to know. "Me too, obviously," I told him. "What else?"

"My dad left when I was nine..my mom wants my brother and me to be gentlemen. And she really wants to meet you. She's heard of your Aunts." He paused. "So you'll have to come over sometime."

"How awful," I said sarcastically.

He chuckled. "I can cook a little bit. I'll make you steak or something."

Steak. Sid liked steak.

No!

I smiled, delighted that he could cook. I wouldn't have to display my kitchen-incompetence. "Thanks, Eric."

"I try to keep my grades up because I want to get into a decent college..maybe have a backup plan if music doesn't work out. I used to be in a band, but the lead singer graduated last year so we don't play anymore."

"Have you written songs?"

Eric shrugged. "A little bit. They're all pretty much shit, though."

"You should play me one sometime."

He smiled. "I will. Anything else?"

I nodded. "Yes. I'll ask you as I think of them," I told him.

"So I get to ask you stuff now?"

"Sure."

"What's your favorite kind of music?"

"That's a terrible question," I blurted out.

"Why?"

"Because I don't have a favorite," I confessed. "I can't."

"I don't either." He leaned away. "So what don't you like?"

I shrugged helplessly. "I don't even know...ummm..devil-worshiper music? I have no idea."

He laughed. "That sucks, because I'm really into that stuff."

I grinned at his joke. "You play guitar at satanic gatherings?"

"Yup."

"No wonder you're friends with Tony."

"Are you religious?"

"To an extent. We're supposed to be Protestant, but I haven't been to church in months. My Aunt Chasey goes all the time though. Are you?"

Eric shrugged. "Nah, not really." He paused. "I just wondered if that was why you haven't made out or anything before this."

I shook my head. "No, that isn't why." I was a little confused. "Why, is that why you're a virgin?"

"No. There isn't really a specific reason." He paused again. "Do you..do you believe in pre-marital sex?"

I almost laughed, having just talked to Sid about this. Having just told Sid I hardly had any feelings for Eric.

"I think so."

"Me too."

We were both silent for a moment.

"Can I ask you what happened to your parents?" he said finally. "Is it too personal for now?"

I shook my head. "It's kind of a long story...you'll probably have to hear it at some point, but I can't tell it all right now. I'll summarize, okay?"

"I was just wondering, because I know you live with your Aunts and a bunch of people but you've never said anything about parents."

I nodded. "It's fine." I paused. "They're just...pretty much gone. They left me when I was 5." It might as well have been true, they did leave me, and they left me in a burning house to boot! "So..my Aunts adopted me. Never saw them again."

"I'm sorry," Eric said.

"Don't be. I'm glad they did. I wouldn't...know the people I know otherwise." I smiled at him.

He smiled and kissed me quickly. "I'm glad too." He looked at the clock. "I should probably show up in the chorus room, just so Mrs. T doesn't think I'm skipping my study hall." He held my gaze. "Can I call you later and ask you some more questions?" He grinned.

I nodded. "Sure."

We hugged and he left.

I tried to figure out "Stairway to Heaven" on the piano. But I wasn't truly cool and couldn't remember all of it.

* * *

As promised, Eric called me after school.

"Hey Phyllis," he said when I picked up the phone.

"Hi." I strategically changed locations to keep from being overheard.

"Sorry I had to go today. You wanna hang out in there tomorrow?"

"Sure."

"You were comfortable and stuff?"

"I would've said something if I hadn't been," I told him.

"My mom told me always to make sure girls are comfortable."

"You said you've been raised to be a gentleman."

"Yep."

"You'll be fine, then," I said, half to myself, relieved.

"What do you mean?"

"Tomorrow. I have a feeling all of the people in my house are going to be watching you."

"That's okay, I'm used to it. I'm not nervous about it, Phyllis. Your Aunts are known for being nice. My mom said they were nice and she's never met them."

And for their morality, I thought. "Just don't tell them you believe in pre-marital sex, please."

He laughed. "Appropriate dinner-table conversation."

I giggled. "Oh yeah."

"I'm definitely going to ask if they mind me having sex with their niece."

"Is that a plan you have?"

"I'm joking, I'm joking."

"I'm sure they'd be thrilled to know it's on your mind."

"Is it on yours?"

Yes.

Wait. This was going too fast, wasn't it? There was an alarm going off in my head. But then, he wasn't asking if I wanted to...he was asking if it was on my mind. Which..well, if it hadn't been before, it was now.

"I'm sorry," said Eric. "That was..that was kinda' forward, I'm sorry."

"It's okay," I said quickly, realizing that I hadn't said anything. "It is, Eric. But don't think it's going to happen anytime soon."

"I'm not...but...I really want to kiss you again."

"I do too," I said, a little bit quieter.

"But I don't want you to do anything you're not comfortable with. I know we just started going out, but I think you should know that. My mom is always telling us that she knows we've only got one thing on our minds, you know? I don't want you to think that about me, Phyllis. I can't say that I'm not going to think about it, though."

"There isn't anyone I know of who doesn't think about it," I told him honestly.

"Good point. I just don't want you to think I'm going to pressure you for anything. Ever."

"Thanks Eric." I wasn't sure what else to say. I swallowed. Might as well dig myself in deep. "I'm really glad you asked me out."

"I'm really glad you said yes."

"I can't wait to see you tomorrow."

"Me neither."

Someone was coming up the stairs. "I've got to go, my Aunts'll tell me to do my homework."

He chuckled. "Been there. See you tomorrow."

"Bye Eric."

"Bye Phyllis."

I hung up.

He was so nice.

I got up and walked out of Aunt Kippie's room to find Sid opening his bedroom door.

"Hey Philly." He turned and spoke to me. "Heard you took my advice."

I shrugged. "I guess."

"It's a good thing. Do you like him a lot?"

I nodded. "Yeah."

"Good."

I nodded to his door. "I thought you were already in there."

Sid shook his head. "Nope, I was doing laundry."

"He's coming to dinner on Wednesday night," I told him.

"Eric?"

"Yeah."

He grinned. "I'll be there." Before I could say anything else, he was in his room, closing the door behind him.

Guess Who's Coming to Dinner.

School on Wednesday rolled by. Mary came to school again. Eric taught me chords on the guitar. And Quincy tried to give me some sort of talk when I got home from school.

"Hey Phyllis, I wanna talk to you." He didn't knock. I glared at him.

"What if I'd been changing?" I chided.

"I want you to know the seriousness of this situation, Phyllis."

I gave him a confused look.

"You got a boyfriend now. You gotta' be careful Phyllis. You know why you see mothers that are 15 years old? Because girls like you aren't careful. Men are fuckin' jerks, Phyllis."

"So why are you gay?"

"I mean straight men, sweetcakes."

"Oh."

"But Phyllis, you've gotta watch out. These teen boys, they don't know what the hell they're doin'. I mean, you hardly know what you're doin' and you're a girl, so you know these boys must be freaking clueless. If you aren't careful, you could end up heartbroken and pregnant!"

"Quincy...you're insulting my intelligence. I'm not gonna go screw a guy I've been going out with for *not even* three days!" He sounded like Sid had the previous evening.

"I know you're smart, Phyllis. But you've never dated before. Guys want to brag to their friends that they got some. So don't give this guy any, okay? Think of Jesus."

"Didn't Jesus say that being gay was a sin?" Sid was standing out in the hall.

Quincy gave him a look. "No honey, that was some asshole who didn't interpret what God told him correctly."

"Did you stage this?" I looked at Quincy. "Are you guys gonna team up and lecture me together."

"Ooh, a lecture." Sid grinned. "On what?"

"I'm tellin' her not to let this guy fuck up her life."

"It's a little bit early to assume she's thinking about those sorts of things, Quince." Sid winked at me.

"Thank you," I said exasperatedly.

"Anytime babes." Sid paused. "Just don't let your emotions get the best of you."

"Oh it's just emooootions takin' me oooover—" Quincy sang.

Sid and I stared at him.

"Don't look at me like that, I have a beautiful voice." Quincy sighed. "Look Phyllis, I know your Aunts aren't gonna talk to you about this. So if you decide you wanna take it that far, use a condom, puh-lease."

I cringed at the word, condom. I did not want to talk about this right now.

"And don't let him go to home base too soon, girl, okay?"

I stared at him. I was almost in pain, I so did not want to hear about this at that moment.

"Okay, okay, I'm leavin'!" Quincy left. Sid shrugged and followed suit.

I wasn't sure what to do before dinner. Shower? Makeup? I didn't wear a lot of makeup at school, why should I have to at home? Should I change my clothes? Should I wear something really nice?

Did I have anything really nice?

I looked in my closet.

Most of my clothes were pretty plain, shirts that were just one color, no pictures or comments like, "You laugh because I'm different, and I laugh because you're all the same." Jeans. One pair of dress-pants. A couple skirts. In the end I just decided leave on what I was already wearing.

Taylor called at four, and again I went into the second section so as not to risk Sid's hearing the conversation.

"I just have to go before five-thirty. My Aunts might decide that I should help them. Or pretend to help them." Taylor knew that I was impaired in the ways of the kitchen.

"Well, you can probably set the table. I—"

"That could be bad."

"Ha. I won't take long, I just needed to tell you something."

"Go ahead."

Taylor took a breath. "Liz threw up in school today." Taylor had been spending more time with Liz, since they couldn't hang out with us when Mary was around.

"That sucks."

"Yeah. Luckily she made it to the bathroom. But she said she couldn't stop for a really long time, and when she did stop, there was nothing more, no more pain or anything. Then she said she thought Mary had randomly touched her in the hall that morning."

I waited.

"It's what she did to Frenchie!" Taylor hadn't actually seen Frenchie vomit, but the entire school knew what had happened.

"How could Mary do it, Tay?"

"I don't know Phyllis, but if *you* can breathe fire, she can be a witch or do magic or voodoo or something!" She paused. "Are you going to tell Eric?"

It took me a moment to realize she meant the fire thing. I swallowed. "I haven't really given it much thought."

"Well, you must not have needed to use it then, right?"

"Yeah."

"So maybe you'll be okay for a while. I don't think you should tell him yet, Phil."

"Why's that?"

"Just...you don't know him well enough yet. I mean, I've known him for longer than you have and I hardly know him at all!"

"Taylor.." I paused. "I've never had a boyfriend before..obviously..and um, I wanted to know...can I ask you something personal about you and Tony?"

"Yes."

"What..umm..." I felt so young, and Taylor was a year younger than I was. "How 'far' have you gone?"

She giggled. "For real or in my head?"

I grinned. "For real."

"I assume you can handle gruesome details?"

"I don't know Taylor, I haven't seen the Hannibal movies as many times as you have."

"Well...our hands have been everywhere. Otherwise, nothing that involved the below the belt area."

"You don't wear belts."

"Exactly. Just kidding," she said quickly. "You've only been dating Eric for 3 days, are you already considering how far you're gonna let him go?"

I sighed. "It's so stupid! Why is it like a damn game?! How far, what base, crap like that."

"I know. I think it's to keep boundaries instilled in us. You know, my mom tried to talk to me about boys and sex once. It was amazing, Phyllis. She actually said all the lines. 'They're only after one thing.'" Taylor did a whiny high-pitched impression of her mother. "She said she wanted me to tell her if I was ever thinking of having sex."

"I think that's stupid too!" I lowered my voice. "Of course we're thinking about it! But that doesn't necessarily mean we're gonna do it either. I hate that older people think they know..."

"Exactly what our intentions are," Taylor finished. "Honestly, I didn't start really thinking about sex until Tony. But it's probably because of Davy's...death..." She paused again, probably to swallow and collect herself. Taylor always looked and sounded pained when she spoke of her brother. She took a deep breath. "I always thought it was one of those things that intrigues people because it's been so forbidden. Like murder, and Satan, and drugs. Though drugs were never intriguing to me."

"Only when we watched 'Fear and Loathing in Las Vegas.'"

She laughed. "Well you know what I mean. It's why people see movies like 'Deliverance' and 'A Clockwork Orange' and pretty much anything involving Quentin Tarantino."

I hadn't seen Deliverance or A Clockwork Orange. But Taylor was usually right about these things.

We were both silent for a moment.

"Anyway, I just wanted to say that, about Mary. Just be careful Phyllis."

"I will, Taylor."

"She really scares me, Phyllis. I don't want her to hurt you or Key."

"We won't let her, Taylor, okay?"

"Okay. Just remember, okay?"

"Don't worry, Tay. I doubt that she's so advanced that she can repel flames, if that's what I have to resort to."

"Advanced in what?"

Oops. "Witchcraft or whatever, right? You think she's a witch."

"Yeah. Well, I'll let you go. It is rather reassuring that you can breathe fire Phyllis, I must say."

I giggled. "Good. See you tomorrow Tay."

"Have a good night, Phil."

"Bye."

I went down the hall toward the back stairs and passed Bill's room. His door was open, his small TV on.

"Hey," I said to him, not yet sure who he was today.

"Oh! Hello Phyllis." Definitely Peter Lorre. "I did not see you."

"Whatcha watchin'?"

"Oh, just a film I found on the television."

"Can I look?"

"Heh. Of course," he said uncomfortably.

He was watching a movie with Cary Grant in it. I'd never seen it before.

"What's it called?" I asked.

"It may be better for you not to know."

"What's your name?"

"Dr. Einstein."

Okay. "Doctor, I'm sorry to interrupt your film, but maybe..do you think you could come downstairs with me? We could watch something else." I didn't really want Bill to be Peter Lorre when Eric was over.

He shook his head. "No no, I must stay here. Johnny might get angry otherwise."

Right. "Will you be down for dinner?"

"Oh umm..will I be able to get a drink?"

Aunt Chasey didn't drink. Aunt Kippie did.

"Yes."

"Oh yes, I will, certainly."

I smiled. "Thanks B—Dr. Einstein." I got up.

"Oh, you're going?"

"Yup." As I left the room I heard him murmur, "Where will we bury Mr. Spinalzo?"

I went into the kitchen and found Aunt Chasey.

"Do you know what Bill's watching?"

"No I don't dear, where is he?"

"In his room."

"Do you know who's in it?" We often had to figure out who Bill would become this way.

"Peter Lorre. That's who he is right now, at least. And Cary Grant."

"Oh goodness. What did he say?"

"He wanted alcohol and said something about Johnny and had to bury someone named Spinalzo."

"Oh! Arsenic and Old Lace!"

"What?"

"Arsenic and Old Lace. What a funny film that was."

"What is it?"

"Two old women poison old men to rid them of their loneliness. They think they're doing a good service." She laughed a bit. "Cary Grant was so wonderful in that movie. He was their nephew. And they had another nephew who thought he was Teddy Roosevelt." She looked at me. "It always reminded me a bit of Kippie and me with Bill, save for the fact that Kippie and I are sane."

"Usually." Aunt Kippie entered. "What are you two girls discussing?"

"Arsenic and Old Lace."

"Oh yes! How funny that film was!"

"I think I'm going to go play the piano," I said quickly. "Incidentally, do you think it's possible that Bill might change characters before dinner? Peter Lorre's a little bit creepy."

Aunt Kippie nodded. "I'll go upstairs and suggest Teddy's appeal to him."

"That has worked several times," Aunt Chasey added.

"Thank you," I said gratefully.

"Anything for you," they chorused.

"Are you telepathic?" I asked, some surprised smoke coming out of my mouth.

"Of course dear. How do you think we supervise you? We simply read your thoughts." Aunt Chasey winked at me.

"Don't play too loudly, Phyllis. We might holler if we need you to set the table." Aunt Kippie went up the back stairway.

I played the piano, and then when the clock said it was five-thirty, I went into the living room. Quincy was sitting on the couch with the paper, Enrique curled up next to him. Johnny hopped up onto Sid's Chair after I sat down in it. He stretched out on my propped up legs.

Quincy peered at me over his paper. "You better hope Sid doesn't come down and want to sit in his chair."

I ignored Quincy's comment and said, "Where's Damien?"

"He's droppin' his mama off at the airport, isn't that sweet? But he'll be here."

I nodded, stroking Johnny's back.

"You nervous?" Quincy asked.

"About tonight?"

"Mmmhm."

"A little."

Enrique rose and meowed.

Quincy rolled his eyes. "I gotta feed this bitch."

Enrique meowed again, a short, loud, "Rowr!"

"Sorry!" Quincy apologized. He rose and Enrique followed him into the kitchen.

I just sat in peace with my kitty, waiting for Eric to arrive.

Eventually Quincy came back.

"So, you ready?"

"I guess."

"He'll be here any second."

"Yup."

"We're all gonna size him up and scrutinize him. The Aunts'll interrogate him. Kippie's the bad cop."

"Quincy."

"We gonna' talk about religion, and politics, and make him eat four helpings. Then we're gonna make him take a drug test, get tested for STDs, and google him!"

I giggled. "Stop."

There was a knock at the door.

"Oooh, he's here!" Quincy squealed, just to get my nerves up.

I rolled my eyes and answered the door.

"Hey," I greeted Eric.

"Hey." He hugged me.

I could get used to this, I thought. I smiled and looked into his bright blue eyes. I could get used to those, too. "We're having pasta in wine sauce, a salad, bread, and whatever else she decides to throw in."

"Wow." He looked in awe.

"What is it?'

"My mom hardly cooks anything that doesn't come in a can."

I shrugged. "My Aunt loves to cook. She doesn't do it because she has to."

"That's really cool. I like to eat." He grinned.

"Hi Eric!" Quincy popped up off the couch.

"This is Quincy, he was at the play?" I introduced Eric uncertainly.

"I remember," Eric told me. Quincy shook Eric's hand.

"You guys can sit down, Chasey's not finished yet," he told us.

"Okay," I said, sitting on the couch. Eric followed my lead.

"Apparently a lot of people are coming to make sure that you're a decent person," I told Eric.

He smiled. "For not having parents you have a huge family. Who am I meeting?"

"I'm not completely sure." I looked to Quincy, who smiled.

"Well," he told Eric, "you're meeting the Aunts, Damien, and me again—"

"Damien's his boyfriend," I added quickly.

"—and Bill, and Sid."

"Who's Sid?" Eric asked.

"He's an old family friend who moved in in January," I said.

"Yeah," said Quincy. "That's all." He gave me a look.

Aunt Kippie came out of the kitchen. "Dinner's almost ready." She saw Eric and smiled. "Hello Eric, it's nice to see you again." She walked over and hugged him.

"It's nice to see you too," he said sincerely, surprised by the hug.

She smiled. "And I see you're a punctual young man, that's good."

"He has to be," I told her. "He teaches guitar lessons."

"Oh really? How much are they?"

"It's mostly just younger kids that anyone could teach..but it's ten bucks for a half an hour lesson."

Kippie nodded. "Chasey always wanted to learn to play the guitar, I'll have to tell her about that." That was something I had not known.

"Well, we just have some guests to wait for, and then we can—" Aunt Kippie was interrupted when Damien burst through the front door.

"Sorry if I'm a little late guys, I had to drop Mom off and then on the way out some girl totally started flirting with me." Damien grimaced.

"Ugh, what an idiot. I was like, sweetie, it was nice meeting you but I'm late to have dinner with my boyfriend. She tried to cover up, like she'd figured it out but she very obviously hadn't." Damien shook his head. "I mean come on. Look at this shirt. Look at these shoes. Two seconds of talking to me should tell you I'm either gay or should have been. Luckily I turned out right." Damien shook his head again. "I'm sorry, that was just disturbing."

Quincy patted him on the shoulder. "Don't worry baby, it's over."

Chasey came out of the kitchen. "Dinner's ready! Let's eat, everyone. Sid will arrive in his own good time, I'm sure." She turned to Eric and smiled. "I'm so glad you could be here tonight, Eric, we're all very eager to know you."

"Thanks for having me," Eric replied with a sincere smile.

Sid was in the kitchen when we all entered. I swallowed. Bill was there too.

"Well hello young man, it's an honor to have you in the White House. Always happy to meet a member of the press." Bill shook Eric's hand rapidly.

"Eric, this is Bill. Also known as Teddy Roosevelt today," said Chasey.

Oops. I'd forgotten to tell Eric about Bill.

I leaned over and whispered in his ear. "Bill's got some mental issues, but he's harmless and he's a good guy, just play along, okay?!"

Eric nodded. "Okay," he whispered.

"Mr. President," Damien shook Bill's hand.

"This is Sid," I told Eric.

"Hi Eric." Sid shook Eric's hand.

"Hello Sid," said Eric, "nice to meet you."

"Likewise."

We all stood around the table, set perfectly (probably by Quincy or an Aunt). There were three tall candles (one of which I fittingly ended up sitting in front) and three pitchers for drinks, and a bottle of red wine that someone contributed.

"Shall we all sit down and eat?" said Aunt Chasey joyfully.

"Bully, that's just bully!" said Bill.

Damien held up a glass. "First, I have to toast you, Chasey."

"This meal is lovely," Kippie agreed.

"To Chastity Sorin," said Damien.

"Hear, hear," said Sid.

Eric and I smiled at each other as we both toasted my Aunt. Then we sat down and ate. I was across from Sid and between Eric and President Roosevelt.

"So Eric," Quincy said. "How long have you played guitar?"

"As long as I can remember," Eric answered, a reminiscent look on his face.

"Phyllis does seem attracted to guitar people," remarked Aunt Kippie. "Taylor plays guitar, if I recall correctly."

I nodded. "Yup."

Eric shrugged. "Everyone plays guitar these days."

"But not everyone can play it well." Sid had almost finished Eric's sentence.

"Can you?" Quincy asked him. It was as if Sid and Quincy had a coinciding attack plan.

Eric smiled. "I don't know, it depends on how you look at it. But I know what I'm doing because I've played so long."

"Which is more than a lot of people can say," Kippie acknowledged.

"Chase this dinner is spectacular."

"Oh, Siddie, do you really think so?"

"Don't try to be modest, you show-off!" Kippie said.

"This is really good," Eric agreed. "I wish my mom did this."

"I'm sure your mother works hard. I myself have a great deal of free time," said Aunt Chasey. "Incidentally Eric, you're welcome over for dinner any time."

I squeezed Eric's hand. Yay! They liked him.

"What's your favorite food, Eric?" Damien asked politely.

Eric smiled. "This, as of now," he said, gesturing to his plate.

Everyone laughed.

"Suck up," Quincy teased.

"I have to say, I agree with Eric," said Sid, lifting his fork. He looked at me and bounced his eyebrows once. I hoped it meant approval.

"You get all the men," Aunt Kippie told her sister in mock jealousy.

"Even the gay ones," Damien added.

"She gets all the men except her boyfriend," Quincy pointed out. "Why didn't you invite Mr. Meneses?"

"Oh, Quincy, he is not my boyfriend," Chasey waved the remark away.

Everyone rolled their eyes.

"Well he certainly isn't! I am far too old for a boyfriend." This was an enormous lie. My Aunts were hardly into their fifties.

"What would you refer to him as?" Sid asked her.

"Yes, do tell," said Damien.

"A good, male friend."

"Aren't I a good male friend?" Sid asked her.

"Sid I'm sure Chasey would romantically link herself to you in a minute," Kippie remarked. I took a sip of my lemonade.

"And I'm a good male friend," Quincy echoed.

There was silence. And then laughter when Kippie said nothing.

I don't know why it was so funny to me. I suppose it was because Quincy is so very...gay. Anyway, I laughed so hard that I started to choke on my drink. Air struggled to get in. And the fire in my lungs...or wherever it came from..struggled to push the liquid out of my airway.

Until some came out, amid cries of, "Are you okay?" and "Don't laugh too hard."

Before I could hold back, small flames burst from my mouth.

As it happened, I thought, Eric's going to see, Damien's going to see, what am I going to say, what am I going to do?

Luckily, I was saved.

Sitting across from me, Sid had stood and reached for me as I coughed. And as I finally coughed out fire, his reaching hand knocked over a candle.

Now it looked as though Sid's clumsiness had set the tablecloth on fire, rather than some freakish burst of fire from my mouth.

On my other side, Teddy Roosevelt quickly said, "I'll get the fire," and splashed his glass of water (the Aunts must not have had whiskey) onto it.

I looked at him. "Thank you, Mr. President." I looked at Sid. I didn't know what to say.

"Sorry about that Philly," he apologized. "I almost set you on fire. You okay?" But his eyes were smiling.

I smiled. "I'm fine."

"What a disaster that would have been, Phyllis is not compatible with fire," Quincy said, completely straight-faced. I saw my Aunt Kippie roll her eyes.

"Whoa," said Eric.

Quincy patted him on the shoulder. "Honey, this is what happens everyday here."

"Laughter ensues. And then something catches fire." Kippie looked upward, presumably at God. "Heaven help us."

"What's your family like, Eric?" Chasey asked politely.

Eric smiled. "Pretty small. Just me, my mom and brother."

"What's your brother's name?" Kippie asked.

"Terry."

"Short for Terrence?" Quincy asked.

Eric grinned. "Unfortunately for him."

Sid laughed at that. "Your mom named him?"

Eric nodded. "She did his first name and Dad did his middle name. They switched for me."

"Lucky you."

Eric nodded. "My middle name is Humphrey."

Damien flinched. "Ow."

"After Bogie?" Aunt Kippie asked.

He nodded again. "Yup."

"Phyllis doesn't have a middle name. When she came to us she was five, we thought about giving her one but I think it should be her choice," Kippie told him.

"You wanted to name her something with an M, as I recall, Kippie." Chasey looked at her. "I told you Phyllis should be the one to make the decision."

"Why an M name?" Eric asked.

Sid groaned.

Quincy giggled. "Her initials would have been PMS."

"I would not have let you do that either, Kippie," Sid told her.

"Oh Sid, you people have no sense of humor."

"Who, men, or just Chasey and me?"

"Chasey and you."

"I don't think it's very funny either," I quipped.

Aunt Kippie sighed. "I'm afraid I'm all alone in the world."

"I thought it was pretty funny," Quincy said.

"Would anyone like more chicken?" Aunt Chasey offered.

"Yes please," Eric and Teddy said in unison, offering their plates.

"Phyllis, I like him," Aunt Chasey said, winking at Eric.

"One down, five to go," said Sid.

"Oh that isn't true, we all like him!" Aunt Kippie declared.

"Indeed!" Teddy raised his glass.

"I think you should teach Quincy to play guitar," Damien said. "Then he can serenade me."

"I can't sing for sh..stuff," Quincy said quickly.

"Philly can serenade you," Sid told Damien.

"I'm afraid she's taken, Sid my love."

Eric squeezed my hand. I squeezed back. Eric was wonderful. I was beginning to feel my heart detaching from Sid and leaning toward him. It only needed a little more coaxing.

"What's your favorite kind of music, Eric?" Kippie asked him.

"Classic rock," said Eric. "What about you guys?"

"Well, I've always preferred classical. And gospel," Aunt Chasey said.

"I agree with you," Kippie said to Eric.

"Madonna!" Damien and Quincy chorused.

"Could you pass the bread, please?" I asked, looking at Aunt Kippie.

"Of course dear, here you are."

"What's your favorite movie, Eric?" Quincy asked.

"No idea."

Quincy nodded. "That's the problem, there are just too many."

"You know what my favorite word is?" said Damien. "Anemone. Isn't that weird?"

"I could never say that word," Kippie told him.

Quincy shrugged. "Butchie's is lollapalooza."

"Butch is one of Quincy's friends, I'm sure you'll meet him soon if you continue coming here," Aunt Kippie told him.

"I hope so," Eric said. I ran a finger across his wrist, just to tell him I agreed.

"Who do you like to play?" Sid asked.

"On the guitar?" Eric questioned.

Sid nodded.

Eric thought. "I like the Stones...Zeppelin..Guns N Roses..Bob Dylan."

Kippie nodded. "Maybe you can give Phyllis the exposure she needs to classic rock. We've tried to give her access to every kind of music...so many different people have lived here...but sadly Chasey and I are not musically inclined as she is. She got that from her father, I believe."

"I liked Guns N Roses until Axl Rose decided to fscrew himself up," Damien said. He scrunched up his face, waiting to be scolded by the Aunts for remotely almost saying fuck. But they didn't, and so he relaxed.

Eric nodded. "I'm a big fan of Slash."

"He is some hot stuff," Quincy said.

"He's got some good music too, Quince," Sid told him.

"I like Peggy Lee," said Aunt Chasey.

"She's not exactly rock, Chase."

"She sang the siamese cat song in the movie with the dogs that eat the spaghetti!" Quincy recalled.

And so on and so forth. More random remarks were made, more questions were asked. All in all it went well, even though I almost choked to death and almost exposed my firebreathing.

After dinner, Eric made a remark to me about the size of the house and the Aunts told me to give him a tour. So I took him upstairs.

The tour took place mostly in my bedroom. On my bed.

As we had before, we kissed and kissed and kissed some more. His lips were so delicious. He kissed down my neck, and pulled my collar aside to kiss my shoulder.

"Your skin is really smooth," he whispered. His hand was at the bottom of my shirt. "Do you mind?"

"No, go ahead," I whispered. He felt good, and if he suddenly went psycho I could burn his eyebrows off. But he wouldn't. He was too good for that.

My thoughts were going a bit too far, but as he ran his hand under my shirt and caressed my side and stomach, I understood why. It felt too good not to want to.

He kissed my collarbone.

"Would you two like dessert?!" Kippie yelled up the stairs.

"Yes please!" I yelled back. "We'll be down in a second, I want to show Eric my piano books!"

"All right!"

Eric smiled. "I think I already had dessert."

I kissed him again. "I think that line was corny."

He ran his hands down my arms. "I think you taste much better than anything they could be serving." He wrapped his arms around me and gently pushed me down onto the bed again, kissing me. "You want to come to my house this weekend and see my guitar books?" he asked between kisses.

I giggled. I felt so warm, and I was getting hotter all the time because I was suppressing the flames. "Yes, please," I said. I could hold them longer.

We went down. Aunt Chasey gave us chocolate cream pie she had made.

"This is delicious," Eric told her. She thanked him and turned to cut another piece for the guys. He leaned over and whispered in my ear, "Still not as delicious as you, though."

I smiled and squeezed his hand again.

As I walked him to his car later, he told me his mother would probably give us more time alone.

"Does she trust you not to do anything?" I asked him.

Eric shrugged. "I don't know. But I don't think she'd bother us, if you wanted to do more of this." He kissed me again.

I grinned. "How's Saturday?"

"Want me to pick you up?"

* * *

"Well I think Eric is quite nice, Phyllis. You have my approval," Aunt Chasey said when I came back.

"And mine," Aunt Kippie added. "He seems to be a very decent young man." She looked at me. "But don't think I'll be leaving you two alone up there for long. And don't think I'll allow you to visit him when his mother isn't at home."

"It isn't that we don't trust you," Aunt Chasey said quickly. "But apparently Kippie remembers being quite a sly young woman back in the day."

"Most young women are," Kippie said in her own defense. "We know you've got a good head on your shoulders. But..well..things happen, you see."

I nodded, reluctant to get into anything near a sex discussion with my Aunts. "I understand. But, I promise not to do anything either way."

They both nodded. "That's good, dear. But our rules still stand," said Aunt Kippie. "I remember what I got away with at sixteen."

Aunt Chasey rolled her eyes. "Don't give Phyllis any ideas, Kippie."

"He invited me over on Saturday. He said his mom will be there, do you want me to have her call you or something?"

"Oh no, I'll drop you off and say a quick hello," Aunt Chasey said pleasantly.

I nodded. "He offered to pick me up. I'll tell him you'll bring me. But he can probably take me home."

"That'll be just fine," Aunt Kippie agreed. She looked at me. "I presume you finished your homework?"

I smiled and nodded. "Yup," I lied. "I'm going to go online to talk to Taylor." I really had an essay I'd forgotten to type.

When I finally finished it, it was time for bed. The living room was empty save for Bill, who was up watching the Rocky Horror Picture Show. I walked over and gave him a hug. "How are you?" I asked.

"Bully, bully. Things are going very well around the White House. I'm very happy to be here." He looked at me. "Do you have anything to report?"

"I just typed up a very important document. It should ensure my...position here in the White House."

Bill nodded. "Glad to hear it, you're a valued member of the Secret Service."

Sweet! "Thank you. Have a good night, Mr. President." I saluted him.

He saluted me back. "Good night."

As I walked up the stairs, Quincy came in with a bowl of popcorn. Damien must have gone home. "I can't miss this movie," he called to me. "It's a classic!"

"Okay," I called back.

I heard coming from Sid's room as I walked by. His door was opened.

I looked in.

Sid was lying on his bed. His eyes slid from the skylight over to me. "Hey Philly."

"Goodnight," I said.

"Night," he replied.

I walked to my room, changed into my pajamas, brushed my teeth, washed my face, and sat on my bed.

Sid opened my door, walked in, and sat in my desk chair.

"Hi," I said. "Do you ever knock?" Not that I wasn't glad to see him. I shouldn't have been, though.

Sid shook his head. "Not on your door, Philly."

"I knock on yours."

"I usually lock mine." Sid looked at me. "Why don't you lock yours?"

Because I don't really mind if you come in, I thought. Instead, I said, "Did you like Eric?"

Sid nodded. "He seems smart. He isn't shy. And he really likes you."

"Which is probably a good sign," I said with mock uncertainty.

"You see a future with this guy?"

I shrugged. "I have no idea. This is our third day as a couple."

"And already he's met your family, eaten in your house, and seen your bedroom." Sid raised an eyebrow. "What else has he seen?"

"What does that mean?"

"You were upstairs with him for half an hour." He grinned. "Were you really showing him your piano books?"

I shrugged. "Some." I eyed the door, not wanting my Aunts to hear, even though their doors were probably closed.

As if reading my mind, Sid reached over and shut it. "Babes I won't beat around the bush. How are you going to handle the fire?"

"What do you mean?"

He leaned closer to me. "Philly honey, when I kissed you your mouth was hot as hell. What are you going to do to control it with Eric?"

My eyes darted about the room. "I've been able to control it so far."

"And how far is that?"

I was at a loss for words. He hadn't seemed to take into consideration that I might not want to talk about these things with him.

Of course, it was probably because he was a genius. Because I did want to talk to him. About everything. How could I be focused on Eric and want to tell Sid all about it?

"He's been here." Sid touched a finger to my lips.

Oh my God, I was going to die.

"Here," he touched my collarbone, "then here," my ribs, "here," my waist. Then he stopped. "And so on and so forth."

"You just think of a girl's body as levels?" I demanded, expressing my aggravation as well as secretly trying to escape his question.

"I don't. But teenage boys seem to. And all bodies have levels if you're thinking that way, babes. Men just have a couple less."

I raised an eyebrow. "Why?"

He grinned. "Men can go shirtless."

"Oh." I hoped my face wasn't turning red, though luckily that wasn't usually the effect Sid had on me.

"Am I right? I smell him on you."

I sighed. I might as well tell him, I thought. I wanted to and he wasn't going to tell the Aunts.

Correction: he'd better not tell the Aunts.

I placed my hand right below my collarbone. "He stopped here."

He nodded. "Are you gonna let him pass that limit?"

I sighed. "I don't really know. I've never done anything like this before."

Sid smiled. "Only with me."

"It isn't the same." I said that a little too quickly.

"Why's that?" he asked, looking interested.

I wanted to grab him and shake him. Why did he act this way, then say, "Don't get any ideas, Philly"?

"When you did it, it was...an accidental thing, I guess," I said.

Sid stood. "Not exactly accidental. But close enough." He looked at me. "Are you going to tell him? Do you know him well enough that you can trust him?"

"I don't know yet. I don't...I don't think I plan on telling him any time soon." I paused. "Thanks for knocking over the candle."

Sid smiled again. "Anytime, Philly. Don't worry about it."

"I don't know what I would have done," I said honestly.

"You would have been in an awkward situation." Sid grinned. "We could have just ignored it and made them think they were hallucinating."

I smiled too. "Maybe that's what I'll do. Eric'll ask, 'Why is there fire coming out of your mouth?' and I'll say, 'The hell are you talking about?!'" I paused again, remembering something. "But that would be like doing what Mary did to Taylor and Key."

"Van asked me about her yesterday. Is there any more evidence that she's a witch?"

I considered. Was the vomiting important? It may not have even been related to Mary at all. It was, however, an excuse to talk to Sid.

But I was getting over him now.

"There might be. Umm..I'll tell you tomorrow. I'm kind of tired."

Sid's face changed a little. He was either surprised, amused, or understanding, or all three simultaneously. "All right," he said. "Sleep is a good idea." He pointed at me. "But you be careful with Eric, babes. I heard what he said to you over dessert." He left.

Damn him and his wolf hearing.

Eric's House.

Mary wasn't in school on Thursday (or for the rest of the week). Key said it was the result of more and more troubles at home. But I didn't mind, because I saw more of Taylor and Liz when Mary wasn't there.

"I think I'm gonna skip math class today," Liz said.

"How come?" Taylor asked.

Liz shrugged. "Math sucks."

Key lay her head on the table. "Everyone sucks."

Liz nodded. "People are pretty much disgusting."

I wanted to see Eric. Every time I thought of him I got the stagefright feeling again, but it was only because of the fire. What if his tongue burst into flames?

I couldn't really express my concerns to Taylor, because first she'd try to be serious about it but sooner or later she'd just burst out laughing.

Sid was different. He understood more, being of odd origins himself.

I decided I would just have to find him when I got home from school.

But first I would get to see Eric. And hopefully, not set him on fire.

When he came to the practice room that day, I ended up being a coward and telling him I was nervous that someone would walk in and see us kissing. He was very understanding and continued teaching me guitar chords. With a few quick kisses in between.

Liar, said the voice.

A few kisses that involved the guitar being set down and me laying on the floor. Yes, I was going fast, but I was doing pretty well holding the fire back.

After school I grabbed a snack and went to find Sid. His car was in the driveway. But he wasn't in the living room (Quincy and Damien were watching "The Poseidon Adventure" and eating potato chips) or the basement (Bill was doing laundry and watching "The Wild Bunch." But he was wearing Teddy Roosevelt garb, with the little glasses and a moustache beginning to sprout up, so he wasn't changing yet). He wasn't in his room, or anywhere upstairs. He wasn't on the back porch.

Finally I gave up and asked Quincy, "Where's Sid?"

Quincy pointed toward the kitchen, engrossed in the movie.

"That movie is terrible," I told them. I felt a chip lightly hit the back of my head as I walked out of the room.

Sid wasn't in the kitchen, which I already knew. So, I checked the back room, and there he was, the man himself, sitting at a table with his laptop.

"Hey babes."

"Hi," I said.

He looked up. "Looking for me?"

I nodded. "What are you doing?"

Sid sighed. "Van sent me an email that one of his employees quit on him the other day and took a sample of some metal with him when he left."

I looked at him expectantly.

"It could become a crisis if it's put into the wrong hands is all. Just like any weapon."

"What is it?"

"The metal's called andrastenite. Everyone has mixed feelings about it. Some people think it might be linked to why the energy exists and some people think we ought to leave it alone."

"I've never heard of it."

Sid smiled. "That's because normal people can't reach it. Apparently it was found at the bottom of the sea."

I raised an eyebrow. "Mermaids?"

Sid nodded. "The deep sea is the only safe place left for mermaids because mankind can't directly get to it. No one who isn't a mermaid can get to it either. But they noticed it because one of them cut themselves on it."

"What do you mean?" What did they care if they cut themselves? They were immortal!

"It's one of the substances that can kill us." Sid paused. "And I don't think it's a coincidence that's it's only at the bottom of the sea. I think it was put there long ago by someone who found it in nature. I think it's so no one messes with it."

"Why does Van have it, then?"

"Van has some and Stacia has some. Sometimes they need it. Stacia has a theory that the force that keeps us going comes from the earth, because of the metal." Sid paused. "But what I'm doing now is telling Van that he'll have to tell Stacia about this himself. They won't talk to each other."

"Why?"

"Van thinks she's a lunatic and she thinks he's an idiot. It's just good old-fashioned sibling rivalry, I'll tell you more about it later Philly. Why were you looking for me?"

Yeah Phyllis, forget about the only metal that can kill the man you love. That's easy.

I thought a moment. Eric. Other man I was supposed to get to love.

"Um..." Everything was fine so far with Eric, no need yet to tell Sid that I'd been felt up today. What else?

Sid grinned. "I think I crashed your train of thought."

"You tend to do that," I said softly, not looking at him.

"Was it about Mary?"

Mary? Mary...Mary! "Yes, thank you."

"What's up?"

"She...um...when I last saw her she had some symbols written on her neck.."

"Probably found them on some know-nothing website. Don't tell me it was a pentagram."

I shook my head. "It looked like a letter."

"No clue. Anything else?"

"She dressed in long, loose clothes..she might have dreadlocks."

"Maybe she's looking for a more natural look. I think she has something, Philly. It sounds like she can't find what she's looking for so she's getting into the closest things she can find. Might be wicca. I know they're big on nature. She may have found something on black magic, too. What else?"

"She might have made two people sick. A girl who told her to watch it threw up nonstop in the cafeteria later that day. And my friend Liz started calling her 'Scary Mary', and according to Taylor, she had the same sickness. It could be a bug, but they're both people Mary had problems with."

Sid nodded. "Do you think she put something in their food?"

I shook my head. "She just touched them."

"She might have put something on them."

"A spell?"

Sid shook his head. "A strand of hair or a nail-clipping or an eye-lash or something from her body. If the victim takes a part of the witch with them, the witch can activate a spell on the person anytime they want."

"I thought you didn't know much about witches."

"I did some research, talked to Van. I have to say, she sounds like a witch to me."

"Should I do something?"

"Not yet. We need something that leaves us doubtless, babes."

I nodded. "Okay."

Sid closed his laptop and stood. "I'm gonna be gone for a couple of days."

"What?!" No!

"I have to check on my house."

"Why?"

"Someone's going to rent it. I feel uncomfortable leaving it alone. It's in the middle of nowhere, but mankind keeps building unnecessarily and they're getting closer to nowhere. So to speak." He paused. "It fits as many people as this place. I've got to make sure everything's kosher before they can move in."

"Oh."

"And the money won't hurt."

I followed him through to the living room and up the stairs to his bedroom. "Do the Aunts know?"

Sid nodded. "Yes. They recommended I have some time to myself."

"Why?"

Sid sighed. "I can turn into the wolf at will. But it's very hard to change back, so I'd never do it here. It'll be safe there, and I won't be pressured to change back. It'll help me put my mind at ease, babes. The wolf's like another person. It always wants to tear things apart, and run, and howl, and it drives me crazy. I need to be somewhere where I can let it be."

My eyes widened. "Where'll you be?"

"In the woods around the house." I was going to ask more, but he cut me off. "Don't worry about it, Philly." He turned and unexpectedly touched my chin. "You just worry about the fire."

"I won't go that far," I told him.

"You'd better not." Sid got out a suitcase.

He left after dinner, and for a day or so nothing seemed as worthwhile.

* * *

After lunch on Saturday, Aunt Kippie brought me to Eric's house. It was a small, cute house on a crowded street, but inside there was a lot of space. His mom was short, at least half a foot shorter than Eric and slightly shorter than me.

"Hi, I'm Jill," said Eric's mom. She shook my hand first, then my Aunt's.

"Hi, I'm Phyllis."

"Hello Jill, I'm Kippie Sorin."

"It's wonderful to meet you both."

"Oh likewise. Thank you very much for having Phyllis."

"It's the least I could do, you made Eric a huge dinner!"

Blah blah blah. We all talked, Aunt Kippie left, and then Eric took me up to his room.

We sat on his bed. His room was under the slanted part of the roof of his house, and there were posters of bands covering that part of the ceiling. Several guitars hung on his wall. Next to his bed was a stereo and under it, he showed me several boxes filled with CDs. Some were mainstream, some classics, some indie, some punk, some emo, some classical, and some were local. The guy certainly loved music. And his guitars. He tuned one as we spoke.

"My mom's room is downstairs so all kinds of stuff goes on up here. She hardly ever comes up. My brother's got a whole fucking stash of marijuana or something in his closet." He shook his head. "He's going to smoke his brains out."

"Do you smoke?"

Eric shook his head. "I've tried it a couple of times, it just made it really hard to see. And it made me really scared. I woke up hiding under Terry's bed."

I laughed.

He grinned. "I did! Never did it again after that. It doesn't help me with anything, so why bother?" He put the guitar back on the wall. "Do you smoke?"

I smiled and shook my head. "It never seemed like a big deal to me. I was never interested."

Eric nodded. "Yeah, Tony used to do that stuff. But then his mom locked him out of the house in the middle of winter when he came home high, he learned pretty fast."

"What?!"

"Yeah, he walked three miles over here to spend the night. My mom talked to him and called his mom and he never did it again." He nodded. "She could probably talk Terry out of doing drugs but she doesn't think she has to. She's never really told us not to smoke. We don't have those sitcom talks, you know?"

I nodded. "I know what you mean. The worst one is the one where the girl's mom tells her she can have sex but she needs to use protection. My Aunts would shoot me if I ever did that."

Eric smiled. "Would you ever do it?"

I smiled back shyly. "Maybe."

"I bet I can make you want to." Eric leaned over and kissed me.

We kissed for a while. Then Eric started to push my shirt upward.

"Whoa, wait," I whispered.

"Sorry," he whispered. He kissed my neck. "It's hard to stop with you."

I considered a moment. "You sure your mom won't come up?"

"She'd yell up the stairs. Even if she came up, the stairs creak, we'd hear her in time, I promise." He looked at me hopefully.

"Okay," I whispered. "Be careful."

"I'm not going too fast for you?"

I shook my head, ignoring the voice, which kept saying, Yes, you are!

Eric took off my shirt. He took off his. I had to use more strength to hold the fire in.

I didn't think about it as far as what base we were running. That would have been stupid and immature.

We didn't go past waist-level, though.

His mom made us spaghetti-os for dinner. After that, we really did play guitars together. Eric took me home around seven.

"Were you okay with everything today?" Eric asked as he drove, sounding a little bit worried.

"Definitely," I told him.

"Did it feel good?"

I squeezed his hand. "No Eric, I just lay there for the hell of it."

He laughed a little bit. "Thanks for coming over. I have to say I'm happier and happier that I asked you out with every piece of clothing we remove."

I giggled. "Oh, I see how it is, that's all you want me for."

"To get naked? No, I want you because you're awesome. You're talented and beautiful and I love being with you. I wouldn't mind though, you know, in case you ever feel like getting naked..."

I rolled my eyes, and laughed.

"Should I call you tomorrow?" he asked as we pulled up in front of my house. Sid's car was in the driveway again.

"Sure," I said. "You can call me anytime, you don't have to ask."

"I'm gonna call you at three A.M. now."

"You know what I mean. I'm...I'm always happy to hear from you."

That was retarded, said the voice.

But Eric didn't think so. He leaned over and kissed me.

"Thanks for coming over," he whispered.

"Thanks for having me over." I ran my hands up the inside of his shirt and he jerked a little, startled.

"You're so warm," he whispered.

"Is that good?" I asked.

"Really good," he said, kissing me more intensely, his tongue coming into my mouth.

"Mm." My whole body was feeling really warm. "I'd better go."

"Okay." He kissed me once more, then leaned away. "I'll talk to you tomorrow."

I nodded. "Okay." We hugged, kissed, and then I got out.

"Phyllis!" Butch stood in the living room, wearing the scarf Quincy had given him, his arms outstretched, waiting for a hug.

I rushed up and hugged him. "Where have you guys been?"

Butch shrugged. "Beats me sweetpea, we've all just been doin' our thing. Did you just get back from your boyfriend's house?"

A pair of crossed, khaki-clad legs topped with a newspaper spoke. "Did you invite him in?" It was Abe.

I shook my head. "No, he had to go back home so that his mom wouldn't worry."

Abe lowered his paper. His hair was slightly darker than it'd been the last time I'd seen him. "Screw that, bad boys are the ones who get all the girls."

"Yeah but this dude plays guitar," Butch told him. "Or, so I've heard." He rolled his eyes. "Quincy didn't even tell us that you guys had a big dinner to introduce him! I was so mad!"

"That's just the way he is now. Either Damien or us," Abe said sharply.

"He's just afraid of another confrontation," Butch told him.

"So he says." Abe sighed. "I think he's growing out of us."

Butch rolled his eyes. "Honey you may be younger than the Quince-meister but you aren't THAT young." He looked at his watch. "Maria and Quincy are supposed to come back with take-out and a Quentin Tarantino movie."

I raised an eyebrow. "Take out?!" Take out in my house was unheard of. Except for pizza. Aunt Chasey loved pizza from the city.

"Chasey's with Mr. Meneses. They went to see a show and then who knows what!" Butch giggled.

"Man, I'm jealous," said Abe. "I haven't gotten any in—" He shook his head. "Never mind."

Butch grinned. "Maybe we should see what Sid's up to."

"Anna would kill us for hittin' on her man."

"Sid would kill you for callin' him her man."

"Hey, hate is just love turned over."

"He doesn't hate her. He just doesn't want to be with her anymore."

"I'm glad to hear that someone understands." Sid entered the living room.

"Christ Sid, I know you have great hearing but do you have to always do the Batman thing?" Butch folded his arms.

"Batman's sexy," Abe said.
"I like Batman," I agreed.
"Sid's sexy too. It works," said Abe.
"You're not so bad yourself Abe."
"Oh baby!" Butch teased.
"Anytime, anywhere, big boy!" said Abe enthusiastically.
Sid rolled his eyes.
"Aw c'mon, can I at least give you a hug?" Abe begged.
Sid shook his head.
"He knows you'll grab his ass, dude," Butch told him.
"You guys know me too well." Abe looked at Sid. "Did Anna ever grab your ass?"
"Nope."
"Neither of you seemed much like ass-grabbers," Butch remarked, taking Abe's newspaper. He frowned and tossed it.
I looked at Sid. "He gets mad because he can't read." Courtesy of Chico Marx.
Sid laughed. I tried not to consider that he may have viewed the Marx Brothers' movies when they were first in theatres.
Butch rolled his eyes. "Very funny little miss."
"I'm fucking hungry, where are they?" Abe demanded.
"Is Kippie at work?" I asked, noticing the use of the word "fuck".
"Yup. So you could yell 'fuck' really loud and not get in trouble," said Abe.
"Good to know," I told him.
"You're such a bad influence," Butch scolded.
Abe sighed. "Don't do drugs. Work hard in school. Don't give in to peer pressure." He thought a moment. "Pray daily?"
I giggled.
Butch clapped sarcastically. "Good job, Honest Abe." He looked at Sid. "I've never once wondered why nobody ever started calling this guy that."
Sid shook his head. "Why don't you two just get together and get it over with?"
Abe raised an eyebrow. "Ex-squeeze me?"

"Me and Phyllis?" Butch grinned and hugged me. "Oh Phyllis darling, where have you been all my life? Oh wait, you're taken." He looked at Sid. "That's why we're not together."

"Not to mention the small matter of sexual orientation," Abe added.

Sid rolled his eyes again. "Life's too short for denial."

"I'll remember that," Abe said dismissively.

How could two people know they're in love with each other and not a do a thing about it? If I somehow knew Sid was in love with me, I would've done something. Now I was mad. How dare they not pounce on the opportunity to be together?

"You guys do some stupid things," I muttered. I sat down and grabbed the remote and turned on the TV.

Sid sat next to me on the couch.

"How was Eric's?"

"Good. How was your house? I didn't think you'd be back by now."

"I didn't either. Van showed up this morning with some guys, they're going to take care of everything. All I had to do was put the important stuff in a safe and get a check from Van. And get the full moon over with." He said the last part softly. He seemed closer to me, too. Not that I minded. "Fire still okay?" he asked very quietly.

I nodded, looking back at the TV.

"You being careful?"

I turned and looked at him. I didn't want to tell him about Eric and me. I wanted to tell Sid I felt unfaithful because I still had feelings for him. But I had to get rid of those. I had to stop confiding in Sid.

"Yes," I snapped.

He raised an eyebrow. "What's up?"

"I just...everything's fine, you don't have to worry."

He continued staring at me. Maybe he could stare answers out of people in his prosecuting days. But I wasn't going to let him do it to me.

"I'm going to go to bed."

"Oh, that reminds me," Abe said suddenly. "I need to ask if you guys can watch my hamster."

Butch stared at him, eyebrows low and eyes wide. "Why does going to bed remind you of a hamster? Did you watch that episode of 'South Park' or something?"

"What?!"

Butch shook his head. "Never mind."

"It reminds me because I thought of the humongous hotel beds I'm gonna be sleeping in this weekend. I'm going to Baltimore on business on Thursday and I'll be back on Sunday morning and I was hoping you guys could keep an eye on Newbert."

"Who's Newbert?" Quincy had entered, followed by Maria.

"Newbert, my hamster."

"Since when do you have a hamster?" Quincy demanded.

"Since forever, dimwit. Maybe if you paid more attention to me.."

"Chill, man!"

"I'm kidding. But I need you guys to watch him. You won't even have to clean his cage, I'll clean it before I drop him off."

"Where the hell are you going?"

"Baltimore."

"What for?"

"I'm writing an article about Baltimore." For a full-time job, Abe worked in an interior-design place, and once in a while he'd sculpt something and sell it. But sometimes he did freelance work for a local newspaper.

Butch patted Abe on the shoulder. "You poor starving artist. You can hardly support your hamster, can you?"

"We've got 'Pulp Fiction' and 'Reservoir Dogs' so it's up to you guys which one," Maria announced.

"Ooh I wanna see the scene where Bruce Willis shoots John Travolta. That always cracks me up," Butch told her.

"And you think I'm disturbed." Abe glared at Butch.

"Things like that happen," Sid told them. "People shoot because they're not thinking or too afraid to think rationally. Or they get startled and happen to have their fingers on the trigger of a gun."

"Mm-mm-mm," Quincy said, shaking his head. "Human race is goin' down the drain. We gotta stop shootin' each other."

"I agree," I said, heading up the stairs.

"Aw, you're not gonna watch with us?" Quincy looked up at me.

I smiled and shook my head. "I've got to get some sleep."

"Have a good rest Phyllis," Maria said.

"Thank you Maria, it's great to see you here."

She smiled. "Thanks honey, see you later."

"Night Phyllis!" chorused Butch and Abe.

"Night." I hurried up the stairs and dove into my bed.

I lay there, looking at the ceiling and listening in the dark to the faint sounds of the TV downstairs and people talking. It was comforting. I was comfortable and sleepy in my warm cozy bed, but I wasn't alone. There were people who loved me just downstairs and if I needed some company, they were there for me. I had a great family and a great boyfriend and..mixed up feelings.

The last thing I heard was Aunt Chasey returning from her date. In my sleep I may have heard the soft sound of someone trying to come quietly up the stairs.

Hot Musicians, Gay Jocks, and the Wrong Moment to Throw Food.

By Friday I was doing a first-rate job of avoiding Sid and focusing on Eric. I suppose it helps when one is rejecting you while the other is making it difficult for you to keep your clothes on.

After school on Thursday Eric had taken me out for a drive, which meant to my Aunts that we were going to visit "safe" parts of the city (locations they'd deemed worthy). To Eric and me it meant making out in the back seat of his car while parked in his garage until 5 o'clock when his mom came home from work.

By this time, Eric had gotten my bra off and I was blowing smoke out of the partially opened window whenever he wasn't looking. I ran my hands through his soft hair while he murmured hard-to-distinguish things about how wonderful my body was. When I picked up something especially nice I'd pull his head back up and kiss him for a while.

All went well (which means my mind was off my morals and guilt and I was thinking, "Wow, someone is holding me and kissing me") until I felt him reach between my legs and press.

I shot up. "Not yet, Eric."

He raised up his hands like an innocent man. "I'm sorry, I'm getting carried away." He kissed my neck. "I won't do it again, but...did it feel good?"

"Yes."

He kissed my lips. "Good."

God he looked great with his shirt off. His arms were toned and a little bit tan. They felt amazing wrapped around me.

But wouldn't Sid look great with his shirt off? the voice had questioned me.

I'd realized something about the voice. No matter what I did, it always disagreed.

Friday morning, Taylor saw me walking toward Key and her. "Hey, you're looking happy. You weren't with Eric last night, were you?"

I grinned. "Yep."

"Aww Phyllis, that's awesome."

Key patted her on the shoulder. "You guys are still young, you have time." She looked at me. "So you like him a lot? You look good together. But then, you both look good alone too."

I giggled.

"What about that hottie who lives with you?"

"Oh, he's like her uncle," said Taylor, than she cringed. "No, no, no, he isn't, he definitely isn't, I can't lie about that."

"I really really like Eric, I'm glad we're going out," I heard myself saying. And it was the truth. But something still didn't fit, if I paid enough attention. So I didn't.

* * *

After lunch, fresh from a midday hug with Eric, I felt pretty happy.

I sat down at my table and noted the absence of Liz.

"Mary's here," Taylor whispered to me. "I'm gonna go to the library now," she said, rising from her seat.

"Taylor—" I started, but she had walked off. I didn't blame her for being uneasy about Mary. It was just easier to be unafraid of Mary if Taylor was nearby. It was easier for me to be unafraid in general when Taylor was with me, come to think of it.

Key, Helen, and Jesse (skipping a class) sat in the seats near mine.

"Where's Mary?" I asked.

Key nodded to my right, and I turned.

There she was, coming out of a lunch line with a tray. I never bought lunch. It was usually disgusting if the school had made it. If I bought anything, it was from a vending machine. Aunt Chasey made my lunch and enjoyed concocting little snacks, like big marshmallows with peanut butter scooped inside and french bread with homemade garlic butter.

We all looked on as Mary came toward us.

Suddenly something whooshed past Mary's head. She whirled around to see that it had come from the jock table. Some kid named Kyle or Richie or Mike. I couldn't keep all those damned jocks straight.

They threw food all the time, but in most cases it was to the neighboring table where Max, the school genius, sat, or another jock table. Never at us, we had never bothered them, we didn't know them, and everyone knew that Key was cool. Plus, just a few months ago Mary had been a pretty, peppy preppy girl.

Apparently though, Mary now had a different attraction. And they obviously didn't know just who she was.

Mary turned back around after glaring at Ted or Steve or Ryan, and kept walking. When the second chicken nugget hit Mary's long, thickly braided and dreaded hair, she turned on her heel and walked right up to the jock table, quickly ducking as someone else pelted a french fry at her.

"Oooh she's mad."

"You're gonna get it, man."

"What are you gonna do, bitch?" the boy sitting next to Jeremy/Greg/Jake yelled.

She grabbed Jeff or Aaron or Mike's shoulders, and stared at him. Suddenly she looked calm. She stood up straight, and put one hand on Jared/Harry/Connor's shoulder, and one on the boy next to him's shoulder.

"Fucking freak, don't touch me!" said the boy next to what's-his-name.

"Why don't you two confess your true feelings to each other?" I didn't hear her actually say this, but later she would tell me. Aloud, she only said, "Fuck you." Then she lifted her hands from the boys' shoulders and walked away.

They all laughed at her as she did so.

She sat down and quietly began eating her rotini.

Suddenly there was an outburst of "Whoa!" and "What the fuck?!" and chairs rustling as the jock table was abandoned. Most of them stood, pushing their chairs away and looking on in horror as the two boys who'd bothered Mary kissed passionately.

"What the hell?" said a girl at the neighboring table. She got up and yanked Joey/Nick/Chris away from the other boy.

"You're gay?!"

"No!"

One of the other jocks laughed. "Dude, you just fuckin' kissed a guy."

The girl slapped Josh/Brian/Jason across his face.

"Hey Crystal, he woulda' kissed Derek earlier if you hadn't given him herpes!" yelled a black guy wearing baggy pants from across the cafeteria. He high-fived his friends.

"I'm not a fag!" cried what's-his-name.

"Dude, get out of here. Go sit with some other fuckin' queers," said one of the jocks.

For the rest of the year, if someone got too close to someone of the same sex, people would say, "Back off Kyle!" (Kyle turned out to be his name) instead of just calling them gay.

Helen said, "Wow," and went back to eating.

"Holy fuckin' shit, I hate that kid," Jesse said. "Now people are going to think I'm a homophobe!"

Key and I were both staring at Mary, who ate calmly in her seat.

"She's doing it to everyone," Key whispered to me under her breath.

I turned to her. "Can I borrow your cell phone?"

Key nodded. "Here, just give it back before school's over. We have to call Jesse's brother for a ride."

I nodded in return. "Okay, thank you."

I went down the hall and searched for a quiet place. I remembered that the music rooms were all soundproof and went into an empty chorus-lesson room.

Surrounded by chairs and music stands, I dialed Sid's cell phone number, which was inscribed in my mind though I had never called it.

I imagined him in his room as his voice came onto the line.

"Hello?"

"Sid."

"Hey Philly, are you okay?"

"I'm fine Sid. But I think you need to see Mary. She just forced some guy to kiss another."

"She forced two guys to kiss?"

"Yes."

"Are you sure?"

"Pretty sure."

"What'd she do?" Sid didn't sound intrigued, but concerned.

"She just grabbed these two guys who were mean to her and muttered something and walked away. And then they started kissing. They were jocks, even if they are gay they would never ever kiss in front of the other guys."

"Jesus." Sid didn't say anything for a moment. "Philly, stay away from her."

"Sid she needs help, she doesn't belong here."

"No she doesn't. Whose phone are you on?"

"Key's."

"After you go, get Mary's phone number if Key has it."

"Can't I just invite her over?"

"Philly, I don't want you near her. You've got a secret that would cause real trouble if it got out."

"Do you think she knows?"

"No, witches can't read minds. They learn all of their tricks, they aren't born with them."

"But you have to have some element of magic or whatever to be one, don't you?"

"Yes, but she wouldn't be able to do everything she's been doing without a book or website or some source providing her information. There are...signs. Symptoms that you have the potential to be an illusionist or witch or mystic. I don't know what they are, but Mary must have had them. The book she's using, if it's a book, must focus on self-profit or revenge. She needs to go to the Frobisher mansion and work with witches who know what they're doing. At least she'd be somewhere where she could do as she likes without being questioned."

"Okay. I'll be fine as long as she doesn't touch me, though, right?"

"Yeah. But don't get close to her."

"How am I going to to get her to you if I don't go near her?"

"Call her up."

"I could find her after school, Sid, and tell her. I'll get a ride home with Eric so I don't have to worry about missing the bus. I'll tell her she can stay at my house to practice witchcraft or something."

"Philly, she's dangerous."

"She was my friend, Sid. She doesn't have a reason to do anything to me."

"Did she have any reason to do anything to Taylor?"

I sighed. He was right.

He was also hot, said the voice.

I don't know what that has to do with it, but it's a good point, I told it.

"It's just...she'll think I'm scared of her if I don't talk to her in person. I left the lunch table to call you almost as soon as she sat down."

There was a pause. Then, "If you do this, you have to be very careful. I don't want you sacrificing your secrets for her."

"I'll be careful." I paused. "You think she'll be okay?"

"If she's exposed to the right knowledge."

"Are there any witches in the CIA?"

Sid chuckled. "Our country might be better off. But it might end up exposing them."

"I just can't believe there's this whole other kind of people, and nobody knows."

"It's surprising how well people can keep a secret when their lives are at stake. And everyone with the energy needs to be able to trust each other. With all of the power that we have and can't share.." Sid stopped. "Philly, you're in school. You need to go, we can talk about this later."

"What if you won't talk about it then?"

"I will, babes. I promise. If I didn't want to talk about this, I wouldn't talk about it at all. You can always talk to me, Philly."

I flinched. "Don't use that tone, it makes you sound like a parent."

I could almost hear Sid's smirk. "I wouldn't be such a bad father."

"Sid." Ewwewwew.

He was laughing at me. "Don't worry babes, it sounds just as wrong to me as it does to you. I'd much rather be your friend."

"Like Quincy? Only trustworthy?"

"And not gay," he added strongly.

I nodded. "Thanks Sid. See you later."

"Be careful Philly." He hung up.

My first phone call with Sid. Ahhh.

As nervous as I was about talking to Mary, talking to Sid had an effect on me that could overcome all my other thoughts and feelings.

I put the phone in my pocket and hoped Key didn't have a tracphone.

As I walked out of the room, I saw Eric.

"Hey Phyllis."

"Hi Eric."

We smiled at each other. "Don't you have lunch?" he asked.

I nodded, and, holding up the phone, said, "I had to call home."

"Are you okay?"

"Yeah, I just had to confirm something." I looked at him. "Can I get a ride home with you today?"

Eric grinned. "A ride home as in.."

I giggled. "Just to my house. I have to stay a couple minutes after school and I might miss the bus."

He kissed my cheek. "Of course, just meet me out front after school, okay? I'll wait for you."

"Thank you Eric." I gave him a soft kiss on the lips.

* * *

After much talk about what had happened during lunch, I said good-bye to Taylor and Tony and gave Key her phone back. I went to find Mary.

It didn't take long. She was outside, on a bench near the front steps of the school. I sat next to her.

"Hi Mary."

She looked over. "Hi Phyllis. Don't you have to catch the bus?" she asked, confused.

I shook my head. "No, what about you?"

She closed her eyes. "I…." She covered her face. Her body lurched and heaved with sobs, but no sound came out.

"Mary," I said softly, "I saw what happened today with..that guy..and I know what you did and...I think I can help you."

"N...no one.."

"Go ahead," I whispered. "Nobody's looking at us, you can cry if you need to."

She shook her head. "Nobody can help me." She sobbed, took a breath, and spoke, her voice quivering up and down octaves. "My par…ents don't…they want me-ee-ee out!" She covered her face again. "I'm not perfect…anymore they…d-don't want m-me."

I hugged her. "Mary I'm so sorry. Where do they expect you to go? What happened?"

"I…don't know…but Key's bringing…me to get my stuff after…she's done tutoring…some kid. They…don't love…me any…anymore." She cried into my shoulder. "And I'm so f-fucked up. I don't know what's going on…and…."

"I think I know where you can go," I said, slowly and quietly.

"There's nowhere to go! I don't h-have any money and the…the whole school thinks I'm a f-f-freak."

"They just don't understand. You have power."

"W-what?" She looked up.

"Come to my house, Mary. I can help you. Remember, my Aunts rent rooms? You could stay a little while with us. We can help you."

She sat up slowly, her dark eye makeup blurred.

"H-how?"

No idea. "We'll talk about it when you get there, okay?"

Mary gently clutched my shoulders.

"How can you help me?"

AH! the voice was shouting. DON'T TALK! DON'T TALK!

No, not the voice. My voice.

"Don't say anything! Don't talk!" I cried, having no control over my words. I closed my eyes, my body jerking away.

She let go. What the hell? What just happened?

"I'm sorry Phyllis. I'll be there at six. I'll bring my stuff."

I nodded. "Okay." I got up and went to find Eric. I'd have to tell Sid about this when I got home. Right now, I had to seem a bit less shocked because someone had tried to break into my mind.

He was right on the steps.

"Was that Mary?" he asked.

"Yeah."

"What happened?"

"She's been going through tough times, I just wanted to tell her I'm here for her," I told him.

"Tony says Taylor doesn't like Mary anymore," Eric said as we walked down the steps and towards the student parking lot.

I nodded. "She doesn't. Mary did something terrible to her."

"So why are you still friends with her?"

"I don't think Mary realizes what she did. I want to help her."

"What'd she do?"

Uhhh... "She...she couldn't let one of Taylor's secrets stay kept."

Eric nodded. "You can't tell anybody anything anymore."

"Yeah. Sometimes I can't even trust my family. But I suppose that's a little different."

"What do you mean?"

"Well, if I were to tell Quincy or Sid or somebody that's lived with us a while—"

"I thought Sid just moved in?"

"Oh, he did, but he's known my Aunts forever."

"Ah, go on."

"If I were to tell one of them about something we did that we're not supposed to be doing—"

Eric grabbed my hand and squeezed it affectionately.

"—they'd probably feel like they had to tell my Aunts."

"Do you talk to everyone in your house a lot?"

I nodded. "Oh yeah. They were my best friends before I had friends. Especially Quincy and his friends, they helped raise me a lot. I didn't have a lot of friends in elementary school, so it was really nice to have friends to go home to."

"That's cool. I've never had a big family, I don't even have cousins or grandparents. Just my mom and Terry. But Tony's kinda' like my cousin, I guess."

I grinned. "So Taylor'll be your cousin-in-law."

"Probably. I can't ever see them breaking up."

"I know. But then, things happen."

Eric looked at me. "Think we'll last a while?"

"I don't know Eric. I've never had a boyfriend. I don't know how it works."

Eric chuckled.

"What?" I asked.

"I was gonna tell you how it works." He grinned.

"I know how that works."

"You sure? I would be happy to show you."

I looked at him. He was such a great guy. So why was Sid still sitting there in the back of my mind? I kept feeling that something wasn't right, but I had to ignore it. I had to get on with my life. Sure, I had plenty of time, but the sooner the better, right?

"Maybe another time," I told Eric.

"Really?"

"I said maybe."

He nodded. "Okay."

* * *

"You're a bit later than usual, aren't you dear?" Aunt Chasey was sitting on the couch, reading a mystery.

"Wow, you're not reading a cookbook?" I smiled at her.

She laughed a little. "No dear, I'm reading. No one gets murdered; it sounded like my cup of tea."

I nodded. "I got a ride home with Eric."

She frowned, only the slightest, subtlest bit. "Why's that, dear?"

"I had to talk to Mary."

"The troubled girl?"

I nodded. "Yes. I told her she could come over tonight and maybe talk to you guys. She's having more trouble than I thought. Her parents have kicked her out of her house, and...Sid thinks he may be able to help her."

"That kind of trouble? Goodness!" Aunt Chasey shook her. "You know Phyllis, when Kippie found out what had happened to Sid, she remarked that she'd like to have some sort of magical ability. But I'm glad we didn't, our parents may have hurt us. They thought anything to do with magic was connected with the devil." She shook her head. "It's ignorant people like that who take fictional stories and such too seriously. They would try to hurt people like Sid simply because of an accident or the way they were born." She paused. "I'm sorry Phyllis, it's just always angered me when people take Christianity too far. My parents never would have let someone like Quincy into their home, not even for dinner. I remember when one of Kippie's friends had an abortion and the town found out. She was never allowed in our house again. Terrible." She sighed. "Kippie's always been pro-choice since that happened. Honestly I still don't think I've made up my mind. But I do know that past mistakes or odd hobbies or simply any disagreement is no reason to treat another person with hatred. Hatred is the only thing we should be protesting."

"You know I never realized this, but you're really just a Protestant hippie, Chase." Sid came down the stairs.

She smiled. "Add 'sober' and 'loves to cook' to that and you're just about right, Dominick."

"Mary's coming at six," I told them both. "Is that okay, Aunt Chasey?"

Aunt Chasey nodded. "Certainly. She's welcome to stay here for as long as necessary, as long as you think she's trustworthy."

"I don't know what damage she could do to anyone here," Sid said.

"So what is your theory about this girl, Dominick?" Chasey asked.

"I think she's a beginner witch."

"Don't they call themselves something else?"

Sid shrugged helplessly. "I don't know Chase, I never learned much about witchery."

She chuckled. "Witchery, eh?"

"When I was your age, we didn't tease our elders like that," Sid said with mock sternness.

Aunt Chasey laughed wildly. "Siddie dear, I apologize."

Sid patted her on the shoulder. "It's okay Chase."

The front door burst open.

"Was that Eric we just passed pulling out of the driveway, Phyllis?" Butch asked. He was carrying a large cage.

"Yeah," I replied.

Butch put a hand to his cheek and smiled as though he might cry. "Oh Phyllis, you are getting to be such a young woman."

Sid was trying not to laugh.

"Is that Newbert?" Aunt Chasey asked, looking at the cage. Inside it was a little orangey hamster nibbling on an empty paper towel roll.

"Why yes it is. Isn't that a wretched name? I never say wretched, but that name is wretched."

"It's not that bad, Butch. He's a hamster," I said.

"Yeah Butch, Quincy did name his cat 'Enrique the Spaniard' and you never had a problem," Sid pointed out.

"What about the Spaniard? What'd that damn cat do now?" Quincy entered, followed by Damien.

"I love Enrique!" Damien said. "Don't call him 'that damn cat'."

Quincy sighed. "Everybody, meet Mr. Newbert. Abe insists that that name is the only thing this hamster will respond to. I figure we can put him in the basement."

"Oh Quincy, no. He'll be all alone. He needs to be in somebody's room, where they can watch him," Aunt Chasey said.

"Okay fine, but I'ma put him in the basement for now so we can watch some stuff down there."

"What is it?" Chasey asked.

"Some kid did a documentary on gays and there might be some awful prejudice...crap in it," Butch said.

Chasey nodded. "I understand, you boys go ahead. I'll try and find Newbert a suitable place."

"Thank you Chasey, Abe really appreciates it," Butch said.

"You know guests are never a problem in our house," Aunt Chasey said pleasantly. The guys took Newby and headed to the basement.

"He could stay in my room," Sid suggested.

Aunt Chasey looked at Sid dangerously. "If you kill that hamster.."

Sid held up his hands. "Chasey, the one time I got loose I couldn't even get out of the garage. I killed a mouse. If I can't even succeed as a wolf, what could I possibly do to a hamster while I'm a man?"

"Sid, I've seen what you've done to your sheets, I don't know.."

"The cats never go in my room, Chase. He'd be safest there."

In the end, Aunt Chasey consented. Then she asked, "Why do you want a hamster in your room, Sid?"

"Hungry."

Aunt Chasey gave him a look.

"I'm kidding. We don't have to put him in my room. But I know it's the only place that the cats don't wander into."

"You're a good man, Dominick."

I wished he wanted me to stay in his room.

What about Eric? the voice demanded.

Would you just make up your mind on which guy you think I should be with?! I mentally yelled at it.

I will when you do.

Ha! Don't have a comeback for that one, do you?

I decided to stop arguing with the voice and go take a shower.

When I got out, there was a knock on my door.

I was in a towel, but I knew it wasn't Sid; he wouldn't have knocked. So I said, "Come in."

Unfortunately for me, I was quite wrong.

"Oh, I'm sorry," Sid said. "I knocked because I thought you might be changing; I heard the water running."

I subconsciously tightened the towel and hugged my arms around me a little. But he didn't offer to come back later.

"I need to talk to you," he said.

"Um, okay. You wanna wait until I change?" I needed to talk to him, too, and tell him about what Mary had done, but facing him with clothing was difficult enough.

Sid grinned. "Well no, if you want my honest answer."

Oh God.

He shut my door and sat on my bed. "Sit down."

I sat a few feet down from him, clutching the towel for dear life, and wished that I could enjoy this a little. Okay, so I was. I just hoped I didn't look fat or that the towel wasn't riding up in certain places and I wasn't noticing. I looked around myself as I sat.

"Don't worry, you're fine," he reassured me. "Listen babes, this is serious. If Mary comes tonight, and if she decides she wants to see the mansion, we're going to be taking her to see Van. And you need to know what Van is like."

"A pervert?" It takes one to know one, Sid, I thought, and tightened my towel.

"Not exactly. He just has trouble with limits when he's around girls. And I mean mental limits more than physical limits, so listen to me right now. Do not look into his eyes. Make absolutely no eye contact. If there's time he'll try to get you to do so. He might even try to make you angry so that you'll glare at him. If you have to, look at his nose, okay Philly? Anything but his eyes. Or he'll get into your head in a way that far surpasses Hannibal Lecter."

That comparison was what scared me the most. I nodded rapidly. "Okay, I won't look into his eyes. Have you told my Aunts that I'd be going with you?"

He nodded. "They said it was fine, it's not a school night."

I looked at him. "They have the utmost trust in you, Sid."

He looked into my eyes. "I would never let anyone hurt you, Philly." He studied my gaze. Then he spoke. "What did you say to Mary? Oh, watch your towel." He gestured toward my chest, where some cleavage was starting to show. I clasped the ends of the towel and pulled them upward a bit.

Jesus, I thought.

He looked at my face again. "Anyway, Mary.."

"I just...I just told her I could help her, basically. And then she told me that her parents have kicked her out of her house and started crying. So I tried to comfort her and said she could stay with us. I told her I knew she had power and that we could help. But then she wanted to know how, and..." I looked down.

"What happened?"

I looked back at him. "She grabbed my shoulders and asked me how."

"Jesus Christ Philly, why didn't you say anything before? What does she know? Are you okay?" He reached over and gently touched the side of my face.

Ahhh, his hands..

"Well...it didn't work."

"What do you mean?"

"She tried to get me to talk and my mouth started moving, but all I could say was 'Don't talk, don't talk!' and I couldn't stop yelling that until she let go of me. She said she was sorry and she'd be here at six."

Sid was staring at me.

"What?"

He shook his head. "Nothing."

"So...am I okay? Did she see anything?"

"No. I think you're fine. She probably thinks you have the energy now, and that's why she was so compliant."

"Why did that happen, Sid?"

He looked ponderous. "I don't know, babes. I didn't think people without the energy could block it." He was staring at me again.

"What is it, Sid?"

He began to speak, then stopped. Then he began again. "Philly...would you mind if I had Van look up your father? Your Aunts didn't really know him. Maybe...maybe he had something."

"But wouldn't I have noticed?"

"I would have thought so. And I should have noticed as well." He looked thoughtful again, then shook his head. "We don't have to worry about it now. Maybe Mary has some sort of limit on her power. Maybe you just have an incredibly strong mind. I wouldn't be surprised." He smiled. Then he was concerned. "Are you sure you're all right, babes?"

I nodded. "Yeah."

"Okay." The ends of his mouth curved just a little. "How are things with Eric?"

"They're fine. Sid, I really should change."

"Sorry about that, Philly." Sid stood. "I can't say that very sincerely, though." He grinned and left.

What was Sid, bipolar?

I shut my door and sighed. My life felt like a really bad movie at that moment. Like what Taylor always said about Spiderman 3. Nothing anybody did made a lot of sense.

Well, at least I hadn't paid to be born.

I got dressed and looked at my clock. There were at least a couple of hours until Mary would arrive. And there was someone who deserved to know about this.

I reached for the phone and began to dial Taylor's number.

No wait..

I hung up the phone. I couldn't call Taylor. I couldn't tell her about Mary without explaining about Sid. I could have said something cryptic like, "You won't have to worry about Mary anymore," but that wouldn't help Taylor. It'd just make her think I was in the Mafia or something. She probably wouldn't be surprised.

* * *

When I heard Aunt Kippie knocking on my bedroom door, I thought it was the early morning, and I was being woken up for school.

Yesterday was Friday, I thought to myself. Shouldn't today be Saturday? No, today must be Friday..

The door opened, I opened my eyes, and I realized it was still light out, hardly dim. I'd fallen asleep on my bed, my comforter over me and the phone on the floor next to the bed.

"Oh I'm sorry dear, were you napping?"

I smiled tiredly and nodded.

She patted my cheek softly. "You've had a long week. It was a good idea to nap. I just wanted to know if you wanted some dinner. Chasey made spaghetti."

We went through the two sections of the upstairs and took the back stairs for a more direct route into the kitchen.

"Kippie, would you like to bring some spaghetti down to the boys?" Aunt Chasey lifted a tray of spaghetti plates to Aunt Kippie.

Kippie took it. "Of course." She went to the basement door. "There had better not be any pornography on that TV when I get down there!" she yelled.

Aunt Chasey put a plate of spaghetti on the table for me. "Let me know what you think of the sauce, it seemed to have a little too much spice to it and less tomato flavor."

I twirled some spaghetti about my fork (drenched in sauce and parmesan cheese) and shoveled it in. The sauce was, of course, perfect, hot and flavorful.

"Did you actually buy tomatoes and crush them to make this?" I questioned.

"Yes dear, I did."

It was the most amazing tomato sauce I'd ever tasted. As I continued to eat, she smiled. "I think I have my answer."

I nodded swiftly.

"My only regret is not having anything to make meatballs with."

"There's a hamster downstairs," Aunt Kippie said, coming out of the basement.

I raised an eyebrow. "You want to make meatballs with it?"

"What?"

"Kippie, I'm afraid your remark came at an odd moment," Chasey told her. "Here, have some spaghetti. Where's Sid?"

"I told him there was spaghetti. You know him, he'll come when he's ready. Maybe he'll bring you some meat to put in the sauce."

I giggled. My mind is dirty, okay? It also has bad timing.

They both looked at me. "What's so funny?"

I shook my head. "Nothing, I'm going to go into the living room in case Mary comes a few minutes early." I took my plate and left.

"Let me know if you want seconds," Aunt Chasey called.

I sat on the couch with my spaghetti. It was nice outside, but it looked as though it might rain, and I had a feeling it would because all of the cats were inside (Wonder Woman was sleeping on top of the TV). It wasn't surprising, though. April was starting.

I heard someone coming down the stairs and turned. It was Sid, of course.

"They want to know if you want spaghetti," I told him.

"Maybe a little bit later," he said thoughtfully. "I'm not that hungry."

Suddenly Xerxes darted out from under the couch and ran up the stairs, past Sid.

Sid looked behind him. "Isn't that cat about as old as I am?"

"In cat years, probably. Maybe he's immortal, too. Can cats be immortal?"

"Not unless Xerxes is."

Johnny came out of the kitchen and walked over to me. He hopped up onto my lap, sniffed my food, and then settled for the spot on the couch next to me.

"My boy," I said in a baby voice, scratching under his chin. He purred like a motorboat.

Sid sat in his chair. "Did you tell Eric about Johnny?"

I smiled. "No. I guess he'll have to find out sometime. Aw, you're so handsome, aren't you Johnny?" He nuzzled my hand.

"Does he have any pets?"

I shook my head. "No." I squeezed Johnny's scruff. He liked that.

"Is everything okay between you two?"

"Me and Johnny?"

"You and Eric."

"Yes," I said quickly, petting Johnny's head.

"Nobody's gotten burned?"

"Hey!" Johnny tried to bite me and I swiftly pulled my hand away. I looked at Sid. "Sid, I don't want to talk about Eric. Everything is fine, okay?"

"Really." He was unconvinced, probably because I was snapping at him.

"Yes." I pulled my sleeve over my hand and dug it into Johnny's belly. He bit and scratched at it. "Nothing is going to happen. I am fine. You don't have to ask me." I took a breath. Why was I getting so mad all of a sudden? Sid was concerned. But he didn't have to ask me about Eric every five minutes! I wasn't telling Sid all about my life anymore. "If something is wrong, I'll tell you."

Sid nodded. "Fair enough."

The front door opened.

Butch stepped in.

"Weren't you already here?" I asked, confused.

Butch held up a grocery bag. "Meatballs for Chasey. And your friend Mary is here." He moved aside and she walked in. They were both a bit wet.

Mary's dreads were pulled back and her dress was long and loose. She was completely covered but could move about freely.

"We just met outside," Butch explained. "I hear she's renting a room?"

I smiled. "Yup, she might be." I looked at Mary. She only had one bag. "Is that all of your stuff?"

Mary nodded. "I don't need much. And my parents wouldn't let me take everything."

Butch reached his hand out to Mary. "Honey, you'll get everything you need here. Welcome."

She shook it. "Thank you."

Butch headed into the kitchen, pausing when he saw Johnny. "Look at that little son of a bitch. Layin' in the nice warm lap of luxury while people are struggling outside in the rain." He patted Johnny's back. "Spoiled cat."

As soon as Butch had entered the kitchen, Chasey came out of it. "Hello Mary!" She rushed over and hugged Mary. "It's wonderful to have you, I'm Chasey Sorin." She let go and smiled. "Would you like some spaghetti, dear?"

Mary smiled. "Thank you so much, I would love some." She walked over to the TV and began petting Wonder Woman.

"That's Wonder Woman," I told her. "This is Johnny," I introduced, pointing to said cat.

"Hi kitty," she said.

"Just make yourself at home dear," Aunt Chasey told her. "I'll be right back with your spaghetti."

"Thank you so much," Mary said gratefully.

"Would you like any, Sid?"

Mary turned and stared at Sid.

"That'd be great, Chase."

"I assume you'd like to wait for the meatballs."

He smiled. "Yes please."

"Of course dear." She went off to the kitchen.

"Sit down," I told Mary, patting the couch next to me.

She did. "I love your house," she told me.

"Thanks. Um...did you want to eat, and then we could talk about how we can help you?"

Mary nodded, not looking at me. "That would be good. I'm sorry about today, Phyllis."

I nodded.

She turned and looked at Sid. "You're the one who can help me, aren't you?"

Sid shook his head. "I can't. I know who can, though. I know where you can go."

"Really?" Mary was relieved. "I knew you had something. When you guys gave me a ride home on Valentine's Day..I knew you were like me." She shook her head. "But...I don't know what I am. I used to be so different, and then..."

"Here you are dear." Aunt Chasey brought Mary her spaghetti and took my plate.

"Thank you Aunt Chasey," I said sweetly.

"Of course dear." She went back into the kitchen.

Sid nodded. "It's okay, you're going to be fine," he told Mary.

I didn't want Mary to love Sid. I concentrated on Johnny. Just then, the front door opened again.

"Hey guys!" It was Clark Kent, or Bill with Clark Kent glasses. He must have watched a Justice League DVD at some point. Taylor's DVDs often somehow ended up at my house for long periods of time.

"Hey Clark," I greeted him. "Chasey made spaghetti."

"Oh that's great, I love spaghetti!"

"Clark, this is my friend Mary," I introduced them.

Bill extended his hand. "Clark Kent, great to meet you Mary!"

Mary didn't seem to notice the Superman's secret identity thing. "You too," she said, shaking his hand.

"How was work?" Sid asked him.

"Oh it was fine. You know. Nothing I couldn't handle." He winked at Sid and me. Apparently we knew he was really Superman. "Well, I'm gonna go get some of that great spaghetti." He went to the kitchen. Johnny hopped off my lap and followed.

"There are people with abilities like yours, Mary. A few of them live normal lives. Most of them live in a place where they can express themselves freely."

Like a nudist colony, said the voice.

Sid began to explain to Mary about the Frobisher mansion. I took in everything I could.

It'd been around forever, as had people with the energy. They had their own mythology about how it all started (though Sid didn't explain what it was), and prophecies had been told about their kind. They had their own apocalypse theory but there was no real religion. Some of them had regular "mortal" religions. People had found out about the "fictional" creatures that had the energy through several people who'd made a living telling their fabricated life stories. Once mortals had gotten wind of it, they'd added on more to it. The silver bullet thing, the sleeping in a coffin thing, etc. The only reason that anyone had any notion that immortals existed was purely for their own entertainment.

Sid told Mary that the people in the mansion were a lot like her, and that she could stay updated with what was going on in our realm while living comfortably in the Frobisher mansion. He explained that Stacia and Van Frobisher were brother and sister. That Van was the most powerful immortal (he made it sound like a Tolkien story or something) in the realm we lived in. He provided news and new products to those living in Stacia's mansion, which some called the hidden realm (Sid mentioned that he thought this made it sound more glamorous than it was). Stacia needed Van, Sid explained, even though she was probably more powerful than he was.

"The mansion is hidden. There are folds—those are like portals—everywhere that lead to the mansion. It's real location is North America. I can't really say where. I always got directions from Van and I haven't wanted to go back there for a long time."

"If you didn't like living there, why would I?" Mary asked.

"I made a mistake while I was there. I got involved in the politics of the place, rumors were spread, harsh words were exchanged..but it'll be different for you. You'll live in a completely different part of the mansion; it's like a tiny city. You'll be with people you can relate to and learn from, and, when you're ready, you can come back and live here again. Or you can continue living there."

Mary looked hesitant. "Couldn't I just live here and learn from you?"

No way!

I listened carefully to what Sid said.

"I'm not a witch. I think that's what you are. I don't know enough to help you. You have a power, and it comes from the same energy that affects me, but I got mine by accident. I was bitten by a werewolf a while back."

Pff. A while back.

"But you were born with yours. You instinctively know how to operate it and as you grow, your knowledge will broaden and your power will increase. But it won't do you any good unless you're in a place where you can use it freely. Philly and I can take you there. Van Frobisher lives in the city, and—"

"Psst!"

The three of us turned.

"Phyllis!" Quincy hissed, peering around the basement door. "You gotta come downstairs!"

I gave him an "Are you kidding?" look. I had to stay and make sure Sid didn't fall in love with Mary. What if she kissed him or something?

"Newbert escaped!" he whispered.

I sighed.

"Quince," Sid protested.

"No! Phyllis has got to help us find him! Come on!"

"Fine." I rose, leaving Sid and Mary alone, and followed Quincy down the basement stairs.

As we neared the TV room and bedroom area, I heard little cries of "Newby! Come out, Newbert!" and "Newie! Daddy'll be home soon! Don't worry!"

I entered the TV room.

They'd pulled out the couch and were running flashlight beams over the wall.

"C'mon Newie, don't worry, it'll be okay. Soon you'll be able to go home," Damien said sweetly.

"Maybe that's why he escaped," Butch muttered.

"Yeah well, crawling into the wall never helped anybody."

"He went into the wall?!" Quincy cried. "Abe is gonna KILL us!"

"It's probably because he named it Newbert."

Damien nodded. "You're right, Newbert sounds weird. Like Sherbet."

"I knew a guy called Northrup once," Butch told him.

Damien giggled. "Northrup."

"Yeah, we called him Nort. Or Ruppy, if—"

"Guys, we got to get this mouse out of the damn wall!" Quincy exclaimed.

"It's a hamster," Damien told him.

"Phyllis, smoke it out. Please."

I looked at him blankly. "Quincy, there's only one hole in the wall. There's no other way to get it out."

"Yeah Quincy, what is it gonna do, crawl towards the smoke? This hamster isn't dumb."

"How exactly would Phyllis smoke it out?" Damien was confused.

Aw crap, said the voice.

Butch's eyes widened and looked at me, petrified.

Quincy's hands flew to his face and covered it completely.

I sighed. "We'll explain later. But we have to figure out how to get him out of the wall." I thought. I couldn't burn the hamster, that would be awful. I could never hurt an animal. I wanted to kill the people who tortured cats and dogs, and probably hamsters too. But was there any other way I could get him out? There was a chance I could push with my breath..the way I'd pushed Jeremy without burning him.

Okay, so I could put force into my breath. Maybe. But all that would do was send the hamster further into the wall. Could I reverse it? Inhale the hamster back out?

Well, it was worth a try. But first I had to make sure I could do it.

"Butch, can you move away from the rocking chair, please?"

Butch nodded and moved over.

I took a deep breath, and then blew. I was about ten feet from the chair.

It flew backward and hit the wall, but did not catch fire when the flames flew past it.

I tried it again, but this time, I inhaled.

The chair moved forward a little, but not with as much force as it had gone backward.

I figured it might work better with the hamster.

I knelt a few inches in front of the hole. Then I set the wall on fire and breathed it in as hard as I could.

As I inhaled the fire, the hamster came flying out and managed to hit my lips before I grabbed it in my hands.

"Okay, that I did not know you could do, honey." Butch reached down and took the hamster. He set him in his cage.

"Bad hamster."

"Now he gets to room with Sid," I told them, and we all sighed with envy.

"Lucky little bastard," Damien said. "Now what just happened?"

And that is how Damien found out that I can breathe fire.

* * *

We carried Newbert upstairs in his cage to the kitchen.

"Hello," Aunt Chasey greeted him, peering into his cage. "Would you like me to watch him in here until Sid gets back?"

My eyebrows shot up. "Did they leave?!"

She shook her head. "No dear, but I'm sure they will soon."

"So...the fire thing..what was you first reaction, Chasey? I just found out a minute ago," Damien told her.

"Oh, so she's decided to tell you? It's about time, Phyllis. I don't think Damien's going anywhere." Aunt Chasey was kneading some dough violently. "Unless he turns and runs when Anna gets back."

"Oh yeah, she's coming back pretty soon, isn't she," Butch remembered.

"She sent me a postcard from the Bahamas man. I'm hopin' she lost some of that stress she had when she left. 'Course she'll get it all back when she catches sighta Sid." Quincy looked at Aunt Chasey. "Did you girls tell her about him yet?"

"Kippie said she would. I've been so distracted lately, I haven't been able to ask her. But she has time. Anna won't be here for another few weeks, judging by what she's said in letters and such."

"Thank God," Quincy said. "It's gonna be bedlam if she doesn't know about Sid. Absolute, pure bedlam."

"I love that word. Bedlam," said Damien.

"If Abe were here, he'd say it reminded him of sex," Butch shared.

Aunt Chasey rolled her eyes. "Phyllis, perhaps you should join Mary and Sid, now that you've rescued Abe's hamster."

I nodded. "Yeah." I turned and went to the living room.

Bill/Clark was on the couch now, but he was entranced by a movie (Dr. Zhivago). Sid was looking at Mary. He was waiting, I could tell from the look on his face. Trust me, I'd studied it enough.

Finally Mary spoke. "I want to leave right away. If I don't like it, I'll just come back. I'll get a job and maybe live here or something, if there's room. But my parents hate me. My friends are afraid of me. And I still don't want to give this up, no matter how bad my life keeps getting."

"It's what you're meant to do."

Mary nodded. "Then I want to go to the place where I belong." She suddenly turned and saw me.

She looked back at Sid. "Do you feel the energy—you call the magic the energy, right?"

Sid nodded. "It's the most common and layman reference used."

"Do you feel the energy coming off of Phyllis? Because I thought you had it when I first met you—" was that a flirtatious tone I heard? "—but I never thought Phyllis had it. And then...today.."

"Today you tried to violate her mind. That's not something you should do to your friends. It's not something you should ever do to someone who doesn't deserve it. You're lucky she blocked it." He looked at her significantly.

Mary looked down, ashamed. "It just feels so good..." She turned around again. "I'm really sorry Phyllis. I just...this power I have..I know you couldn't ever have experienced this but..I just have this thing and it feels so good to use it."

Well, at least I knew Sid hadn't told her about my breathing problem.

I nodded. "It's okay Mary. I forgive you."

She smiled gratefully. "You still helped me, even though I did awful things. You're the best friend I've ever had." She rose and hugged me. "Thank you," she whispered.

I hugged her back. "Hey, you invited us to sit at your table the first day, even though we were freshmen. I figured I owed you something."

She laughed a little. "Back when I was Miss Popularity. You cared about me even though I changed."

"I don't mind change. I do miss your hair though. You had amazing hair, Mary."

She smiled. "I'll see what I can do. Maybe when you see me again it'll be back to normal." She glanced at Sid and then she looked at me. "Have you ever been to this place?"

I shook my head. "No. But I trust Sid with my life, so I'm certain you're doing what's best for you."

She smiled again. "Me too." She turned back to Sid. "Can you take me tonight?"

Sid nodded. "Of course. Let's go."

We grabbed our things, told Bill/Clark we were leaving, and left.

Mary and I sat in the backseat. As we drove, I realized I might never see her again. She was going to some weird hidden place that I would never know. We hadn't been the closest of friends, but I was used to her, whether it was preppy her or witchy her. Now there would just be no Mary at all.

And I wouldn't be the only one who'd notice, would I?

"Sid!" I said suddenly. "What are we going to tell everybody? What if the cops come?"

"Mary's going to deal with that," Sid told me.

"I'm going to call my parents and tell them I'm moving away. I'm sure they won't care," she told me.

"Thank you."

Mary looked out her window. I looked out of mine.

Sid turned on the radio. "Philly, remember not to look into his eyes. He's waiting for us."

Oh crap. Psychic vampire. Oh my God, I was going to be with someone who could read my mind...dirty thoughts would automatically float in if I looked into his eyes.

Nose, I thought. Nose, nose, nose. Maybe collar, to be on the safe side.

"What about me?" Mary asked.

"I'm willing to bet you'll be able to block him. If he starts to go into your mind, you'll be able to tell. The sooner you get used to those kind of mental invasions the better. Stacia Frobisher is a stronger psychic vampire than Van is."

"But I'll be living with witches, right?"

Sid nodded. "Yes. But don't refer to them as witches. I'm sure there's a better name they use for it, but I never got close enough to find out."

A little while later, we pulled into the large parking lot of a strong-looking, old stone building that went up 13 or 14 floors.

Sid led us to the front door, through what seemed to be a lobby, and into an elevator. He pressed the button for the third floor.

Down a hall, in a large room, a tall, lanky man with white blonde hair was waiting for us, standing in front of a desk. To his right were some cushiony chairs. He was pale and sinister-looking. Just as Sid had said, he looked the way people expect a vampire to look.

"Hey Van," Sid greeted him.

"Hello Howls." Van had the smallest British accent. They shook hands.

"Howls?" Mary asked.

"Wolf," Sid reminded her. He gestured to her. "This is Mary."

Van nodded. "Hello Mary." They looked at each other.

Mary clutched her head. "Get out get out get out get out GET OUT GET OUT GET OUT!"

Van smirked. "Well she's rather potent, isn't she?"

"I won't go," Mary told Sid and me firmly.

Sid was staring at Van. "He won't do it again. Van's just got some issues. You won't be living with him."

"Yes, I'm afraid I'm rather nosy. I do apologize, and may I compliment you on being so far along while knowing so very little? My sister will love you." Van turned to me.

Ah! Collar, collar, collar..It wasn't that hard because he was so tall that looking at his face could have damaged my spine.

"And you must be Phyllis. I've been hoping to meet you." He held out his hand.

I'd been trained to give eye contact when shaking hands, but I remembered Sid's words and looked at his nose.

"You too," I said civilly.

"I like you, Phyllis. You're polite. I don't encounter many like that anymore," Van told Sid.

Sid smirked. "She won't be polite once she gets to know you."

Van shrugged in admission. He looked back to Mary. "I'm very sorry Mary," he said, actually sounding sincere. "But I think you may understand why I might be tempted to look into the minds of those around me. My self-control is very weak, I'm afraid." He paused. "But you'll hardly need any at the mansion. They're all used to it there. You'll be able to practice."

A young woman with long brown hair appeared. No, she didn't just appear, although I wouldn't have been that surprised. She came in through the door, from the hallway.

"Hello Alanna," Van greeted her.

She scowled at him. "I'm not here to see you. I'm hear to see Sid and his friends." She had an Irish accent, one I'd never heard in person. She turned to Sid. "Hi," she greeted him.

Sid looked confused. "Alanna Castle?"

She nodded. "I came to pick up Mary." She looked at Mary. "Mary."

Mary nodded. "How did you know?"

Alanna took her hands and looked at her hopefully. "We all know each other. A sorceress always knows when another sorceress is present."

"Which isn't always a good thing," Van added.

"Can you please explain why a woman whose mother tried to poison me is here to help us?" Sid asked, looking at both Van and Alanna.

"My mother worships Stacia. That is the only reason she tried to kill you, because you insulted her idol. I don't worship Stacia. And Natasha asked me to come here before Van even suggested it."

Sid nodded. At the mention of the name Natasha, he smiled faintly.

Jealousy flared up within me, literally. But I didn't let any smoke out. I didn't know how any of these people would react.

"She thinks very highly of you, Howls. Wonder why." Van smiled slyly at Sid. "And my sister does not. It couldn't possibly be for the same reason."

"Don't start with your sister," Alanna warned. "Mary deserves our full attention." Alanna looked at her. "She has great power."

Oh God, please don't say "and with great power comes great responsibility," I thought.

Van nodded. "Mary, this charming young woman is Alanna Castle, the daughter of one of the most powerful...ahem..sorceresses we have. Rhonda Castle, her mother, is my sister's right hand. Alanna is going to tell you more about what's in store for you at my sister's home. I myself haven't been there in a century, so I thought it better that you speak to someone who knows the place and what goes on. It would seem Natasha felt the same way. I can tell you one thing, my dear. You will become part of a family whose loyalty will remain with you, no matter how much you change."

Mary looked at him. "Stay out of my head."

Sid chuckled.

Alanna held Mary's hand. "Are you ready to leave?"

Mary swallowed and nodded. "Yes."

"You're going to leave your entire life behind when you come with me. It'll be worth it, but you should know it will never be the same again."

Mary nodded. "Good."

Alanna smiled. "Okay."

Mary turned to me. "Bye Phyllis." She embraced me. "Thank you so much for this."

"Don't worry about it Mary. I wish things could have been better for you. I didn't really do anything, except know Sid."

"And let me talk to him." She whispered in my ear. "You're lucky to have him and vice versa. You're a great person, Phyllis." She was starting to sound more like the old Mary. She leaned away. "I really do owe you though. If you ever need my help and you know where to find me, let me know. I'll never forget that you helped me."

"Good luck," I told her. "Thank you. I'll let you know if anyone bothers me," I said with a grin.

She smiled. "I'll miss you. I know you can't tell anyone where I really am, but...can you tell Key that she was my best friend? Tell her I'll miss her and I'm sorry that I treated her badly. But don't say too much about how you know or where I am."

I nodded. "I'll tell her, I promise."

"Thank you Phyllis." Mary looked to Sid. "Are you going to get into trouble for this? I mean, even after I call my parents, what if they search for me and trace it to you?"

Sid shook his head and gestured to Van. "Van'll take care of everything. Don't worry about us."

"Yes, we're just restoring the balance to society," Van said flatly.

Sid looked at Mary. "Just remember that you don't have to use your power for what others tell you to use it for. Use it for the right things. Remember how lucky you are."

I bristled as she hugged him. "I will, Sid, I promise," she vowed. "Thank you so much. I hope I see you again."

Van was giving me a look as he said, "Good luck, Mary. Alanna, my regards to your mother."

Alanna scowled once more and then, looking welcomingly toward Mary, led her out of the room.

"Well, there's a woman who is about to become her mother. I pity her greatly. Those witches are just a lesbian cult," Van said sourly, looking at the doorway through which they'd left with distaste. He turned to Sid.

"Now Howls, thank you very much for your continually dedicated services to our community. But don't leave yet. I need to speak with you."

"I promised the Sorins I'd bring their niece home, Van."

"Oh, it won't take long. It's about the andrastenite." He paused. "Since Phyllis already seems to know a great deal about our realm, I see no reason why she shouldn't be present."

"Nor do I," said Sid. "In fact, I have a favor to ask you that concerns her."

Van looked at me. "Anything you ask, my dear."

Favor? What was the favor? I looked at Sid.

"Your father," he reminded me.

The head invasion. I remembered now.

"We were wondering if you could look up my father, and see if he's someone you've...ever known."

"You wish to know if he's connected with anyone who has the energy?"

"Actually," Sid said, "we wanted to know if he has the energy."

"Certainly." Van grabbed a black planner book from his desk. "What is his name?"

"William Caramie," I said. Then I spelled it.

Van looked back at me, and I struggled harder not to make eye contact. "Now my dear, I'm aware that you don't live with your father and I'm also aware of the reason why. But I had thought that reason was purely scientific; I don't feel the energy when I'm near you. Not the type of energy you're inquiring after, anyway." Van grinned.

Sid shot him a look that could cause deep physical pain.

"Do you?" Van asked Sid.

He shook his head.

"Then, what's the reason for your inquiry?"

Sid looked at me expectantly.

Staring at Van's tie, which shouldn't have been so hard because he was at least a foot taller than I was, I explained in a basic manner what Mary had done and how I'd reacted. Then I explained that none of my friends had been able to fend her off when she'd asked them questions.

Van nodded. "I understand your curiosity." He was thoughtful. "I'm not certain of why that happened. I will see what I can find out about William Caramie and I will do it personally, Phyllis. You are a very interesting young lady. I can see why Sid is so fond of you."

"What did you need to say about andrastenite, Van?"

"Stacia has deigned to inform me that *Roger*," Van said the name with great disgust, "has heard several occupants of the mansion discussing Dunn's villainy with great vigor. She believes that he is planning something. I'm going to have to wait while she finds out about this, but in the meantime, I've sent for the Cliffords to guard this building. Dunn had no knowledge of you or any others that live outside of this building or Stacia's home, so you need not be concerned for yourself. But I may need to call for you if this turns out to be a serious matter or threat, Howls. Keep yourself on the lookout, would you?"

Sid nodded.

Van sighed. "Well, I suppose I can permit you to leave. Though I have been feeling rather lonely lately."

"You ought to try having a conversation with your sister," Sid told him.

"You've had some very deep conversations with her yourself, my friend. Look how nicely things between you two have turned out, Howls." Van looked at me again. "I'm glad to see you've become much happier living with the Sorins."

Sid nodded. "We'd better be going."

Van shook Sid's hands. "Very well, then." He looked to me. "It was quite nice to meet you, Phyllis." He nodded to Sid. "Always a pleasure, Howls. Thank you for bringing Mary. Farewell."

As soon as we were in the elevator, Sid asked me, "You didn't look into his eyes, did you?"

I shook my head. "No, of course not."

He nodded. "Good. Because he certainly was interested in you."

I raised an eyebrow. "Is he a rapist?!"

Sid sighed. "No, but he has his moments. I'm sure he's come close."

"So..why are you friends with him?"

"He's never actually done it, unless you count mind-fucking. And he's never wanted to rape me."

I don't know why not. "Always a plus," I said dryly.

"And he's got a connection to everything. He's dependable. And he's harmless if you avoid eye contact."

"So we just...go home?"

"Yep."

We were silent for a moment, but I couldn't keep that way for long.

"Who's Natasha?" I wanted to know.

Sid glanced at me. "She used to be a friend of mine. We had to say goodbye when I left Stacia's mansion. But she's a good person to have on your side. She's the most clairvoyant connection in the world."

I wanted to ask if she'd ever told him his future, but first I had to figure out if he was in love with her or not. "What did Van mean when he was talking about Stacia and her?"

"When?"

"He said Natasha liked you and Stacia hated you and it couldn't be for the same reason."

"You know for a girl who's attached you sure do seem to pay close attention to the women I've known."

Direct hit, that. Yeah, well, I'm still in love with you, I thought.

No, wait!

You said it, the voice told me.

"I just want to know about the things you've done. Wouldn't you be curious about a completely different type of people if you were still...uhh..mortal?"

Sid sighed. "Babes, it's a long story. Basically I saw that Stacia was a terrible person and decided not to trust her. Natasha saw that as a good decision."

"Did she ever tell you your future?"

"Yes."

"What'd she say?"

Sid grinned. "Not all that much, unfortunately for me."

"What did she tell you?"

"She told me that I was going to leave the mansion of my own free will. Which I did, after Stacia decided she had it in for me and her cook—Rhonda Castle—put wolf's bane in my salad. Not that that has ever worked, but she was trying to kill me nonetheless."

"That's Alanna's mom?"

"Yup."

"Is Mary going to be okay?"

Sid nodded. "She won't have much direct contact. And trust me, there's no way she could get into the same situation as I did."

"Why's that?"

"Babes that's rather personal. Do you really want to know?"

"Yes."

Sid shrugged. "I slept with Stacia. But I refused to continue being with her because she was evil. And I know kids call their teachers evil and religious fanatics call Jews and gays evil. But Stacia really is evil. She got even worse when I stood up to her." Sid swallowed and breathed carefully. He looked enraged but trying to keep as calm as possible. "So she took up with a kiss-ass blood-sucker named Roger and whenever she looked at me, my mind...just...lost control. I saw horrible things and thought horrible things and soon everyone was saying horrible things. So finally I left. And Van was very happy to hear that I was going to live in the real world."

"Why did you sleep with Stacia?" I blurted out.

"Young, stupid...I didn't think she'd take it seriously. I wasn't even sure she had emotions."

We were silent again for a few moments.

"If something happens with the andrastenite, will I have to meet her?"

"I hope not." Poor Sid sounded distraught, to say the least.

"She can't be scarier than Anna," I remarked, trying to lighten the conversation.

Sid groaned. "Anna. I forgot she's coming back in, what, 3 weeks?"

"Probably less."

Sid shook his head. "Somehow I attract the most frightening women."

I gave him a look.

"Philly, you're wonderful. But you have the power to turn the earth into hell." He pointed at me. "And we're not in a relationship."

"You were in a relationship with Stacia?"

Sid sighed. "I don't know, babes. I don't know what it was." He sounded so worn, so tired. I couldn't ask him anything more.

Expect the Unexpected.

Eric came over the next day. When he arrived, Bill and Sid were watching the news in the living room, so after a polite greeting and the grabbing of a snack, we went down to the basement.

"Mary left last night," I told him.

"Really? Where'd she go?"

Uhh..

I shrugged. "She didn't say. But she assured me she had friends up north, and she'd let me know she was okay when she got there."

"Why did she leave?"

"Her parents kicked her out."

"She should have just come here. You have like, what, 8 rooms you aren't using?"

I counted in my head. "Yeah, we'll go with that."

"Maybe I should move in. Then nobody would ever get pissed if I woke up and played guitar at 3 in the morning."

"Do you actually do that?"

"Sometimes I want to, but Terry would slaughter me. He's a menace when he's tired."

"I'll remember that."

"He'll probably be home if you come over this week, so you'll have to meet him."

"Is he really that bad?"

"Yes. Just trust me."

I giggled. "Okay. What do you want to watch?"

In the end we decided on nothing.

For what seemed like hours we kissed, our hands moving over each other.

"Phyllis! Eric!" Quincy called suddenly.

Eric's lips rose off mine (at that point he was above me).

"Yes?" I called back.

"Come up here and have some lunch! I made burgers!"

I looked at Eric. "Do you like burgers?"

"I love burgers."

"Okay." I smiled and we went upstairs.

"Where are your Aunts?" Eric asked as we got out some plates.

"I'm not sure. Quincy?" I looked at him.

"They went shoppin'. Kippie needed a break and Chasey's angry with Sid," he explained.

"Why?" I wanted to know.

Quincy shrugged. "Who knows?" He subtly moved behind Eric and nodded to him, then he shook his head. It was about something that he couldn't say in front of Eric.

I nodded in comprehension.

Bill entered. "Well, Sid's—hey, those burgers are looking pretty good, Quincy." He was still Clark Kent. He had the glasses and the good-natured manner.

"Have one, man. What were you gonna say?" Quincy handed Bill a plate.

"Hello, Phyllis, Eric. Good to see you again."

"You too, Bill."

"Oh, I'm sorry." Bill extended his hand. "Clark Kent."

Eric smiled and shook Clark's hand. "Sorry about that," he apologized. Luckily I'd been able to explain to him about Bill. Despite our constant physical contact when we were together, I had managed to have some long conversations with Eric. He was great to talk to. There wasn't that tiny bit of excitement that I felt when I spoke to Sid, but I had decided that I couldn't expect my love for Sid to go away within a matter of days. I had to be patient.

"Hey, no problem." Clark waved the apology away.

"Clark!" Quincy folded his arms.

"Yeah Quincy?"

"What were you gonna say?"

Clark took a bite of his hamburger. "Sid left a minute ago. He went to give some legal advice. You know, I think he might be hiding something, Quincy. I'll have to consult Bruce." He took another bite. "Great burgers Quincy." He looked at his watch. "Well, I'm off to the Daily Planet."

Quincy looked at his own watch. "Yeah, I gotta be at the store in like, 3 hours. The Aunts better be back by then because I'm not supposed to leave you two alone in the house."

"They don't trust us?" I questioned.

Quincy gave me a look. "Sweetie you're sixteen, of course they ain't gonna trust you with a boy. No offense intended towards you, Eric, I'm sure your intentions are noble."

Under the table Eric squeezed my hand.

"Bye everybody!" Bill left.

Quincy sighed. Then he looked at me. "Did you show Eric the hamster?"

Eric looked at me expectantly.

I shook my head. "No, I didn't."

"You have a hamster?"

I shook my head again. "It belongs to our friend Abe."

"I think they finally put it in Sid's room. He probably locked the door anyway."

"I have the keys. But do you really want to see the hamster, Eric?"

Eric shrugged. "Whatever, I've seen a hamster before."

Just then, the phone rang.

Quincy picked it up. "Hello? Oh yeah, sure." He put it down. "It's for you Phyllis. It's Key."

Uh oh.

What if she knew about Mary?

I took the phone. "Hello?" I don't know where she is, I swear!

"Hey Phyllis. Jesse's brother's having a huge party. Apparently his best friend is freakin' loaded and they're having it at his indoor pool. Taylor and Tony are coming. You and Eric should, too."

Hmm. I loved swimming. I felt slightly wary of parties, but I figured my best friends would be there. It was very unlikely that other freshmen like the boy who'd thrown punch on my head at my last pool party would be attending.

"Hold on, let me run it by Eric."

I asked Eric.

"As long as you don't mind stopping at my house to pick up my trunks."

"Tell him he can skinny dip," Key told me.

"He might like that too much," I told her, grinning at Eric.

"Like what?" he asked.

I shook my head, gesturing to Quincy, who was now engrossed in Time magazine.

"So when's the party?" I asked her.

"That would be six. Til whenever. You can stay the night if you need to. There'll be pizza and racing around the pool and shit."

"Okay, we'll be there."

"We'll probably be late," Eric told me.

"We'll be there late," I told Key.

"Sounds good. See you tonight!"

"All right. Bye." I hung up.

"Is there gonna be alcohol at this party?" Quincy asked, still staring into the magazine.

"Oh I doubt it," Eric said.

"You just tellin' me that so I'll let you two go? I'm the parental figure when the Aunts aren't here."

"Like hell you are," I muttered.

"Don't you take that tone of voice with me young lady. Eric? Are you just saying that?"

Eric shook his head. "No. Rumor has it that Jesse's family can't hold their liquor. To the point of embarrassment. As in, last year Jesse's dad wrapped his car around a tree and since then they haven't even had rubbing alcohol in the house."

Quincy nodded emphatically. "A frienda' mine drove drunk once. Tragedy like I've never seen."

I was confused. "Someone died?"

Quincy grinned. "Nope, but she destroyed her week-old Mercedes-Benz."

"Fancy cars aren't worth it," Eric said.

"Don't tell Sid that. He loves his cars."

I looked at Quincy. "He has a Civic."

"He's watchin' his budget. When that car goes he'll get himself a Mustang convertible, you'll see. Or a Jaguar." Quincy stood. "I gotta start getting ready for work. I'll be upstairs. Could you guys stay in the living room so that I don't get in trouble?"

"Of course," I said agreeably.

Eric and I sat on the couch for a while, watched some TV, fell asleep on each other. Then we went into the sewing room.

"You should teach me to play Toccata and Fugue."

"Eric, I can't even play that."

"I have a guitar in my trunk, do you want to play something?"

"Sure." I loved music. And I was really starting to enjoy playing music with Eric, even when it didn't lead to or follow making out.

Nevertheless, he gave me a kiss before running out to his car.

We played a while, some stuff of mine, like Fiona Apple, Alicia Keys, Tori Amos, Billy Joel that Eric improvised on. Then we played some old rock and I improvised. Then we tried to figure out some modern rock songs but it was hard to find one with a good piano part that didn't have whiny lyrics.

"We should start a band," Eric said.

I laughed. "Taylor and I always say we're going to do that."

"Yeah but we really should. I can't play with other people like this."

I gave him a kiss. "I think you're just nice."

His hand wrapped around the back of my neck. "You're pretty nice too."

Just then, the phone rang.

"Hold on, let me get that." I ran to answer the phone.

"Hello?"

"Hi."

"Hey, Taylor."

"Key called you, right? I just wanted you to know there's definitely going to be beer."

Oh Jesus H. Christ.

"Okay..."

"And I wanted to know if you ever drank before?"

I shook my head. "No."

"Okay, well, I don't think you should, Phyllis. You might explode." Her tone was extremely serious.

I giggled. "Teenage Girl Spontaneously Combusts at Pool Party."

"Exactly! So...please don't drink, okay?"

"Are you really being serious, Taylor?"

"Of course! Honey, if you exploded, I'd be Taylor minus my best friend!"

I laughed. "Okay, I promise not to, Tay. But I wouldn't have anyway."

"Why not?"

"I've always thought I'd explode."

"There you go. Sorry about that, I just wanted to make sure."

"Don't worry Tay. I won't."

"Okay. Thanks Phyllis."

"Thanks Taylor."

"See you."

* * *

Eric and I went to get his trunks and drop off his guitar, then we went to the party. We were about twenty minutes late, but only because I had to find a dry bathing suit (my other one was wet from school).

We entered the pool room.

It was huge. I don't know how rich those people were, but their pool was enormous. I'd hardly be able to fit it in my backyard. There were so many people, eating, swimming, talking. There was a drink table, a stereo, a diving board, all kinds of things to float on.

"Hey guys!" Taylor shouted to us above the music and splashing and talking. She walked over.

"You're just in time to see Jesse and Tony race across the pool."

"CLEAR THE POOL!" A tall red-haired guy standing fully clothed on the diving board shouted. It had to be Jesse's older brother.

When everyone had moved to the sides, I could see Jesse and Tony sitting in inner tubes at the deep end of the pool.

"On your mark!" Jesse's brother shouted. "Get set!" Then he did a two-fingers-in-the-mouth whistle.

Jesse and Tony splashed desperately across the pool.

"C'MON TONY! C'MON! GOOOOOO!" Taylor screamed.

"GET 'IM JESSEEEEE! GET 'IM! YOU GOT THIS ONE!" Key shrieked.

"YEAAAAHHHH!" I yelled, having no preference.

"GO TONY!" Eric offered.

Key looked at him. "Hey."

Eric shrugged. "Sorry, best friends."

Jesse won the inner tube race by a hair.

"I challenge the winner to a game of beer pong!" Key shouted, and everyone cheered. "And anyone else who wants to join," she added.

Eric eyed the table. "I'd better not," he told me. "Do you want to?"

I shook my head.

"I can't drink!" Jesse called to Key. "I have to drive Gabe!"

"Jess! Let me meet your friends!" Jesse's brother came over.

"This is Gabe," Jesse said, gesturing to him with his thumb. He told Gabe our names.

"Nice to meet you," I said.

"You too," he said. "Now, I have to go and judge the beer pong!" He strutted off to the drink table.

"He means he wants to drink all the beer before they can start playing," Jesse explained.

"Helen and Liz were supposed to come, and I called Mary," Key told us. "But her parents said she left."

"Left?" Taylor questioned.

Key nodded. "Well, her parents kicked her out yesterday but when she left my house she said she was going back home to try to work things out."

Huh? "How did she get there?"

"She took a cab."

"Oh."

"They said she called. They said she's moving up north with some friend." Key sighed. "She didn't leave a number or anything and...and I couldn't even say good-bye to her."

Jesse wrapped an arm around Key's shoulders and squeezed her.

"Thanks," she said softly.

"Key..." I began.

"Yeah?"

There were too many people, I couldn't talk about Mary here. "Let's go in the pool."

"Okay."

We all jumped in.

"Dude if I ran away from home I'd just leave a note and be like 'Screw you guys!'" Jesse said, grabbing a tube. "Short and sweet."

"Is Jesse short and sweet, Key?" Tony asked. He and Eric burst out laughing, and it took me a second to realize, Oh. Penis size.

"Shut the fuck up!" Jesse splashed Tony, and soon a full blown splash fight erupted among the three of them.

"I don't understand guys. We don't stand here and talk about how big our boobs are," Key said.

"Well that's because we can see how big they are. It isn't really insulting if they don't know it's true," Taylor told her. "Is he short and sweet?"

"Oh shut up," Key said, rolling her eyes. "I don't even know."

"I don't know about Tony either. I don't plan to for a good long while either," Taylor said strongly.

They both looked at me.

"I don't know either," I told them. "We've only been dating for two weeks!"

Key grinned. "She's totally lying, Taylor."

Taylor rolled her eyes. "Just don't, Key. Mary's bad enough."

"If she ever comes back," Key countered.

"Key.." I started again, then looked around. Everyone else that was in the pool was splashing or throwing around a beach ball, and everyone outside the pool wasn't paying attention.

"Key, Mary..called me last night."

Key's eyes widened. "Is she okay? What'd she say?"

"She said..." Think fast, Phyllis. "She said she couldn't call you because you might tell her parents, but she was leaving and had to get out of town before her parents found out. She thought they might have her arrested or something, I guess they had a really bad feud. She said the same thing, she was going up north. She wanted to tell you...she wanted to tell you that you're the best friend she's ever had. And she wanted to apologize to both of you for...violating your privacy. She sounded really sorry...but...at peace with herself. Like she was making a new start. She said she'd miss you, Key. She wanted to thank you."

Key smiled sadly. "I guess she had to leave. I didn't know how to help her. I don't know what happened to her. But maybe she'll write me a letter or something."

I nodded. "Yeah."

"Ah!" Taylor shielded her face as the boys forced us to take part in the splash fight.

Just when I thought I was going to die from over-splash, a blonde girl yelled, "PIZZA!"

The six of us cheered.

"Thank God, I am SO hungry!" Taylor cried.

"Pizza is God," said Jesse.

"Dude," said Tony. "That's blasphemy. Dr. Pepper is God."

"We should fill the pool with it," Jesse said thoughtfully.

Everyone got out of the pool.

Eric pulled me toward him.

"Hi," I said.

He ran his hands down my thinly-suited sides. I leaned in and kissed him.

"Do I get a kiss too?" Gabe yelled.

Tony laughed. "Yeah, you better kiss him, Eric!"

There was a lot of wet chaos. At one point, I threw Taylor into the pool, then Eric threw me in, then Tony threw him in. Then Taylor pulled him in and they got into some sort of argument which somehow indirectly caused Jesse and Key to argue. After endless eating, tube-racing, swim-racing, Marco Polo, dancing, diving contests, making sure people didn't throw up in the pool, and talking to lots of random people who were probably half-drunk, Taylor and I snuck outside. She handed me a can of grape soda.

"I don't think I've ever been to a party this big before," Taylor told me.

"Me neither." A strong smell made me wrinkle my nose.

We looked over to see two girls smoking at the end of the driveway.

"Ugh," I said.

Taylor smiled. "They're not as smokin' as you are."

I rolled my eyes. "Please."

"I can't believe we're so uncool that we didn't drink," Taylor said.

I laughed. "Yeah, we didn't give in to peer pressure!"

"Woohoo! So what's been going on?"

"Nothing too much..just stuff with Mary last night and Abe's hamster." I told her how Damien had found out about my firebreathing.

Taylor nodded. "I think you can trust him. Quincy seems to have friends that are good people."

"Yeah. Anna's supposed to come back soon. I'm a little nervous."

"Why?"

"I don't know. Just the way everyone looks when they talk about her and Sid..."

"You think they'll get back together?"

"I guess. I don't know."

"I want to meet her. You have to invite me over when she comes back." Taylor smiled. "She must be gorgeous."

"Oh, she is."

"Not as gorgeous as Sid."

"Nobody is." I smiled a little, then caught myself. "But Eric comes pretty close. We've been hanging out a lot. I really like him."

"Hanging out, or making out?"

I grinned. "Both."

The door opened.

"Hey Eric," Taylor greeted him.

"Hey," he said. "We should go Phyllis, it's almost eleven and I told my mom I'd be back by then." He had a towel around his neck and his hair was sticking up. He handed me my own towel.

"Thanks," I said, taking it and nodding. "Okay."

"Do you have everything?" Taylor asked.

I nodded. "Yeah, wore my suit under my clothes."

"What a resourceful young woman." She grinned.

I gave her a hug. "Thanks for caring about the fire," I said quietly.

"Of course," she said. "See you later."

"See ya. Call me or something."

"I will."

Eric and I got into his car.

"Bye!" I yelled to Taylor from the window.

"Bye!" She yelled back, and went back into the pool room.

"Are you dry enough?" Eric asked.

I nodded. "I think so."

"You want to come back to my house and dry off or something?"

I smiled. "Thanks Eric, but I should go home. I don't want the Aunts to be more suspicious than they need to be."

He smiled back and nodded. "Okay.

He dropped me off a little after eleven, warm and dry for the most part (except for my hair which seemed to be getting longer every minute). He kissed me, running his tongue over my lips.

"Mmm," I breathed. "I had fun today."

"Me too." His hands slid down my back, and he kissed my neck. "Want me to call you tomorrow?"

I squeezed his shoulder. "Yes please."

He kissed my throat. "Okay." He hugged me. "I really love being with you, Phyllis."

We kissed again. "Mm, me too, Eric." And I meant it. Maybe there was more to this than moving on. Eric was a great person. I kissed him again. "Talk to you tomorrow?"

"Okay." He kissed me again.

I opened the car door. "Thank you, Eric." I kissed him again. "Bye."

"Bye Phyllis."

I walked to the door and waved to him before I walked in.

Quincy, Butch, and Bill were playing some card game in the corner of the living room and each gave me distracted greetings. They would've asked all about the party, but there was a considerable amount of money in the middle of the table.

I noticed a light peeking out from under the kitchen door. I hung up my towel on a coat hook by the door and walked across the dimly lit living room to the kitchen. I opened the door.

Sid was sitting at the table with his laptop. He looked up. "Hey babes." He was wearing an old T-shirt and plaid pants. He still looked sexy as hell.

But so did Eric. And I could have Eric.

"Have fun?" he inquired.

"Yeah, did you?"

He smiled. "Sure. Anybody mention Mary?"

"A little. Key called Mary and her parents told her she was moving up north."

"And?"

"So I said that Mary had called last night and told Key what she said."

"Good." He began typing.

"I heard you got into an argument with Aunt Chasey."

Sid sighed. "Yeah, it's okay now, though."

"What happened?"

"She thinks I should check in with Stacia to make sure Mary's okay there. She's a very caring lady. But I'm sure she's fine. Van would tell me otherwise. Or Natasha, if she could."

"Why wouldn't she be able to?"

"She's not exposed to many modern devices. She's kind of a hermit. It's a privilege to know her in that realm. But she doesn't have a great life." Sid shook his head. "Anyway, Mary is fine. But Chasey was nervous because I'd never mentioned Alanna Castle before. There wasn't really a way to convince her until she wasn't angry anymore."

I nodded. "Oh. So how well do you know Natasha?"

"Not so well anymore, I haven't seen her in over sixty years."

"Oh."

He started typing again.

"Sid?" I sat down at the table.

He stopped and looked at me. "Hmm?"

"There was beer at the party."

"Did you have any?"

"No."

Sid grinned. "I'm glad you told the truth. I would have been able to smell it on you if you had."

"If I did..do you think I'm justified in being afraid it might hurt something? Do you think there's a chance I'd spontaneously combust?"

He chuckled. "I don't think so, Philly. But it might cause some sort of bad reaction. None of us really know how you're built, like you've said before. Maybe someday you'll want to visit your parents and you can ask them."

I took a deep breath, not wanting to think about my parents.

"But until then, you're right, you probably shouldn't do alcohol. You shouldn't be drinking anyway."

"I know."

"I know you know."

"So...how do I smell?"

"Like chlorine. And Eric." Sid's eyebrows rose slightly. "Long goodbye kiss?"

"Is it that bad?"

"Am I still a better kisser?"

What the motherfucking hell? God, he had to say things like that. Why? Didn't he know how it made me feel?!

Why don't you ask him to show you? You don't know how good a kisser he is, he only kissed you twice. Quickly, the voice pointed out.

I have a boyfriend, I told it.

"No," I told him sincerely.

Liar, said the voice.

Sid grinned and looked back at his computer. "Surrre."

I folded my arms. Now he was just being cocky. "Would you like to prove me wrong?"

Oh. My. God. I just said that, I thought.

He looked up. We stared at each other for a few moments. I was trying to look stern. I couldn't decipher his expression.

"Go to bed, Philly," he finally said.

So I did.

The Wrong Decade to Live.

I came down the stairs that Sunday morning, well-slept and happy. For once I had nothing to do. I could just sit around, maybe watch a movie, maybe eat some stuff, maybe take a walk...it was already eleven, anyway. Today could be a great, quiet, lazy day.

I should have known.

I entered an unusually chaotic kitchen.

Aunt Chasey was rushing around the sink and stove, stirring and mixing and switching things off and on, pouring, opening, closing. Not at all her usual orderly self. Something felt off.

"Do you need any help?" I asked.

She smiled nervously. "Oh no, dear, thank you."

"What's wrong? Is Mr. Meneses coming?"

"Oh dear, of course not. I don't have to make anything for him. But I'm a little busy Phyllis. Kippie is in her room, you should go speak to her, I don't have much time."

I nodded uncertainly. "Okay." I rushed up the stairs. Obviously something was happening. Maybe Aunt Kippie was sick. Aunt Chasey was probably making her something and she was in bed.

I knocked on Kippie's door.

"Come in."

I opened it. Kippie wasn't in bed at all. She was in front of the mirror, piling her hair on top of her head.

"Aunt Kippie, what's going on?"

She looked at me, visibly strained. "Oh Phyllis, Anna called late last night. She's arriving this morning!"

"So why are you both so..." Uh oh. "Even then you didn't tell her about Sid?!"

"I didn't even think of it Phyllis! With all that's been going on, the play and Mary and Eric, and the call was so quick! I just didn't think swiftly enough."

"Is Sid even here?"

"In his room."

"Does he know?"

"He doesn't know either." Aunt Kippie sank into a chair by her bed.

I came over and hugged her. "It'll be okay Aunt Kippie, don't—"

"Are you two talking about me?"

We looked and saw Sid standing in the doorway. "I heard Philly come back up the stairs. I heard 'Anna,' and I heard 'He doesn't know either.'"

We looked at him in silence.

"Aw, Kippie. Kippie, don't tell me Anna's coming back today."

"I'm afraid so." Kippie's hand came helplessly to her face.

"God dammit. I picked the wrong decade to meet you, Kippie."

"Oh no Sid, I'm sure I picked the wrong decade to live."

"She isn't that much of a problem, is she?" Anna got mad a lot, and loud, yes, but I wasn't afraid of her.

They both looked at me with pity.

"You were never an adult when she was around," Sid told me. "I'm sure she'll consider you old enough to witness her full wrath now."

"Are you afraid of her?" I demanded.

"I'm afraid of her giving me a migraine."

Kippie nodded. "Sid's had his fair share of Anna."

"What's her problem?" I raised an eyebrow.

"I am. No, everything is. Anna finds a problem with everything," Sid decided.

"I wish you were only saying that because you're still in love with her," Aunt Kippie said sorrowfully.

"I consider myself superhuman, Kippie. Not because I can't be killed, but because I survived a relationship with Anna for two years."

"What did she do to you?" I wanted to know.

"You'll see soon enough, Phyllis. Now go get dressed, we don't know when exactly she'll be here. And wake Quincy!" Kippie ordered.

Sid was smiling as I headed for my room.

"You just like to see me get bossed around," I accused him.

"You could use more of that," he told me.

Standing in my doorway, I asked, "What do you think she'll say to you?"

"I don't know, Philly. With Anna it could be anything from, 'Good to see you again,' to shooting me in the face just because she knows it won't kill me."

I raised an eyebrow. "Has anyone ever done that to you?"

Sid grinned. "Probably, I can't remember my entire life."

"Well I don't remember all of mine but I think I'd remember getting shot in the face."

"You get back to me after you've been alive for 160 years, babes."

Was that an offer?

I went into my room and tried to find something nice. I settled on a black t-shirt and jeans. It was just Anna.

I went out and down the hall to the door that divided the upstairs, then down the next hallway to Quincy's room. The door was closed. I knocked loudly. "Quincy!"

"HMFPrrffWHAT?"

"Wake up!"

"WHY?!"

"Wake the hell up and I'll tell you!"

"I'm SLEEPING!"

Duh. "I know! Wake up! Anna's coming!"

"WHATTHEFFffffI'mgoingbacktosleep..."

"QUINCY!"

"Okay okay FINE! I'll be there in a minute!"

Somehow Quincy managed to appear well-groomed in fifteen seconds. Or he had fallen asleep well-groomed? Either way, he came out in less than a minute looking nothing like the trainwreck I did when I woke up.

"Did you say Anna is coming?" he demanded.

I nodded. "Yes, I did."

"Jesus Christ!"

Jesus Christ indeed. I exhaled some smoke. "Yeah. So, get ready."

Quincy sighed. "The preparation's all mental, baby. I'ma go check out her room. Go ask Sid if he wants to move the hamster down there with all of Anna's inevitable pets."

I shook my head. "No way. If she still has the snake, Newby'll get eaten."

Quincy reconsidered. "You're right." He patted me on the shoulder. "She's gonna' be surprised to see how you turned out Miss Phyllis. Happy, lotsa' friends, a boyfriend..on the verge of stealing her ex.." Quincy winked at me and I rolled my eyes.

Quincy headed down the hall and, sans knocking, opened the door to Bill's room. "Bill, whatcha..oh." He looked at me. "Dracula."

I shrugged. "It could be worse."

I went downstairs and received an order from Aunt Kippie to put a new quilt she'd made several weeks earlier on Anna's bed. When I came back upstairs, Quincy, Dracula (Bill's hair was gelled back dramatically and he was wearing his cape), Sid, and Aunt Kippie were all arguing.

"Kippie I am sorry but what the hell in God's name were you thinking?!" Quincy screeched.

"I wasn't thinking at all, Quincy! I just wasn't! I made a mistake!"

"How would you suggest she tell her, Quincy? Precisely what, praytell, would be a pleasant way to tell Anna all of this?" Dracula inquired calmly.

"Just freakin' say, 'Oh, and Sid's back.'! It's not easy, but it's gonna be harder for all of us now! She is going to flip out! What if she has a gun?! Kippie, I'ma be pissed if we all die. Phyllis is only sixteen! We're all gonna go out Tupac-style because you were too scared to tell her something!"

"Guys, don't worry about it, I'm going to bear the brunt of this either way, okay? Don't be so hard on Kippie, Quince," Sid said, sitting down.

"Excuse me, but you've been writing her for years, Quincy. You never mentioned it in any of your letters?" Kippie gave him a look.

"We talk about guys in our letters! We talk about celebrities and clothes and and and...not complicated relationship issues!"

"Oh really."

"I just can't understand why you wouldn't tell her! She lives in the house you own! Why didn't you call her back as soon as you realized? She has a cell phone, Kippie!"

"I didn't know that! She's always called here."

"Quincy, if you know her number, why don't you just call her up now and tell her?" Sid folded his arms.

Quincy was about to say something when Sid raised up his hand in a stopping motion.

"She's here." We followed him down stairs.

Quincy sighed. "Aw Jesus. I'll go out and help her with her bags. You guys can figure out what the hell to say." He went out the door and we could all hear two loud screams of "Hiiiii!!!!"

Chasey rushed out of the kitchen. "Oh goodness gracious, I can't believe she's back."

"What are we going to say?" Kippie asked.

"About what?"

Chasey shook her head. "What is there to say now? We can all just say hello and focus on her, what she's been doing. We don't need to make a big showing of Sid." She glanced at him. "Though that may be difficult."

"Sid, any suggestions?"

Sid shook his head. "I would say there's no point in worrying now. She's almost at the door."

Kippie looked worriedly at Chasey. "Maybe we can hide him."

We all heard the door open and we knew it was too late. This was the moment of truth. Sid remained in his chair.

Quincy came in first, carrying two large black bags.

"Hey Count Dracula, can I get some help with these?" Bill rushed to his aid.

And then Anna entered.

Anna hadn't changed. Still the beautiful, bright-eyed yet serious face, slender tall build, skin like coffee, and long flowing black hair. And, of course, the pointy red nails. As Quincy said, "Now those damn things'll leave a mark."

"Oh Anna!" The Aunts rushed to hug her, and then I did. The four of us greeted for about five minutes.

"So good to see you!" "How was your trip?" "My, have you gotten more beautiful?"

"My trip was considerably smooth, girls. It's so good to finally see everyone aga—" She stopped, her mouth agape. She'd seen Sid.

Anna set down the large black bag she'd been carrying. "Well, if it isn't the big, bad, wolf."

Sid grinned. "Hey Anna."

I saw the Aunts exchange distressed glances. I moved next to Quincy. Anna liked Quincy, she wouldn't throw anything at him if she got angry.

Anna started singing, a dadadada tune without words, and after a second I realized it was the wolf's theme from "Peter and the Wolf." Sid chuckled. "How's the music business, Anna?"

She nodded. "Good, good. So you're back."

"Yeah. I came back a month or so ago."

"Huh. A month or so. I heard nothing about this, but...wow. You're exactly the same."

"So are you."

"I guess we won't have to worry about them getting back together, then," Quincy whispered to me.

She smiled. "I know this is hard to believe, but..I'm actually very happy to see you."

"Some bad shit's about to go down," Quincy told me under his breath.

"Glad to hear it," said Sid.

"I just hope you're not as disagreeable as you were when we last spoke," Anna said, seemingly genteel.

"*I'm* disagreeable?" Sid questioned.

"Quincy, why don't you help Anna set up her room. You too, Count." Kippie suggested, a bit loudly.

"Yes," agreed Aunt Chasey at similar volume. "And then we can all have lunch in an hour or so and Anna can tell us of all her travels."

"Reminiscing can come later," Quincy muttered to me. He gave Anna a big smile. "C'mon girl, let's go spend some quality time. You gotta tell me about all those sexy dancers you met."

"And you've got to tell me about this sexy dance club owner you met," she countered. "Let's go."

Aunt Chasey put a hand to her heart and exchanged relieved looks with her sister.

"That was interesting," I commented.

"I'm afraid it's going be very interesting for a good long time, dear," Kippie told me. "Especially if Sid provokes her!"

Sid held up his hands helplessly. "Here, I'll go up to my room so I don't cause any more trouble!" I could tell he was trying not to laugh, though.

Chasey rolled her eyes. "Oh Sid, don't be a martyr."

Sid sighed. "Let me know when lunch is ready, would you Chase?"

"Of course, Sid."

I watched Sid go up the stairs. After he was out of sight, I decided to follow him.

"Don't you interrogate him, Phyllis." Aunt Kippie warned.

"I won't, Aunt Kippie," I promised.

Not.

"Philly," I heard Sid say as I reached the top step.

"Yes?"

"C'mere."

I went into his room.

"What is it, Sid?" I asked him innocently.

"Keep Anna's attention off me as much as possible today. The wolf is going crazy. I'm not going to be nice."

"How is it going crazy? It's not the day of the full moon."

"It remembers Anna." Sid shook his head. "It wants me to fight with her in some way. I feel like a mental patient. It's hard to even be civil with her because of the damn wolf. And of course it's the first thing she mentions."

"You're lucky you have that excuse. Do you ever have control over yourself?"

Sid grinned. "Yeah, though it may not appear so at times."

"Well how does the moon thing work? Like..in what state of the moon are you most in control?"

"When the moon's really big, or hardly there, the wolf has more influence. But I'm pretty much all me when it's a half. That would be the best time to ask me to make rational decisions." Sid smiled. "I can't use the wolf as an excuse during a half-moon."

Half-moon, half-moon. I'd remember that.

"But that doesn't make sense. Wouldn't it work..wouldn't it be like, more moon, more wolf?"

"I don't make the rules babes. I think it has to do with the moon in its entirety. If the moon isn't completely there or completely gone to us, the wolf becomes weaker."

I nodded. "Do you ever use it as an excuse when it's not really doing much?"

"Only if I want to avoid trouble. Usually with your Aunts, or Anna." Sid grimaced. "There's going to be a lot of that these days."

He was quite right, as I would soon find out.

Just then, the phone rang. It was Eric.

"Hey," I said, taking the phone into Aunt Kippie's room.

"Hey," he said. "How's it going?"

I sighed. "Oh, we just had an unexpected visitor."

"Oh really?"

"Yeah. Well not a visitor, a tenant. She lives here on and off, the opera singer I told you about once."

"Yeah, the one with a temper. I remember."

I smiled. "Yes, the enormous temper. She and Sid almost got into an argument as soon as she walked in the door."

"Oh, they know each other?"

"I guess they went out years ago when I was little."

"Wow. Why doesn't one of them move out of your house? I would never want to live with an ex-girlfriend."

I sighed. "Sid.." doesn't really have a choice because it's hard to explain to other landpersons that you're a werewolf. "Sid's known my Aunts longer..it's just a very convenient situation. And Anna...I don't know, maybe she's just cheap, I'm sure my Aunts charge less than anywhere else. They've both just always called the house home."

Eric and I talked about my house a little bit more, and I realized I actually did have some funny stories. Or at least, interesting ones. I told him all about Sarah Lagano, leaving out details about my fire-breathing ("I guess my Aunts just really influenced her to be good, because we saw her later at a shoe store and she's completely changed. She even thanked us!"). We talked until Chasey called me down for dinner.

Happy, I headed down. Hopefully everything would be okay with Anna. I mean, maybe everyone was overreacting. I knew how easy it was to remember the bad points in people rather than the good ones.

Butch had come, and was sitting with Anna and Quincy at the table talking as Bill and the Aunts put the food onto the table.

"This is so great, Chasey. Thank you so much for this meal, I know I must have caught you off guard." She saw me. "Hi Phyllis." She stood. "My God, I hardly got a look at you. You're so much older! You look so mature! Look at this figure! Look at that style!"

"She got that from me," Quincy told her.

"She certainly didn't get her figure from me, I'm afraid," Aunt Chasey said grimly.

Figure? Yeah, right. Maybe hiding under all the extra padding.

"Oh hush Chasey, you're gorgeous," Butch told her.

"This is why we keep you around," Kippie told him.

"Man, let's eat. Now that you're here we have tons of time to reminisce and marvel at how much time has gone by. But this chicken's getting cold," Quincy said. He began forking pieces onto all of our plates.

"Did you summon Sid?" Butch asked my Aunts.

"Yes, he said he'd just be a moment, he's in the middle of some work," Aunt Chasey told him.

"He's not eating the hamster is he?" Quincy bit his lip.

"Oh stop it Quincy," Kippie scolded him.

"Yeah, I'm tired of hearing about the damn hamster," Butch said.

"Hamster?" Anna asked.

"It's Abe's. Do you remember Abe?" Butch asked her.

Anna shook her head.

"Ah, blonde, angelic looking man who dated Quincy for a short time years ago? Anyway, it's his hamster."

"Ah. I had a hamster once, Gonzo ate it."

"Oh, how is Gonzo, Anna?" Aunt Chasey asked, finally sitting down.

Anna sighed. "I had to give him to a friend, it was too rough to take him all around those islands. But I'm told he's still alive."

"Islands?" Butch asked.

Anna nodded. "Yup, I traveled a bit after we finished the run of Phantom."

"Oh my God, I forgot you were in that! Sing something for us!" Butch insisted.

Anna sighed, and started singing. Her voice was strong, beautiful, but at times rough on the ears. Like now. I was thinking about Sid and Eric and what would happen when Sid came downstairs. Anna's opera voice could shatter any train of thought.

When she was finished we all clapped.

"Bravissimo!" Quincy cheered.

"Thank you," Anna said. "I actually won an award for my performance as Carlotta, but I have to say I wish I could have been Christine."

"Why's that?"

"It's just a better part to me. You know why I didn't get it? It's because I'm black."

"Oh pish tosh, Anna," Kippie told her.

"Do I sound like I would be refused that part for any other reason?"

Modesty is a virtue, said the voice.

Of course we all agreed with her. Then Anna unexpectedly looked at me.

"So Phyllis, what's been going on now that you are sixteen!" Anna practically screamed the word. "My God, I can't believe I missed that. You got a boyfriend?"

Gah!

I nodded.

"She does and he is a musician." Quincy looked at her as though he expected her to be impressed.

"What kind?" Anna asked.

"Plays guitar," Quincy told her.

"Oooooh." She looked at me. "Is he hot?"

I laughed a little. "Yeah, he's great."

"What's his name?"

"Eric."

"That's a nice name," she said with an agreeable nod.

"So who was that dancer Quincy mentioned earlier today?" I asked quickly. If there was one thing Anna loved to talk about, it was men.

Kippie helped herself to some potatoes. "Yes, tell us about him, Anna."

Anna smiled. "His name is Julian. He's a ballet dancer. He came to Aruba with us. He said he was living in the city," Anna gestured out the window, "so that might be interesting." Anna bounced her eyebrows once subtly. Carmen Electra would have been proud of her. She took a sip of her drink and her eyes widened, staring at something behind me. She put the glass down. "Hello Sid."

"Hello Anna. Good to have you back." Sid sat down.

Quincy looked at me and mouthed what looked like, "Liar!"

"Would you like some chicken francaise, Sid?" Aunt Kippie passed the plate to him.

"Thank you." He smiled and took it.

"So do you have a lot of friends this year?" Anna, I could see, was hiding her shock. I had a boyfriend? When she'd left, I'd been in my outcast stage, friends with only two girls.

I shrugged. "Enough, I guess. I'll have to have my friend Taylor over to meet you, she was very interested."

"Is she your best friend?"

"Yeah."

"Oh, Taylor might as well be part of our family," said Aunt Kippie. "She's a wonderful girl."

"You met her in school?" Anna asked.

"Mhm." It wasn't completely accurate, but I didn't feel like telling the whole story.

"So how were all of your travels, Anna?" Aunt Chasey asked.

"Oh Chasey, they were great. When I got finished with the show, my friend Carla and I went to the Caribbean. We went everywhere. The Virgin Islands, Antigua, Martinique, Bonaire..it was just beautiful."

"Any nude beaches?" Butch asked.

Anna laughed. "Oh no. But it was okay. The tourist men were not very impressive. But the native men were gorgeous."

"Oh really?" Quincy looked at her expectantly.

Anna giggled. "It ain't dinner table talk, Quincy. I'll tell you about it later."

"Oooh girl!"

"You met a lot of men down in the Caribbean, Anna?" Kippie asked.

"Mmhmm."

"Kippie, Anna meets a lot of men wherever she goes," Quincy said matter-of-factly, taking a sip of his drink.

Anna raised her glass and grinned. "I'll drink to that, baby."

She and Quincy clinked glasses.

"So Anna," Butch asked. "Where else did you go?"

Anna shrugged. "The Bahamas, Aruba.."

Quincy shook his head. "Nonononono." He looked at her expectantly. She looked at him as though he were insane.

He grinned. "Aruba, Jamaica, oooh I wanna take ya. C'mon Phyllis, Anna doesn't know you can sing!"

I shrank back. "I can't."

"I'm sorry to say this Aunts, but that is bullshit," Quincy said.

"Incredible bullshit," Sid said with a nod.

"Oh I do agree," said Aunt Chasey, looking at me.

"C'mon Phyllis, I'll do the background, you take the lead."

"Aruba, Jamaica, oooh I wanna take ya, Bermuda, Bahama, c'mon pretty mama," Anna sang, motioning for the guys to join in.

"Key Largo, Montego, baby why don't we go," sang Butch.

God, if you exist, help me. Help me please, I prayed.

And I swear on my own life, right at that moment the phone rang. I ran from the room.

"Aw c'mon, no answering the phone during dinner!" Quincy called after me.

Out of their hearing ranges, or at least the ranges of the mortals, I picked up the phone. "I don't know who you are, but I love you."

"Oh, I knew that, but thank you very much."

I grinned. "Hey Taylor. Your call just saved me from an awful moment. Anna and the guys were going to make me sing at the dinner table," I explained.

"We must have a psychic link!" she said excitedly. "This is awesome! Wait, Anna's back? You're in the middle of dinner?"

"Yup, but please, talk as long as you want. Maybe they'll forget what they were doing."

"I thought she was going to argue with everybody, anyway."

"Not when it's advantageous for me, it would seem."

"That sucks."

I sighed. "But my Aunts'll probably scold me for being rude during a special dinner. Can I call you back in about an hour?"

"Yes. But you have to tell me everything, especially if it involves Sid. Oh, and can bugs be rabid?"

"I wil—what? I don't think so."

"I swear to God, one just attacked me and then it started, like, flipping and bouncing all over the table. So I killed it."

"I don't think so Tay, but if you start foaming at the mouth, call a doctor."

"Heh, okay, I will. Will you fill me in on everything?"

"Of course Tay. You should come over after school this week and meet Anna."

"I'll ask and get back to you tonight."

"All right, talk to you soon."

"Indeed. Bye!"

"Bye." I hung up and went back into the kitchen.

"Taylor?" Sid questioned.

"Oh don't ask Sid, we all know you could hear it," said Anna.

"You don't know that," Butch told her. "What if Sid had never told Phyllis? You'd be in big trouble, missy."

"Now I know it," Anna shot back.

"I was just making sure. I could only hear Philly's side."

"She's going to come over this week, I told her she has to meet you," I said to Anna.

"I'd love to meet your friends. And your boyfriend."

Why are boyfriends so incredibly interesting to everyone?

I nodded. "Yeah." I tried to sound excited or happy or something. But I felt annoyed. I hated being asked a lot of questions by people who hardly knew me. Although, come to think of it, I suppose Anna was just trying to get to know me. I didn't really want to be her buddy or anything. I didn't want her to be there at all, and I didn't know why.

Luckily, Anna then turned to Sid.

"So Sid, what are you doing for work these days? Or are you just hiding out for the usual reasons?" She smiled at him.

Sid looked thoughtful. "Well..I've been giving some legal advice, discreetly. But I can't go out and do lawyer work for the public for a few more years. I hid here, then I went traveling, and in a few more years it might be safe to start practicing again."

"Uh huh, and under what name?"

"My own if I'm lucky."

"I see. So what have you been doing in your spare time?"

Sid smirked. "Are you asking if I'm seeing anyone?"

Anna frowned. "Of course not. Why would I ask that? It's no business of mine. I was just wondering how you occupy your time. It must get so dull without being able to do what you love."

Sid shrugged. "It's nice not to have to deal with people on a regular basis."

"But people are the main part of your job. How could you not enjoy that and still love the job?"

"It isn't only the people. It's the satisfaction, the work, the discovery." Sid waved his words away. "But I won't bore you with details, especially when I haven't actually practiced in what, thirty years maybe."

"I'm not bored hearing the details of court cases, Sid."

"It's not always all that interesting, Anna."

I wasn't sure what to do. They were probably going to start arguing. My cowardly fellow diners had all conveniently started talking among themselves.

"This country shouldn't be open to just anyone who wants in," Aunt Kippie was telling the guys.

"America should be a sanctuary," Butch said.

"But only for those who are willing to live here. People shouldn't come in here, to us, and expect us to start speaking their language! You wouldn't go to Italy and expect them to stop speaking Italian. If people want to come here, they need to show that they're willing to live an American lifestyle, at least somewhat! Otherwise, go back to Mexico! Or, wherever. No offense, Quincy."

"None taken, baby."

Aunt Chasey and Bill..er..the Count, were talking about their daily lives.

"I try to pray twice a day, once when I wake up and once before I go to sleep," she said.

"I try to feed every morning before bedtime." Bill smiled and I saw that somehow he'd acquired the slightest of fangs.

And then back to Sid and Anna.

"Even I'm not always interested in my cases. Sometimes the people I'm prosecuting are just so disgusting, and they only get worse."

"You mean as time goes on?"

"Of course. Mankind would rather indulge itself than try to make any real changes."

"What would you suggest?"

Sid sighed. "I honestly don't know. I'm not saying we were any better 50 or more years ago but I have to say, crime is getting worse and more frequent and meanwhile we have to worry about outside countries attacking us.." Sid shook his head. "Mortal men are doomed to destroy themselves in the end. And I'm just going to have to sit back and watch!"

"Are you kidding me? You immortal people aren't any better."

"We're just harder to kill," Sid said.

"The world has more promise now than we've ever had before, Sid!"

"Yeah, more promise to kill each other."

"You never had faith in anything."

"I just don't believe we'll ever achieve our full potential, whatever it is, if we keep going in this direction."

"And what is that? What are you saying? That every generation is just making it worse? That's an insult to me and an insult to Phyllis and an insult to all the good people that you are including in your generalizations!"

"I'm not saying that there aren't any more good people! There are millions! But there will never be enough."

Until Superman shows up, I thought. Or Batman. Batman was cooler. Or Wonder Woman...

"Sid there is so much beauty in the world! It was made for mankind and I have faith that in the end, that will stop us from ever destroying it."

"One fool in the right place can destroy an awful lot."

"What is that supposed to mean? Who are you referring to?"

"Anna why the hell does this even matter? You only wanted to know what I've been up to lately, why do we have to start talking about world affairs?!" Sid said. Quite loudly.

Everyone stared at him.

Sid sighed. "Sorry."

"Damn, you two can argue about anything!" Quincy observed.

Aunt Kippie stared at him. "Had you forgotten?"

Anna sighed and sipped her wine, and, completely serious, said, "Sid argues with everybody. It's just how lawyers are, I suppose."

"This chicken is delightful, Chasey. Thank you so much!" said Butch, loudly.

Sid didn't say much for the rest of the dinner, and the Aunts made a point of dually pressuring Anna to tell us about tropical fish and all that she encountered on her trips.

I wasn't yet convinced that Anna and Sid were as monstrous to each other as everyone kept saying. Of course Anna was annoyed; no one had told her her ex was here. And anyone could argue about political stuff and the direction the world was headed in. On top of these two things every person all day was extremely nervous, and that probably increased the bad vibes.

Sid and Anna were mature adults. With ten years between now and when they'd been in love, whatever feelings that were between them had to be gone. They couldn't hate each other and they certainly didn't love each other.

I hoped.

But it really didn't matter; I had Eric.

After dinner Anna and the guys went downstairs, and Sid sat in the living room, drawing.

I walked in.

"I don't know who you are but I love you?" Sid said, not looking up. "Was it really that bad that you'd answer the phone with that? What if it'd been a child molester?"

"What, like your good friend Van?"

"You know what I mean."

"Yes it was that bad. It was terrible!"

Sid looked up. "Sorry. Next time I'll insist that your singing is terrible, too." He grinned.

I rolled my eyes. "Thanks."

"Sid..."

"Hmm?"

Do you think you still have any feelings for Anna?

What do you care babes, you have a boyfriend.

"Can bugs be rabid?"

Mature Adults.

The next two weeks crept by, even with Easter Sunday in the middle of them; we'd never had an enormous celebration for Easter, just mass and the big church egg hunt. It was fun, but I wasn't having much more of that. I was so ready for the school year to be over; I kept hearing people say "It's April already! Only two months left!" and I knew they would be two of the longest months of my life. My math teacher was already raving about the finals.

"I'd better not see any of you in this class next year!" the teacher yelled.

"But what if we just miss you?" asked Max Spalding, not only a genius but a suck-up. He was actually being sarcastic, but sometimes it was hard to tell.

I exchanged looks with Taylor. Neither of us would ever voluntarily come back to this class.

Mr. Hamil was giving us more and more work.

"Now I want you all to choose two of these five essay questions and write a two to three page paper for each of them. Staple them to your split-notes and chapter summaries. I'm extending the dates for the quote analysis sheets, because I know those take a lot of time."

We all stared at him incredulously.

Meanwhile at home, both Anna and Sid seemed to be hiding. Anna would head out with Quincy and when they came home she'd complain about how she still hadn't met Damien. Abe had debriefed her when he'd come to claim Newbert and she was very obviously irritated with Quincy.

"You never told me you guys broke up! Why didn't you tell me?"

"Girl, we got back together! It doesn't matter anymore!"

When she didn't go out with Quincy, she went out to meet this person and that person and this guy and shop for this friend's birthday, etc.

Sid holed up in his room with his law work or just left, especially when Anna was practicing her opera singing in the cellar. When it seemed like Anna had left for the night, he'd come downstairs and watch movies with Bill while I sat on the couch and did my homework. We didn't talk much, and this was not my doing. I had to finish all the damn work. The only teacher who was letting up a bit was Mr. Busch. At least I didn't have to worry about my friends; Key seemed to be over Mary's leaving, despite the fact that every once in a while she zoned out at the lunch table. Taylor and Liz were back at the table for good.

Eric and I didn't see much of each other, though. He had to prep himself and other kids for end-of-the-year music competitions and exams, and that meant using all his free period. I had so much homework that I could only afford to get together with him on the weekends. I missed him. We only spoke on the phone for a couple of minutes and hugged for as long as possible in the hallways.

When I told Taylor about not seeing Eric, she nodded and replied that she and Tony were busy as well.

"At least I get to see you on Friday night," I told her, in reference to the sleepover we'd set up after the celebratory dinner for Anna. Originally it had been the first Friday after she'd come home, but Miss Highman had given us a surprise weekend project to do and we both agreed the next weekend would be better. We would celebrate the beginning of spring break.

Taylor snapped her fingers. "We can invite the guys, too! They can come over and watch movies and then leave at like, ten!"

I loved Taylor. "You are so smart," I told her. "I have to run it by my Aunts but I don't think they'll mind. They like Eric and Tony."

And I was quite right.

"Oh of course Phyllis, you know you can always have Eric or Taylor over, provided there is an adult in the house," said Aunt Chasey.

I raised an eyebrow. "You're afraid to leave Taylor and me alone together?"

She rolled her eyes. "You know what I mean, dear."

"Not that there's anything wrong with being in love with another girl," Aunt Kippie said quickly. "We just hope you'd inform us first."

I grinned. "What would you do if I were a lesbian?"

"Nothing at all," said Aunt Chasey.

"Thank God that we wouldn't have to pay for an expensive wedding," said Aunt Kippie.

"What if we wanted to get married?"

"I suppose we could do that," Aunt Chasey said thoughtfully.

"We wouldn't have to worry about her getting pregnant, Chasey," Aunt Kippie pointed out.

"Very true. And Quincy could take her to all of the gay gatherings and what not."

"You're not trying to tell us something, are you Phyllis?" Aunt Kippie asked me.

I rolled my eyes now. "Yes Aunt Kippie, I'm coming out of the closet."

Aunt Chasey smiled. "To tell you the truth, I'm glad you're not a lesbian, Phyllis."

"Why's that?" I wondered.

"Perhaps in about fifteen years or so you'll fall in love with Sid!"

"Oh Chasey he's too old for her. I like Eric. But remember this Phyllis; no woman needs a man."

"Yes, they're only a convenience," Chasey said sarcastically.

I grinned. "Oh, I know."

"Thanks a lot." Sid entered the kitchen. "Sorry to interrupt girl talk, I need some coffee."

"You hate coffee," Aunt Kippie said.

That I hadn't known.

"It isn't for me. Quincy just woke up and he looks like death."

"Huh?" I was confused.

"Oh dear, don't follow his example but Quincy was out quite late last night with Anna," Chasey told me.

"At least he came home. I haven't seen Anna yet," Kippie said. She sighed. "Take it from an oldhand, Phyllis, promiscuity does no good."

"I don't need to know, I don't need to know!" I held up my hands. I never ever wanted to hear about my Aunts' sex lives.

Sid grinned. "I think Philly's gonna be okay, Kippie."

"Yes and why would you assume that Anna's with a man, Kippie? She might have gotten intoxicated and gone home with a trusted girlfriend."

Aunt Kippie gave her sister a look. "I know you're as straight as they come, Chasey, but would you leave Anna be if you were a man?"

Chasey shrugged. "Ask Phyllis, she's the one who just came out of the closet."

Sid snickered. "I didn't hear that part of the conversation."

I sighed. "So everything's okay for Friday night?" I asked my Aunts.

"Of course," they chorused.

I grabbed some juice and went to call Taylor. And finish my stupid English papers so that I didn't have to worry about them on Friday.

Stalking Sheep.

I came home on Friday to a battle in my living room.

"You almost hit the fucking cat!" Sid cried. Apparently my Aunts were not at home, as I heard no scolding words from the kitchen or sewing room.

"He moved out of the way! He was fine!" Anna yelled.

"You come home driving some huge fucking gas guzzler and you dent my damned car and then you almost kill the damn cat!"

Ah. That explained the hummer in the driveway.

"I'm borrowing it from a friend for the night while he has mine! It's none of your business what car I drive!"

Sid looked at her in disbelief. "It's my business when you hit my car!"

"There's hardly even a mark!"

"There's a white line across the side! You're lucky I'm not insisting you PAY for repairs! You don't fucking show up here in some asshole's fucking army truck and fucking act like I should have been watching out!"

"Your HIDEOUS car was parked practically across the driveway, Sid! How in hell could I miss it?! You're lucky I don't sue you for blocking my way into my home!"

"Sue me?! SUE me? I parked in the middle of the driveway, leaving room on the side for your convertible, and you come home in an SUV, dent my car, which you very easily could have AVOIDED by parking on the side of the ROAD, and scare the hell out of Phyllis's cat!"

"Oh there are enough fucking cats in this fucking house, I'm sure she'd be okay!"

I coughed.

Sid grinned as Anna whirled around, eyes wide.

"Is Johnny okay?" I demanded.

"Phyllis, he's fine. Sid just parked his car irresponsibly and I bumped it. When I swerved away the cat was in my path, but he ran out. These cats are smart enough to run when they see a car coming." She shot an angry look at Sid.

"They shouldn't have to be on alert in their own yard! The cat wasn't even in the driveway!"

"Well where the hell else was I supposed to go when your precious car was in peril?!"

"When you have a vehicle that size, you park it on the side of the road. That way you don't take up four other peoples' parking spaces! And why in HELL are you TRADING cars?! Are you planning to get it back? Or are you just gonna fucking plow over the cats every time you come home!"

"Would you just SHUT the hell UP, Sid! The goddam cat is fine! My parking was fine! If YOU hadn't parked your stupidass car TOO FAR OVER then THIS would NOT have happened."

"Because it's NEVER your fault. All YOU did was dent my fucking car and just miss killing a fucking cat!"

"I'm going downstairs, I'm not going to fucking deal with this, I don't have to deal with this anymore. Your car is fine, the cat is fine."

"The hummer's a little lopsided," I told her. "You should probably park it on the other side of the road." It wasn't as if anyone lived across the street from us.

Anna turned and glared at me. "The only reason I couldn't park correctly is Sid's damn car and all of the damn cats!"

"It's just going to be hard for other people to back out, there isn't going to be any room. Don't worry about the cats." Some smoke flew out of my mouth, as I was getting a little angry with her too.

Anna sighed. "I can't believe your Aunts didn't tell me about this, Phyllis. I just can't believe it. This is the most irresponsible thing they've ever done."

"Just ignore him," I told her sternly.

Sid chuckled.

Anna whirled around. "Oh go stalk some damn sheep." She stomped out the door, slamming it behind her.

I stared at the door. "Damn."

"Oh it gets better babes. It gets better." Sid shook his head. "She's right about your Aunts though, Philly. I think that just made it all worse. Although why Anna would decide to borrow a hummer is beyond me."

"I've never seen her so mad," I said.

"She shouldn't have spoken in that tone to you. You haven't done anything." Sid smiled. "But you could take her, I'll bet."

I shook my head. "She'd scratch me to ribbons."

Sid rubbed his shoulder. "She poked me a few times while we were fighting. It's a good thing my skin doesn't break."

Huh?

"What?"

"My skin doesn't break."

"It doesn't break?" It wasn't registering in my mind. What did he mean?

Sid smiled. "Yeah Philly."

I followed him into the kitchen.

"I don't understand."

Sid poured himself a glass of water. "How do you think immortals survive so long, babes? We can only be hurt by andrastenite, remember? And suffocation."

"So you can't..be cut?"

Sid nodded. "Here, look." He took my Aunt Chasey's largest, sharpest, scariest butcher knife out of the wooden block that sheathed its blade. He pulled his shirt sleeve to his elbow.

My eyes widened. "Oh my God, Sid.."

"Don't worry Philly. Just watch." He took the knife and pushed the point hard into his skin. He dug it in and dragged it down the inside of his arm. His beautiful arm.

My eyes were popping out of my head. He put the knife down and touched my shoulder.

"It's fine Philly, look." He held up his arm.

There was no blood, no cut, just a long crease in the skin like when I poked my arm with my fingernail for a long time.

"Oh my God," I said again. "Your skin's like..kevlar or something." I looked at him. "Does it feel a lot different than human skin?"

He shook his head. "Not at all, haven't you felt it before?" Not waiting for an answer, he held out his arm. "It's just the same."

Since I knew I might never have an opportunity to do it again, I touched his arm. I ran my finger down the crease. His skin felt so good.

"See?"

Pulling my finger away, I nodded.

"That must be pretty handy."

Sid grinned. "Yup."

"Does it still hurt when you get scratched?"

"Not as much as it would on regular skin. I can hardly remember those days, though." Sid put the knife back. "So you're having some friends over tonight?" he asked.

I nodded. "Yeah, Taylor and Eric and Tony."

"Tony's the blonde guy?"

"Yeah."

"What are you guys gonna do?"

"Probably watch movies. We can do it in the back room if anyone needs the living room."

"The living room's probably better, as long as you tell them about Bill. I doubt Anna's going to stick around tonight; Quincy's been talking about taking her to Damien's club."

"He must have been pretty happy that you were the one taking care of him yesterday."

Sid groaned. "Oh, he was."

"Is he all better?"

Sid nodded. "Yup. Healthy as ever."

Something occurred to me.

"Do you get hangovers?"

Sid smiled. "Nope."

We heard a door slam.

"She's going to the basement," Sid said. He looked at me. "You didn't look so calm yourself, Philly."

"She insulted my cats." I smiled and went upstairs the back way. I grabbed the phone and called Aunt Kippie at work.

"Oh hello Phyllis! Is anything wrong dear?"

"No Aunt Kippie. I don't mean to bother you at work—"

"Well if my own niece can't bother me I don't know who can."

"Thanks Aunt Kippie. Anna and Sid just had a fight."

"Oh really?"

"Yeah. I think she's really mad at you guys for not telling her about Sid..so..I guess I just thought I'd let you know."

"Oh sweetheart, she already let us know, don't worry. I'm sure she'll be letting us know for years to come. Still, I have to say it was nice to have her back, she's a very dependable girl."

"Ah ha. Well, okay Aunt Kippie, I just wanted to let you know..and I love you." Dependable, eh.

"I love you too, dear."

I hung up. For a moment I was struck with shock, realizing there was nothing I had to do for a few hours. No more papers, no more math problems..what should I do with this newfound free time?

I went to take a nap.

* * *

When I woke up it was nearly time for everyone to show up. I rushed downstairs and set out some bowls of chips.

"I'll be in here if you need anything, dear," Aunt Kippie called from the sewing room.

"Thanks Aunt Kippie."

"Lucky you woke up in time. I went to check on you when I came home, you looked so contented to rest I just couldn't wake you."

I rolled my eyes. "Where's Aunt Chasey?"

"I believe she's doing something with the humane society today, but I'm sure she'll come in through the side door so that she can get to the kitchen as soon as she's home. She'll want to make something for your friends."

"And you are one lucky girl, most parents complain about cookin' for other peoples' kids." At some point while my attention was on the sewing room and my Aunt, Quincy had come into the living room.

I turned around. "I thought you guys were going out tonight?"

"Yeah I am, in about an hour with Damien. Anna might come to but we ain't goin' together. She wants to drive herself and I ain't ridin' in no hummer to a dance club." He strolled over to me and called to Aunt Kippie, "J'you see that thing, Kippie? It's e-friggin-normous! S'ridiculous!"

Aunt Kippie chuckled. "Sridiculous indeed."

"Did you hear about how she scratched Sid's car?"

"I did, Sid was kind enough to inform me himself."

"I haven't seen Anna since it happened," I said.

"I was just talkin' to her downstairs. Man she is not thrilled that Sid is here Kippie. You shoulda told her. Yeah, she would have come anyway, but still. The girl wasn't prepared," Quincy said.

Aunt Kippie sighed. "I know Quincy, I really do feel bad about that, but it's been 2 weeks. There's nothing we can do about our past mistakes at this point."

Quincy nodded. "You are right Miss Kippie." He turned to me. "You need help with anything?"

I shook my head. "I don't know what they want to drink so I'll just do that when they get here."

"And when's that?"

As if on cue, there was a knock at the door.

It was Taylor.

"Hey," I said, giving her a hug.

"Ohh doesn't it feel great to have a vacation?" she said, squeezing me so hard I coughed and a puff of smoke came out.

She patted me on the back. "Sorry Phyllis, I've just been so stressed with everything."

I nodded. "I know what you mean."

Quincy put his fits on his hips. "I don't get a hug?"

Taylor smiled. "Of course you do!" She hugged him. "Sorry Quincy, I thought maybe physical contact with women repulsed you."

Quincy grinned. "I can only handle small doses." He looked at me. "Did she meet Anna yet?"

"No I haven't," Taylor said.

"I'll go get her!"

"No Quincy," I said. "Don't get her yet, I think she might be mad at me. Let her come up on her own."

Quincy squinted. "Why would she be mad you Phyllis?"

"I told her to park the hummer across the road so it wouldn't block the driveway."

"Oh my God, is that big yellow thing Anna's?!" Taylor asked.

"Yeah, she switched cars with her friend for a couple days. He's got her convertible, which I have to say is much more chic. Anna is the queen of chic. I don't know why she wanted the hummer. In fact, I didn't think she knew how to drive it," Quincy told her. He looked at me. "I'll let her come up on her own hon."

There was another knock on the door.

"Which one do you think it is?" Taylor asked.

"Both of them. Eric's giving Tony a ride, I thought he'd have offered to give you one?"

"Oh yeah, Tony told me that this morning. I wanted to walk."

I answered the door.

"Hi." Eric hugged me.

"Hey Phyllis," said Tony. He brushed past Eric and me and hugged Taylor.

Quincy giggled. "How cute."

"Quincy, this is my boyfriend, Tony." Taylor let go of Tony. "Tony, this is Quincy. He lives here."

Quincy shook Tony's hand. "Hello."

"Hey." Tony was always friendly to everyone.

Aunt Kippie came out of the sewing room.

"Hello Tony, I'm Kippie Sorin, Phyllis's Aunt. Make yourself at home." She smiled warmly at him.

"Nice to meet you Ms. Sorin, thank you."

"He's a regular Eddie Hascal," Taylor told Aunt Kippie.

Aunt Kippie chuckled. "As long as I don't see the other side." She looked at me. "I think I'm going to head upstairs Phyllis, if you need anything I'll be in my room." She went up.

Quincy looked at us. "You want me to leave you guys alone?"

I shook my head. "No, you can stick around, we're gonna watch a movie."

Taylor brimmed with happiness. "Yes, I have 'Hannibal Rising'!" She held up the movie for Quincy. Taylor looked at me. "And I have explained to Tony about Bill, so if he joins us you don't have to worry."

Tony looked at me. "Is she making that up? That he thinks he's dudes from movies?"

I shook my head. "I'm afraid not."

Tony looked at Eric.

"It's true man, and he's pretty good at it too," Eric told him.

Tony looked us all over. "This could be some kind of conspiracy to mess with my head." He looked at Quincy.

Quincy nodded. "He's been crazy as long as I've known him. You'll see in an hour when he comes home from the donut shop."

"Who was he today?" Taylor asked.

Quincy sighed. "I'm not sure, he was watchin' some Jim Carrey movie...aahh I can't remember." He winced. "I hope to God it wasn't 'Dumb and Dumber' or some shit. Not that he would do anything...just...ugh I don't want to live with those guys." He held out his hand. "Let me look at the DVD."

She handed it to him.

I exchanged smiles with Eric.

"Oooh, I haven't seen this one yet!"

"Oh, Quincy, you'll love this guy, he's such a hot...I mean, he's such a good actor." She grinned at Tony.

"Hey!" he protested.

"Maybe you should take up cannibalism so that your girlfriend is insured," Quincy suggested to Tony.

Tony looked at Taylor. "I love you Taylor, but I don't think I can go that far."

Taylor sighed dramatically. "Well, I'll just have to break up with you."

"Aw no." Tony looked at Eric. "Eric, I'm sorry man.."

Quincy and Taylor laughed.

"You're not allowed to eat my boyfriend," I told Tony.

"Yeah, that's your job, huh?" Tony said with a grin. "Or no, it's the other way around.."

"It best not be either way if these two want to live a nice long life," Quincy said, folding his arms.

"Let's put on the movie," Taylor said quickly.

Bill did indeed join us when he returned from the donut shop but he wasn't Jim Carrey at all; quite the contrary, he was William Wallace. His Scottish accent wasn't bad, but he didn't talk much. He was, however, wearing a kilt; I couldn't tell if it was the correct colors, though. All he said when he walked in was, "I'm not gonna stay in here with you and set in front of that idiot box. I'm only here ta fight for Scotland's freedom. What film are yeh watchin', lass?" He'd asked me.

I told him.

"Aye, yeh've chosen well," he said, and sat down.

We all exchanged looks and then went back to watching the movie.

Not long after Bill came back, Quincy looked at his watch, hissed, "Aw shit!" and rushed out the door.

"He's going to meet his boyfriend," I explained quietly.

"Men are pigs," said Tony.

"Seriously," said Taylor.

"Hey!" Tony protested.

Taylor smiled sweetly. "I was just agreeing with you, puddin'."

"Nice," said Eric. It took me a moment to realize he was talking about the movie. Hannibal was drowning a guy in formaldehyde.

"I think that was the worst one," Taylor said.

"I don't know Taylor, I wouldn't want to get squeezed to death either," I told her.

Eric couldn't resist but reach over and hug me as hard as he could.

I grinned. "Except by you." I gave him a quick kiss on the cheek and we went back to watching the movie.

When it ended, Bill bid us goodnight, still the Scottish warrior, and went upstairs.

"That guy's awesome," said Tony. "And he isn't just Scottish?"

I shook my head. "Nope, he's been a lot of people."

"Yeah, when I met him he was Jack Sparrow!" Taylor told him.

Eric looked at me. "I think he was Teddy Roosevelt when I met him, right?"

I nodded. "I believe so."

Taylor got up. "I'm gonna grab some juice," she told me.

"Do you want me to get it for you?" I asked.

She smiled. "Nope, I know your kitchen pretty well now." She went into the kitchen.

"Hey, make me a sandwich while you're in there," Tony called.

"She's gonna hit you when she gets back," I told him.

He shrugged. "Oh!" He jumped into Taylor's seat. "Stole the chair!" He pointed at Eric. "Tell Terry that I'll give him back the Pick of Destiny whenever I see you next."

"Yeah right. You've been saying that for about three months, dude."

"Yeah, well, Terry still has my Justice League Heroes game from like, three years ago, man."

"It hasn't been three years."

"It's been at least two."

"You're full of shit. And don't you have his Nine Inch Nails CD anyway?"

"Well he has my Godsmack!"

"Who cares? Godsmack isn't that great anyway."

"That's not the point."

They went on for a little while longer about the various things Tony had of Terry's and Terry had of Tony's.

"You took his tickets to Ozzfest!" Eric argued.

"Bullshit! That was a gift! He said so himself."

Taylor walked back in with her cup of juice. She set it on the coffee table and whacked Tony in the back of the head.

"Outa my seat, puddin'."

Tony sighed and stood. "Can I sit on your lap?"

Taylor was skeptical. "You might squish me. And it'd probably disturb the Sorins."

Suddenly Anna emerged from the basement. "Oh hey," she said, looking a bit taken aback.

"Hi!" Taylor said. "I'm Taylor."

Anna smiled. "Phyllis told me about you." She spotted Eric, sitting next to me on the couch, and guessed that it was him.

He nodded. "Yup."

"This is Tony," I said quickly, gesturing to our long-haired blonde companion. "He's Taylor's boyfriend," I explained.

"Hello," she said.

"Hi," said Tony. I couldn't help but notice that both of the boys also seemed taken aback.

"I'm Anna," she introduced herself. "I live in the basement."

"You're an opera singer, right?" Eric asked.

"Mmhmm, and you're a guitar player?"

"Yup."

Anna nodded. "That's pretty cool. Well, I will see you all later; I'm off to meet Quincy and Damien at the club." She winked at me and left, her long black hair flowing radiantly down her back.

Taylor looked at me. "Jesus Phyllis, no wonder she dated Sid. She's gorgeous!"

"Sid's that guy who was at the play, right?" Tony asked.

"Yeah," I said.

"What are you implying Tay?" he asked.

She looked at Tony. "They're both beautiful people!"

He grinned. "Just like you and me!"

"And Phyllis," Eric added.

"Aw, you're beautiful too," I reassured him.

He kissed me. "Thank you."

Taylor giggled. "It sounded kind of funny though, when she said 'I live in the basement.'"

"Wanna watch cartoons?" I asked suddenly.

"Definitely," said Taylor.

"Sure," said Eric.

I nodded. "Okay, I'm just going to go grab some water."

Eric stood. "That sounds good."

Taylor grimaced. "Right after milk and cookies?"

I shook my head. "So that I have it a little bit later."

The previous weekend, I'd tried drinking a bottle of water before Eric came over, to see if maybe it would calm the firebreath. Don't ask me what I was thinking; water's never affected it before, and it didn't then, either. But it'd gotten me started drinking a bottle a day. Water was becoming more irresistible than my Aunt's cookies.

I went to the kitchen, Eric in tow, and grabbed two bottles out of the fridge.

Eric closed the refrigerator door and pinned me up against it. We kissed.

"I've been wanting to do this all night," he whispered.

"Me too," I said honestly. The fact gave me hope that I could and would get over Sid, but whenever I felt that hope, I felt a little bit of pain as well.

His hands slid up my back, under my shirt, and his tongue slid gently into my mouth. After kissing me a bit more, he leaned to my ear and tugged on the ends of my shirt.

"I wish I could take this off of you." He kissed my neck. "I wish I could take everything off of you."

"Maybe you can sometime," I heard myself say. As hot and heavy as Eric and I had been going, my jeans had yet to be removed. Apparently I was ready to change that.

He kissed my cheek. "Really?"

I nodded. "Mmhmm." And kissed him.

He ran his tongue over my top lip and said, "We'd better go back in there." He ran his hand down my side and squeezed it gently.

I giggled and led him back into the living room.

"I think we should watch Justice League," Taylor announced.

"I think we should watch Looney Tunes," said Tony.

"Ah, so this is what you two argue about," I realized.

"Oh!" Eric interjected as though he'd just remembered something. "Terry let me bring Robot Chicken."

"Hmm," Taylor said uncertainly.

"It has the episode with all the superheroes on the Real World," he said, as if it were the most tempting thing in the world.

Taylor's face brightened and she gave in. "Okay!"

For the remainder of the boys' time, which was until eleven, we watched Robot Chicken. Then they got up and headed to Eric's car.

While Taylor and Tony kissed goodbye, Eric gave me a tight hug.

"I'll see you Sunday," he said, kissing me quickly.

I nodded. "Okay."

He flashed me a smile before turning toward the door.

Tony gave me a wave. "Bye Phyllis, thanks!"

"No problem, Tony."

"Bye."

"Bye guys."

And then it was just Taylor and me.

We sat in silence for a moment. Then Taylor said, "You know, we didn't walk them out to the cars. They could have been attacked by some wild animal on the way to Eric's car and we didn't even notice. They could be dead."

We looked at each other and shrugged.

"You think they are?" I asked.

She shook her head. "Nah." She looked at me. "So have you told Eric yet?"

"About?"

"The firebreathingness you have acquired."

"No. I don't know how long I'll wait. I guess...I mean, relationships don't last forever...what if I tell him, then we break up, and he tells everybody or something?"

Taylor nodded. "I see what you mean. Eric seems like a really decent guy though Phil, I think you could tell him eventually."

"I think I could too."

"They're so cute," said Taylor, settling into the couch. She yawned. "Want to watch more Hannibal movies?"

I grinned. "Yes."

She giggled. "'Silence of the Lambs'?"

I nodded. "Definitely."

Suddenly, there was a loud crack and we both yelped, startled. We heard a low chuckle.

"Sorry girls, can't sleep." It was Sid. "I'm just gonna get some work done in the back room."

"We're gonna watch 'Silence of the Lambs.'" I told him.

He rolled his eyes. "I have never met two girls so obsessed with a cannibal." He looked at me and smiled a bit. "And you know from me that says a lot."

"So you're not going to join us?" Taylor said disappointedly.

Sid grinned. "Of course I am." He came and sat in his chair, his laptop appropriately propped up in his lap.

"We should ask Bill, too," said Taylor.

"He might be asleep," I reminded her.

Moments after we popped in the DVD, a British gentleman who turned out to Maxim de Winter from "Rebecca," joined us.

Taylor, as always, was fixed like a heroine addict as soon as the film logos rolled, but I zoned out while Jodie Foster ran through the obstacle course at the FBI academy.

I realized that as close as I was getting to being completely over Sid, no matter what, he would always fascinate me. His dark eyes, and his dark chestnut hair that had the slightest auburn tint. His smooth impenetrable skin. The way he spoke, the boldness of the things he said. And his connection to the full moon.

I often wished I could tell Taylor about Sid. Especially since sometimes she whispered things to me in his presence, thinking he was a regular human and wouldn't hear her.

One of those occasions was this night.

As soon as Clarice had gotten into the elevator on her way to Crawford's office, I was sucked back into the movie. A bit later on, as she neared the doctor's prison cell, I felt relieved to have Bill, Sid and Taylor nearby. I had learned that it was always better not to watch Hannibal Lecter movies alone.

We had gotten to the scene where Dr. Lecter mimics Clarice and mocks her.

"All those tedious sticky fumblings in the back seats of cars while you could only dream of getting out, getting anywhere, getting all the way to the F.B.I." He emphasized each letter.

Taylor leaned over and whispered, "Sounds like you," in reference to my making out in the backseat of Eric's car. Taylor was the only person I really spoke to about Eric.

I looked at her, not yet realizing that Sid could have heard us. "What do you mean?" I whispered. "I don't want to be in the FBI." I smiled.

She giggled, then looked back at the TV.

Grinning, I turned as well. And as I did so, I saw Sid's eyes shining at me, the light of the TV reflected towards me in them.

Another interrogation would be coming.

The next day, in hopes of avoiding Sid, I suggested to Taylor that we walk to the cemetery not far from my house, and then go to see a movie at the tiny movie theatre.

Taylor was up for it, of course.

As we walked through the graveyard in our light sweatshirts, we examined each headstone carefully.

"Cemeteries usually aren't haunted," Taylor told me knowingly, an expert on all things strange.

I nodded. "I've never felt uncomfortable here."

"It's so peaceful."

"Yeah."

"I'm not sure I want to be buried. I might go with being cremated."

"There's nowhere good to have your ashes thrown anymore," I said.

"What makes you say that?"

"Well, for a while I thought about having mine scattered over the ocean. I went there once when I was, like, eleven or so, with Quincy and my Aunts. I loved it. So later on I thought, 'Well, if I get cremated I'll just have them toss me into the ocean.' But it wouldn't be as special now, though. It'd just be more crap that got dumped in there."

Taylor nodded. "Mother Nature deserves better." She snapped her fingers. "Phyllis! I just thought of the perfect career for you!"

"What is it?"

She grinned. "You could cremate people!"

"Ew!" It was disgusting, but I laughed anyway. "I think that would tire me out. Ugh." I quickly exhaled some fire. "That must be the worst job."

"Yeah, unless you're the lethal injections guy."

I wrinkled my nose.

"Not fun," said Taylor. She looked at me. "Anna didn't seem so bad."

I smiled. "Speaking of executioners."

"I didn't mean it as a continuation."

"I know. I didn't think she was bad either. But I guess now that I think about it, she's been okay. I've only heard her get angry three times in the two weeks since she's been here."

"What about?"

"Well first she and Sid started arguing about politics."

"Was it a sexy argument?"

"What?!"

"I figured if anybody could make politics sexy, it would be Sid."

I shrugged. "I don't know. It's mostly just annoying and scary when they argue."

"Oh. I hope I get to see."

I rolled my eyes.

"What else did she yell about?"

"She yelled at my Aunts for not telling her Sid was here, and then yesterday she scratched Sid's car with the hummer and just missed one of the cats so they argued about that for a while, then she stormed out." And Sid showed me that his skin can't be cut, I wanted to tell her.

"She must be having a hard time keeping her hands off him."

"Jesus Taylor."

"I'm just saying! They must have had sex! Look how great-looking he is."

Thank God we weren't in the house.

"I think right now she's having a hard time keeping from punching him in the face. She gets so angry, from what I've seen. He said she jabbed him with her nails."

"You think she'd hit him?"

"She might slap him."

"How do you think he'd react?"

I considered for a moment. "He'd probably laugh. Then she'd stab him or something. Not that it wo—"

Whoops. I'd been about to say, "Not that it would do anything."

"Not that what?"

I shook my head. "I don't know, the rest of the sentence disappeared."

Taylor giggled. "I hate when that happens. The last time it happened to me, I was giving a presentation in English class. I'm pretty sure it cost me six points off, too."

"That's stupid," I said sympathetically.

"So's my English teacher."

"At least she isn't as strange as Mr. Hamil."

"I wish I had Mr. Hamil! I bet he's related to Mark Hamill, and he did the voice of the Joker in some of the Batman cartoons. He was also Luke Skywalker, but that doesn't matter," she said sarcastically.

I started to hum the Star Wars theme, then realized that I was humming the Superman theme instead.

"I do the same thing," Taylor confided. She gasped and pointed at one of the headstones. "Oh my holy Jesus Christ! Look at that!"

I looked. The stone read, "Phyllis Taylor."

We looked at each other.

"Bad omen?" I questioned.

"It could be a good sign. Like maybe it means that we'll be best friends til death!" Taylor said brightly.

When we got back from the movies, Sid was gone. We hung out with Quincy and Damien in the living room until Taylor left. Apparently Damien and Anna had become fast friends.

When I went to bed, Sid hadn't come back yet, and I hadn't seen Anna since the previous night.

* * *

Eric came over on Sunday morning and brought his acoustic guitar. We went up to my room, played some songs, talked about school and movies. Then we started making out.

I got up and closed my door.

"Are you allowed to do that?"

I shrugged and smiled. "They never said I wasn't. I don't think anyone'll come up, anyway."

We kissed, gently at first and then intensely, lying on top of each other, rolling over each other, grabbing each other.

"Whoa," Eric said when I touched him. He looked at me. "Double standard?" What he meant was, why couldn't he touch me in the same place?

"For now," I whispered.

Our hands continued to explore when suddenly there was a loud SLAM! that should have been accompanied by the word slam highlighted, Batman-style.

"Holy shit," Eric whispered, working his hand under my shirt. "What was that?"

I listened. All I could hear were loud, "RAH RRRBRR BRR BRR!!!"s that were probably words. But I recognized the voice; Anna, of course.

"The opera singer?" Eric questioned.

"Mmhmm." And the werewolf, I thought. I heard Sid's low, vicious growl (not meant in the literal sense at this time) replying to Anna's more high-pitched scathing tone.

Then I heard footsteps coming up the stairs. Anna's voice was still yelling in the distance, so it must have been Sid coming up.

Eric began to draw his hand back. "Is he..?"

"He's probably just going to his room, he has no reason to come in here," I whispered. "Go ahead."

So, Eric's hand crept up over my breast.

And Sid burst in through my door. He was about to say something, when he noticed Eric's hand. His eyes widened, and he stuttered.

"Oh, I didn't know..Philly, don't go downstairs for a while...Anna's..."

Anna yelled something up the stairs about Sid being a "granny eater." Wolf insults, I guessed.

He shook his head. "Anna's going nuts, just stay up here." He shut the door.

Eric and I stared at each other. I could feel the "Oh my God holy shit what the hell am I going to do?" look on my face and I saw a similar look on Eric's face.

The door opened again.

"Get your fuckin' hand out of her shirt!" Sid hissed dangerously.

Eric's hand flew out of my shirt.

Sid looked at both of us with a poisonous glare as he shut the door again.

Oh. My. Lord.

Eric and I looked at each other again, breathing heavily. Then I started laughing. I couldn't help it. I was just so glad Sid hadn't killed Eric. The whole situation suddenly seemed hilarious, and then Eric began to laugh, too. We laughed and laughed until our sides hurt. When we tried to speak we just started laughing again.

Finally Eric managed to stammer between giggles, "I think...we'd better save...that stuff for my h-h-house."

I agreed. So much for trying to avoid Sid asking about Eric and me. But at least now he knew firsthand (heh) that I could handle my firebreathing just fine in that type of situation. Eric playfully headbutted me in the stomach and we started laughing again.

We stayed upstairs a while longer. Eric taught me to play a Tom Petty song on the guitar.

"Hey," he said when I'd finished, "do you like AC/DC?"

I shrugged, recalling seeing their CDs in Sid's room.

"I haven't ever really listened to them. But have you ever heard of Cannibal Corpse?"

Eric raised an eyebrow. "Yeah. They didn't seem like your..cup of tea."

"They're not, but Sid listens to them."

Eric cringed. "Is he a violent man?"

I shrugged again. "I've never seen him get violent..." ..in human form.

He winced. "Do you think he's gonna shoot me or something?"

I laughed. Then I bit my lip. "No, he'd be more likely to shoot me."

"I didn't realize you guys were that close."

"What, for him to shoot me?!"

He laughed. "No, for him to come into your room randomly...and for him to care that you were...you know.."

"We're kind of...pals." I grimaced privately at the word. "He helped take care of me when I was younger."

"How old is he? 23?"

Crap. I tried to quickly do the math in my mind. "He's 30, I think."

"Whoa."

"What do you mean whoa? He doesn't look that young."

"I figured he was an old soul, with the way he talks and stuff. But I was sure he wasn't more than like, 26."

Heh. "Nope. He's a lawyer."

"Oh no! Fuck, Phyllis. He's gonna put me in jail now!"

I giggled. "Don't worry Eric, it was consensual." I kissed him.

"That guy scares the hell outa me," Eric said.

"He won't tell anyone," I promised. "He might yell at me later but I think the worst is over for you." I had no idea what Sid would do. And why the hell had he just barged into my room? Hadn't he noticed Eric's car? No matter how much cause Sid had to yell and interrogate, I would be interrogating him right back. What in God's name could Anna have been yelling about to the point of distracting Sid so much? If he'd just noticed the car or listened, if he'd been paying attention, he would have known Eric was in my room.

"Are you sure he won't tell your Aunts?"

I wasn't completely certain, but I was hoping Sid and I had some sort of tacit agreement not to tell each other's secrets, no matter what. I nodded.

"Okay," he said hesitantly. "Uh..do you want to see something? There's a place in the woods I wanted to show you."

My eyebrows narrowed. Eric lived in the city, nowhere near the woods.

"When have you gone out there?"

"I go with Terry. Sometimes Tony and his brother come, too."

After listening for Anna or Sid, we carefully went downstairs. I alerted Aunt Kippie as to where we were headed, and we left.

Eric took me to a little brook, and we sat together there for a while. Sometimes we'd talk, and sometimes we just sat there, leaning against each other. It was nice to have some peace.

As it started to get later, Eric suggested we go to his house. Once we were there, it wasn't long before we were kissing again. My Aunts would not have been proud.

Then my shirt was off, his shirt following quickly behind it. Then he was at my waistband.

"Can I..."

"Yes," I replied, and he took my jeans off. Then his. And then we were making out in our underwear, something we'd never done before. It felt so good to feel his skin on mine. We kept it up for what seemed like hours (and honestly, it probably was). Suddenly Eric stopped kissing me, though his hands kept moving.

"Phyllis...Terry gave me...I have something, in case you..." He didn't finish his sentence, but reached over to the table beside his bed.

And pulled a condom out of the drawer.

"Oh..no, not today," I said quickly. I shrank away from him. "I think it's getting dark, my Aunts are going to be wondering where I am..."

"Oh..okay, well—"

I pulled on my pants. "Do you mind if we leave now?" I didn't know what else to say. I wanted to explain myself. But I couldn't. It was just so soon, didn't he realize that? Didn't he realize how good he felt?

"Uh, no," he said. "No problem Phyllis." He put on his clothes and gave me a kiss, then led me down the stairs and out to his car.

Eric took me home quietly. I went into the kitchen to have a small dinner with my Aunts. It was nice to have some time alone with them, but it didn't last long.

Anna came in, up from the basement's back stairs, which meant she must have wanted to come right to the kitchen. The other stairway was closer to the bedroom.

"Hey," she said to me.

"Hey, Anna," I greeted her in return.

"Anybody seen Sid?"

Aunt Kippie shook her head. "I think he may have left not long after you chewed off his head. What happened between you two?"

Anna sighed. "Sid was just having trouble minding his own business." She looked at me. "Did you see? I got my convertible back."

"I did notice the hummer was gone."

She sat down. "Your boyfriend's a cutie, he seems like a nice guy, too." She looked to my Aunts. "Listen, girls. I'm sorry for turning on you a while ago because of Sid."

"Oh pish tosh dear, you had every right," said Aunt Chasey. "We really should have told you."

Anna sighed. "Quincy could have let me know, too. But..I really shouldn't have been so surprised. He had to come back eventually."

I saw my Aunts exchange cautious glances.

"He doesn't have anything else to do," she said.

"What do you mean?" I asked.

"He never dates. He won't take any jobs, he can't very well get involved in the community, he's probably been all over the world by now. I pity him, really. But I think he tends to hold himself back. He doesn't trust himself anymore." She shrugged, and, shaking her long, sleek hair back, she went upstairs the back way to talk to Quincy.

Kippie shook her head. "I think she's more angry with Sid than ever before."

"But why? What were they arguing about?" I asked.

They both held up their hands helplessly.

"Neither of us know!" Aunt Kippie said frustratedly. "I was in the basement doing laundry and Chasey was getting groceries. Our only hope was that you heard, but it seems not."

I shook my head. "Eric and I were playing music in my room for a while. We tried to block them out, but Sid did come up and tell us to stay upstairs til Anna calmed down, I guess."

"Well," Kippie said as though she were trying to convince herself, "it really isn't any of our business, anyway."

"I think the real honest truth is that we may be better off not knowing," Aunt Chasey said, and she seemed to genuinely believe her words. She rose and took her dish to the sink.

I certainly wasn't better off not knowing. I finished my chicken and sipped down the rest of my juice.

I went outside and sat on the front steps, scanning the road for Sid's car. If he came from the city, he'd come from around the corner. If he came from anywhere else, he'd come from the side, straight down the road that passed my house. Directly across from my house were trees and a field, and not far down the road was the cemetery, and further on, the movie theatre.

I glanced at the driveway, then got up off the steps to get a better look. His car wasn't there.

Spring was in the air, hot weather was on its way. The feeling usually made me effortlessly happy, but I couldn't feel good right now.

What if he didn't come back at all? What if Anna had driven him off? What if I had? What if he was angry with me for not having strong enough morals? He was the one who'd been talking about levels on a girl's body! I hadn't thought he'd get mad at me for that sort of thing. I just didn't want to talk about it with him, why would I?! Aaaah!

Stop worrying. He'll be back, said the voice. But it'd probably be better if he did leave.

I sighed. I didn't ever want to go back to not having Sid.

He'd probably wondered to himself why the hell he was staying in the same house as his ex and couldn't come up with a good reason. Who did he have to stay for?

I closed my eyes. Sid must be so lonely. Maybe staying here just made him feel worse. Maybe he would find another place to hide.

And then he pulled into the driveway.

I stared in relief at Sid's Honda. He saw me and smiled, giving me a little wave.

I smiled and waved back, then went into the house again.

The living room was empty, and my footsteps echoed in the large room as I walked across it to the staircase. I went up to my room. Then I changed my mind and went into Sid's. I sat at his desk.

Within seconds, he was there.

"Waiting for me?" He looked me over. I looked him over. Neither one of us seemed to know what to say.

"Yeah," I finally said. "I was kinda'..kinda' worried you'd left."

"I did."

"I mean...for good."

"Why?"

I shrugged. "Mad at me and Anna."

Sid half-smiled. "Philly, I would never leave without saying goodbye. No matter what un-Christian activities I saw you taking part in." He gave me a look. "You better be careful, babes. I haven't left a scar on anyone for a while. I don't want to have to do it to Eric."

"Well why did you just come right in like that?! Didn't you see Eric's car?"

Sid shook his head. "I was distracted," he muttered. "And why the hell was your door shut?! Your Aunts would never let you have a guy in your room with the door closed! I figured you'd be alone!"

"Why didn't you listen?!"

"Because *someone* was screaming in my *ears*!" Sid almost shouted. Then he took a deep breath. "Sorry babes. I just wasn't at my best this morning, all right?" He sighed, and sat on the side of his bed. He looked at me again, his eyes serious. "But Philly you had better watch what the hell you're doing."

"I am."

"Phyllis, people make mistakes." He looked me squarely in the eye.

That's right, said the voice. He called you Phyllis.

Holy shit he did, I thought.

He continued. "I still make mistakes, and I'm 160 years old! I know 500-plus-year-olds who are still fucking up their lives. You're too young to deserve the consequences of the kind of mistake you could make!"

"Sid. I'm fine. Everything is fine. I'm 16 years old, being felt up isn't going to hurt me."

Sid grinned. "Oh really?"

"Yes. Nothing Eric does will ever hurt as much as your kiss did," I felt myself spitting the words at him. Luckily they were not accompanied by smoke or fire.

Whiner, said the voice.

Sid's face fell. "Aw, Philly."

"I'm fine now," I added quickly. "I really like Eric. Being with him is great."

Sid nodded, his face still solemn. "Good."

We were quiet for a moment.

Sid started to speak. "Phi—"

But my mouth had already opened, working against me. "What were you and Anna arguing about?"

"Oh." Sid scowled. "She did something stupid and I got her out of it."

I looked at him expectantly.

Sid sighed. "You don't need to know this, babes."

"But you should tell me anyway."

Sid rolled his eyes. Then he told me.

"I got home last night, just as Damien and Quince were leaving. They invited me to go to Damien's club with them, and I figured, why not? All I've been doing lately is working. The wolf isn't so strong right now, I'll keep alert, and I'll be able to drive the couple home if they indulge themselves.

"We all rode to the club in Damien's car. It was a pretty nice place, there were a lot of colorful types. Butch was there, uh…only he was…."

"Beatrix?"

Sid chuckled. "Yeah. I had some drinks with Maria and her husband. Everybody was dancing, it was a good time. Then I saw Anna walk in and wave the keys to the hummer at some guy, and they walked out." He paused. "A few hours later, Damien's leaving the place with his staff and loading Quincy into the car. I came outside and saw the hummer.

"My sense of smell is pretty keen, even when the wolf isn't so strong. As soon as I got out there, I caught a huge whiff of marijuana." Sid ran a hand through his hair. "But it wasn't being smoked. It was just sitting. I walked over to the hummer. It was stashed, bags of it were stashed under the seat of the car! I'm surprised there weren't already three canine units there. And Philly, that weed hadn't been there before.

"Anna comes out with some guy and he's telling her 'You can have it for a while longer. I love the convertible.' They walked over to the hummer and Anna spotted me. So I told her, 'Anna, give the fucking car back.' And she asked me why, so I told her, 'It's full of marijuana, I can smell it. This guy's gonna turn on you, you better get your car back.'

"So the man she was with grabs me by my jacket," Sid said, illustrating by grabbing his collar, "and asks me how the hell I got into his hummer, what I'm doing there, to stay away from his shit." Sid winced. "And then I got a little carried away."

"Carried away?"

"I uh...threw him off me. I push a little harder than most guys. He landed on the ground, and started yelling at Anna, saying how can he lend her shit if she doesn't trust him? She told him she did and he said 'Then why're you having people check out my stuff?!' He takes his keys and walks off. I yelled at him about her keys and he threw them. At Anna."

"Wait, if the hummer was his, where was he walking off to?"

"He lived right there, by all the clubs in that area. Must be how Anna met him." Sid shook his head. "So we were out in the streets at about four a.m., yelling. Finally Damien came over and said he didn't think he should drive." He put a hand to his forehead. "Then we couldn't find her convertible for another few hours. After a while I drove Damien and Quincy to Damien's house, and then Anna and I had to track down the fucking drug dealer again so he could tell us where the car is. So he drives us to the other side of the city to get her car from another fucking friend he traded with. Then she drove us back here and told me I needed to mind my own goddam business."

"But..." I was confused. "You saved her from having trouble because of the marijuana in the hummer. You got her car back..what if she'd never seen it again? She should have been mad at the guy. In theory she should have been saying thank you."

"In theory," Sid agreed with a sigh. "But instead she was furious. I lost her a night's sleep over something she said she could have solved herself." He shook his head. "And then we just kept fighting. Until I left." Sid sighed.

"So...why did you come upstairs?" I asked him, still not sure.

"I was going to tell you what had happened because I didn't see anybody else who wasn't exhausted to the point of insanity."

"You're not tired?" I questioned.

"I don't need much sleep."

"Oh. Yeah."

"So when you...weren't available.." Sid gave me a look. "I just warned you about Anna and left."

I nodded. "Thanks." I looked at him. "Why do you think Anna got so mad?" I asked him.

"Oh she hates to know when she's fucked up." He smiled sadly. "That's one of the reasons she doesn't like to see me around, remember? Proof of a mistake."

It just didn't make sense to me. I didn't think it was possible for anyone to look at Sid and see a mistake. Quite the contrary.

A voice called up the stairs. "Phyllis! Phyllis, Eric's on the phone!"

I looked at Sid. "You're not going to tell my Aunts—"

He looked at me carefully. "No."

I nodded quickly and got the phone from Aunt Chasey's room.

"Hi," I said. My Aunt hung up.

"Hey," said Eric. "Listen, I don't want you to think—"

"Oh Eric no! I feel the same as you do, it was just..you know.."

"Soon?"

"Not just soon. Listen Eric, I've never even had a boyfriend before this so it's a big step. And it freaked me out a little," I told him.

"I'm so sorry, I didn't even give you time to say you weren't ready for—"

"But that's what freaked me out, Eric. I think I am ready." And there you have it, folks.

"Really?"

"Yeah. But..let's just wait, just a little while longer, it's hardly even been a month."

"Okay. I'm really sorry Phyllis. We don't ever even have to make out again if you want to take it slow."

I laughed. "Eric, come on."

"I was just so stupid."

"Eric, listen. I felt the same way. That's why I made you stop. Because if I hadn't, I would have..." I paused.

"Lost your virginity right there?"

"Yeah."

"So then...as of now, what am I allowed to do?"

"Everything you did today. Except for the last part."

"Really?"

"Mmhmm."

"You sure?"

"Yes."

"Then the double standard is abolished for good?" He must have been beaming, I could almost hear his smile.

"Yes." I couldn't help but giggle a little myself.

"Phyllis, I didn't mean to go this far this soon but I think it's because I'm in love with you."

Awww, he was so—did he just say he loved me? I asked.

It sure sounds that way, said the voice.

"Really?" I asked him.

"Yeah." He paused. "What about you?"

"I feel the same way."

That wasn't true. I loved Eric. But I wasn't in love with him. I was still trying to recover from being in love with Sid!

"Do you want to come over sometime this week?"

"Definitely." That was true.

"Okay. And I won't take any condoms out unless you request it."

I smiled. "I might not be able to help it."

"Good." He paused again. "I love you."

"I love you, too," I replied. It felt great to say it. But it still wasn't quite the way it should have been. I hung up. I had taken a big step. But maybe it was just what I needed to do.

Closer.

As the weeks went by, I observed the consequences of my decision. I'd thought saying "I love you" to Eric would help me make it true. And while we were spending lots of time together and having fun whether or not we were, uh, running a few more bases, the fact that I felt so natural with Eric hardly discouraged my feelings for Sid.

In fact, I felt closer to my animalistic housemate. After that talk we'd had, knowing each other's secrets made me feel that we were closer. Somehow what Sid did in his spare time seemed like a much bigger secret than the fact that he was a werewolf. And I felt comforted by Sid's promise not to tell my Aunts what he'd seen. It made it less difficult to keep his secrets, even from Taylor.

Before I knew it, it was Memorial Day weekend. Eric and I went to watch fireworks and eat hotdogs in the city. I like my hotdogs extra-burnt; it was very tempting to just do that part myself.

We had the day after Memorial Day off, and since Taylor was staying with her grandparents for the weekend, Key and I decided to hang out at my house. We sat on a blanket in the backyard, which was completely green aside from the delicate blanket of my Aunts' flowers, and gave each other funky manicures. Key's idea.

"I broke up with Jesse," she told me as she painted my nails lime green. We'd just been talking about hair dye, so it was a very random statement.

"What?!" I'd gotten to know Jesse, I liked Jesse. "Why?"

Key shrugged. "It just wasn't working. He wanted to get serious, he was talking about taking a trip this summer and stuff. I don't plan ahead. I don't even know what I'm doing after I leave your house! I'm in my sophomore year of high school, I can't make commitments. So I had to let him go. And I just gave Liz my blessing to pursue him."

"Isn't that against the rules?" I asked.

"Nah. Not if I say it's okay and mean it." She sighed. "You know, sometimes I really miss Mary, Phyllis. She would have understood all of this. You haven't heard from her, have you?"

I smiled sadly and shook my head. "No. But I'm sure we'll see her again. When Taylor's famous—"

"For what?"

I shrugged. "I don't know. It's Taylor. She'll probably make a movie or something."

"Yeah, a superhero flick with Batman somehow needing advice from Hannibal Lecter to catch the Joker."

Man, Key had Taylor pegged.

"But the Justice League and Johnny Depp would all be in there somewhere, too," she added. "Anyway, you were saying?"

"We'll all be at some fancy party, like the one after the movie's premiere. And Mary'll be there. She'll have a psychic show or something."

Key smiled. "So what happens to us?"

"Well, you'll write a book about how to date 60 guys within a month."

Key laughed. "Shut up! I'm not that bad."

"No, you're not," I agreed, satisfied that I'd cheered her up.

"Are you and Eric serious?"

I shrugged. "I don't know. I guess right now we're just having fun and winging it."

"A girl after my own heart. You know, this guy I'm into now is friend's with Eric's brother."

"Who is it?"

Key pursed her lips.

Oh boy.

"Jesse's older brother."

* * *

Key's mom picked her up around 3, and I walked her through our full living room to the front door. We waved and she walked briskly to her mom's van.

I sat on the couch next to Quincy, who was doing a crossword puzzle.

"Sid!" he called, even thought Sid was only about three feet away in his chair. "Five letter word for implied, with a 'c' in the middle?"

Will Hunting, who sat on the floor watching the TV screen intently, quickly turned and answered at light speed, "Tacit." I wondered if he'd been writing equations or formulas on his bedroom walls.

"There you go," Sid muttered, not looking up from his newspaper.

Anna and Aunt Chasey were playing a card game at the table. Aunt Kippie was in the rocking chair, sewing and watching the movie that was on, a Lifetime courtroom drama.

Even the cats were all there. Johnny had followed Key and me inside. Wonder Woman was in her favorite spot atop the television. Enrique was on Quincy's lap, rubbing his face against the corners of the crossword puzzle. But the strangest thing of all was Xerxes's presence. He always avoided being in plain sight, let alone being in crowded rooms. But there he was, curled up in a chair. It was like the Loch Ness Monster walking out of the loch and waving to the tourists. He even hopped up to be with Aunt Kippie without being summoned. She was the one who'd found him, before I'd even been born. His age was showing; he was getting thinner and he wasn't as quick as the other cats. But he had no trouble jumping onto my Aunt's quilt-covered lap.

Suddenly we all heard the piercing sound of a motorcycle coming down the road.

"Sounds like a nice bike," Anna remarked.

"It's almost as loud as you are," Quincy teased.

She grinned. "You shut your mouth," she said, playfully threatening him with one long red fingernail.

Though the nail was nowhere near him, Quincy shrank back, hiding behind Enrique the Spaniard. "Save me, Spaniard!"

The motorcycle stopped. Within seconds, there was a knock on the door.

We all looked at each other.

"I'd rather not disturb Xerxes," Kippie told Chasey.

"Oh it's fine, girls. I'll get it." Anna rose and walked over to the door.

Upon opening it, she revealed a very solid-looking man with short reddish blonde hair. He wasn't a big guy by means of height, but he looked like he could level somebody if he really wanted to. He wore a leather vest and a white T-shirt, and his arms were lined with tattoos.

He was holding a helmet under his arm, and as he smiled at Anna I almost expected him to be missing some teeth. He wasn't though. Quite the contrary, as he looked as though he'd just gotten out of braces. He was probably in his mid-30s.

"Hi," he said. His voice was gruff but friendly. "Name's Jud Bunyan. Heard you guys got rooms?"

"We certainly do," Anna said. "Come on in." She peered past him. "Is that your bike?"

"Yep, that's my Harley."

"Oh, is it a Harley-Davidson or do you name your bikes?" Anna asked flirtatiously.

Sid, behind his newspaper, rolled his eyes.

"It's a Harley-Davidson named June," he told her with another smile.

"Hello sir," Chasey greeted him as he walked in. She introduced herself and Aunt Kippie. "Please, come sit. How long are you planning to stay?"

"'Bout a month."

"Ah, and where are you from, Mr. Bunyan?"

"Any relation to Paul?" Aunt Kippie asked with a smile.

Jud thought for a moment, as though he thought she were serious. "No, don't think so. I'm from Michigan."

"Is a weekly charge all right for you, Mr. Bunyan?"

"Sure."

"And what brings you here?"

"I'm an artist."

We heard a laugh very poorly masked as a cough. It was Quincy. He covered his eyes, his teeth gritted and his grin ear-to-ear. "I'm sorry!"

"You got a problem with that?" Jud demanded.

Quincy's lips stuck together in a shaky smile that threatened to give in to laughter. "No man, not in the least. Just...you know.. you look more like an assassin." He laughed loudly.

Jud shrugged. He wasn't uncomfortable, though. "The Harley makes for good traveling. I paint all over the place. And nobody ever gives me any problems when I'm dressed like this."

Quincy nodded. "I totally understand, man." He got up and shook Jud's hand. "Quincy Herman Smith, good to know you."

"Thanks."

Aunt Chasey spoke again. "I'll have to ask some routine questions," she told him. She made sure he had no problem with gays or the mentally ill and what not.

"Do you use any drugs?"

Jud's mouth twitched. "I have the occasional smoke."

"Please don't smoke here. Our Phyllis," Aunt Chasey pointed to me, "has a respiratory problem."

"That's fine," said Jud.

I looked at them and smiled uncomfortably. Then I glanced at Sid. He winked at me. I subtly blew him a smoke ring.

"What about alcohol?"

"Yeah, I do drink."

Quincy spoke. "Good, 'cause so do we." He high-fived Anna.

Once Aunt Chasey had finished with her questions, she introduced everyone.

"Phyllis is our niece, Bill and Sid are two old friends, you've already met Quincy, of course. And this is Anna Xesly. She stays here when she isn't doing a show."

"A show?" Jud looked at her, curious.

"I'm an opera singer," Anna explained. "But I'm also interested in auto machinary. I'd like to get a bike, maybe you can advise me on the best price?"

"Oh yeah, sure. I've been workin' with bikes since my late 20s, haven't even driven a car in at least five years."

"Wow."

"I'm sure you'd like to see your room," Aunt Chasey said, getting out a key and standing up.

Anna took it. "Here, I'll take him up."

Sid chuckled softly, but Anna caught it and glared at him briefly before disappearing up the stairs with Jud.

"Girl works fast," Quincy remarked. "She's not even gonna touch that dude but he's probably gonna end up handing that damn bike right over."

"My prime concern is why Anna's been trying to do Kippie and me so many favors," said Aunt Chasey. She felt her face. "Am I looking older?"

"Oh honey, I'm sure she just feels bad for yellin' at you when she got here," Quincy reassured her.

"But Quincy, that was over a month ago. Nearly two months."

Aunt Kippie spoke. "Did you see the way he reacted when I asked him about Paul Bunyan? Do you suppose he's never heard the joke before?"

Sid lowered his newspaper. "Kippie, he had a tattoo of a blue ox on his arm."

"Did he really?"

Sid nodded. "Yeah, right there on his bicep."

"Well, that's a relief." Aunt Kippie stroked Xerxes's back. "Sid, any idea why this old cat's decided to come out today?"

Sid stared at Xerxes for at least a minute. The cat stared back. Then Sid shrugged. "Nope."

Not much later, Anna and Jud returned.

"Thank you ladies," he said to my Aunts. "It's perfect."

"I'm glad you think so. You'll be sharing that portion of the second floor with Quincy and Bill."

Jud nodded. "All right." He opened the front door. "Well then I'll just get my bags." He returned with two bags and a portfolio, and headed back upstairs.

As soon as Jud had gone, Anna turned to Sid, her hands on her hips and her black eyes shining with rage.

"You feel you can criticize everything I do?"

Aunt Kippie picked up Xerxes in her arms, and he curled up comfortably. "I'll be in the back room if anyone needs me," she said.

"I think I'll start dinner," said Aunt Chasey. They both left.

Anna continued to stare, seething, at Sid. "Well?"

"Anna, don't."

"What were you laughing at?"

"Nothing."

"Sid godammit you're a coward."

"I'm a pacifist."

"If you're a pacifist—"

"I don't want to fight."

"I don't want to fight either! Just tell me what the hell you were laughing at!"

"It isn't important."

"Tell me!"

Sid set down his newspaper and folded his arms. "I just find it amusing that you flirt with every man you see."

Obviously Sid did want to fight.

"You have no right! No right! I smiled at a man! I asked him some questions! Are you jealous, Sid? Is that it? Or do you have something against me?!"

"Anna, calm down. You asked me!"

"You know what, Sid? You don't care. You don't care about anyone! You don't care about their feelings or their thoughts or fucking anything!"

Quincy leaned over. "I'ma go get some popcorn girl, this is entertainment."

Sid glared at him and growled. "The fact that Anna is still angry about something that happened ten years ago is not entertaining."

"This has nothing to do with ten years ago! I let go when you left, you son of a bitch!"

"You wanted to end it just as much as I did. But the blame was never on your shoulders," Sid said sarcastically.

"That's because it was your fault!"

"We made a damn mistake!"

"You made a damn mistake!"

Quincy raised a hand. "Uh-uh honey, it takes two to tango."

"Quincy, shut up!" Anna ordered.

"Ooh!" Quincy scowled.

"You're the most inconsiderate bastard I've ever known, Sid. You never really cared. Never!"

Sid's voice got quieter, more sensible. "You know that isn't true, Anna." Then it rose a bit again. "You could never admit you were ever wrong."

"I WASN'T WRONG!"

We were all silent for a moment.

"We both were, Anna," Sid said, softly but certainly. "But now it's behind us."

Anna blinked and paused before shouting, "I didn't know you were going to be here!" She stormed down into the basement, yelling, "Go blow down a house!"

"Boy, she still loves you," Quincy told Sid.

"Damn it Quince, it isn't that. She just doesn't want to admit that we weren't compatible, because at the time she was so sure that we were. She just wants to think she wasn't wrong about us." Sid sank into the couch.

I looked at him. "Is she going to ask for you to come back?"

Sid squeezed my arm. "We'll never get back together," he assured me.

"Think I should go comfort Ms. Drama Queen?" Quincy wondered.

"It's up to you, Quince. She needs to know that's not my job anymore." Sid massaged his temples. "Ten years and she's as mad at me as if it'd happened yesterday."

Quincy patted Sid on the shoulder. "You stressed out, Sid? You want a back rub?" Quincy asked in mock sweetness.

Sid whacked Quincy's hand away. "Get out." He smiled a little bit, but it didn't last long.

"Man that'd be fun," Quincy said.

"You'd better tend to Anna," I told him.

If I couldn't have Sid, neither could Quincy.

"I s'pose you're right," Quincy said with a sigh. He left.

"What happened between you two?" I asked Sid. "You told me it was a mistake, but...I don't really understand."

Sid thought a moment. "In the beginning, I told her everything about myself, and I warned her not to expect anything. I can't commit. I don't commit. But we decided to try it out anyway. And for a while it was great. In the end though, it was just a relationship that didn't work. We were constantly hurting each other. We ended it together."

"So why is she still hung up on it?"

"She's a perfectionist. It can't be her personality that split us apart. Only mine. Never both of us." Sid sighed. "But then, a lot of things were my fault."

I looked at him expectantly.

"I left once for three days and didn't tell her where I was. Only that

I'd be gone."

"You have trust issues."

"Yeah, I do."

"Where were you?"

"I was at my house."

"Why didn't you tell her?"

"I would've had to tell her why."

"Can you tell me?"

"Not now."

"When?"

"Another time."

"If I guess, will you tell me?"

Sid grinned. "Let me hear some of your guesses."

"You had werewolf business to attend to."

"Next one."

"You were with another woman."

"I never cheated on Anna."

"You needed a break."

"I did," Sid said with a grin, "but that isn't why I left."

"You were with another man."

"Philly."

"I don't have much to work with here, Sid."

"I know, that's why I'm letting you guess."

"You're mean, Sid."

"I'm half-wolf, Philly."

"Lousy excuse."

"You wouldn't say that if you were one."

"A werewolf?"

"Yeah."

"Is it really that hard?"

Sid looked me in the eye. "I'm going to be alive long enough to see all the people I love in this house die."

Oh. Yeah.

I hugged him. "I'm sorry, Sid."

He squeezed me. "It's not something anyone has to be sorry for, babes. That's just the way it is."

"Why do you stay here?"

Sid grinned. "I might as well enjoy you people while you're around."

"Do you?"

"What?"

"Enjoy us."

"Yeah, I do."

Well..that's good.

"There's no way to turn back into a human." Thought I'd throw that out there.

"No," he confirmed.

"No like...spells or serums or anything?"

"Nothing so far. Once the energy touches someone, it's never gone. That's how I can tell who has it and who doesn't."

"But I don't, right?"

"I never noticed anything, which makes it all the more baffling when I try to figure out how you blocked Mary."

"Oh."

"But you seem like someone who it would come to very easily. Don't get any ideas from that, though."

"I'm not, Sid, I won't. Besides, I can't get bitten because you'd have to agree to it." I smiled. "I wouldn't force you to get stuck with me for all of eternity."

Sid looked amused. "It would be an interesting eternity."

Interesting. Interesting could be good, I could work with it.

"But it's not easy being immortal. Unless you're in a life-threatening situation. Then it's kind of entertaining."

"Have you been in a life-threatening situation?"

"Yes." I was so glad he wasn't Taylor, who would have said, "Technically, any situation could be life-threatening if you think about it."

"More than once?" I supposed the time he was bitten by the werewolf would be considered life-threatening.

Just a little, remarked the voice.

"Oh yeah."

"Will you tell me about one?"

"Living with Stacia Frobisher was always life-threatening."

"Van's sister with the mansion?"

Sid nodded. "Yeah. She and a lot of other people refer to it as the 'hidden realm' but it sounds too much like some fantasy novel for me. I never thought my life would turn out that way."

"Which?"

"Like fiction."

"It's only fiction to the people who don't know it exists."

"And for that reason it might as well be."

I sighed. "Well why was living with Stacia so dangerous? I remember you said she made you see awful things, but could she really hurt you?"

Sid glanced at Bill, who was still entranced. "You know how regular vampires suck blood?"

"Yeah."

"Psychic vampires aren't bloodsuckers that can hear your thoughts. They're mindreaders who suck your energy out. They only need eye contact, and then they can kill you."

So now they can hear my thoughts and kill me?! I sighed hopelessly. "Great."

"They're not everywhere, babes, don't be afraid to make eye contact with people. There are only one or two psychic vampires who don't live with Stacia or Van."

"Why so few?"

"She's killed most of them."

"Oh. But..how? If your skin is impenetrable.."

"She's had a lot of practice."

"What does she do?"

"Once she has your eyes she can start absorbing the energy right out of you. You get a little tired, then exhausted, then unconscious. And if she needs it or just is in a bad mood that day, she can kill you in less than a second, whether or not you're immortal."

"But she liked you for the most part, right? Until you..rejected her?"

"Yeah."

"What was she like when you were...friends?"

"She was still cruel, just not towards me. I think it comes from hundreds of years of hearing what people really thought of her."

"Did she listen to your thoughts?"

"Sometimes."

"How did you handle it?"

"I just gave in. I stopped caring about what she heard. And then I learned to block it."

"How?"

"I got help."

"From Van?"

"No." Sid stood. "I have to say I'll always prefer mortals for company."

"Why?"

"They're just as interesting as anybody, but they usually can't read your mind." Sid smiled and pulled on his jacket.

"Where're you going?"

"Van has some people who need legal advice."

"What exactly does Van do?"

"He does everything. Bye babes." He left.

I went to call Eric.

* * *

The next day when I arrived home from school, Anna was in the kitchen with my Aunts. They were making a huge pot of soup. Anna sprinkled in some spice, Aunt Kippie provided encouragement, and Aunt Chasey did the rest. Anna kept taking a different spoon and tasting it.

"Hello dear," said Aunt Chasey as I walked in. "How was school?"

I grunted and sat at the kitchen table.

"Well, try to finish your homework before dinner, Phyllis. Everyone's coming tonight."

"Why?" I asked.

Anna answered, "For fun." She smiled and hugged my Aunts. "I missed everyone so much. It's so great to be doing this again."

"It certainly is, dear." Aunt Kippie smiled at Anna. Then she looked at me. "We're eating at six when Quincy and Bill get home." She looked at Chasey nervously. "I did mention it to Jud but I don't know if I told him the time!"

Aunt Chasey sighed. "Well, I'm sure we'll have another big dinner before he goes on his way." She looked at me. "Anyhow Phyllis, you'd be best not having anything you need to do after dinner, we may need your help cleaning up and such."

I nodded. "Okay." I looked at my backpack. I only had history; I'd done everything else in study hall. Until Eric had shown up.

I groaned. Mrs. Highman gave terrible homework. It could drive you to suicide if you were having a bad day and didn't have a loving family and friends.

First it was vocabulary fill-in-the-blanks with no wordbank or hint as to what chapter the words were from. Then it was explain the words and their definitions and significance (assuming you got the fill-ins correct). Then there were several questions. Then there was reading. But before I left, I had to ask.

"Where's Sid?" I asked the three women.

Anna scowled at her soup.

"I'm not sure, dear," Aunt Kippie said. "He went out."

"One can only presume that he's with Frobisher," Anna muttered.

"Anna, Sid may work for whomever he likes. He doesn't have the luxury of being able to always do as he pleases. He might as well find a plausible job that suits him."

"Frobisher is a dictator. He pays off half the city."

"You make it sound like the Mafia!" Aunt Kippie cried.

"They aren't killing anyone. They're keeping a secret, Anna. Not everyone is open-minded."

"What exactly does this guy do?" I asked.

Aunt Kippie pondered a moment. "Well Phyllis, he keeps control over those people with Sid's...talents. He provides them with homes, jobs, money, identities. Didn't Sid tell you when.." Aunt Kippie looked at Anna, unsure whether or not she should speak of Mary in front of her. "Didn't Sid tell you?"

"Yeah, he said the same thing. He doesn't sound like a bad guy."

"Rumor has it," Chasey said, glancing at Anna, "that he is rather rude."

"And speaks lightly of murder!" Anna cried.

"He's never killed anyone!" Aunt Kippie insisted.

"Never when it can be proved."

"Anna! That is not a minor accusation!" Aunt Chasey scolded.

"I'm aware of that."

"You have no basis."

"I know he has."

"Have you seen it? Has Sid?"

I spoke. "Why do you guys care?"

"The man is Sid's friend. Sid would not befriend a murderer."

"Sid became a murderer the moment he became a werewolf," Anna said calmly.

"Now STOP IT, Anna!" Aunt Chasey shouted.

Kippie sipped a glass of water. "She's just still in love with Sid, Chasey. Don't overreact."

"I am NOT in love with him!" Anna stormed out of the kitchen.

"Are too!" Kippie called.

"Tell me when dinner's ready!" Anna yelled angrily.

Kippie giggled.

Chasey rolled her eyes. "She just comes right back and there isn't even a pause before she attacks Sid!"

"Oh Chasey, he can take it. I just like to jerk her chain. Everyone does."

"But Kippie, what if she really is in love with him again? Her heart must be breaking terribly!"

"I'm gonna go finish my homework," I declared, and went to my room. I didn't want to start feeling compassion for Anna as far as Sid went. How could she have let him go?

But why would he have left for three days without telling her why? What could his reason have been for not telling her if he hadn't been having an affair?

I sighed. It was probably something that had to do with having the energy that I hadn't learned about yet. Maybe he'd gone to run around the woods as a wolf? No, Anna probably would have understood if it'd been that.

Of course he can't just tell me, I thought.

I peeked out of my bedroom. Sid's door was opened, he wasn't in his room. I considered going through it for a brief moment, and then I shook my head. No. Sid and I could tell each other things now, I didn't have to snoop. If he wouldn't tell me now, maybe he would when we were older. He must have had his reasons. I just wished I knew what they were.

The dinner went...interestingly.

We ate outside in the backyard because it was a beautiful evening, too beautiful for my Aunts to waste, they said. Plus, they could use paper plates and I wouldn't have to help clean up.

At first, everyone seemed in good humor. Anna and the guys were talking about Damien's club, and Damien was undoing Quincy's tie. Sid and Jud were talking about different places in America; it sounded as though Sid had seen them all and Jud had seen quite a few. I talked to Bill about how nice it was out. And filming. He was Ricky Fitts from "American Beauty." My Aunts fussed over the food.

"Can I borrow this?" Damien asked Quincy, holding up the tie.

"Yeah sure baby, I got tons. In fact, sometime you should go through 'em and just take a bunch, I hate ties. I feel so constricted."

"No bondage then," Abe said, looking at Damien sympathetically. "Maybe you can reach a compromise."

"I was never into that stuff," Damien said.

"Me neither," said Butch. "The only thing I like around my neck is my feather boa."

"Yeah, I never even watched gay videos. In fact, I thought I was straight for a while," Damien admitted.

Abe looked at him, appalled. "When did that end?"

"Unfortunately when I tried to have sex with a woman." Damien winced.

"The vagina just didn't do it for you," Butch understood.

"Gentlemen, please. We're about to eat dinner," Aunt Kippie scolded.

"Oh, Kippie, don't be such a prude. Just because you haven't had sex in twenty years," Anna said.

The guys all gasped.

Surprisingly, it was Jud who spoke first, standing up defensively. "Don't talk to the lady of the house that way! Show a little respect! Look at all the trouble they went through to make us this dinner!"

"Yeah Anna, don't bite the hand that feeds you," said Butch.

"That was uncalled for, Anna. We'd love to have you with us, but if you've already decided you're going to be undesirable tonight you can climb into your convertible and leave." Aunt Chasey looked Anna squarely in the eye. She hadn't said it meanly, more matter-of-factly.

"Besides Anna, you can't say anything. You been gone. Kippie's a pimptress!" Quincy insisted.

I couldn't help it. I giggled.

Aunt Kippie looked at me and smiled. "Yes Anna, if you don't shape up I'm going to have to go up to my closet and get my riding crop."

"Sorry Kippie, I must have missed out on a lot." Anna grinned. But it didn't look all that good-natured.

My Aunts let the dinner commence, and we went back to talking.

Sid raised his eyebrows and widened his eyes briefly, sighing and stretching his arms out for a moment. "That was tense." He picked up his spoon.

"Man that was scary. I don't ever want to see Kippie and Anna fight again," said Damien.

"Yeah, Kippie's so good-natured all the time. She wouldn't waste time yelling, man. You know if she got angry she'd start whippin' out some crazy kung fu moves," Abe told him.

"I don't know man, I've seen Anna practicing kung fu down in the basement. She don't look it but she could kick Sid's ass," Quincy said.

"Yeah but he'd secretly enjoy it," said Abe.

Sid rolled his eyes.

"As long as we don't have to see Kippie and Anna in a girlfight," said Butch.

"I don't know, it'd be kinda' hot," said Jud.

Wait for it, wait for it, I thought.

"Oooohhh," the gays chorused.

"Jud likes older women!"

"Kippie, here's your chance to use that riding crop, girl!"

"Jud's into that girl-on-girl action."

"*Somebody* here likes bondage."

"You should come to my club, Jud, we got lotsa' middle-aged divorcees looking for a good time."

"What are we talking about, guys? Sid'd probably enjoy it too."

They looked at Sid expectantly.

"They'd have to fight fair, I'd have that condition," Sid said, glancing at me. New subject.

I looked at my Aunts. "This is really good soup. Taylor's gonna be mad she missed this."

"Oh Phyllis, you should have invited her!" Aunt Chasey told me.

"It looks like you guys have enough people. I wasn't sure if there'd be enough food."

"You know there's always enough food, even if we were all tasting the soup in the kitchen. Besides, there isn't just soup. Taylor likes my bread. You should call her and have her over for dessert."

"I will. Could I have a piece of bread, please?"

"Of course." Aunt Chasey passed me the plate.

"Would you like some steak, dear?" Aunt Kippie offered.

"No thanks," I replied, contented.

"Could I get another one, Kippie?" Sid asked, holding out his plate.

She smiled and forked it onto his plate. "There's an extra saved for you in the freezer, dear."

Sid grinned. "Thanks Kippie. You ever really want to use that riding crop, let me know." He winked at her.

"Oh Sid, you always did make me feel younger."

"Jud, man, you got some competition," said Butch.

I never did call Taylor, because after dinner, Anna started an argument with Quincy that ended up becoming an argument between Quincy and Damien. I couldn't tell what it was about. At first I thought it had something to with Damien's past straightness, because I heard someone yell something about sexual preference as I quickly retreated into the house from the porch. But as I came out of the kitchen, I also caught something about wearing ties. I still didn't want to stay and listen, though. I was tired of arguments.

Unfortunately, Anna decided to stay on the rampage for the rest of the week.

Past and Present Controversial Decisions.

On Saturday, Eric went to a concert with some of his friends. He called me that night.

"Hey," he said. "Can I pick you up tomorrow?"

"Sure. How was the concert?"

"It was fun. The sound was a little off though. It was really loud but we couldn't hear what the band was saying. Of course, they might have been stoned."

I smiled. "Maybe they play better that way."

"Have you ever been to a concert?"

"Yeah, but it wasn't anybody I knew, just some random singers with Quincy and my Aunts. But Quincy says he'll take me to see Alicia Keys if she ever comes to the city. Or Madonna. Last time she was here he told me I was too young a for a Madonna concert."

"I hope I'm always too young for a Madonna concert. She's weird."

"Because none of the bands you like are weird."

"You have a point."

"Well, you do too," I admitted.

"Only when you're around."

It took me a second to get the joke. "Eric."

"You set yourself up, Phyllis." I could almost hear his smile. "Want me to show you what I mean tomorrow at my house?"

I bit the inside of my lip. "Maybe."

"I didn't mean—"

"I know." It'd been almost two months since I'd told Eric I wanted to take it slow. But on Memorial Day I'd decided I was ready to speed up a bit again. I'd seen him naked for the first time after the fireworks. He'd seen my whole body now, too. "But I did."

"I love you, Phyllis."

"I love you too."

We stayed on the phone a while longer, until I went to bed.

I lay there, thinking.

Had I really meant it? Was I ready?

What if I got pregnant?

I flinched at the idea. I wouldn't. If the condoms he had weren't good ones, I'd buy some myself. I didn't need any fire-breathing babies.

I was also looking forward to it. Not just seeing Eric and being with him, but getting out of the house. Thank the Lord we'd be at his house because I didn't know how much longer I could stand my own. Earlier that day, Anna had even attacked Quincy.

"Damien," Quincy had been talking to Damien on his cell, "I don't have your stupid tie! If anyone took that hideous fashion faux pas, it would be Butch." There was a pause. "Because he's like a ferret, he likes shiny things. And I don't have to restrain my judgments just because I'm talking to you, hon. Uh huh? Well then you can just go find the damn tie by yourself! Ugh!" Quincy angrily pressed the END button and shoved the phone into his pocket. "How in hell did I end up dating someone who can't even keep track of his goddam ties? How am I supposed to tolerate someone who expects me to put my opinions on hold all the time?" He sat down in a chair and ripped an issue of People off the coffee table.

Anna slammed her own issue of Elle down. "Maybe if you stopped bitching for once you'd learn how to have a stable relationship, Quincy," she said in a sensible tone.

After a second or two Quincy peeked over his People. "What?"

"I said maybe if you focused on someone other than yourself and your nonsensical meaningless fashion judgments and clothes, you might actually be able to stay with someone."

Quincy, wide-eyed, was speechless. But not for long. "Excuse me?"

I saw Kippie open the sewing room door a crack, not wanting to miss this. It had to be the first time in history the two of them were having a serious argument.

"Did YOU just call ME unable to hold onto a relationship?"

"Yes I did. Because YOU break up with men when they wear TIES you don't like."

Quincy put his hands on his hips. "Sweetie, I don't know how long you haven't been here but I've been with Damien for months now. We are in love. We have some trials and tribulations, so what? At least I have a relationship I commit to. I ain't goin' out all the time, sleepin' with every man I meet because I can't get over PAST MISTAKES."

Anna was raging now. "You can't say shit about me."

"And why not? I'm the one who knows all your shit. You know what?"

"What?!"

"You need ta lighten up! The hell are you doin' in my business anyway?"

"My relationships are built on what really counts, Quincy. Not just a mutual love of Dolce and Gabbana and cheesy movies." She pointed at him. "You know you make it harder for other gay men? You're the reason that people expect homosexual guys to talk a certain way, think a certain way. You're the reason people think that all gay men act like the ones on 'Queer Eye for the Straight Guy'! You're the reason that gay hasn't overcome its stereotypes yet!"

Quincy stared at her in disbelief, his face scrunched up as though he were either going into battle or about to cry. Finally he said, his voice quivering just a little, "Just because you're never satisfied with yourself doesn't mean you need to try and make me feel the same." He turned and went into the kitchen.

Just then, Sid came in through the front door. "Hi girls," he said, hardly even looking in our directions as he hung up his jacket.

"Ugh just...go chase some pigs," Anna huffed, stomping down to the basement.

Sid sighed quietly, then sat in his chair. "Is she just being herself? Or am I looking particularly wolfish?"

"You look fine," I said honestly. "She just got into a fight with Quincy."

"Really? With Quincy?"

"Yup."

"Yes, they did fight." Aunt Kippie said, coming out of the sewing room with a quilt. "And I wish they wouldn't use such obscenity." She shook her head, then looked at me. "Phyllis, how do you like this?" She held up the quilt. It was brightly colored and had funky fabrics that my Aunt would never hang up around the house.

"I like it. It's kinda' cool."

She dropped it into my lap. "I thought we could put it in your room, on the wall. Next to Johnny Depp." She grinned, then looked at her watch. "All right you two, I'm off to work." She kissed me on the cheek. "Steer clear of Anna." She left for the hospital, hastily grabbing her purse on the way out.

"Your Aunt knew to lay low, I see," said Sid.

I nodded.

"So what happened?"

"Anna insulted Quincy's ability to hold onto a relationship and he told her she needed to get over past mistakes. I guess he thinks that's why she's been so volatile for all this time."

Sid grinned. "Blaming me, eh?"

I hesitated. "Can I ask you a question?"

"Sure."

"Why..did you go out with Anna?" There, I asked it.

Sid sighed. "She isn't always as bad as she's been lately. When she doesn't have you on her hit-list, she can be fun. She can be sophisticated. She's also very smart, we always had engaging conversations. And she was funny as all hell. But there just ended up being something that made us clash. Plus she wasn't.." He stopped as if he'd been startled.

"Are you okay?"

"Yeah fine, thanks babes. I'm gonna head upstairs and get some work done." He went upstairs.

I wondered what Anna hadn't been. And right before I kicked the thought out of my head, I wondered if I could ever be whatever she wasn't.

* * *

The next morning, Eric came to get me, and before I knew it we were kissing on his bed, half-dressed. His hands moved with finesse, he'd learned quickly where I liked to be touched. With him it was a little bit more obvious. As I kissed him, I made my final decision. I wanted Eric.

"Eric..?"

He looked at me, stopping suddenly. "Yes?"

"I'm really..I really want to.." I kissed him. "I want this." I reached down and touched him.

Eric smiled and touched me right back. "Are you sure?"

"Yes."

Eric reached over to his bedside table, his bare chest brushing mine. He took out the condom.

Luckily he had more than one.

* * *

When I got home, I had so much to think about. The first time hadn't been very impressive, but afterwards...

I'd always thought my first time would be huge, dramatic, emotional. But it wasn't. I felt great...but not changed, even though I'd probably just made one of the biggest changes you can make. I wondered why. I didn't feel sinful, but I didn't feel any sort of ecstatic epiphanies coming on. I wanted more..I'd liked it, obviously..but it didn't feel like as much of an emotional jolt as it should have.

Then, coming up the stairs, I passed Sid on his way down. And I gasped, feeling a pang of awful realization like I'd been kicked in the chest.

I'd made love to Eric, more than once. But I still wasn't in love with him.

Was it wrong that I didn't regret it?

I got into the shower. I didn't ponder my decision but tried to remember every detail, every move Eric and I had made.

When I got out, I grabbed a towel and headed into my room to get dressed. As I walked back into the bathroom to hang the towel I'd dried myself with, I noticed my hair, getting longer than usual, was dripping onto the backs of my ankles. I smiled, remembering Eric's hands running through it. Then I reached into the small closet for the special towel I used on my hair only. It was small and maroon with black wavy lines on it. I dried off my hair with it and looked at myself in the mirror.

Maybe I had made a bad decision. But, in my opinion, it was the best bad decision to make.

* * *

The next day at school, Eric and I exchanged secret smiles in the hall. Our hugs were just a little bit tighter. Taylor and Key asked me why I was in such a good mood during lunch.

"Phyllis, how in hell can you be so happy?!" Taylor demanded frustratedly. "We just had a pop quiz in history," she explained to Key. "And I'm absolutely positive that I failed it! I'll bet everyone failed it! But here's Phyllis, smiling away." Taylor folded her arms. "You *are* a genius, Phyllis, but you still hate school more than anyone I know. Why are you so happy?"

I shrugged. "I had a good weekend."

Key grinned. "What, did Sid propose to you?"

My heart sank. But only for a moment. "No," I said. "I spent it with Eric. It was really nice."

"Because you don't see Eric every weekend," Key said sarcastically. "Or every day, for that matter.

I shrugged. "I guess he just makes me really happy."

Taylor beamed. "Aw Phyllis, I'm so glad!" She hugged me tightly. "Key, she's in love!"

You sure are, said the voice. But not with Eric.

I pretended not to hear the voice.

In study hall, I stopped playing immediately when Eric came in and we kissed.

"Everyone keeps asking why I'm so happy," I whispered in his ear.

He smiled. "Why *are* you so happy?" He kissed me again. "It's not something *I* did, is it?"

"Maybe."

"I must be pretty good if you stayed happy this long."

"Mm you should come over this week," I told him.

"No, I think *you* should come over." He kissed my cheek.

I giggled. "Okay."

We kissed a little bit more.

"I'm glad you were my first," he whispered.

"Me too," I said genuinely. It made me even happier to know he felt the same way.

After school, Taylor and I walked to our buses together.

"So how do you think you did on that quiz?" she asked worriedly.

I looked at her. "Taylor, are you serious? Are you actually panicked?"

"Yes! If my grades go under a certain point my parents will try to cut me off from the world. And Mrs. Highman has me hanging on the edge!"

"Taylor, history's your best subject."

"But if she keeps doing awful surprise things like this—"

"Taylor!"

She looked at me.

I patted her on the shoulder. "It's going to be fine, I promise."

"I don't know, Phyllis."

I sighed. "Look, do you want to come to my house and study or something? Would that make you feel better?"

She brightened. "Why yes, yes it would. Thursday after school sound good?"

I grinned. "Sure."

"Okay then." Taylor started toward her bus, then turned back around. "Is Eric really the reason you were in such a good mood?"

I smiled. "Yes."

She nodded. "Good. Bye Phyllis!"

When I got home, Sid pointed out my prominent smile.

"You're in a good mood for right after school," he remarked. "What happened?"

"Nothing," I said cheerfully.

He smirked. "Uh huh."

I shrugged, still smiling, and walked past him into the kitchen to make myself a fruit salad. I figured that, even with my inherited anti-kitchen gene, a fruit salad couldn't be that hard. I mean really. You cut up some fruit, you throw it in a bowl, you mix it around..

Well, I tried my best.

The pieces of peach were too big and the banana slices kept falling onto the floor. When I tossed the salad, the grapes would hop out because I'd put the salad in a bowl that was too small. Johnny spotted one rolling across the kitchen floor and started playing with it.

"You know Phyllis, you're a lot like your Aunts in a lot of ways."

I looked up and saw Butch.

"But I think you lean slightly more toward Kippie when it comes to making food."

Luckily, I was still in my good mood. "I just need a little practice. I don't think I'll ever be as good as Aunt Chasey but maybe someday I'll surpass Aunt Kippie."

Butch grinned. "I like a girl with ambition. You want some help? I can slice up an apple and throw it in."

"Sure." Maybe then some of the salad would end up in the bowl.

Butch and I finished the salad (after Butch dumped what I already had into a larger bowl) and then we ate it.

"Thanks Butch," I said gratefully, spooning a strawberry slice into my mouth.

"No problem sweetie. I know how to handle fruits." He winked at me.

I smiled and rolled my eyes.

Suddenly we both heard a loud, high noise. For a second we froze, unsure of the source. Then realization came.

"Anna's practicing," I explained.

"Oh. Oh yeah, I keep forgetting she's a singer. Ever since Quincy mentioned her doing kung fu I keep thinking of her as a ninja or something." Butch paused. "Hey, she's not so bad."

I laughed. "Did you think she would be?"

"Well you'd think she'd have worn out her voice by now."

We heard a low chuckle and turned to see Sid entering the kitchen. "That voice never wears out." He strode to the refrigerator and opened it. "I need meat," he muttered.

"You carnivorous beast," Butch said, with way too much relish.

"Yeah Sid, ever consider being a vegetarian?" I asked jokingly.

"That's about as possible as you freezing to death, babes." He opened the freezer and pulled out a large chunk of steak. "Besides, better I eat an animal than take a bite out of somebody in the house."

"You can take a bite out of me anytime, sweetcakes," Butch said in a deliberately feminine voice. Then he went back to his regular one. "Sorry Sid, couldn't resist."

Sid cut off a piece of the steak and threw it onto the stove, Rosemary's Baby-style.

"Aren't you gonna eat it raw?" Butch asked.

Sid smiled. "Not in here."

"I think we could handle it."

He grinned. "It wouldn't be very well-mannered of me."

Butch rolled his eyes. "I'm sure Phyllis is grateful that you're trying to set a good example."

Sid chuckled, laughing at a joke only he fully understood. He forked the steak out of the pan and tossed it onto a plate. He began wolfing it down, no pun intended. (Maybe a little.) It had to be the sexiest display of bad table manners I'd ever seen. I stared.

When he'd finished he noticed me looking and laughed.

"Sorry about that, Philly."

I smiled, caught off-guard. "Uh, no problem." I rose quickly and left. Time for some homework. Ugh.

"Hey honey."

I passed Quincy in the living room.

"Hey, I thought you were at work?" I said, confused.

"They let me off early today, sales are slow and I wasn't feeling so well."

"Are you sick?"

Quincy shook his head. "Nah, I just dressed improperly. It's damn hot outside today. I just needed to put on some light clothes and take it easy. And.." He held up a brochure. "..I'm gonna have Chasey and Kippie take a look at *this*."

I took it. It was for a place that installed jacuzzis and above-ground pools.

"I think this house needs a pool. And there's at least five us that live here regularly, we could help pay for it and clean it and all that."

I looked at him. "You must have been really hot."

"Yeah. I could use a pool. If we got one, girl, I'd use it all the time. Whatchu' think your Aunts'll say?"

I blinked and shrugged. I had so many other things on my mind, not being a virgin anymore, sex in general, Eric, school, homework, finals...and Sid devouring that piece of meat.

Bet you can think of some other things you'd like him to devour, said the voice.

"Aw c'mon, give me some more support than that," Quincy pleaded.

I blinked again. Right. Pool.

"Well, I don't know what they'll say exactly," I told him. "But they're usually pretty open to any suggestions you guys have, you know that. And I'll back you up, I'm ready for a pool."

Quincy nodded. "We could get 'em to say yes." He paused. "You think Sid smells like wet dog when he gets out of the water?"

I shook my head. "No way."

He grinned. "I know, he probably smells like sexy no matter what he does. But that'd be pretty funny, wouldn't it?"

I smiled and gave Quincy a little hug. "You'd just better hope he didn't hear you."

"Honey I wouldn't mind Sid getting rough with me one bit."

Good old Quincy.

The next evening at dinner was when he chose to bring up the pool idea with my Aunts. He'd gotten the approval of Anna, Bill, Sid, and the rest of the guys beforehand. Now, he had even more reason for them to accept. He walked dramatically into the kitchen, where the Aunts and I were eating from a plate of sandwiches.

"Kippie, it's *hot.* It's burnin' outside. *But...I* have the solution!"

Kippie smirked. "Oh really?"

Quincy held up the brochure. "We can get a pool!"

"Quincy.." Aunt Chasey began.

"You don't have to make the decision now, girls. But Anna and Phyllis and I all think it's a great idea. We could all split the costs, and the cleaning. The yard is big enough for *any* kind of pool! And these are above ground so they don't take much construction."

"Well, I—" said Aunt Kippie.

"Sh! Don't decide yet! Give it some thought. And remember, it wouldn't just be your money. We'd make it all worth it. And that's all I have to say." He sat down and grabbed a tuna sandwich from the plate.

The Aunts looked at each other.

"I think it's a lovely idea," said Aunt Chasey. "Especially with all of the outdoor activities the church has scheduled for the summer. It would be nice to come home and jump into a pool."

"Yes, but I think we'd be better off investing in an inground pool," Aunt Kippie told her. "That way, should the inheritance somehow run out or I lose my job, we can sell the house for even more than it's worth. *And* we'll be able to dive and do cannonballs."

Quincy and I looked at each other in shock.

"All right then, I'll go into the city and see about construction for this summer," said Aunt Chasey happily. "Would you be so kind as to hand me that pamphlet, Quincy?"

* * *

"We're getting a pool," I told Taylor the next day.

"That's it, I'm moving in," she said. "I seriously am. I turn 16 this summer and I'm moving into your house. I mean it. I'll take one of the empty rooms near Quincy and Bill. Or whatever's cheapest."

"That'd be the downstairs bedroom, but my Aunts have been using it for storage."

"Then I'll stick with whatever else is cheapest, I guess."

"I'll move into Sid's room," said Key. We were sitting at our table in the cafeteria.

"Key, you've seen him like, twice," Taylor scolded.

"Well I'm sure he's as sexy as he looks." She turned to me. "But just so you know, once the pool's set up or finished or whatever, I'm going to be at your house all summer." She smiled with realization. "Do you think Sid'll swim?"

I rolled my eyes. "Jesus, Key." Key had been boyfriendless for nearly two weeks, longer than ever for her.

"Sorry. I'm just a little boy-crazy these days."

"No, really?" Helen questioned, checking herself out in her compact mirror.

"Hey, just because *you're* a tightass," Key began. Then she reconsidered. "Or maybe a lesbian?"

"Shut up, Key."

"She's just trying to get your goat," Taylor assured Helen. Then she raised an eyebrow. "That's an expression, right?"

I shrugged helplessly as Key glared at Helen. "You're just jealous, Helen. You're just jealous of people that are happy!"

Helen looked at Key, befuddled. "What?"

"Ever since Mary left you've been a complete bitch to me! Well you know what? I miss her too! But there's nothing we can do! We have to live in the present now, Helen."

"Somebody's in the middle of a speech," Liz remarked as she sat down with her lunchtray.

Helen sighed. "It's just Key ranting again."

Liz patted her friend on the shoulder. "Key just needs to get laid."

Taylor put an arm around Key protectively. "*Key* is too young to get laid."

Liz snorted. "Oh, like you and *your* boyfriend aren't doing it."

Taylor looked at her blankly. "We aren't."

Liz's eyebrows shot up. "Really?! I guess Phyllis isn't the only virgin here, then."

"Whoa, hold on a second there Liz, *I'm* still a proud member of the V-club," Key told her.

I sighed. Should I tell my friends of my recent change in virginal status?

Helen and Liz looked at each other. Liz coughed and they both laughed.

No, I thought. Not today. In fact, I didn't know if I'd ever tell them. They'd just assumed I was a virgin, so they must not really have wanted to know. I folded my arms as I thought to myself. What if I'd lost my virginity *before* meeting them?

You've only been dating Eric a few months, the voice reminded me, and your Aunts attempted to raise you with high morals. What else would they think?

Hmph.

I wanted to tell Taylor. I knew she'd take it seriously without being judgmental. But at the same time..I wasn't sure yet. The only person I'd talked about it with was, well, Eric.

Speak of the devil, said the voice as Eric entered the cafeteria.

"Hey," I greeted him happily.

"Hi," he said, leaning down to give me a hug and a brief kiss. "I just wanted to let you know I won't be there today, I have to watch some kids take their final exams in music; Mrs. Reygor just left."

I nodded. "Okay."

"I'll call you after school, okay?"

I smiled. "All right."

"I love you."

"I love you, too."

He gave me another kiss and left.

Everyone at the table was silent for a moment. Then Key sighed.

"Phyllis, you are so lucky. I wish I had a boy who liked me that much."

"*Oh my God!*" Helen cried. "Key, you're SO STUPID! YOU dumped JESSE."

"Jesse was too serious," Key explained feebly.

"He wasn't serious, you idiot! He just really liked you! Almost as much as Eric likes Phyllis, but we wouldn't know because you would *never* say 'I love you'!"

"Like it really means anything in high school, anyway," said Liz.

"Exactly! So don't sit complaining about not having a boy who loves you when you made it that way yourself!" Helen stood and stalked over to the vending machine.

Key lay her head on the table. "Blahhh."

"You shouldn't do that, do you know how dirty these tables are?" Taylor told her.

"I don't care."

Liz patted Key on the shoulder. "Don't worry about her, Key."

Key sighed. "No, I should have known better. The guy she likes just started dating another girl." She was fibbing. She and Helen tried not to talk about Mary with Liz.

Liz's eyebrows shot up. "Key!"

Key blinked. "Oh, but Phyllis is getting a pool!"

Liz rolled her eyes. "You'd better go talk to Helen, Key."

Key sighed and went to get Helen. Liz followed.

Taylor and I looked at each other and shrugged.

"Still on for tomorrow?" I asked her. We were still going to do a study session even though Taylor had gotten a nearly perfect grade on the pop quiz.

"Of course."

"Good."

We had already decided we were going to study history because Mrs. Highman was the most brutal grader and she'd probably be helping grade our finals; from what we'd been told, several people would. We would have sessions once or twice a week for the next two weeks.

Of course, we both knew we wouldn't really be studying. And we were right.

"I'd be better off studying with Eric!" I told her the next day after an hour had gone by and we hadn't even opened our books.

"Oooh, how are you guys?"

I still hadn't told Taylor about Eric and me. Why? I don't know. Maybe because I was used to keeping secrets. Maybe because I was afraid she'd say something that would make me worry. At the moment, I hadn't had any worries about pregnancy just yet, and I was pretty sure Eric didn't have any diseases. But Taylor always knew things like that; she would probably tell me about some STD that shows no symptoms for fifty years and then causes the victim to grow horns on their genitals or something.

"Pretty good," I told her.

She grinned. "Oh really?"

Of course, you never knew with Taylor. She might tell me it was a great idea and give me some techniques to use that she'd read in one of her million books.

I smiled. "Yeah. Mostly we hang out at *his* house."

Taylor bounced her eyebrows. "How's *that* going?"

I smiled and avoided her eyes suggestively. "Good." Then I looked at her seriously. "Especially since it means I'm not *here*."

"What's wrong with here?" Taylor asked, concerned.

"Ugh. Anna. She's just.." I shook my head. "When she isn't attacking Sid she's flirting with Jud or some guy over the phone. She hardly ever sings and she hasn't really spoken to Quincy since they fought." Taylor had of course heard about the words Quincy and Anna had exchanged. "Though Quincy did ask her what she thought about the pool. But they're still not really friendly anymore."

"That's awful."

"Yeah, I know."

"So why is she flirting with Jud? He doesn't look like her type." To put it nicely.

"I don't know," I said helplessly. "I don't know what's up with her, but...I kinda' think she might be trying to make Sid jealous."

Taylor was alarmed. "Is it working?"

"I don't know, it doesn't seem to be. He told me he'd never get back together with her, but..it's not like she's straight-out asked him back. Yet."

"Yet," Taylor agreed. "So you're not over—"

"No. Of course not. But Eric and I have started saying 'I love you' and I think it's helping a lot."

"Do you love him?"

"I really do love him, Tay, but—"

"You're not in love with him."

"Yeah." But I'm trying to be. "I don't think I can feel that serious about a high school guy when I've already had such strong feelings for Sid," I said suddenly, surprising myself.

"So don't get too serious."

God damn it.

I smiled at her. "You give good advice."

She grinned. "I know, you never would have thought of that yourself."

Suddenly, the sewing room door (we were in the sewing room) opened.

"Girls, I'm finally doing it. I'm finally giving my dream a shot," said Butch. He was wearing the blue scarf Quincy had given him back in

March, even though it was nearly 80 degrees out.

"What?" Taylor asked.

"You're going to call Brad Pitt?" I guessed.

"Even better." Butch took a deep breath. "Abe and I were in the store today and Quincy introduced us to a GQ contributor! I guess he's a regular. And he's going to let me know when there's an opening so that I can get an interview!"

"Oh my God!" I was excited. Butch was the reason Quincy read so many magazines; he dreamed of working for all of them. Except for Glamour. That had been Anna's subscription that somehow kept coming even when she was gone.

Anna came up behind him and handed him what looked like a martini.

"Let's drink to it," she said, holding up her own glass.

They clinked.

"Hey, where's mine?" Abe's voice came from the living room.

It seemed that Anna had improvised a small party for Butch. The guys, Maria, and Bill were there. Sid was on his way down the stairs; I never would have had that conversation with Taylor if he'd been in hearing distance.

We abandoned our so-called studying and joined them in the living room. Anna was actually fun to be around when she wasn't screaming. When Jud came back from painting on the rooftop of some building, she didn't flirt with him at all. In fact, once Aunt Kippie came home *she* started talking to Jud. It was all very strange. But I was happy to see that Anna and Quincy seemed to be friends again.

"If you get an interview and they hire you, you have to write an article about Quincy," she told Butch.

"I'd have to call it 'A Well-Kept Secret' and it could be all about the shop."

"And there could be a dramatic picture of Quincy like this." Damien posed, his hands folded beneath his chin and his expression serious. "And then in the middle of the article there'd be a picture of Quincy and me together doing something casual. And Anna could be in there somewhere too making a comment since she's already famous."

Anna put an arm around Damien. "I knew I liked you."

"*I* think you should do a dual article on Abe and Sid," said Quincy. "You could call it, 'Sensations for all Orientations' since one of them is straight and one is gay, but they're both just as sexy."

Abe shook his head. "Sid is a love god, do not compare me to him."

"Jesus Christ," Sid muttered.

"Or 'Men Everybody can Love,'" said Butch, genuinely considering the article. Then he looked at Abe. "Oh shut up Abe, look at you. You look like you just walked out of an Abercrombie ad."

Quincy leaned over and whispered something in Butch's ear. Butch looked nervous but laughed off whatever Quincy had said. "Honey you are tireless," he told him.

"He sure is," said Damien suggestively.

"Gag me with a spoon," said Abe.

Taylor giggled.

Eric called a few minutes before I was going to walk Taylor home. I rushed up to my Aunt's room to answer it.

"Hey," he said, "do you mind if we go to the mall on Saturday?"

"No, why?" Eric didn't quite seem like a shopping kind of guy. Maybe for video games and music supplies, but he didn't seem that attracted to the mall.

He sighed. "Terry spilled soda on one of my amps and I promised the kids I'd let them try out one of my electric guitars next week for their lessons."

"Why don't you use the other amp?"

"I don't want to use my Marshall with kids. Terry's just lucky he didn't spill soda on *that* one."

"How'd he do it?"

"I think he was high."

"Shouldn't *he* buy it for you?"

"Oh he's paying for it, and then some so that I don't tell mom about his stash. The new amp won't cost too much but ugh, he's an idiot."

"I'm sorry about that."

He chuckled. "Yeah, me too. So that's all right?"

"Of course."

"Then after that you can come to my house again."

I smiled to myself. "Sounds good."

"Yeah it does," he agreed.

"I'll see you tomorrow."

"Okay, I love you."

"Love you, too. Bye." I hung up and looked around to make sure Sid wasn't nearby. Somehow he could have heard. Things like that worried me often, especially after the feeling up incident. I didn't want Sid to know Eric and I were having sex.

I went back down and found Taylor and Sid having a friendly discussion.

"There shouldn't *be* plea bargains!" she was saying.

"Without plea bargains every trial could take *years*. Decades, even."

"If someone murders a child, or *any* innocent person, they should *not* be able to *bargain*."

"Sometimes people deserve second chances. And what about manslaughter?"

"People who commit manslaughter should have been more careful," Taylor said bitterly.

Sid grinned. "So I'm guessing you believe in the death penalty."

"Yes," she said certainly.

"I do, too," said Quincy. "If somebody shot Abe or Butch or my Damien, I'd kill 'em myself."

"The death penalty is *wrong*," said Anna. "Who are *we* to choose who lives and who dies? It makes *us* murderers too."

Sid looked at Anna, confused. "*You* don't believe in the *death* penalty?"

"I can understand personal vengeance," Anna said calmly. "But not death doled out by the government."

"That'd be an awesome song!" Taylor exclaimed. "We could call our band 'Casualties of the Sane' and 'Death Doled out by the Government' could be our first hit!"

Jud grinned and said, "She's on to something," in his gruff voice.

"Haven't you ever seen 'The Life of David Gale'?" Abe demanded. "Innocent people get sentenced to death all the time!"

"Yeah, and guilty people *bargain* out of the jailtime they deserve," Taylor said. "Or they don't get convicted at all."

"Not when Sid's on the case," said Quincy.

"When *were* you a lawyer, Sid?" Taylor asked curiously.

"Right now," he said with a grin. "But for now I only do office work and some paralegal stuff."

"Oh. That's cool." She saw me. "Who was on the phone?"

"Eric," I told her.

"Good, you should tell him about the band."

"What'd Eric have to say?" asked Aunt Kippie.

"His brother broke one of his amps so he has to buy another one on Saturday."

Taylor nodded. "How'd he break it?"

"Spilled soda." While high.

"Nice."

We were all quiet for a second. Then Quincy folded his arms and looked at Anna. "I *still* can't believe *you* don't believe in the death penalty."

"Well, some people don't believe in death at all," said Anna, glancing subtly at Sid.

Jud made a "tuh" sound, grinned again and raised his glass. "Amen to that."

Everyone raised their glasses. Except Sid, who looked at me and winked.

I glanced at the grandfather clock and looked at Taylor. She nodded, and we wordlessly set down our cups.

"Bye everybody!" she called. Aunt Kippie, Bill and all the guys hugged her (she congratulated Butch one more time) and Sid, Anna and Jud bid her farewell.

"Be back in a little while," I told them as we walked out the door.

"So when do they start on the pool?" Taylor asked.

"Monday."

"I'm assuming Quincy and Anna made up."

"It looked that way. I'm glad. I didn't like them mad at each other." I sighed. "It's strange...I never thought she'd yell at Quincy."

"Well, she did leave for a few years," Taylor said. "Maybe some things have changed." She looked at me. "I mean, you looked a lot different when you were thirteen."

I bit my lip. "How so?" Taylor had seen the pictures in Aunt Chasey's room, chronicling me from age five to present.

"Well, you're much more.." She moved her hand in circles, waiting for the right word. "Sophisticated-looking. And you have bigger boobs. And longer hair. Basically that's it. But that can be enough. You probably look even more different to Anna since she didn't watch you grow."

"You have a point."

"She's probably jealous of how close you are to Sid." She put up a hand. "But that is over because you now have Eric."

"Indeed I do."

Hidden.

Once I got back home Abe and Butch had left. Quincy was on the couch with Damien while Sid played cards with Bill, who was someone named Desmond from the Lost DVDs he had recently purchased.

"You sure you want to take your chances with that hand?" Sid was asking.

"You're gonna fold, brother," Bill said with a Scottish accent.

"Quincy?" I looked at him.

"Yes ma'am?"

"You and Anna..made up?"

"Yeah. I finally went down into the basement and started saying everything I could think of that is stereotypically gay for like twenty minutes. She laughed and apologized, and it was history, girl." Quincy made a cutting motion with his hand.

"Thank God. You were one miserable bastard," said Sid.

"Yeah, you were," agreed Damien.

"But now it's all better and we're gettin' a pool!!" Quincy exclaimed.

Sid laid down his hand in front of Bill/Desmond, who grinned and laid out his flush. Sid sighed. "Can't say I'm a big swimmer."

"Noooo!!!" the gay couple moaned, then looked at each other.

"Well, there's one thing we can agree on," said Damien.

"Sid is one smokin' hot pieca' meat," Quincy agreed. "I don't think any of us here would mind seeing you shirtless, Mr. Siddons."

Sid sighed again and handed Bill/Desmond five bucks.

"Thanks brother."

"Oh my goodness! Anna didn't yell at Sid tonight!" Damien realized.

Sid looked at him, confused.

"Quincy said she's been a real bitch to you."

Sid shrugged. "I probably deserve it somehow." He took a deep breath. "Maybe something I fucked up in a past life."

His cell phone rang, and he pulled it out of his pocket and answered it, hurrying up the stairs to his room.

"Man," said Damien with admiration. "But Quincy, I am glad he isn't gay."

"Me too, baby, me too."

* * *

The phone rang unexpectedly on Saturday morning as I was getting ready for Eric to pick me up. I rushed down to the living room to answer it. It was Eric.

"Phyllis, the brakes on my car stopped working, it had to be towed. They're looking at it right now. But I can't pick you up, and I can't get to the mall." He sighed. "Every goddam thing keeps breaking on me!"

Poor guy. "Oh Eric, don't worry about it, maybe I can get somebody to drop me off at your house."

"That'd be great. But I don't know what I'm gonna do about my amp! Mom's gone with Terry." Eric groaned.

"Gone?"

"He came home stoned and she caught him. So she took him to a drug counselor." Eric groaned. "Terry's always doing this shit. He's a loser and I hope he has to go to rehab for like fifty years. I swear Phyllis, I want to kill him right now. He breaks my amp and *then* he's the reason I can't go get another one!" He sighed. "I have to disappoint at half my lessons this week, I promised the kids they could start on electric guitar!"

"Do any of them have their own amps?"

"I don't know. And it's a lot of extra shit for their parents to lug to a lesson that only lasts half an hour. Plus if I bring mine every kid is guaranteed a try."

"Hey, Philly." Sid was in his chair, turned towards me.

Great. I hadn't even noticed him.

I hadn't even noticed him! I thought. That's a good sign, right?

No, said the voice. He could just be stealth. And he can still hear every word Eric's saying.

Oh, yeah.

"Hold on, Eric," I said, and looked at Sid.

"Yes?" I replied.

"I'm going into the city. I can take you guys to the mall and drop you off at Eric's house afterwards. I need to get some work done anyway."

"Really? Are you sure?"

"Yeah babes, why not?"

I shrugged and smiled. "Thanks, Sid."

"Anytime." He turned back around. He was reading a book.

I relayed Sid's message to Eric.

"Is he sure?"

"Yep."

Eric sighed with relief. "Tell him thanks. That just makes my whole day." He paused. "So I'm forgiven for feeling you up then. I guess it's—"

"Eric," I said rapidly, "I'll call you right back!" I hung up, thanked Sid one more time, and ran up the stairs to use the phone in my Aunt's room.

"Hey," Eric answered. "What happened?"

I sighed, nervous smoke rushing from my mouth. "Listen Eric, this is going to sound really weird but you have to do it, okay?"

"You're not gonna ask me to break up with you, right?"

"No—"

"You don't want to have sex anymore?"

"No no not at all. Just listen. Sid has really, *really* good hearing. You can*not* say anything at *all* about...us while we're in the car with him, okay? If he picks anything up, I don't know what he'll do."

"Okay."

"Don't say *anything*. Don't even whisper. He *will* hear you no matter what, okay?"

"It's no problem, Phyllis." Eric paused. "So how do you know his hearing's so good?"

"I live with him. When he's in the kitchen, he can hear what I whisper in the living room."

"Really?"

"Yes."

"Has he been exposed to any heavy radiation?"

"It wouldn't surprise me. But just please don't say anything about sex, okay?"

"Don't worry Phyllis. I'm not going to try to piss him off, especially since he's doing me a favor."

"You promise?"

"Yes."

"Thank you. Sorry, but if my Aunts find out...I don't know what they'll do."

"I understand."

"Thanks Eric."

I went back down the stairs. Sid already had his jacket on.

"Let's go."

I gave Sid directions to Eric's house from the backseat. When we pulled into the driveway, I went and knocked on the door to get him. Then we climbed back into Sid's car.

"Sorry to hear about your amp," said Sid.

"Thanks. I'm a little more worried about my car."

"What's wrong with it?"

"Brakes are out and there's an alignment problem."

"Ah, they're gonna screw you on the bill. Those things are simple to fix."

"Yeah, I probably am gonna get screwed." Eric squeezed my knee. Then he quickly added, "But my mom's helping me pay for it. She knows all the tricks to car economics."

"Those are good tricks to know." Sid turned on some music. Guitars shrieked.

Eric looked at me and grinned. I shook my head at him, afraid he would say something. I was also afraid Sid was going to slide in some sort of secret attack. So I asked him boring, normal questions.

"Who's this?" I asked him, in reference to the music.

"Dio," he said. "I borrowed it from Jud."

"Who's your favorite?" Eric asked.

"My favorite as far as rock or metal goes?"

"Your favorite out of everything."

"I can't answer that, I listen to too much music. Philly knows. She's seen my collection."

"Yeah, his Alice in Chains CD is right next to Duke Ellington," I said.

"Do you play anything?"

Sid shrugged. "Not really."

For some reason the conversation was odd to me. But I had to remember that Sid was only ten years older than Eric, physically.

Sid dropped us off at the mall and we walked in.

Eric looked at me. "How long do we have?"

"Probably about two hours."

He hugged me and quietly said, "I can't believe I have to wait two hours to touch you again."

I smiled and kissed him on the cheek.

"I need to get condoms too," he remembered.

"I'll get them," I said. "I have ten bucks." I had more but I was putting it away. I was saving up for a car. Or a grand piano. Or a trip to Paris. Whatever happened.

Eric nodded. "Okay. You wanna meet me at the music store?"

"Sounds good," I told him.

I scanned the drugstore for people I knew as I strode toward the "Family Planning" isle. That would just be great. Excuses formed in my head in case I ran into Anna or one of Quincy's buddies. "They're for a friend." "They're for a health class project." Yeah, right.

Oh no. What if Sid had followed me in? I looked around. What if he was someplace where I couldn't see him? He did have, like, a century on me.

I glanced about as I bought the box and when I walked out I threw away the receipt. I looked behind me again, and shoved the condoms in my pocket.

I subtly glanced upward. God, I thought, if you could please make Sid not have been there, I'll be very thankful and uhh..well, I won't ever do drugs or kill anybody.

I couldn't very well promise Him my chastity or churchgoingness.

* * *

After spending the majority of our two hours deciding on what amp to buy and then fooling around with the different keyboards and guitars, Eric and I were driven back to his house by Sid. We were all quiet for the rest of the ride.

In his room, Eric gently pushed me onto his bed, reached into my pockets and pulled out the box of condoms.

After two of them were gone, Eric's mom returned, and so did the mechanic in a tow-truck with Eric's car. Terry was staying at the counseling center for the rest of the day.

"Ugh. I'm so glad I have *one* productive, well-behaved child," his mother said lovingly, giving Eric a one-armed hug. She and Eric paid the mechanic and thanked him for bringing back the car, and he left.

"You think it's really all better?" Eric questioned.

Jill nodded. "Oh yeah, I've been going to Henry's for years, Eric. They're the best." She sighed. "So did you get your amp?"

Eric nodded. "Yep. Phyllis's friend gave us a ride."

"That was nice of him." She looked at me. "Eric says you've got a lot of people in that house."

I smiled. "We've got a few."

"But the house is pretty big anyway, right?"

"Yeah Mom, it's huge."

"I'm sure my Aunts would love to have you over for dinner sometime if you'd like to see it," I said. Aunt Chasey would have been proud.

"It sounds wonderful," said Jill.

"Just let us know," I promised. I looked at Eric.

"I should burn Sid a CD. I bet I have a lot of stuff he'd like, if his taste is as widespread as you said."

"What made you think of that?"

Eric shrugged. "I want to thank him for driving, I guess. And make a peace offering."

I smiled. "I have a feeling you were already off the hook, but if you're going to burn something we better do it now."

"You're right, if we don't do it now I'll get distracted," he said, kissing my neck. "Or you could distract me first, and we could burn it after..."

I kissed him. "Sounds good." I just had to concentrate on not burning *him*.

* * *

"Thanks Philly." Sid took the CD I handed him when I got home.

"Yup."

He looked up from his laptop. "How was Eric's?"

Ahhh. "Pretty good. Thanks again for taking us to the mall."

"No problem babes, like I said, I had to be in town." He studied me.

"What?" I asked.

"Nothing."

Sigh. "So what'd you have to be in town for?" I couldn't help myself.

Sid closed his eyes and leaned back into his chair. We were in the sitting room near the back stairway.

"I had to talk to Van. And Jud."

I raised an eyebrow. "Jud?"

Sid nodded. "Jud's a guard for Van. Or, he used to be. He's really doing this as a favor."

"What?"

Sid smiled. "Jud has the energy. He's part hypersensitive—that's when all your senses are heightened about a hundred times more than mine are. Some hypersensitives are so sharp they can pick up people's thoughts and emotions. The thing with *Jud's* hypersensitivity is that it only affects his eyes and ears. So he's staying with us until Van's sure the man who stole the andrastenite and whoever is with him are far from this area." Sid shrugged. "It's a win-win situation for Jud. He gets some painting in and gets paid to watch over our surroundings."

I raised an eyebrow. "Do the Aunts know this?"

"Of course Philly, I told them the moment there was any chance of danger." Sid sighed. "They've never been phased by my warnings."

"Wow." We were being guarded? Until now everything Sid had told me about andrastenite and the Frobishers had just sounded like some story. But *we* needed protection? That meant all of our lives could be in danger, even Sid's.

"Is there anything I can do?"

"I wouldn't ask you for help babes. You're not supposed to be worrying about this kind of stuff at this point in your life."

"Sid. Please. People worry about all kinds of stuff at every age."

"I should let you enjoy your life and I shouldn't make you worry about anything besides petty teenage-girl stuff." Sid grinned.

My nostrils flared and smoke came out.

"Sorry," Sid apologized. "Ever since..well, lately I've just been having to remind myself that as unique as you are, you should and *can* have the life of a normal kid."

Yeah, parties, homework, screwing around, all kinds of things that couldn't ever compare with the things Sid told me, the things that no one else could ever know. Now that I knew about all this, I should be allowed to help. Sure, sometimes I needed the normalcy. But I could do both, couldn't I?

"That doesn't matter. I'm sure all normal teenagers want to help their fr—" In some cases, calling a person your friend means everything in the world. But with Sid, it didn't seem like enough. "—the people they care about," I finished quickly. "And who said I *want* to be considered normal?"

You did, said the voice. You were so happy once you started going out with Eric. You were excited about being normal.

Oh yeah. I did, didn't I?

Sid shrugged. "Sorry Philly."

"Sid, come on. I can breathe fire! I can shoot heat from my fingertips! I'm completely fireproof! I can't ever have a safe, quiet life and I never want to!"

Sid stood. "But you don't want to die either, do you?"

"I won't die!"

Sid glared at me. "Phyllis, these *things* don't *care* whether or not you're human. If andrastenite can penetrate my skin, God knows what it could do to you! I don't want you looking for anyone or trying to help because if they're here, I don't want them to know you're involved and try to *kill* you because you're the *easiest thing to kill*." Sid paused. Then he pushed a strand of my hair out of my face. "Do you understand babes? I *refuse* to risk your life. I appreciate your offer, though."

I sighed. "I don't want you to risk your life either, Sid."

"He won't have to." Jud had entered.

Sid turned around. "You know already?"

Jud nodded. "They scoped the entire area out. And so have I. There's nobody dangerous within at least a 300 mile range of this place. And there's been no sign of them since the stone was stolen. But Van will have the Clifford twins watching out full-time until the bastard's caught." Jud grinned. "I'm still here because I've been getting in some good painting." He looked at me. "And I have a little crush on your Aunt. Don't tell her though."

I smiled. "You can stay as long as you want."

Sid nodded. "Long as you pay the rent on time." He grinned. "Just kidding. They're great here, Jud. Why do you think I keep coming back?"

"Well when Van told me about you I figured it was for the opera singer. But now I can see why you're not with her. Men might as well be her hobby."

"Ouch," I said.

"Yeah, and I ain't even interested in serious relationships. Not with young *mortal* women." Jud nodded to Sid. "Come outside with me for a second n' take a look at my bike."

I couldn't tell if that was really what Jud wanted or if he just wanted to talk to Sid alone. I watched them go, and wondered if he'd been telling the truth when he said Sid wouldn't have to risk his life.

That night Eric called and after I hung up the phone, I realized that I couldn't remember anything he'd said.

After the next Saturday passed I realized our relationship was changing. Sex was now a regular thing. And we both enjoyed it. In fact, it was awesome, or at least what I would estimate to be awesome for two people in our age group. But Eric and I changed in other ways. When he called, I had nothing to say, and neither did he.

This was the conversation we'd had the previous night:

"Hey," Eric answered the phone.

"Still up for tomorrow?" I asked.

"I'm always up for you."

"Heh." Uhh.. "Is your car still working okay?"

"Yeah, I think so."

Pause.

Eric spoke. "We should play some music soon."

"Yeah, definitely."

Pause.

"So I'll pick you up tomorrow morning?" he asked.

"Sure," I replied.

"All right. I love you. Bye."

"Bye," I said, but he was already hanging up.

At school, we always had excuses not to spend long periods of time together. We hugged and then we kept walking. Physically, when we were alone, we were great.

But I was sixteen years old. I had just started high school. This wasn't something small; Eric wasn't planning ahead with me as Jesse had done with Key. This *was* serious. I wasn't supposed to be in a relationship that was based on solely on sex.

No, you shouldn't, said the voice as I headed up to my room after visiting Eric's house a week later. Things had been strange and awkward for over two weeks. And I was feeling more and more bored with Eric and more and more interested in Sid.

But it feels good, I reasoned. And I should be fooling around with someone. I *should* be a normal teenager. Normal teenagers do bad things. They make mistakes like this. They have *fun* instead of wishing for someone else who is about a century their senior.

But you're wishing for him anyway, the voice pointed out. And if you aren't thinking of yourself, think of him. It isn't honest or fair. Not if you love someone else.

But eventually that love will wear off, I argued.

You sure about that?

...no.

I went into the living room in my pajamas. Bill was on the couch watching a movie. I sat in Sid's Chair, curled up.

I really liked Eric. We had so much fun. And he wasn't like most of the high school boys I knew. How could I break up with someone so good? True, the person I wanted more was better, but he was unattainable. Eric was *there*. Eric loved me. Eric was concrete.

Anna, Quincy, and Damien entered, each greeting me and heading, amidst chatter, into the kitchen. A few moments later, Anna re-entered. She was alone and had a bowl of strawberries.

I glanced at them and my mouth watered. But I just didn't want them enough to get up. I didn't want to think about breaking up with Eric. I'd just started having sex with him. That doubled how horrible a person doing this would make me. Plus everyone would start asking me why I'd broken up with him, why I didn't go out with anyone else.

Anna sat down and looked at me. "You're looking very lost in thought. Is everything okay?"

I shrugged. "Yeah."

She nodded. "Listen Phyllis, I know I've probably seemed like a bitch lately, what with Quincy and all. I'm sorry about that. But you should know that if you want to talk, I'll lend you an ear anytime."

I sighed, looking at my bare feet. "Oh, I'm just not sure if I should stay with my boyfriend. I don't think...I don't think I'm doing the right thing by being with him."

Anna raised an eyebrow. "What do you mean?"

"I don't think I feel as much for him as he does for me. But I'm afraid I'll be weird and lonely without him." I was being honest; people expected you to have a boyfriend when you were 16.

Anna smiled. "Phyllis, I didn't have a boyfriend until I was nineteen."

My eyebrows shot up. "Really?!"

She nodded. "I was never asked out. I had crushes on guys but they never seemed to return my feelings. Of course, when I think about it now, there were only one or two that I really could have dated." She paused. "But I had friends. Good friends. And when people asked me why I didn't have a boyfriend, I just said, 'I haven't found anybody worth the trouble,' or, '*Should* I have one?' Eventually people got off my back, and I stopped being self-conscious and worried about it. I focused on my friends and my life. And I think I turned out all the better because of that."

"Did you make that up?" I wondered.

She laughed. "No! I promise. You can call up my mother and ask her. There's nothing wrong with being single, Phyllis. It's normal. Having a serious boyfriend or having sex when you're a teenager is what tells you you're screwed up."

Oh shit. That isn't good.

Haha, you're screwed up, said the voice.

I smiled. "Thank you Anna."

"No problem, Phyllis. I can't believe I missed three years of your life. You're so beautiful."

I laughed. "You don't have to go that far."

"Hey girls." Quincy came in from the kitchen and sat next to Anna on the couch.

Anna raised an eyebrow. "You don't know you're beautiful or are you just being modest? It's okay to admit you're beautiful, girl. I do." She grinned, and high-fived Quincy.

"Sid doesn't, though," he reminded her. "And that's who she's been hangin' out with."

Anna rolled her eyes. "I know, Quincy. But I'm sure he's told Phyllis she's beautiful."

Now Quincy rolled his eyes. "Well what do you expect her to say? What did *you* say, Anna? 'Thanks baby, I know I'm beautiful.'?"

Anna gave him a look. "I think my relationship with Sid is different from Phyllis's, honey-buns."

Hmph.

"You'd be surprised."

We all whirled around. Sid had come in the front door.

"Yeah Anna, Phyllis is Sid's new flame," Quincy cracked.

"Jesus." Sid cringed at the joke.

Anna cringed too, but not at the joke. "That would just be too disgusting for words. You're like her father!"

Sid winced. And so did I. I hoped we were wincing for the same reason, but I wasn't going to get my hopes up.

Quincy patted Anna on the shoulder. "Girl, you've been gone a long time."

"Ah, she's just jealous because I'm younger than she is," Sid said, referring to Anna.

"Sid, you're 130 years older than I am."

"That's an estimate," Quincy told her.

"Not in appearance," Sid said, grinning at Anna's displeasure.

"I wouldn't become immortal if you asked me, Sid," Anna seethed.

"Calm yourself, girl," Quincy muttered to her under his breath. Of course, Sid would hear it anyway.

"I wouldn't ask anyone," Sid said calmly. "And I don't think I would compare myself to Philly's father."

I nodded. "I think in my case it'll be good if I never find *anyone* like my father."

"I only meant in the sense of your relationship. How would *you* define your relationship with Phyllis, Sid?" Anna wanted to know.

Quincy gave her a disturbed look. "What's up with your tone?"

"If Sid's doing something he shouldn't, I wanna know!"

"What could you possibly think he's *doing*? What the hell's wrong witchu?!"

"I didn't mean *that*!"

"Guys, calm down!" Sid motioned his hands in a downward shushing motion.

"Anna, I was just complaining about my boyfriend," I reminded her.

"Yeah Anna, what exactly are you implying?" Sid demanded.

Anna sighed. She didn't say anything for a moment. "I just remember, ten years ago you would have been thrilled to be called a father figure to Phyllis. And now it repulses you?" She stood, not looking at any of us. "I guess I've been gone too long." She went downstairs in, as usual, a huff.

Quincy sighed. "I guess I'll have to go comfort miss princess." He stood. "I'ma get some cookies first, anyone want some?"

Sid and I both shook our heads.

Quincy nodded. "All right, see yas. Hey Sid, at least she didn't tell you to go blow down a house or chase a granny or somethin'." He went into the kitchen, presumably entering the basement from there.

Sid looked at me. "Why were you complaining about Eric?"

The man picks up every little thing, the voice noted.

"I just...I don't think I..I don't think I'm being fair to him." I stumbled over my words.

"Why's that?" Sid sat down.

"I think he..deserves someone better." I shook my head, knowing he'd come to my defense if I put it that way. "I mean...someone who cares more for him. I try really hard but I don't think I'm as interested in him as he is in me."

Sid nodded. "When did this come to be, babes?"

When we started having sex. But I'm not going to tell you that.

I shrugged. "Just...a random moment a couple weeks ago."

"What happened?"

"I don't really want to talk about it, Sid," I said firmly.

"Don't you?" He looked at me.

I took a deep breath. "I..." don't know what to say.

Suddenly a trumpet sounded.

"TEDDY!" Aunt Kippie shrieked from the kitchen.

"CHARRRRGE!" Bill shrieked, and we heard him bounding up the back stairway.

"Where did he get the bugle?" I wanted to know.

"I don't think we'll ever know," said Sid.

We sat in silence for a moment.

I stood. I was going to go up to my room. I needed to think and Sid's presence didn't help me to focus on anything but him. I turned to go up the stairs.

"Philly."

I turned.

"Did you talk to Anna about Eric?"

I nodded.

"What'd she have to say?"

"She said not to take it seriously or have sex with him because that would be screwed up."

"She's half-right."

"What do you mean?"

"When you're young,*everything* you do is screwed up."

I raised an eyebrow. "What constitutes as *young* to you?"

Sid grinned. "Good point, babes."

I smiled a little in return and then turned, heading up to my room.

I couldn't figure out what to do. There was only one person who just might be able to help me.

I went to Aunt Chasey's empty bedroom and called Taylor.

"Hi!" she answered happily.

"Taylor, I need to talk to you."

"Uh oh. What'd I do?"

I laughed.

"Are you breaking up with me?"

"Yes Taylor, I can't see you anymore," I said dramatically.

"You must be going blind. Ah ha ha haaa. So what's up?"

"Well..I..I think I need to break up with Eric."

"What?! Aw why?"

"We've been..we've been getting serious and I don't think it's done any good for my feelings for Sid. Plus it seems like the more serious we get, the less..chemistry we have, I guess."

"How do you mean?"

"Conversations just don't come naturally."

"That's happened to me and Tony. Are you still happy to be talking to each other? Because sometimes we'll just sit there and hardly say anything and then one of us'll just be like 'I love you' and then—"

"No. It's awkward and one of us initiates goodbye as soon as plans are made. Neither of us call just to talk anymore. I feel like I used up my feelings for him already."

"That's not good. Maybe you should talk to him."

"Maybe."

"Do you feel like you should break up with him right away? I mean, Eric's a good guy."

"It's been like this for the last two or three weeks and I just don't feel that it's right to be with him anymore. He says I love you and I say it back but I don't love him! It isn't fair to do that to him."

"So why haven't you broken up with him?"

Deep breath. "Because..we had sex."

There was a pause. "Really?"

"Yeah."

"Nice."

I giggled.

"How was it?"

"Good. That's the only part that *is* good."

"You used something, right?"

"Yeah, of course."

"Okay good."

"Do you think that I should give it more time because of that?"

"Well, have you had morning sickness?"

Jesus. "Thank God no."

"Then do what you feel is right, Phyllis. Seriously." There was another pause. "So did it hurt?"

"Just a little."

"Was he a virgin too?"

"Yeah."

"Nice."

"It was."

"Awesome."

"But that's when things changed between us."

"Well...maybe you'd be better off as friends."

"I don't know. It might be a total shock to him. I think I'm gonna wait til this weekend. Just in case something changes."

"Whatever you do, don't use a post-it or a text message."

I laughed. "I'll do it in person." I paused. "I feel really awful. He's such a great guy, and I'm going to hurt him."

"Yeah. Don't worry too much though. He's a musician. He'll just write a sad song and get over it."

"Hey!" I pretended to be insulted.

"But..what are you gonna do about Sid?"

"I don't know, Taylor." Suddenly there were footsteps on the stairs.

"Speak of the devil," I muttered under my breath. "I have to go," I told Taylor. "Thank you so much."

"I didn't really do anything. But just so you know, I hope everything goes all right."

"Thanks Tay."

"Of course. Bye!"

"Bye." I hung up and went into my room.

I showered. And inside my head, I quarreled with myself. What the hell was I supposed to do?

I got out of the shower and dried off and dressed. My hair, which I had neglected to have cut, still hung against my back. Water dripped from it down onto my ankles. I went back to the bathroom to grab my towel from the closet.

It wasn't there.

Towel, towel, towel. It must be on a hook. I looked around.

No towel. That could only mean one thing; it had been taken from the hall closet and mistakenly put on a rack in the other bathroom.

So, with my wet hair leaving drops on my ankles and leaving a wet spot on my shirt, I went out into the hall. I was headed down to the end where the bathroom was, when I found Sid.

He walked out, clad in his red robe, and..

Wow. Breathe easy, I told myself.

...using my towel to dry his hair.

"Oh, sorry Philly," he said, moving to the side so I could get by.

"Sorry, never mind," I told him turning around. I'd just use one of Aunt Kippie's towels for my hair.

"No, what do you need?" he asked.

"Uh, well..I was going to get my towel, but.." I pointed to the towel in his hand.

His eyebrows went up. "Is this yours? I'm sorry, I didn't know."

"I don't mind. I can get another towel."

He smirked, and smoothly placed the towel around my head, gathering my hair up into it carefully.

"I only used it on my hair, I promise."

You'll never wash that towel again, said the voice.

Not likely, I agreed.

I swallowed, staring into his eyes. He stared back. His finger came up and touched my lip.

Then he pulled it back and went down the hall to his room.

I blew out some smoke.

Ah, Sid.

The kick in the chest came again.

When you were in love, maybe you didn't need sex to validate it, or intensify your feelings. Not that I'd mind, of course. I felt more satisfied, more in awe, more in love just looking at Sid than I did having sex with Eric. How could I have been so stupid?

I had to end this thing with Eric, and soon. It was not only unfair to him, it was dishonest to me.

Why the hell would I ever have wanted to be typical?

If It Weren't for Bad Luck...

I still gave Eric the rest of the week. Besides one not-so-hot make-out session in his garage, we hardly interacted. I could feel it coming. If I didn't do it soon, he probably would.

Still, he did say "I love you" each time we said good-bye.

But now I was starting to feel that it was losing its meaning for him, too.

So on Saturday I called him up and told him that when he came over, I had something important I needed to talk to him about. He said, "All right."

I couldn't tell if he knew what was coming.

I went into the living room, past where Sid and Quincy were playing poker or something, and outside to sit on the front steps and wait.

What would I say? What was there to say? How do you break up with the person you lost your virginity to? How could I explain that I tried to love him and it just...hadn't worked. That I'd done the wrong thing, and I didn't regret it..but now it had to be over.

When he pulled up I still hadn't worked out the perfect response. But it was now or never.

Smiling, Eric approached me. He gave me a hug.

"What did you need to talk to me about?" he asked as we pulled away from each other.

I swallowed. "I'm sorry."

A serious look came upon him. "What is it?"

"Eric..I don't think I'm ready for this."

"What?"

"I'm not ready for this kind of relationship."

He paused. "Really?"

I pursed my lips and nodded. "I'm sorry. I..I love you Eric, but not in the way you deserve. It's not fair to you if I stay here. I'm too young, I guess."

"We don't have to—" he started.

I looked at him, my eyes pleading. Please just understand. Please don't make this worse.

He swallowed and said, "Are you sure about this?"

"Yes Eric. I'm just not ready. For any of this."

He nodded, looking down. "Okay. Well...see you later then."

Eric turned and walked down the path to his car.

I looked down at my feet as he drove away.

And then bad things started happening.

* * *

The weekend passed, dull and slow. And quiet, mainly because Anna was invited to speak at a university and was gone for the weekend.

On Monday morning when I woke up, I reached over to grab a glass of water I'd brought up the night before and knocked it over onto my math homework. I dried it out with my breath but it still had wrinkles in it. I tripped climbing up the stairs to get onto the bus, and I could hear high-pitched giggling as I walked to my normal mid-bus seat.

I entered school and saw Tony look over at me, give Taylor a kiss, and walk away. Already, I knew Eric had spread the news.

Taylor looked at me. "Hey," she said.

I gave her a look, gesturing with my head to Tony.

She held up her hands helplessly. "You dumped his best friend, it's gonna be a while before it isn't treacherous to hang around with you."

I closed my eyes. "Does he know we had sex?"

Taylor gave a short, quick nod.

"Great. Now he must think I'm a bitch *and* a slut."

Taylor patted my shoulder. "Phyllis. He knows you. He even admitted to me that he knows you're a decent person and he told me he's sure there's a part of the story that Eric is leaving out."

I looked at her weakly. "Do you know what he *has* said?"

"I guess..he just made it sound like you guys had sex and then you broke up three weeks later."

I looked down. "This is a bad day, Taylor. A very bad, bad day."

"Breaking up is always bad. But good will come of it Phyllis, it always does."

I looked at her doubtfully.

She nodded. "Yes, yes I *am* full of shit."

In English, Mr. Hamil was kind enough to give us an essay to be written in the period about something we'd read and how it illustrated some literary element or other. I couldn't concentrate. I felt awful. Maybe I really was a bitch. And a slut. What could I do? Apologize? Would I ever be able to talk to Eric again?

My math teacher was not happy with what had happened to my math homework, saying not a word but giving me a look that said, "Failure."

I could feel Tony watching me every time he came by to see Taylor in the hallway or in the cafeteria. By the end of the day, I had a stomachache. When I got home, I spent the rest of the evening throwing up and then in a fitful sleep.

Aunt Chasey woke me up a little bit later than usual, sitting at the end of my bed.

"Phyllis, did you want to stay home today?"

My eyes half shut, I shook my head. "Nope," I muttered. "That'll just make things worse." The Aunts knew I'd broken up with Eric, so everyone else probably did but no one had spoken to me about it. Jud and Sid had been gone for most of Sunday and Monday so Sid hadn't tried to have a discussion with me about it. Quincy hadn't either, because he and Damien and the rest of their friends were constantly "supervising" the men working on the pool's construction. Although most of them were older and fatter, a couple were cute.

"What happened yesterday?"

I closed my eyes more tightly. "Tony is avoiding me because he and Eric are friends. Just general bad day stuff."

She moved my hair out of my face. I opened my eyes and she was smiling. "Well darling, the good thing about bad days is that the next day has to be better."

I sighed and smiled weakly. "I hope so."

There was a "Meow" from the hallway and small pats of little feet.

"Xerxes is going in to wake up Kippie." Aunt Chasey looked at me. "Tell me that isn't odd."

"It's very odd," I agreed.

"He's been very outgoing lately. He comes into the kitchen and eats in plain site now." Aunt Chasey smiled again. "All right dear, well dress quickly, there isn't much more time before the bus comes."

As I walked out of the house, my foot—in my red sneaker—submerged in a mud puddle. I knew this day wasn't going to be better.

Again, Tony walked away as I walked toward Taylor. She shrugged helplessly.

"He'll get over it," she promised. "He's a boy, he doesn't know how to deal with things." She looked down. "Oh no! Your shoe."

I nodded sadly. "I think it's ruined. But I can't exactly change it."

Taylor sighed. "It's so rainy today. It's June, we have like five days of school left, and it hasn't been hot at all in the last few days."

I just nodded. I hadn't noticed the weather the previous day, having spent it in school and then in the bathroom, puking.

Taylor looked at me. "Hey, it's gonna be okay Phyllis. Today will get better, I promise."

I looked at her and tried to smile. I was exhausted and worried and I hadn't eaten breakfast. "Thanks Tay."

For the most part the morning was fine, until English class.

"Phyllis." Mr. Hamil stopped me on my way out and handed me a paper. It was the previous day's essay. My grades, at the Aunts' urging, are usually above 90. This was well below that number, about three points above a passing grade.

"Phyllis, you are your own greatest ally. You turn on yourself, you don't have anyone. You need to work on your writing. You've been doing a great job, do *not* write like this on your final exam, okay?"

I nodded solemnly and walked off. My Aunts were going to lecture me for this one.

I sat quietly for the rest of the day. I figured that if I hardly did anything, nothing else bad could happen. I hadn't seen Eric at all; he'd obviously been avoiding me. It didn't make me feel any better, but it was probably for the best.

As I carefully walked into my house, I saw Quincy on the couch, surrounded by friends and tissues.

"Anna was right," he sobbed. "I can't hold onto relationships!"

"Quincy, she admitted she was wrong about what she said to you! That has nothing to do with you and Damien!" Butch said, handing him another tissue.

"Yeah dude, you guys'll probably work this out. You did last time. Then we'll all sit here and tell Damien about how you cried on the couch."

Quincy giggled.

"And you don't want that. So stop bawlin'."

Quincy nodded, then sobbed again. "I can't! He broke up with me for someone else, I just know it!"

Ughhh I couldn't get involved with Quincy and Damien stuff right now. I walked quietly past them to the basement door.

I walked down into the basement to watch TV by myself. I didn't want to have to talk to anyone. I didn't want to deal with anything more than this.

As I entered the small TV room, I saw a familiar sight. Xerxes lay across the floor in the corner of the room, oddly not in his usual spot on the couch.

"Hey Zerks." The sight of a cat always cheered me up. Maybe he would sit on my lap the way he'd sat on Aunt Kippie's.

Xerxes didn't look up.

I sighed. Cats.

"Xerxes," I called. "C'mon, I could really use your company."

His ear didn't even twitch. Was he completely asleep? He had pretty sensitive hearing. I went over to make sure everything was all right.

His eyes were open, and he lay across the ground comfortably.

But he wasn't breathing.

Xerxes, the cat I'd known since before my memory began, was dead.

My hands went over my mouth.

Damien and Quincy hadn't been getting along again. My essay'd sucked. My math grade was falling. My shoes were ruined. Tony was treating me like a stranger. I'd initiated the break up with Eric; now I no longer had him as even a friend.

I could handle that.

But this was too much.

I wailed. I sobbed and cried and covered my eyes, wishing I could have pet him one last time and said good-bye and thanked him somehow for teaching me to care for a cat, for being patient with me as a little girl even when I'd pulled his tail once. For making me an eternal cat-lover. But his eyes were blank, strangely contented but lifeless. I mumbled, "I love you, I'm sorry," and felt terrible. He'd been old, he'd been at least seventeen, but he'd always been there.

Suddenly I felt hands on my shoulders, pulling me upwards.

"Hey," Sid whispered gently, holding me tightly close to him. "It's okay."

"No," I whimpered. "No, he shouldn't be dead."

"He had a great life, babes, he had everything he wanted. Don't be sad."

"What if he suffered?" I whispered.

"He didn't, babes. He knew what was coming, don't worry. He was ready. And he was a happy cat."

"Everything is awful," I whispered.

His hand crept up behind my head, and he held it up, leaning away from me and looking down.

"Everything?" he asked softly.

I closed my eyes then opened them, looking downward. "I don't know. I just..wish I could have given him a good-bye."

"He said his goodbyes."

"Huh?"

"A couple weeks ago he came to say good-bye to everybody, walked around the living room, sat on Kippie's lap. He knew what was coming, Philly. You don't need to worry." He kissed me on the cheek. "And you don't need to cry."

I nodded. "Okay."

Sid got an old blanket and wrapped Xerxes's body in it. He carried it up the stairs to tell the Aunts.

I sat on the couch, my head in my hands.

That evening Sid, the Aunts and I put Xerxes's body into a box and buried him next to the garden. Aunt Kippie cried.

The next morning, a rare picture of Xerxes on Aunt Kippie's lap was prominent on the mantel.

* * *

The week wasn't getting any better. Every time I passed a group of people, it seemed like they were talking about me. Some girl tried to trip Taylor as we were walking by. I still hadn't figured out how to tell the Aunts about my essay grade. I'd hardly studied for the upcoming final exams. I still hadn't seen Eric and I didn't know what I would do about Tony. I was afraid I was going to cause arguments between Taylor and him.

I walked out of the school that afternoon. Could things get any worse? Not only had I screwed up the end of my freshman year but I'd completely butchered the faith my Aunts had tried to instill in me. It wasn't right. And speaking of screwing up the end of my freshman year, when the fuck was this school year going to end, anyway?

And I had walked past my bus. Sigh.

"Let go of me!"

I turned, but didn't see anything. I came around the corner of the school and saw two girls attacking another one. One girl held the victim's hair and the other girl punched her in the stomach.

I looked around but there weren't any teachers or security guards anywhere, conveniently enough. They were behind the school, in an area where people didn't usually venture, near the boiler rooms and such.

"Stop!" I yelled.

"Go away, this ain't your business!" one of the girls yelled.

I put down my bag and stomped over to them. I wasn't thinking. I was just angry as all hell.

"You want us to kick your ass too?!" yelled the girl who was holding onto the victim's hair.

I grabbed the other girl's shoulders and forced all of the heat I could muster into my fingers and pulled.

She fell to the ground. "What the fuck?" She rubbed her shoulders. "She's got a fuckin' knife!"

I held up my bare hands. I was wearing a T-shirt and sweatpants despite the crappy weather.

"I have no place to hide a knife," I said.

The other girl came from behind me, wrapping her arms around my waist and tackling me to the ground. Then she kicked me.

Without any thought, I blew at her. Hardly any fire, just force. She flew back and landed on the first girl.

"Get the fuck away from us or I'll fucking throw you through the goddamn windows!" I hissed.

The girls looked at each other and for a second I thought they were going to retaliate. I was angry and scared and didn't know what the hell I was doing.

Then the girls stalked off, heading for the buses and muttering things like, "Fuckin' weirdass bitch."

"Are you okay?" I asked the girl they'd been hitting.

She nodded, gathering her things.

They must have really wanted to hurt her. Most people started fights for attention, but they knew no one would see them here. There weren't even serveillance cameras back here.

"What happened?"

She shrugged. "My little sister..one of them fucked with my little sister so I told her I'd beat her up. But I didn't know she'd have her friend with her." She looked at me. "What'd you do?"

I shrugged. "I just pushed them."

"You must have crazy-strong arms." She smoothed her hair back.

I smiled and shrugged. "I just don't like cowards."

"I'm Kendra."

"I'm Phyllis. Shouldn't you get to your bus?"

"Nah, I live a few blocks from here, I don't ride the bus." She shrugged again. "So..thanks a lot."

I nodded. "Yeah."

She walked off.

I turned around to catch my bus. I could hear them starting up and driving away. And then I saw Eric.

"What happened?" He came toward me. "Are you okay?"

"Yeah, fine, they were just beating up a girl—"

"Yeah. I just saw one of them go flying. What the hell did you do?"

"I just...got angry."

"You didn't even touch her."

Oh shit.

"Phyllis, what happened?"

I sighed. "It's a long story."

"Well, tell me in the car." He motioned with his thumb to the bus lot. "The buses just left."

"Of course they did. I'm having the worst week of my life."

"Here, tell me about it."

"Eric, look, I can't—"

"Listen Phyllis. Maybe we're not in love. But I don't have the musical chemistry with anybody else, and I saw you go this way and I wanted to ask you. Can we be..friends?"

The poison word.

I looked at him. "Is that possible, after.." I pursed my lips.

He half-smiled. "I don't know Phyllis. I've never done it before. But we could try." He grinned. "Maybe you'll be more than one first for me."

I looked at him. "I love someone else."

He nodded. "I do too."

We looked at each other.

I smiled and shrugged. "Why not?"

* * *

By the time we arrived at my house, I'd told Eric what'd really happened with my parents.

"So..you can breathe fire?"

I nodded. "Yeah."

"How did I never notice that?"

"I tried to hide it. And it's not exactly something you look for."

Eric nodded. "Wow." He looked at me. "I'm sorry about everything Phyllis. I went too fast—"

"Eric."

"Yeah?"

"I don't regret it...I'm still glad my first time was with you. And I'm glad that we both wanted to end it. I was as..un-ready for a serious relationship as you were."

Eric leaned in and hugged me. "Thanks Phyllis."

I hugged him back. "Trust me, if I hadn't wanted to do anything with you, I would have set fire to your hair."

He laughed.

"You can't tell anyone, Eric."

"Who would believe me?"

"Still."

"I wouldn't."

"Thank you Eric."

"No problem." He looked at me. "So who's the someone else you love?"

I sighed. Why even bother lying? "It's Sid. I just have to work on getting the feeling to be mutual."

He nodded and smiled a little. "You want to hang out sometime?"

I nodded. "Sure."

"Okay, I'll give you a call."

"Sounds good." I paused. "Who's *your* someone else?"

Eric smiled sheepishly. "Mika Henderson."

Rizzo from Grease.

I nodded. "I approve."

We hugged and I got out of Eric's car feeling much better. I hadn't made a mistake.

Because having sex with someone you don't love isn't a sin at all, said the voice sarcastically.

It had a point. But at least my first time had been with someone trustworthy, honest, and who had a good heart. It was almost too bad that I wasn't in love with Eric, I thought as I entered the house.

But then I shut the door behind me and saw Sid. He gave me a smile and a small wave.

I waved back.

Yeah...Eric was best as a friend.

* * *

"So what happened?" Sid said after I got home from school on Thursday.

I looked at him expectantly.

"You got happy." He smiled and closed his newspaper. "You hardly did anything this week, and then yesterday you started playing the piano again. And you got a ride home from Eric on yesterday." He studied me. "Aren't you broken up?"

"Yeah, we are," I told him.

Sid nodded. "I assume you've gotten over it."

"Well I was the one who did the breaking up."

"You were still sad, babes."

"We decided to be friends."

"Ah, *that's* why you got a ride home with him."

I raised an eyebrow. "How'd you know that anyway?"

Sid grinned. "I could smell him on you."

"Oh."

Sid patted the couch cushion next to him. I set down my bags and sat down.

"Why'd you break up with him?"

I hesitated. "It was the right thing to do. I didn't want to string him along." Sid raised an eyebrow. I shrugged. "He liked me more than I liked him from the beginning, I guess. And then after a while our feelings just kind of wore off, I suppose. I didn't think it would be fair to him to pretend."

"Sounds like a good decision. Think you'll be good as friends?"

"I'm pretty sure we will. It's not like he broke my heart."

"Not like me," Sid said in his teasing tone. Like my feelings weren't serious.

"Not like you." I felt a little less resolved, a little more reminded of why I'd tried to get over Sid. Because I really couldn't have him.

Damn it.

Quickly I changed the subject. "Are Quincy and Damien back together yet?"

Sid shook his head. "Nope. He's out there with Kippie picking out a design for the border of the pool."

"I hope they finish before the end of July," I said. "I think it's gonna get hot tomorrow."

Sid nodded. "Summers here were always nice. Except for when Anna started yelling. Or Quincy saw a bat." He sighed. "They'll be here soon."

I looked at the photo on the mantel. "No Xerxes to lurk around the attic and get them."

"One of Kippie's friends called and asked us if we wanted a puppy. Quincy was all for it but your Aunts said they weren't ready for a replacement." Sid cringed for some reason.

"*Especially* another dog." I turned and saw that Anna had entered, silent as the grave.

"You're back," I said, surprised.

She nodded. "Yup."

"Did you have fun?" I asked.

"Oh yeah, it was great. I love colleges, so much energy. And this was such a musical place. I didn't go to music school for undergrad."

"But wasn't that your major?"

"No," she said calmly. "I started out with political science. I wanted to go into law. It's still interesting to me. It's one of the reasons I ever got involved with *this* mongrel." Anna patted Sid's head the way she would a dog and ruffled his hair.

Sid fixed his hair, then turned and smiled at her. "You better watch it Anna, or I'll blow your house in."

"My what a big grin you have."

If he replied with "All the better to eat you with, my dear," I was going to shoot myself in the face.

Sid bounced his eyebrows once. "All the better to eat the lamb chops Chasey's making me."

Anna nodded and looked at me. "Don't be fooled honey, he's a wolf in sheep's clothing."

"That was terrible," Sid told her.

"You mean it didn't make you *howl*?" Anna smiled sweetly. "Well, I'll manage somehow." She leaned down and kissed him on the cheek. "I'm sorry for the way I've been treating you," she said softly. She rose and went to the kitchen.

I looked at Sid. "Was she flirting with you?" A non-virgin and I still didn't understand flirting.

Sid looked tired. "I hope not." He stood up. "I've got to get some work done for Van, babes. You wanna have somebody let me know when that lamb's done?"

I shook my head. "How can you eat anything as cute as a lamb?"

Sid grinned sinfully. "The cuter it is the better it tastes. Why do you think I'm so tempted to bite you?" His grin disappeared. "But don't get any ideas." His eyes flashed and he went up the stairs.

I sighed. The man was devastating.

I went to play the piano. I dug out a classical book from the times when I'd taken serious lessons.

Right in the middle of a Turkish March by Mozart, Quincy burst in. He shut the door.

"Quincy you scared me!" I put a startled hand to my heart.

"I'm sorry baby, but I got *news*!" Quincy sounded very serious.

I looked at him. "What news?"

"Well—" he began.

"Are you and Damien back together?"

"No, don't even say that name to me. No baby, it ain't about me, it's about Anna and Sid."

Anna and Sid? I was confused.

"Yeah. Look, I heard...Anna was talkin' to me in the kitchen a little while ago...she said she's gonna ask Sid back tonight, that trip made her crazy or some shit, I don't even know. She's been hanging around him all day."

"So what? She's gonna ask him back like..at dinner?"

"No! No, not tonight at dinner. She's gonna go up to his room after everybody's asleep so she can talk to him in private. Baby, you gotta do something for me."

"What's that?"

"Well, you'd wanna do this anyway since it's the man you love—and you're gonna have to fill me in on that Eric situation later—you gotta leave your door open tonight and stay awake and listen. I don't know when she's coming up, but you gotta hear what happens, I have to know."

"Well, Quincy.." I was about to say he'd know the next day if they were back together. But then, I wanted to know just as much as he did. "All right, I'll listen. Hey, thanks for telling me."

"Hey no problem baby. You know I'm just as nosy as you are."

"That's true," I said. "You better not say anything to him about this. Did you tell Anna how I feel? Is that why she was flipping out the other night?"

"No, I haven't said anything. Phyllis, you scared me into silence."

"Good, you *should* be scared."

"I know!"

I gave him a look. "Now let's just hope Sid hasn't told anybody."

"I'm sorry, I'm sorry!"

"Yeah well, maybe I shouldn't even tell you what happened with Eric."

Quincy sighed. "What if I tell you what happened with Damien first?"

"Done."

"Well..he told me he couldn't take it anymore. And I think he left me for another man. He didn't give me the pleasure of knowing the whole reason why though." He shook his head. "All right, enough of that. Eric, details!" When it came to Damien I could hardly expect more details from Quincy than had just been divulged.

So I told Quincy the Eric story minus the sex and any other inappropriate details. When I got to the part about the fire I skipped over it. I wanted to tell Sid first and I hadn't yet.

When I finished Quincy seemed impressed. "It's always been hard for me to stay friends with exes. 'Cept for Abe. Good luck Phyllis." We stood there for a few moments.

I finally spoke. "You think they'll get back together?"

He sighed. "I don't know. He didn't seem to dislike what she was saying, you know?" He shook his head. "I don't know." He pointed at me. "But you make sure you leave the door open. Don't open it when she comes or he'll respond based on knowin' that you hear him."

I nodded. "Okay."

He nodded in the direction of the kitchen. "You wanna get something to eat?"

"Sure."

Through dinner and then homework, Sid and Anna were always in my mind. He wouldn't say yes, I told myself. He's said that over and over. But then, he didn't exactly reject her today. And Anna's gorgeous, smart, a good singer, sexy..the list probably goes on and on. And she's *fun* when she's not *angry*. What if she's changed and Sid wants to give her another chance?

I showered and went to bed worried. I stayed up reading, worried. Finally I turned out the light. Worried.

I began to drift in and out of sleep, but I would not let myself go. I had to hear this.

Around midnight or 12:30 I started to wonder if she was coming up at all. Maybe she'd chickened out, or hadn't ever intended to come up in the first place. Or maybe I'd missed her somehow.

Then, around one, I heard soft footsteps on the stairs. Then the sound of a door opening. Sid must have heard her and opened his bedroom door.

"Hi." He sounded surprised. Confused, even.

"Hi." There was a pause.

Oh God, please don't let them be kissing, I thought.

"May I come in?" Anna asked softly.

"No thanks." Sid must have started to close the door because I heard the unmistakable sound of Anna's nails on wood.

"Wait. Is that it?"

"Yeah. What else is there?" They both sounded eerily calm.

"We used to be so good, Sid," she said gently.

"Anna, I have the utmost respect for you. But we ended this a long time ago, and it's over."

"You'd never even *consider* trying again?"

"Nope."

"Sid," her voice was still gentle, "have you had *one* successful relationship since you left?"

"I try to avoid those," Sid said honestly. "But I also try to avoid ones that I know will be *un*successful."

"Maybe you just can't *be* with anyone else. Maybe you just can't imagine yourself with anyone else."

"I can see myself with someone else."

"Who then?!"

"That's not your concern, Anna. I don't want to argue. I don't want to shut this door in your face, and I don't want to yell. Look, Philly and Chasey's doors are open. We'll wake them up if we go at it here."

"So you *do* want to."

"What?"

"Go at it."

Sid chuckled. "I didn't mean in *that* way."

"But don't you miss it Sid? There's not really anyone else. You just can't admit to yourself that you don't *want* anyone else."

"Anna, here's what you need to understand. I'm not perfect. I'm no fuckin' saint, I know. I know when I made things difficult they didn't end well. I can't always do the right thing, I made mistakes. 160 years old and I still make mistakes. But I know *myself*, Anna. I know what *I* want. And you know damn well that if it was you, you'd be in here."

Damn it! I wasn't in there either!

"Don't be an idiot," she said.

"I don't play the fool twice, Anna."

"You know it wasn't my fault, Sid."

"If I say it was all mine, will you go back to bed?"

"Sid, what if you're passing up the best relationship of your life?"

Sid sighed. "Anna?"

"Yes?"

"I *need* you to listen to me. I wouldn't lie to you. You're wonderful,

Anna. You have a beautiful face, body and voice. You're an amazing woman. But I've had love before. I've had love and I've lost it, and I've had to pass it up. Our feelings were strong for each other. But they weren't love. I am *not* the love of your life."

There was a pause.

"Hey," he said softly. "Anna, I'm telling you this so that we don't dwell on the past anymore. You can still go out and find your man. You've still got a whole life ahead of you, to find someone you can grow old with." His small laugh was faintly sad. "You know it's impossible with me."

There was another long pause. Then Anna spoke.

"Love or not, you know you still want me in that room with you Sid. You've denied yourself all your life."

Sid sighed. "Now I'll be blunt. I haven't had sex in years, a few more won't hurt me. I'm not denying myself; I'm *sparing* myself. I told you before, I respect you and I'll always care for you. But that doesn't mean I want to sleep with you. Go back to bed, Anna."

Anna was steaming. "You know, I only think I'm always right because it's true. You're going to doom yourself someday." She stormed back down the stairs.

I sniffed and pulled up my covers. The conversation had both disturbed and comforted me. While it had scared me to death that Anna'd asked Sid back, I was glad to have heard that he'd said no. And that he didn't call her "babes."

Suddenly there was a presence in my doorway. I jolted in bed, then saw it was Sid.

He looked at me, exasperated. "Did you *hear* that?"

I nodded.

He nodded back. "Great." He looked at me. "You're not one to mind your own business, are you."

"You could've told her to.." I stopped, unsure of where I was going. I was very tired. "No, not when it comes to you, Sid." I looked at him. "Are you mad at me?"

Sid breathed deeply, in and out. "No. It's probably a good thing you heard that. I don't want you to worry about me going back to Anna. But don't g—"

"Get any ideas, Philly," I finished his sentence absently. "You should tuck me in."

Sid rolled his eyes, I think. I'd started slipping in and out of dreamland.

But then, to my surprise, he stepped into my room and stood over my bed.

Or you could climb in, I thought.

He pulled my covers up to my shoulders and tucked them under.

"Warm enough?"

"Yes. Thank you, Sid."

"Anytime babes."

"Hey...Sid.."

"Hmm?"

"Don't take this..uh..I know this might be bad but...I love you. Not just in the way Quincy said, but..." I rambled on sleepily.

Sid's face went very soft. He touched my arm, even though it was covered. "I love you too Philly, you've always meant a lot to me. You always will." He kissed me on the cheek. "Night Philly."

"Goodnight."

Sid closed my door. And I fell fast.

A Motorcycle Ride and a Turtle Named Ozzy.

I spent the next day at school wondering exactly what had happened between Anna and Sid that made Sid so certain he would be a fool to go back to her. Obviously they'd argued a lot, but Anna must have been like that before they thought about dating each other.

Maybe she has back hair, said the voice.

No, she wears too many back-baring dresses, I reminded it.

Plus Sid would probably *like* back hair anyway, being part wolf, said the voice.

Ew, I thought.

I decided not to discuss it with Taylor or Key. I hadn't even discussed it with Quincy yet. Plus, all of my friends were too excited. Next week was the last two days of school. Taylor was getting ready for a family vacation by the beach, and Key was now with some guy named Trevor. They were both looking forward to summer.

"Thank GOD!" said Taylor. "Summer's here, bitches!"

"I am going to spend the entire summer learning to drive," said Key. "Then I'm driving to Phyllis's house to swim in the pool."

"Are they almost done?" Taylor asked eagerly.

I snorted. "No. It'll be at least til July."

"Man. Well, we'll figure out something until then," Key decided.

Taylor giggled. Later she said to me, "How would you ever keep cool, with your firebreathing plus a man as hot as Sid?"

"And a man as flaming as Quincy," I cracked.

She laughed but wagged a disciplinary finger at me.

We said good-bye and got on our separate buses. Tony waved to me as he came to meet Taylor. That made me smile and distracted me. But not for long.

My thoughts continued until the bus stopped on my corner and I saw Aunt Kippie and Jud Bunyan standing next to his bike in front of the house.

It wouldn't have been strange to me at all. If Aunt Kippie hadn't been holding a helmet.

I gave them an inquisitory look as I neared them.

She smiled and held up the helmet. "Jud just took me for a ride on his bike Phyllis! Isn't it exciting? I'm a regular hogette!"

I laughed and went inside.

Quincy was waiting. He stood as soon as he saw me. He'd missed me that morning when I'd left for school.

"So...?"

"You haven't seen them today?" I questioned.

He shook his head. "I been at work."

I told him the jist of what had happened the previous night. I didn't relay that Sid had found out I'd heard them and tucked me in. That part I still wasn't sure whether or not was a dream.

He nodded. "Strong man, Phyllis. If you get him you'll be the luckiest fuckin' woman on earth." He turned and headed out of the room, muttering, "Maybe he *is* gay."

"I called you flaming today!" I called after him.

He flicked me off as he went into the kitchen.

I giggled and sat on the couch. It was then that I realized that it was the last time I'd think "thank God it's Friday" until the summer ended. The last day of school was a Tuesday.

* * *

The next morning, I plopped down in the same spot on the couch next to Abe and we ate Cinnamon Toast Crunch, because Aunt Chasey was off volunteering somewhere with Mr. Meneses.

"Cartoons?" I asked him, picking up the remote.

Abe looked at his watch. "Whatever you want Phyllis, I have the day off and any break from thought would be great."

Spongebob was on. My eyes teared up at the thought of watching it with Xerxes in the basement, but I contained myself.

"Where's Quincy?" I asked. "Is he coming back?"

Abe shrugged. "Who the hell knows? I just came here for breakfast."

The doorbell rang.

I got up, then looked down at myself. I was still in my pajamas. Oh well.

I answered the door.

I saw before me a girl with the wildest hair I'd ever seen and big eyes the color of a forest. A guinea pig sat on her shoulder and she held two large bags.

"Hi! I'm Lacey! I heard you guys rent rooms?"

I nodded. "Yeah, come on in, you can set your bags down, they look heavy."

"Thanks! They are." She stepped in, set the bags down, and picked up the guinea pig. "This is Super Secret Agent Spiffy."

I patted him on the head. "Hi Spiffy."

"Do you guys allow pets?"

I shrugged. "It depends on the pet. We have fo—three cats."

"Oh." Lacey sighed. Then she brightened. "Do you maybe have a room that's a little out of the way? Your house is huge."

"Oh I'm sure they'll be able to figure something out for your guinea pig."

"Well, I have a couple of others."

"How many?"

Lacey swished her hair back behind her and counted on her fingers, her eyes rolling upward as though she was trying to look into her head.

"Well, there's Chippy and Skippy..Benatar...Ozzy...Grim...Riff Raff...umm.."

Oh boy.

"Wow. Well, have a seat and I'll go find one of my Aunts. They own the house. I'm Phyllis." I held out my hand.

She placed Spiffy back on her shoulder and shook it. "Nice to meet you! Lacey Streemer." She glanced at the TV. "Spongebob!" she squealed, and rushed to sit next to Abe.

I shrugged and went to find Aunt Kippie.

In the kitchen I found Sid, Quincy, and Bill.

"Well done," Bill was saying to Sid. He was Teddy Roosevelt again. "You may have saved yourself from certain death."

"Yeah you're telling me," said Sid. He saw me. "Hey Philly, what's up?"

"Yeah baby you have that look in your eyes, you huntin' someone down?" Quincy said.

"Do you know where Aunt Kippie is?"

Sid smiled. "She's in the garden with Jud, babes."

"I will summon her," said Bill/Teddy. "You can't decline a presidential summons." He went out through the back porch.

"Whatcha need her for?" Quincy asked.

"New tenant, maybe," I said.

"How is there a maybe? Who WON'T these ladies take in?"

"Well...she seems to have a lot of animals."

Sid chuckled. "She'll have to keep them away from the cats. Anna learned that the hard way."

"What is it dear?" Aunt Kippie had entered, Jud and Bill in tow.

"A girl wants to rent a room," I told her, pointing with my thumb to the living room.

"How wonderful!" Aunt Kippie walked to Lacey. "It's wonderful to see you my dear. What's your name and what brings you here?" She was cheerful and did not drill her questions in the usual way.

Of course, some of this was made so because Lacey was so eager to talk.

"My name is Lacey Streemer and I'm a paranormal investigator! I just came up here from Florida. I was working in a marine place but my boyfriend and I got engaged and decided to move here to be in a city and be near my family. Well sort of, they live like an hour away. I just got a job at the zoo but I don't have a place to stay yet and all of my pets are with my mother and I needed a place fast because who knows if she's going to feed them. And Ethan— that's my brother— he might step on one of them or something. My iguana used to be his but he could hardly take care of her so I took her." She sighed. "Anyway, I need a room but I need a big room because I have a ton of pets. If you don't take pets I understand, but I really, really hope you do." Lacey reached up to pet Spiffy.

Aunt Kippie was thoughtful. "Well dear, what kind of pets do you have?"

"They're all small and can be kept in cages or terrariums. I can keep them away from cats easy, Phyllis told me you guys have a bunch."

"We certainly do."

"Oh I love kitties! I love animals as much as I love paranormal stuff, they're my passion. Spiffy is my bestest friend in the whole world. Besides Craig, that's my fiance."

Aunt Kippie smiled. "It sounds like you'd be a welcome addition Lacey. We have a large attic room that the cats rarely visit because there's only one way up. It's usually locked. It'll be a little extra compared to what we usually charge tenants, I'm afraid, because of size."

"I understand. Money really shouldn't be a problem, as long as you don't mind all my an-yamals!" She picked up Spiffy in her hands and nuzzled him. She wore wristbands that had cartoon characters and flames on them. She wore a ring that held a large emerald supported by rose gold. (I found this out later on, when she told me all about her fiance's proposal and the ring he'd given her.)

"I think everything will be fine. Now dear, do you have any prejudices? We have a variety of people in this house."

"A variety of nutjobs in this asylum, you mean," Abe said.

"Yay! Asylum!" Lacey clapped her hands. Spiffy sat lazily in her lap. "Nope, no prejudices!"

Aunt Kippie shrugged. "Enough for me." She was unusually happy and carefree as she led Lacey up to the room. The attic room was enormous, bigger than Sid's. Bigger than one whole section of the upstairs.

As they disappeared, Abe turned and looked at me. "Too much PCP in that one," he remarked.

"She's not a very good paranormal investigator," Sid mused.

"I liked her hair. I think it beats out Anna's by a zillion," I said.

"Oh yeah, j'you see how long it was?! It was like a huge, well-conditioned mane!" Quincy was impressed. "I wonder what shampoo she uses."

"Smelled fruity," said Sid.

"Then we MUST know what it is, Quincy," said Abe.

Sid sighed. "That was not a gay reference."

Quincy giggled. "Sure it wasn't."

"You guys never stop," Jud observed of the gays.

"No honey, we don't." Quincy put his hands on his hips. "So *you're* the reason Kippie's so happy."

Jud shrugged. "I'd like to think so. I gotta leave soon though, unfortunately."

"Aw man come on, you'll be like all the other men that broke the lady's heart!" Quincy pointed at Sid. "Sid knows, he was there. You gotta stick around man."

Jud half-smiled sadly. "She knows I'm leaving. And I'll miss her but I think we both did each other a service."

Sid snorted. "Is that what you young people call it these days?"

"Yeah baby, Jud took Kippie for a ride on his *motorcycle*," said Quincy, nudging Sid in the arm.

"Okay, no more talking about my Aunt having sex please," I said, nudging Quincy in the arm.

"Aw come on Phyllis, it's a natural part of human life," said Abe, nudging me in the arm.

"I'm with Phyllis," Jud agreed.

"Okay fine," said Quincy. "But if she gets depressed after you leave, Sid WILL hunt you down, Jud."

"Well I could understand why." Jud patted Sid on the back. "Good luck with your opera singer."

Sid groaned. "Jesus Christ, stop making fun of me for that."

Jud grinned. "I heard her yell at you to go chase a granny today. I can't be sure if it was a wolf joke or a cut on your age."

Sid rolled his eyes. "Thanks Jud."

"You know my name would have been Judy if I were a girl?"

We all looked at Abe.

He shrugged. "I'm just saying, you'd know people named Judy and Jud."

"Okay then," I said.

"You watch too much TV man," said Quincy. "It's gettin' to your head."

"You're the one who watched all the Flavor Flav shows!"

"I did not! That was Butch."

"Oh shut up, you loved it."

"Yeah well, you love Butch and that doesn't mean you're gonna say so."

"And you love Damien, but as soon as I say his name—"

"I'ma go talk to the pool guys." Quincy walked out.

"You walk the fuck away!" Abe yelled after him.

"Abraham! Do not use that kind of language in this house!" Kippie was coming back down the stairs.

Jud smirked. "Busted."

"What was that Jud?" Kippie gave him a look.

He smiled chivalrously. "I was wondering if you wanted to go for another bike ride today."

Aunt Kippie smiled. "Why, I'd be delighted."

Sid looked at me and winked.

* * *

Jud left on the last day of school. I had to say goodbye to him in the morning before I got on the bus. He was outside, binding his bags to the back of his motorcycle.

"It was good to meet you Phyllis. Nobody's ever gonna believe I met a girl who can breathe fire." He smiled. "Take good care of your Aunts for me."

I smiled back. "I will. Thanks for watching out for us."

"My pleasure."

"Where are you going now?"

"Somewhere new to paint. I got a month's vacation from watching out for Van."

"That's cool."

"Yeah." He looked at me. "Don't worry too much about all this stuff with andrastenite. There shouldn't be any trouble for Sid, and you probably won't be involved at all."

There's another past conversation I would look back on and laugh at.

I nodded and wished him luck. He did the same and then I went to my bus stop.

Nobody took anything seriously in school that day, not even the teachers. Mrs. Highman wasn't even in school.

Zorro and Delia gave me their phone numbers and I promised to invite them over to swim in the pool when it was finished.

At the end of the day I knew I had to say good-bye to Mrs. Reygor. She was the teacher I liked best. And if I made a good impression maybe I'd get a lead in the musical the next year. I went to see her during my very last study hall.

Instead I found Eric.

"Hey," he said. "Practicing again?"

"Yup." I grinned. "Just the piano this time."

He chuckled. "What are you playing today?"

I shrugged. "I didn't bring any music, so I guess whatever pops into my head."

"Can I play with you? I'll just grab a guitar."

"Sure. But first, do you know where Mrs. Reygor is?"

"Yeah, come with me." We went into another room and found Mrs. Reygor.

"Mind if I borrow a guitar?" Eric asked, picking up a guitar.

"Of course not, don't be ridiculous." She looked at me. "Phyllis! I hope you're signing up for Fiddler on the Roof?"

I raised an eyebrow. "Who's doing that?"

"The school is! It's our summer musical! You ought to try out." She winked at me. "You'll get a good part."

I nodded rapidly. "Okay, when are tryouts?"

She gave me audition sheets, I thanked her, and then Eric and I went back into the other room to practice.

We played a bunch of songs and it was great. We'd play a song he knew and I'd improvise, and then vice versa. I didn't feel uncomfortable or hesitant about playing with him. If nothing else, Eric and I were still good for expanding our musical skills.

We finally stopped, with only a minute or so left.

"So how's everything going?" I asked him.

"Pretty good. Terry's off weed. But Mom's started coming upstairs all the time."

"That sucks. I guess you won't have the same luck with Mika."

Eric smiled and shrugged. "We're taking it slow."

I grinned. "Probably a good idea."

He nodded. "Yeah. It was hers."

I laughed. "Well I'm glad you're happy."

"Thanks." He looked at me. "You're not...with Sid, are you?"

I laughed again. "No. Just in love with him."

Eric smiled. "I'm going to tell you something then. I like Mika a lot, and I think I'll probably fall in love with her." He leaned forward and spoke softly, close to my ear. "But she's not as good a kisser as you were." He leaned away and grinned. "Don't tell anyone." We hugged and promised to hang out over the summer.

I left school beaming.

Maybe Sid would think I was a great kisser too.

* * *

"So tell me this story again? You broke up with Eric but now you're friends?" Sid looked at me as I set my bag down in the living room.

I nodded. "Yes."

"He's giving you an awful lot of hugs, Philly."

I rolled my eyes. "I hug Taylor, too."

"Point taken."

I sat on the couch next to him. He had been typing on his laptop when I'd walked in. "There was something I didn't tell you about how Eric and I became friends, though."

He gave me a sideways glance. "Oh really?"

"Yeah."

"And what's that?" he asked.

"Well..he saw me breathing fire."

Sid's face was suddenly serious. "WHAT?"

"Yeah."

"How did THAT happen?!"

"There was a fight and I was mad.?

"WHAT?" Sid stood. "You got MAD, so you showed someone that you can breathe FIRE?! Are you out of your mind?! Who else saw you?!"

"It was two girls beating up another girl behind the school, where nobody could see."

"Then how the hell did ERIC see?!" he yelled.

Quincy and Bill entered. "What the devil is going on in here?!" Bill demanded.

"Philly just decided it was okay to publicly display her firebreathing." Sid gave me a look.

His immediate rage shocked me for a moment. And then it made me angry, too.

"It wasn't a PUBLIC display, Sid. I was having a horrible week—"

"That doesn't give you an automatic excuse to put yourself in danger!"

"Let me finish." I glared at him. "I was already angry. *No*, that's no excuse to show people this. But I hadn't been paying attention and I walked past the buses and I heard the girls fighting. I went around the corner. NO ONE was there but the three girls. I told them to stop. Sid, it was wrong of them. They were holding down one girl and punching her in the stomach. What if she'd been pregnant? What if they'd seriously hurt her? I was furious! Not only was it wrong, but it was cowardly. So I told them to stop, and when they didn't, I touched one of them. And then I blew the other one into the school wall. They ran away. The GIRL wasn't even sure what happened. She thanked me and left. And then I turned around and saw Eric. He was the ONLY ONE who saw."

"How can you be sure someone wasn't watching from a window?"

"Do you really think they'd believe what they saw Sid? There's no one who can PROVE that I can breathe fire except for ME. I have control, Sid." I paused. "Thanks to you."

Sid sighed heavily. He sat down and looked away from all of us, through anything in front of him, deep in thought. Then he looked at me. "You burned one of them with your touch? You got it to be that intense that quickly?"

"It may have been because I was feeling a lot of strong emotions."

"And you blew a girl off of the ground WITHOUT burning her?"

I nodded.

He looked at me intently. "That's amazing, Philly."

Quincy held up his hands. "Whoa now, what's goin' on? ERIC knows you can breathe FIRE?"

"Yeah," I said reluctantly. "That's how we got started on deciding to be friends."

"You didn't tell ME that!"

"I wanted to tell Sid first."

Quincy put his hands on his hips and huffed.

Sid looked at me and smiled slightly. He understood.

* * *

The arrival of all of Lacey's pets marked the beginning of summer. She said as she brought them in that she was disappointed that Jud had left, because she'd always wanted someone to teach her how to ride a motorcycle. She also almost dropped the cage she'd been carrying when she heard Anna's booming voice from below us.

Lacey Streemer was the first female tenant we received in a while who didn't cause any trouble. She didn't have an active volcano for a temper, and she had never been in a gang. She was actually rather sweet. She loved cartoons and observed that Jud Bunyan spoke like someone named Pickles on a show called "Metalocalypse."

She did kind of bounce off the walls a little bit.

The first time I was in her attic bedroom after she'd moved in—I was bringing up an empty aquarium that had arrived—I walked in on her dancing all around her humongous room to "Take On Me" and other eighties rock music.

"Lacey!" I yelled.

She didn't stop, but replied, "Hey Phyllis! What's up?! Sorry I didn't answer, I'm thinking I might install a doorbell." She wasn't yelling. It seemed that her voice was just naturally high and loud. But not in an irritating way.

My voice, however, was not loud or high, so I had to turn it up to above stage-voice level in order for her to hear me. "This big box came for you!"

"Oh! It must be the aquarium for Sherman! Wanna dance?"

I wondered who Sherman was. "Sure! I can't dance though!"

"All you have to do, is jump up and down! See?" She hopped up and down.

I giggled. "Okay!" I shouted, putting down the box.

We danced and danced. We probably made a racket for Sid and whoever else was upstairs. When we were too out of breath to keep dancing, Lacey pulled a mini-fridge out from under her bed and handed me a bottle of grape soda.

That day I decided that Lacey and I would be good friends.

Unfortunately, the endorphins I'd built up dancing were shot as I went back downstairs to the kitchen.

"You need to MIND your own business! You have plenty of things you never told me, Sid!" Anna snapped at him.

"You don't need to tell me *anything*," Sid said. "I'm just telling you you need to be careful! You can't go around promising anybody you want that they can have a room in this house! You hardly know this guy and you haven't even talked to the Sorins about him."

"He's a friend of mine, they know they can trust my friends."

"Like your drug dealer friend?"

Anna folded her arms. "Oh just stop! Stop acting like you care so much! Like you're out here to protect everybody. You know what Sid? You're not here for our protection, you're here because you're *hiding*. You're hiding like a coward. Like a sad little *dog*. You've never cared about our feelings more than your own. Stay out of my goddamn life." She turned around.

"Don't do this Anna. You know what Kippie and Chasey have done for me. You know I'd do anything for them." He gestured to me. "And for Philly. You know I care, about *everyone* in this house."

Anna stopped and turned back to face him. "You didn't even care about me when we *were* together."

"Anna I cared a hell of a lot about you, but you were obsessive! I couldn't do a damn thing without you looking over my shoulder."

"I never knew what you were going to do next!" Anna shook her head, looking downward. "And someday you're just gonna leave us again, aren't you Sid? You'll just be gone, like before. Despite the people that care for *you*."

"What?!" Sid shook his head. "Anna that was three days, and I came back."

"And where were you?! The island of the wolves?!"

Quincy opened the kitchen door. "Would you two kindly SHUT THE HELL UP, please?" He was quite frustrated. "We can hear you in the living room! Sid, be more considerate."

Sid rolled his eyes again.

Quincy looked at Anna. "Anna, it's Sid's business! It's nona' yours! Calm the hell down for once, girl. Everything is fine. Let me talk on the God damn phone without screamin' in the background, God damn it!" He shut the door, and we heard him say loudly, "Sorry about that Damien. Oh no, just a couple of RUDE people. Oh really? Not at all, I'm glad to get out of here."

Anna slammed open the kitchen door. "You know where he was, don't you Quincy?" she said as Quincy put his cell back into his pocket.

Sid closed his eyes. "Why can't women ever forget anything? It was ten fucking years ago!"

"Watch your language!" called the Aunts in unison from different parts of the house.

"He's sorry!" Quincy yelled back to them. "You owe me for that Sid. Now if you two are finished re-breaking up what you never had, I'm gonna go meet some friends. Toodles." He left.

"I missed you and *Damien* getting back together!" Anna yelled after him. She looked back at Sid. "You're never gonna tell me why you left, are you? Why you left for those days with no explanation."

Sid shook his head. "Anna, it didn't have to do with you. It was something I had to do alone and it doesn't matter now. I'm going for a walk." He strode past Anna and me to the side door, then glanced back. "Sorry Philly." He shut the door and left.

Anna plopped down into a chair at the kitchen table, exasperated.

"I'm sorry too, Phyllis. Sid makes me so angry." She shook her head. "I just don't understand him. If something like that..like what he did..if that didn't matter, he'd tell me. Nobody keeps secrets that aren't significant. I'm sorry you had to hear all of that."

"It's okay Anna. But..what happened?"

Anna chuckled. "If only I knew." She looked me in the eye. "But I'm sure of one thing, Phyllis. Sid is keeping something from us. And he's been keeping it from us for a good long time." She blinked.

Poor Anna. She was a drama queen, true, but she was utterly convincing. Especially, I'll wager, to herself.

"I'm trying out for Fiddler on the Roof tomorrow," I said in an attempt to cheer her up.

Anna beamed. "I'm so glad! You know, it was me who got you started singing." She rattled off some story about my childhood that probably happened, but hadn't gotten into my memory.

And that got me started thinking about my parents.

Then I went into the living room and almost sat on Lacey's turtle.

"STOP!" she screamed as I began to sit next to her.

"Why?!" I jumped back up. She'd sounded like I'd been stabbing her.

She snatched her turtle from under me. "You almost killed Ozzy!"

"Whoa, he's big," I blurted out. Then I shook my head. "Sorry Ozzy, my mind was someplace else."

Lacey smiled and looked at Ozzy. "She didn't mean it Ozzy." She looked back at me. "Ozzy forgives you. He also says he's glad to meet you, but please don't sit on him." She held out one of Ozzy legs. "Shake hands with him."

I grinned. "Nice to meet you too, Ozzy."

* * *

Soon I went upstairs. I took a long, hot shower, and when I got out I could hear Sid's voice again, downstairs. Then I heard footsteps coming up. I rushed and closed my bedroom door, as I was in a towel.

I put on my clothes and heard the door to Sid's room shut.

No goodnight for me.

I read for a while, listened to some music, and then turned out the lights.

Ah. No homework during the summer, bitches!

I could hear voices downstairs, and bats behind the walls of my bedroom. They were scratching, trying to get out. Mice with wings.

Quincy must not have opted for a night out on the town, because he suddenly shouted, "Oh my God! They're in here!" I heard him squealing. I was glad I was upstairs.

"Quincy you'll wake everyone in the house! It's just a little bat!" Aunt Kippie said.

Aunt Chasey was in bed, and Bill probably was, too. Anna was in the basement.

"Someday you're just going to leave us again, aren't you Sid?"

So Sid had left them once. With no warning. And no explanation.

"Anna, calm the hell down. Let me talk on the God damn phone, goddammit!"

Gotta love Quincy.

"It's Sid's business. It's none of yours."

So Sid had a few secrets here and there. It just made him all the more intriguing to me. And now I had some cold, solid, loud proof that he and Anna were not compatible. He may not have been mine. But at least he was single.

He's 160 years old, Phyllis, said the voice.

I breathed out flames, immersing the ceiling in them. Then I inhaled them all back in.

The perfect age, I told the voice.

There was a knock on my door.

Sid has come to seduce you, said the voice sarcastically.

I told the voice to shut the hell up.

I didn't answer, and the door opened.

"Phyllis, I never said good night to you. Do you mind?" It was Aunt Kippie.

"Not at all." I turned on the light.

She leaned down and kissed me on the cheek. "I love you Phyllis. You're the best thing that ever happened to me, you know."

"What makes you say that?" I wondered sleepily.

"I was just thinking how I would never have had the experience of raising a child without you. And you've grown into such a wonderful person." She hugged me. "There now. You go to sleep." She sighed. "And if you hear any more commotion about bats, ignore it."

I smiled. She smiled back, and turned away.

"Aunt Kippie?"

"Oui, mademoiselle?"

"Will I ever see them again? My parents?"

"My dear, that is entirely up to you. If you're ever ready, we're glad to take you to see them."

"All right."

"Anything else?"

"Nope, I think that's all," I said, even though I knew I should have told her how glad I was to have my Aunts as well. Instead, I yawned. "Night, Aunt Kippie."

"Good night, Phyllis." She shut the door.

I turned the light back out, and again realized how boring my life would have been had I been born into any other family.

Epilogue

We came to a red light.

Aunt Chasey had sausage-curled my hair for the play. For the most part it had been kept back in a kerchief, but it had gotten so long that the curls were still prominent. Now that I'd taken the kerchief off, it seemed that they were rebelling.

Sid reached over and tugged on a curl. It bounced back.

I looked him menacingly in the eye. "If you had been anyone else, I would have blown smoke in your face."

"Gee, I feel lucky."

I opened the window and blew smoke out into the dark night air.

"Do you really *have* to do that?"

"What do you mean?"

"You've always been able to hold it back. Could you get by without doing it at all?"

I shook my head. "I don't think so. It's like holding my breath, only I can do it for a lot longer. I have pretty good control over it."

"Thanks to me." Sid gave me a look.

"I wish I could remember that," I said sincerely.

"It's stayed with you somehow. It'll probably come to you eventually, babes." He half-smiled. "I loved having you around."

I looked at him. "Likewise." No use covering anything up now.

Sid sighed.

Suddenly he pulled over. He turned and looked at me.

"Listen babes, I'm not gonna do this often. It isn't right and it doesn't do either of us any good." Sid paused. "But I can't stand it if I *don't*."

I raised my eyebrows.

He leaned forward and kissed me.

I can't describe Sid's kisses. Long, slow, more than wonderful..and experienced. Hot. I could feel smoke rising in my throat, up into my mouth, as his lips stroked mine.

"Whoa, careful Philly," he murmured. He put his hand on the back of my neck, his fingers lightly brushing my skin. Then he gently pulled away.

"I won't burn you," I told him.

"I know." Sid put the car back in gear and pulled back onto the road.

Great, I thought. It's probably close to the full moon, I realized gloomily. He wouldn't let himself kiss me otherwise.

You got *that* right, said the voice.

Quietly, I looked out the window to see if it was whatever kind of gibbous that comes before the full moon, or a crescent, or a new moon.

It was a perfect half.

I looked at him. "Sid....if I were older..would things be different for you and me?"

Sid glanced at me and bounced his eyebrows twice. "We'll see, won't we?